THE HILL, '67

In the Beat of a Heart

A Novel

Roger Johnson

ISBN   979-8-9872510-4-1

Email: rogerj47@gmail.com

To those classmates who, in their own way, nurtured a naïve, introspective, but curious young man who found himself in over his head in Boulder in 1965. Specifically, Kal Fallon, Steve Hatchell, Bob Stailey, Dick Buell, and Flip Unger Farrar. Heartfelt thanks for giving me the confidence to continue. I haven't forgotten you.

To David Weil (and the entire Weil Family), my first favorite student.

To Chick Ritacco and the rest of my basketball buddies at the Sixth Street Gym in Leadville, Colorado.

And again, in memory of Dr. Gail S. Rowe (University of Northern Colorado), my Professor Orr.

Acknowledgements

The following offered insightful comments, copyediting, and critiques on various stages of the manuscript:

> Jay Johnson
> Steve Cogil Casari
> Jane Becker
> Stephanie and Jody Olson

Formatting and cover design: Joe DesGeorges. He has provided these services and artistic talents for all ten of my novels, and I am extremely thankful for his patience, professionalism, and friendship.

Cheryl Johnson, my wife, who does not critique my work but offers support in many other more important ways.

Books in Print

Historical Fiction

Laments for the Dead
Layers of Darkness
America's Soul
Refugees Among the Lines
The Why Intersection
The Hill, '67: In the Beat of a Heart

Girls'/Women's Basketball Novels

On Point
Gifts: The Return
Coach Izzy
Hoops and Seeds: A Pause in the Harvest

The HILL, '67

In the Beat of a Heart

by
Roger Johnson
IngramSpark
2025
(first draft 2004)

Dual journeys
One of the mind
One of the heart
Traveling laterally . . . safely.

World crises swirl
The Winds of War
Eddying
Like a river at a bend.

That vortex of events
Couples these journeys.
A convergence
Mind <u>and</u> Heart.

Two paths become one
Merged . . . fused
Embarking on a venture
Daring . . . risky.

. . . and then I asked him with my eyes to ask again yes
and then he asked me would I yes . . .
and first I put my arms around him yes
and drew him down to me . . .
and his heart was going like mad
and yes I said yes I will Yes.

James Joyce, *Ulysses*

"Take me to bed."

Sarah Phillips

The University consists of all who come into and go forth from her halls, who are touched by her influence and who carry on her spirit. Wherever you go, the University goes with you. Wherever you are at work, there is a University at work.

George Norlin, CU President, 1919-1939

PART I

UNIVERSITY OF COLORADO, BOULDER, SPRING SEMESTER, 1967

Wednesday, January 11

The student demonstrators that huddled around the fountain outside the University Memorial Center dispersed, and the activists loosely marched up to The Hill, the hub and heart of this college town. Boulder's University Hill: fifty shops, ranging from theaters and restaurants, bookstores and record shops, shoe stores and stylish clothing boutiques, pharmacy and grocery stores to bars that legally served 3.2 beer to eighteen-year-olds. As the neighborhood fanned out toward Chautauqua Park, the Flatirons, and old Boulder, there were fraternities and sororities, rooming houses and rentals, and finally, the residential homes. The Hill: where students went for excitement and exploration, for alcohol and drugs, to dance, to mingle and maybe get laid, to ask questions. For truth and lies. The Hill: directly west of the campus, across Broadway, within walking distance to where much of the tangible education for CU's students took place. Many universities had such a district; at CU in the sixties, it was "The Hill," and at the start of 1967, its heart pulsated as if on uppers.

The protesters reassembled fittingly in front of Clancy's Bookstore (F*ck Censorship buttons) where a protest song was sung before the activists merged with students who were largely unconcerned about the issue. Finding little ideological support from these students, most of the demonstrators scattered to bars and rooming houses to make plans for their next political action. One marcher went to a Greek house, where a semi-impromptu function was occurring, celebrating something contrived and unrelated to the early evening's demonstration. Calm would return to CU's campus, but storm clouds were forming over the Flatirons.

A week earlier 11,510 students returned from their winter breaks to begin the spring semester. Boulder sat in the shadow of "The Flatirons," a unique geologic rock formation that this evening was glazed under a recent light snow. The Flatirons were the town's and the University of Colorado's recognizable landmark, unique and a bit slanted, sort of like CU itself. For much of its history, Boulderites welcomed these students into their cozy town, but because of the controversial Vietnam War, an undercurrent of resentment had developed toward many of these students, especially the long-haired males, who seemed to flaunt their protected status, their privileged condition. Unfair generalizations certainly, but real tensions and resentment.

At the Sigma Delta Tau sorority house, that one marcher slid past the crush of obnoxious Greeks who were pushing against an oversized card table where cups of beer were available. Paul Garrity had no intention of waiting in line for a drink, especially tonight. The Sig Delt coed working behind the table was obviously unable to keep up with the demand. In her frustration she called a few of the more obnoxious male students dickheads and threatened to shut down the keg. Having her jet-black hair done up in pigtails held by yellow rubber bands did not help to enhance her stature as the person in charge. She looked puzzled when Paul suddenly appeared at her side with a towel draped over his left shoulder.

"I've been hired to help, so let's see if we can restore a little order and sanity to this function," he said to the frazzled server. Paul stacked the overturned paper cups lying on the table and set them on the counter behind him. The bottles of hard liquor were also put on the counter. He used his towel to wipe up the spilled beer. To create more space in "the bar," he moved around to the front of the table, picked it up, and walked backward into the crowd a few steps.

"What do you want me to do?" asked the server.

"Get a couple of pitchers from the kitchen and fill them with beer from the keg and see if you can grab one of your sorority sisters to help, maybe a pledge." The young woman did as she was told, while Paul made the announcement for the function to continue.

For the next hour, Paul, the server, and the recruit worked smoothly as a team to supply the function with its liquor needs until the keg was emptied around ten. As quickly as it began, it ended, with couples leaving to walk to the real bars on The Hill. Paul dismissed the recruit politely, then turned and smiled at the server.

"Who hired you?" she asked as she leaned forward across the counter to take his towel.

"No one actually, I just came to meet you."

"That was a pretty good move," Sarah Phillips said as they finished cleaning up the kitchen and parlor. "It couldn't have been planned."

Paul laughed. "It wasn't. Would you like to go to Tulagi's and dance until curfew?"

"I would, but I can't." She took Paul's arm and led him to the opposite end of the parlor near the fireplace. "I'm beat," she said as she sat them both down on a two-seater couch. "Dancing would be great, but I'm kind of restricted this week."

"How come?" Paul asked as Sarah held his arm for a moment longer than necessary on the couch.

Sarah shook her head. "Oh, I've been rude to my mother, and the house mom found out. I'm not a nice person just now."

"I didn't know you could be grounded for being rude to your parents. If that was the case, I'd never get out of my house. My dad and I can get pretty nasty to each other."

"I'm not technically grounded. It's a sorority expectation to be nice to one's parents, but my mother calls all the time, and I just get tired of her probing and correcting. Her world is so confining. She called my house mom and told her I sassed her."

"Did you?"

Sarah nodded. "Yes, I did, and she deserved it!"

Paul sensed frustration in her tone more than anger. "Why don't you just not take her calls?"

"I'm not this week. Part of Mrs. Meyer's plan. A cooling off period, but I'm supposed to stay here at night and think about my attitude. Tonight's the last night of the restrictions."

Paul smiled. "Is it working?"

"Not yet. What do you and your father argue about?"

Paul sighed and looked away, into his own thoughts. "The war, my politics, my being here at CU where the communists are instead of CSU where the sons of patriotic Republicans go, my support for my drug addicted brother." He turned back to Sarah's eyes. "Maybe not the same conversations you have with your mother, but it's still about control." Paul knew he had said too much with the addition of the information about his brother.

The couple paused to reflect, and then Sarah changed the subject and tone, putting on her best sorority face. "Okay, I'm kind of interested in finding out about a guy who's willing to pour beer just to meet some girl. What fraternity do you belong to?"

"I don't. Long story, but briefly, I was asked to pledge Sig Ep last year about this time, but my dad said no until I got my grades up. They were pretty bad first semester. After that, I just never got around to it."

"Did you ever get anything to drink?" asked Sarah.

"I didn't come here to drink," said Paul. "How come you were serving tonight?"

"Oh, this function wasn't well planned, so I kind of volunteered at the last minute. No big deal. It's not like I was looking for a date tonight." She flipped one of her pigtails to emphasize her claim. She shifted on the couch, putting her left leg beneath her, and then removed the rubber bands from her hair, shook it out, allowing it to fall over her shoulders. "Where do you live now? In a dorm?"

"No, I live on The Hill near The Sink. Why Sigma Delta Tau for you?"

"This is a Jewish house mostly. My mother belonged to a chapter back east and steered me into this house. She didn't want me to move so far away but consented if I promised to pledge CU's chapter. It's worked out well being 2,000 miles away, and I'm moving back to my parents' faith a little." Sarah held up her thumb and index finger about a half inch apart to indicate how much.

"Where's back east?"

"New York. Can't you tell by my accent? What about you?"

"Lakewood. West Denver suburb. Just down the road. I came here for the physics program."

"So, you're a science major?" asked Sarah.

"Not anymore. History. I need to know what's going on these days, what all this is about, and history and poly sci seem to be the best path."

"Why not philosophy then?"

"Too abstract. I'm trying to figure out the events of now."

"Sounds like you're in a hurry . . . and that you're carrying a bit of extra weight."

"I am. I'm trying to make up for lost time. What about you?" asked Paul.

"Sociology, with an emphasis in early childhood development." Sarah related a few stories about the children at the local school where she worked, some funny, some poignant. Paul listened with his eyes as much as his ears, watching Sarah light up with excitement about her kids.

The couple was interrupted by the housemother who was preparing to get the girls checked in before the eleven o'clock curfew. "Sarah, introduce me to your young man." Both students stood.

"Mrs. Meyer, this is Paul . . ."

"Garrity, ma'am. Nice to meet you."

"I'm sorry." Sarah turned a bit red.

The housemother eased the moment. She had experience with these first encounters and their awkwardness. "Paul, I'd like you to formally meet Miss Sarah Phillips. She gets a little nervous around handsome young men." They all smiled, and Paul shook Sarah's hand.

"I'd like to see you again if I could," Paul said, deciding to take a chance.

"How about lunch tomorrow at the UMC? I'm done at noon for an hour."

"That'd be great, but I can only stay for a half hour or so. I've got an SPU committee meeting around twelve-thirty. Maybe you'd like to come with me?"

"Ooh, the Student Peace Union. You're into anti-war politics, huh?" Sarah flashed a knowing smile. "I'll meet you just inside the UMC doors closest to Hellems at noon. I'll think about the meeting. Mrs. Meyer is getting impatient." Sarah steered Paul to the door. "It was very nice to meet you, Paul Garrity. Thanks for helping, but I had it under control, you know."

"Yeah, I could see that."

Sarah leaned in, placing her right hand on his upper chest. "I'll see you tomorrow."

This girl could be a handful, Paul thought as he jogged back to his apartment just as the wind picked up and snow flurries began. He wondered if Sarah would develop into one of his three-week relationships. He scaled the stairs at his apartment two steps at a time. He found his roommates arguing and laughing. "What's so funny?"

"Well," said Dan, "if it isn't CU's SDS commie. I saw you in the march. Did you accomplish anything, Mario?"

"Ignore him, Paul. He's drunk again," said Mose.

"Cute guy," said one of Sarah's sorority sisters. "He doesn't look Jewish?"

"No, his name is Paul Garrity. Yeah, he is cute, isn't he? I think he might be my boyfriend for a few months, only he doesn't know it yet." *Boyfriend? Really, Sarah?* she thought. *How about just a date or two?* Sarah turned to walk upstairs to her room, nodded slightly, and smiled wryly at herself, thinking how that might be a novel experience.

Thursday, January 12

Paul's last Tuesday/Thursday class for the spring semester was Intro to Art History, an elective class to meet the Liberal Arts requirements, and it ended at eleven-thirty. He was making up for his freshman year's deficiencies. The snow had continued throughout the night and early morning, dropping about five inches of fresh powder. As he left the Hellems classroom building for the UMC to meet Sarah, he wondered if she would show up, with the weather so bad. He had twenty minutes to wait, so he picked up the *CU Daily*. Two stories grabbed his attention, the first about seven CU students arrested in a marijuana raid, and the second about the continuing border clash between Israel and Syria near the Sea of Galilee. His history professor had advised his students to watch for events that might impact the United States in the months and years to come.

Sarah's class was a 100-level math class, part of the Arts & Sciences degree requirements. She carried a 3.4 grade point average, a combination of brains and effort. She was hardly recognizable when she entered the first set of doors at the UMC, snow covering her fur-tipped ski parka. "Hi. Have you been waiting long? It's just miserable out there."

"Want to get something warm?" Paul took her coat and shook the snow off.

The half hour passed quickly for them. "If it's okay, I'd like to go to the SPU meeting with you, at least for a little while," said Sarah.

The Student Peace Union was a political action organization formed in the early sixties in the Midwest. At the University of Colorado, it included Rockefeller Republicans, Northern Democrats, liberals, socialists, communists, civil rights enthusiasts, and anti-war protestors, most of whom were young males. As the war in Vietnam became increasingly unpopular, the SPU emerged as the focal point for campus protests. Paul was initially interested in civil rights issues but drifted into the SPU as the civil rights movement seemed to depart from non-violence into Black Power.

He was confused about his thoughts about the war, since he was never a radical or a pacifist, but he saw the war pulling funds from LBJ's Great Society programs and national attention away from civil rights. Paul and his freshmen friends on the second floor of Brackett Hall had discussed politics as part of their university transition, and it was with Moses Robinson and Dan Savage that Paul gained some clarity about his positions.

"Shit, Garrity, SNCC doesn't want white boys anymore, unless they need foot soldiers to register voters," said Mose. "Black Power's the new way, and your kind is out."

"What is your kind, Paul? Why don't you just support America and forget about all these protest movements. You're in college to learn, not waste your dad's money," said Dan, echoing the words of so many of CU's professors.

"Paul, I have to go," whispered Sarah while the SPU meeting's leader was ranting.

"I'll go with you. I know what I need to do before next week," Paul whispered back. He stood and interrupted the speaker. "I'm out of here, Cohen. Call me if something new develops. I'll let you know about the Freedom Boys, and I'll try to pin Professor Kennedy down."

John Cohen was having the last word, something about the Associated Students of the University of Colorado, the official student government, being left out of the mix, but both Paul and Sarah had enough and were out the door and heading towards the main entrance on the south side of the UMC on their way to the Lab School.

"You've dealt with Cohen before, I see," said Paul as he helped Sarah on with her parka.

"One of my sisters set me up with him last year. Blind date. She thought she was doing me a favor, you know, important upper class-men, fellow Jew. It was awful! He's so full of himself, such an asshole, but I must say that I really admired how you interacted with him, especially when he tried to dictate the policy on demonstrations, and you said it had to be a consensus. I'm not sure any of the other members had ever stood up to him. Kind of put him in his place. Cool." She bumped Paul's shoulder. "Now you have to be my guest. I hope my little kids behave better than yours." They both laughed.

Not all the children made it to school that afternoon, nor did some of the student aides. Paul was welcomed and immediately put to work reading to two little boys. An hour and a half passed quickly. One of the boys had fallen asleep with his head on Paul's lap, but the other, Ricky, was intrigued by Paul's reading of a *Little Golden Book* for the third time. Paul did not see Sarah for the entire session until she brought in the two boys' mothers at three-thirty.

"You're a natural. I was watching you earlier, before I was pulled back into the little girls' fashion show. You really bailed me out of a jam. I owe you bigtime." Sarah opened her eyes wide like she was offering Paul a gift. "Did you enjoy yourself?"

"Yeah, I'm glad I came. Maybe you can drag me back again sometime."

Sally Long was the fourth resident on the second floor at 1203 Pennsylvania where Paul, Mose, and Dan lived. She rented the room in the fall when she transferred to CU from Southern Colorado State College at Pueblo. She kept to herself at first, but rooming house living requirements broke down her early isolation, and she became one of the gang.

That evening, just after eight as planned, the gang living at 1203 Pennsylvania went to The Sink for a study break, a half-block away. It had been crowded earlier, but the band at Tulagi's was drawing off the pack. Sally had once offered her thoughts about The Hill's two most prominent bars late one night when the second floor was drinking and philosophizing over its place in the universe. To her, Tulagi's and The Sink were like the yin and yang, those interconnected forces keeping everything in harmony. While the Tule rocked to live bands on one of the nation's largest dance floors, The Sink's attraction was the dark backroom, a cavern with low ceilings where students drank, smoked, and mingled anonymously. "They're such different bars, but they feed off each other. We've all spent lots of time at both, sometimes on the same night. Start at one, end up at the other." Sally had taken a class on comparative world religions the year before while she was a freshman in Pueblo, so she insisted she was the expert. "They're the opposite sides of the 'Ultimate Oneness,' keeping order and harmony in this cosmic universe we call CU." Paul wanted to know which bar the yin was and which was the yang. "I'm not sure yet," she replied. Dan asked where The Huddle fit in. "The universe is not static, my dear. Its place is still to be determined."

Ever the pragmatist, Mose offered his succinct conclusion. "Works for me."

On this night Sally used her charm to talk two drunken guys out of their booth, so the four of them could have a front booth.

"So, what's the progress with the new girl?" asked Dan.

Paul nodded, "So far, so good, I guess. Seems pretty nice. Definitely a sorority girl."

"Made your move yet?" teased Mose. "It's been a year."

"Working up to it, big guy. I'll let you know when," said Paul.

"Just don't let her interfere with your time with us," warned Sally.

"Game's at one on Saturday. Everybody goin'?" asked Mose. "Except you, of course," nodding at Sally. She had never attended a CU basketball game.

"I'll go when you're reinstated. These two tell me you're good, but I haven't seen your name in the paper yet," said Sally.

"Me and coach just don't see eye-to-eye. When he understands what a gentle soul I am, everything will be okay." Mose finished his first beer. "He might have a problem with these casual beers I share with you guys."

Finishing the pitcher, they went back to the apartment, where Paul returned to his history books. "Yalta, Potsdam, and the Decision to Drop the Bomb." The Cold War had begun. Like President Truman's demands on Japan to end WWII, Professor Orr's demands were unconditional.

Homework was taken seriously at 1203. Paul, in whose apartment they often gathered, staked out the old green recliner along the inside wall beneath the bronze metal lamp. His apartment, room 2A, was the largest, and it had a refrigerator. It was also nearest to the only phone on the second floor. As the apartment manager, Paul had scoured garage sales, flea markets, and the want ads for furniture to furnish the eight apartments at 1203 Pennsylvania. The renter's ad had read, "Partially furnished." The owner budgeted twenty dollars per room for Paul to buy used furniture.

"Is homework supposed to get easier as I get smarter or is it going to get harder because they expect more from me as I get smarter?" asked Sally.

"I hadn't noticed you gettin' smarter," teased Mose.

"You really ought to put gees on the end of those words," said Sally.

"It's a hard habit to break; I've been cool since junior high." Mose laughed.

The bantering ceased and the studying resumed.

Friday, January 13

"Was Vietnam France's war or America's war by proxy as part of the containment of communism?" Professor Orr was boring in on his Cold War students. "Think! President Truman had already decided on a Europe first foreign policy, but did this fit the program?" His eyes scanned the room. Most of the students dropped theirs, but Paul kept his up, directly at his professor. "Mr. Garrity."

"It wasn't his priority; Berlin and Europe were, but the US was funding most of France's effort. I'm not sure if de Gaulle was having second thoughts by this time or not."

"Anyone else? What about de Gaulle?" The class stayed silent. Again, Paul raised his hand. "Someone besides Mr. Garrity. Know your facts! Let's go over it again."

After class and a brief exchange with his professor, Paul went to the UMC for a quick bite but ate it in the entrance where he had met Sarah the day before. Just as he finished, Sarah entered and acted surprised to see Paul. She told him that she needed to buy a few supplies downstairs in the bookstore and invited him to join her. She bought a fancy pen and two notebooks, and then they went back upstairs for Paul's second lunch where he asked her out on a date for Saturday.

CBS reported the same details as NBC. The continuing American offensive into the Iron Triangle northwest of Saigon was devastating. Nearly 15,000 Marines and about that many ARVN were leveling every structure in the region in their assault on the Viet Cong and the civilian population, which was caught in the middle. Operation Cedar Falls would win the day, but the resentment among the local farmers would be long-lasting.

In his office at the Pentagon, Secretary of State Robert McNamara waited for the reports of the assault in the Iron Triangle. He was concerned about the course of the war, and on this day, he felt alone and unable to persuade those around him that the war in Vietnam was not furthering the cause of freedom and democracy or the security of the United States. The 50-year-old McNamara was an architect of the war, but he now doubted many of his own basic assumptions. He had been overconfident and cocksure a few years earlier.

Paul generally watched the evening news by himself in the first floor TV room, although Dan sometimes joined him for the first few minutes. Today, Paul was alone, but he muttered, "Shit! Information is so controlled. If the army is kicking the shit out of the VC every day, why does this thing keep getting worse?" He was deeply upset by the indiscriminate bombing campaign and the increasing reports of civilian casualties in free-fire zones. "It's your fucking war, McNamara, you lying bastard. Have you ever seen it up close and personal? All you care about is a Cold War domino. Don't you care about the women and children who are dying?"

Two men 2,000 miles apart and 30 years in age difference wondered what might be happening to the soul of America as the war in Vietnam continued. Neither man trusted the other, but for the younger man, Vietnam was not about legacy but . . . breath.

Saturday, January 14

The CU Buffalo basketball team played it closer than maybe it should have against Kansas State but won 71-68. Mose joined Paul and some of last year's Brackett Hall buddies in the stands; Mose not yet being allowed to sit on the end of the bench until he proved his desire to the coach a little longer. A projected starter at the beginning of the season, Mose had fallen out of favor and suspended due to his "lack of fire" and perceived disinterest. Paul knew both evaluations were wrong, that his best friend operated on a unique plane and saw competition in a different light. Watching Mose when he played on the freshman squad a year ago, Mose played best when he played freely without artificial motivation, i.e., threats and yelling. Only when playing pickup games did Mose trash talk; otherwise, he was a student of the game and gentleman on the court. Stoic, self-controlled . . . yet intricate and improvisatory. On and off the court.

Paul picked up Sarah for their first date at eight-thirty at the SDT house, a casual meeting for one drink at Bennett's, the anti-Sink. He had walked the five blocks to her sorority house since the weather was unseasonably warm. Butterflies! Sarah bounded down the stairs into the foyer where he was waiting. She kissed him on the cheek and handed him her leather jacket. He felt a surge within and wondered whether she acted like this toward all her dates.

At Bennett's the table conversation initially revolved around their university studies as it had the night they first met. They probed for common interests—of which there seemed very few—but they both liked CU. They laughed at how different their experiences had been for their year-and-a-half at CU, almost as if they attended different universities, yet here they were in Boulder at age twenty. Neither volunteered much about themself, but both answered the questions posed by the other. Sarah seemed fascinated by Paul's participation in the current "movements" and asked if he was a hippie. He laughed that off. Sarah revealed that she helped in several community projects, especially with her Greek affiliation. She said that Paul's curiosity reminded her of Valentine Michael Smith, but Paul had never heard of him, asking if she had dated this guy with the weird first name. She laughed aloud before explaining. On the walk back to her sorority, they held hands, laughed, and shared a meaningful kiss.

When Sarah's roommate asked about her date, Sarah offered that few things were sexier than a guy who showed genuine interest in a girl, a guy who didn't talk mostly about himself. She tapped her roommate on the nose and said, "And he's funny too."

You wouldn't recognize him from last year, Sally," said Mose.

"How so?" She seemed concerned about Paul's new girl.

"The whole package. I thought he was kinda small and immature to be in college last year when I first met him. He was an inch or two shorter than Dan and skinny"

"Paul's good looking, you know," said Sally.

"Nah, I wouldn't know about that," smiled Mose. "He combed his hair over from one side with a flip in front, and it was really short over his ears. If it hadn't been for basketball, we'd never have hung with each other. It's strange how people fall together. We were playin' ball over at the gym, and he kept passin' the ball to me, so the next time we played, I picked him for my team. I found out we lived in the same dorm, so we started hangin' out—two totally different guys. I'm streetwise and cool, and he was naïve and goofy. A good fit." Mose smiled.

"How long was he like that?" asked Sally.

"Not long. He grew up fast. Even though we kid him, he's not so much now. He still has that enthusiasm, and he's so perceptive."

"This new girl sure has him excited."

"Don't worry. He hasn't kept a girl longer than a month since he's been here."

"Has he always been so serious about his studies?"

"Last year was just so hard for him with the math. He tried, but he'd get frustrated and give up. His grades that first semester were terrible. Slept a lot too." Mose shook his head. "We started studyin' together, kind of to help each other out, and we both got tutors second semester, but it was a steep hill to climb to get out of his mess."

"He hardly ever sleeps now. I hear him late at night and early in the morning moving around. I just assumed he's always been like that." Sally knew Paul had taken a chance on her as a tenant at 1203 that fall, arranging the room assignments to protect her a little. To her, Paul was the responsible apartment manager.

"He walks when he's frustrated or mad," said Mose. "He's usually got a bug up his ass over somethin' that's wrong in the world. He just seldom lets it out. Just before Christmas, he looked up what it would cost to fly to Cambodia just to see what that part of the world looks like. You know, a peaceful country in Southeast Asia that isn't getting bombed by the US of A. He said he might want to spend a little time there . . . get to know the people."

Sunday, January 15

Just after nine, Paul called Sarah, their first phone call. He told her what a good time he had had on their date and asked if she wanted to meet him again for lunch tomorrow. She agreed to the meeting but declined any food, saying she just would have a soda but that he could get something if he liked. "Sorority girls are always on a diet, you know."

Monday, January 16

"Good morning, Paul. Coffee's ready."

"Morning, Dr. Orr." Paul hung his coat on the back of the wooden chair in front of the professor's desk and rubbed his hands together. "It's cold out there!"

"Here's your cup. My wife thinks they ought to be washed at least once each semester." Even in winter, he wore white short-sleeved shirts with his tie.

Dr. D.R. Orr's office was a small space in the basement of Hellems, but it was unmistakably the workplace of a scholar, a passionate teacher who took his craft seriously. Two floor-to-ceiling book-shelves anchored the ends of the office, and each was crammed full of history books and historical journals. One shelf directly behind his desk at eye level was orderly, and it held fiction. There was also a baseball almanac on that shelf. His desk was crowded, but neat. A blue IBM Selectric typewriter anchored the left side of the desk near the wall, and a well-worn dictionary, thesaurus, and book of quotations stood behind the typewriter. Two family pictures also sat on the desk, one of two little boys and the other of a college man and his bride from about fifteen years earlier. To the right of his chair against the wall was a microfilm machine on permanent loan from the library to its most prolific user for research. There were only two chairs in the office, both sturdy wooden ones, and there was a metal TV tray by the door for his coffee pot.

Dr. Orr closed his notebook at eleven-fifty and adjusted his eyeglasses. The Cold War class began to stir, thinking this day was over after just five pages of notes. "For the last few minutes of class, I'd like to question you about your political leanings." The class grew quiet again. "Are you a Republican or a Democrat? Maybe a liberal or a conservative? Maybe you label yourself an independent or haven't become political yet." He paused, looked about the room, and then moved around the podium, closer to his students. He fixed his eyes on an older female student near the door, a senior political science major with long straight hair and hoop earrings whom he had taught in other classes and who was not timid about her political beliefs. "Or maybe some of you are New Leftists who believe that the US took the wrong path after World War II and hasn't corrected its policies since?" He smiled at her and moved his gaze elsewhere, settling on another senior, a young man with short-cropped hair and a thick neck. "Maybe you're about to graduate and are facing the draft. Will that influence your political philosophy?" The student under the spell of Orr's eyes shifted uncomfortably at his desk. The professor returned to the podium, allowing the silence to do its work. His eyes canvassed the room again before settling on Paul.

"Dr. Orr, if I call myself a Democrat, does that brand me as a socialist too?" Paul was not afraid to be the first to answer the professor's challenges.

Katie, the senior by the door who was also SDS, responded. "Some might, but I'd call you a pampered, 2-S, secret right-winger. You probably want to end the war, but you don't fully know why." She turned back toward Dr. Orr. "If his daddy's a Republican, chances are he is too. Maybe not for the few years here in Boulder but scratch the surface and he will be. These guys think they're entitled to run the country." She paused. "Privilege . . . and history."

Two minutes to noon. Paul picked up on Orr's earlier New Left comment to Katie and took a chance. "Am I supposed to become part of your Marxist, revolutionary proletariat, that kind of old New Left, or are you new New Left SDS like Mario Savio who romanticizes this . . . I don't know . . . revolution against the establishment?"

Katie nodded to Paul. "Clever, but don't be naïve. Go out and get your hands dirty and your face bloodied. The real world is messy, unlike our pristine CU." She turned back to Professor Orr. "Ask the class about their political views in a couple of years—or after this war ends. I won't be the only leftist then. The truth will come out about American atrocities in Vietnam. Time and events are with me. They all think it's just 'over there,' the poor boys fight, but when they graduate, the reality will smack them in the face." She returned to Paul. "You've probably been given it all up until now. I wonder what you'll give back when you're older."

Dr. Orr did not need to check his watch to know the time. "Make sure you've completed your reading before class on Wednesday. I've put one article for you over at the library. See you in two days." Like most days when class ended, Paul exchanged a few words with Professor Orr.

It was Orr who spoke first. "Did I note a bit of smugness in your expression just now?"

"No," answered Paul. "It was an honest question. I really wasn't trying to be clever, as Katie suggested. I think Savio and Hayden believe that students can make a difference. She is right about me being naïve though."

Dr. Orr wondered about his student's comment as that student left the room. *Most students are naïve, but few are willing to admit it. Much of the college experience centers around losing that naivete. I'm going to enjoy this one.*

Sarah relented and had a salad. Their small talk touched on the sociology of children, music, the Peace Corps, and voter registration. Sarah talked Paul into working with her children at the Lab School again.

Tuesday, January 17

It was cold on Tuesday, Colorado cold, and the snow was flying. A native Coloradoan, Paul knew January was the coldest month. He stopped in the UMC for coffee before class. The University Memorial Center was Paul's favorite building on the CU campus. It was not the most magnificent, although in keeping with the architectural style of sandstone walls with limestone trim and red tile roofs, it was beautiful. But it was not Macky Auditorium, Sewall Hall, or Norlin Library. What made the UMC special to Paul was the energy within and at the adjoining fountain. It contained the offices of the *Daily* and the Clearing House. It was the scene of the lunchtime harangues and the gauntlet of information tables on the ground floor through which students needed to pass to get to the Grille or bookstore. Concerts on the front deck or teach-ins in the Glenn Miller Ballroom; SPU meetings in upstairs rooms. Always the impassioned, impromptu sermons at the fountain. Free speech! It was the first building that Paul entered when he visited CU as a high school senior, and it remained his focal point.

After getting his coffee, Paul returned to the gauntlet to study the men in uniforms fortifying the ROTC table. He wondered about their sense of duty: nation above self. He found a seat and settled in to watch fellow students prepare to be officers after graduation . . . in a war many Americans thought a mistake.

For the first time since meeting Paul, Sarah confessed to her roommate that he was not just a temp but could become a serious boyfriend. She really liked him and was sure he was infatuated with her. "I think about him most of the time, and he is so interested in me. He came to the Lab School with me last week and worked with a couple of the kids. He's so different from anyone I've ever dated. This is the first day since we met that we haven't talked." Sarah's roommate grinned at Sarah's giddiness and asked if his being a Gentile played a part of the mystic. "Honestly, Anne, except for when I first met him and found out he wasn't, I don't think I've thought about it. He's just such a nice guy. He makes me feel special."

Wednesday, January 18

Sarah told Paul she could not meet him at the library until nine because of a house meeting, something about drug education. Still, she said she wanted to see him even if it was just for an hour or so. "I'll walk over so you can walk me back home," she said on the phone just before dinner. "What will you be studying?"

"History, probably. I have two classes from the same professor, and he's tough. On Fridays, we discuss the Vietnam War. He forces us to be specific about our views."

"What's your biggest complaint about the war?" she asked.

Paul thought for a moment. "Besides the brutality of a war that's so ill defined, probably that it takes money from domestic programs started during the Great Society, but I have lots of concerns about how the war is even being fought. How do you feel about it?" It was the first time since the SPU meeting that they had talked about Vietnam.

"I know we have to fight communism, but I just don't understand how Vietnam threatens us. After all, China's communist, and I hate seeing the pictures on TV every evening." Her voice indicated an uncertainty about her position.

"It's complicated, but hopefully my Cold War class will clear it up for me," Paul said.

"Look for me early; I'll try to sneak out. I'm certainly not the one Mrs. Meyer is worried about with drugs."

Sarah could not skip out early from the drug education meeting, but she still walked over to Norlin Library to see her new boyfriend. They pretended to silently study for another hour, but touching got in the way of concentration. A ten-minute walk back to the Sig Delt house took about thirty minutes.

Thursday, January 19

Weather-wise, Thursday was the pick of the week, so the children at the Lab School had group play on the north lawn. Ricky joined with a few other boys to play tag with Paul. Sarah's attempts to organize a kickball game went largely ignored, but all the kids seemed to have fun. The afternoon passed quickly, and Paul and Sarah were able to spend a few moments together during that time. At three-thirty Ricky was tuckered out and sitting on Paul's lap again listening to him read about their favorite baseball player, Rootie Kazootie. His mother was late, but when she did arrive at four, Ricky had fallen asleep on Paul's chest.

On the way back to the Sig Delt house, Paul and Sarah agreed to meet at Tulagi's at four-thirty on Friday for FAC and go to a movie on Saturday evening. No specific one, just a date. He could not get her to go to the basketball game later that night, even though it was Kansas. Studying came first. At the door Sarah gave Paul a kiss that seemed like a promise. "I had a wonderful afternoon. Call me tonight before ten-thirty; I'll need a study break. If the line is busy, keep trying."

"Sigma Delta Tau house, Pledge Susan speaking."

"Could I speak with Sarah Phillips, please?"

"Just a minute. SARAH PHILLIPS! TELEPHONE! IT'S A GUY!"

Sarah answered after about 40 seconds, "Hello?"

"Hi. It's Paul."

"Did you get something to eat?" asked Sarah. "By the way, Mrs. Best called me this evening. She's in charge of the pre-school kids at the Lab School, and she wants me to bring you back. Guess I wasn't the only one who noticed your abilities. She thinks we need more males to work with the little boys. Anyway, think about it."

"Every day won't be as easy as today, but I'll try to make it when I can. Tuesdays and Thursdays are usually open for me."

"John Cohen called, but I wouldn't take his call. I have a feeling that most of my free time will be spent with this other guy I just met. At least, I hope so." There was a pause on the other end of the phone. "Paul, are you still there?"

"Yeah, I'm not hiding my feelings about you too much am I?" He laughed.

"No, and I like that," said Sarah. "I'll be sitting in a booth near the band with a couple of my sisters tomorrow at the Tule. Come find me and we'll dance until I have to go to synagogue. You did say that you dance, didn't you?"

Friday, January 20

FAC at Tulagi's was the property of King Louie and the Laymen. Other bands were booked for the evenings, and some of them were very good. The Boenzee Cryque, the Beggar's Opera Company—both remnants of the old Moonrakers—Avanti and even The Astronauts, but FAC on this afternoon belonged to King Louie.

Sarah sat on the top of the booth like a lookout, right where she said she would be, along with a half dozen of her Sig Delt sisters who were there to check out the "new guy." Mose and Sally came to check out Sarah. The sisters were not drinking, due to the Jewish-Hillel meeting at seven-thirty, but they all danced. Sarah and Paul got closer and closer as FAC progressed, and he nursed a single beer out of respect for her abstinence. When most of the sisters chose to leave, Sarah stayed, attached to the arm of her new man. Paul realized that she would have some explaining to do later that night at the house.

Avanti replaced King Louie around eight. By then, their dancing became much more physical.

Around nine they all had enough beer and smoke, so they went across the street to Bennett's for a bite to eat. A folk trio played to an older crowd, and despite Mose's overdone protests about staying, Sally found them a table in a corner where they could talk. "I was afraid Paul had found himself a girlfriend who didn't drink. You put a scare into us, Sarah." Sally was sitting next to Mose across from Paul and Sarah.

"I don't drink that much. I may have overdone it tonight with two beers." She rested her head on Paul's shoulder and closed her eyes. "Ooh, can't do that. Everything starts to spin."

"Pizza okay?" asked Sally. She knew it was good for Paul and Mose, since they often came to Bennett's to talk politics, religion, and personal problems, and pizza was the meal of choice. Sarah nodded that it was, but suggested they get an order of fries too. Pizza and fries.

Mose laughed. He knew that Sarah would be happy with anything if she was snuggled up to Paul.

"Fire away," said Sarah. "Ask me anything tonight and I'll probably tell you." They were about to learn one of Sarah Phillips' most endearing characteristics, her curiosity and self-deprecating humor about herself. After a few questions about her background, they moved on.

"D'you know what a 'Leslie Smith' is?" asked Mose deliberately.

"No, don't, Mose," begged Paul with feigned concern. "Don't get drawn into this, Sarah. He's just trying to embarrass me."

"We just want to warn her about you before she gets in too deep," added Sally with a glance to Mose.

"Who's Leslie Smith, an old girlfriend?" asked Sarah with a slight tilt of her head.

"Sorta. Leslie Smith's a fantasy woman. She was our freshman orientation guide, and we all fell in love with her, from a distance, except Paul. Somehow, your stud here thought this gorgeous, sexy senior was payin' special attention to him."

"God! Am I ever going to live this down?" Paul slumped in the booth.

"Hush!" said Sally. "I want to hear this too. Again."

Mose slowed his sentences. "Anyway, the Paul Garrity you're sittin' next to has grown up a bit since then. He was probably three inches shorter and 30 pounds lighter and proportionately dumber last year." The pizza and fries came, along with sodas. Sarah was glad for that. "We had the residence advisor's wife call Paul and pretend she was Leslie Smith. Asked him all kinds of stuff, you know, to make sure school was goin' okay."

"Let me guess." Sarah turned to Paul. "You asked her out, didn't you?" Paul, still slumped in the booth, covered his forehead with his hands. "You did! What did she say?" Sarah turned and pulled Paul's hands from his face. Sally bumped Mose's shoulder and smiled. "What did she say?" Sarah asked again.

"She admitted this was all made up, that the whole dorm floor was in on it. She was nice, but the damage to my self-esteem was done. You're the first girl I've asked out since then."

"Right," said Sally, "and I'm a virgin."

"Immaculate conception," said Mose.

"Michael Row the Boat Ashore" was being sung in the background, as the pizza and fries were devoured. Afterward, they walked the block and a half to 1203 Pennsylvania. When they climbed the stairs to the second floor, Sally said, "Goodnight," and went to her room. Mose said he'd had enough "cover rock" and "stupid folk" music for the month and excused himself to listen to jazz.

Paul opened his door to Sarah. "This is home." It was ten-forty.

They learned a good deal about each other that night: their music interests, politics, family, class schedules, that Sarah had never been to a CU basketball game, that Paul didn't know much about Jewish traditions, and that they wanted to know more about each other. Most of the information was shared while they slow-danced and kissed. Around midnight they found out even more about each other. Paul drove Sarah home in his Ford pickup.

"You might not believe this, but I've never ridden in a pickup truck before." She paused. "Another first."

It was quiet for the rest of the brief, five block ride to the Sigma Delta Tau house. Paul parked across the street. "You okay?" he asked gently.

"I'm more than okay, my dear," Sarah replied softly. She put her right hand on his cheek. "When we left Bennett's for your apartment, I thought this might happen, and . . . I was excited. You were perfect." Her eyes glistened and then the tears rolled down her face, a face she then laid on Paul's chest. He held her both tightly and tenderly.

Mrs. Meyer flicked the porch light twice, a signal that her girls needed to say goodnight. Paul walked Sarah to the door. "I'll call you tomorrow and we can pick a movie."

"I'm sleeping in. Paul . . ."

"Yeah?"

"I've been waiting for you."

They kissed once more, and Paul returned to his truck.

Paul pulled the Ford into the driveway behind his apartment. RESERVED FOR MGR: TOW AWAY ZONE. Mose's light was on.

Paul knocked once and stuck his head in. "Let me hang up my coat and get a cup." He returned after going to the bathroom. "I shouldn't drink your coffee. It tastes like shit and will keep me awake. What are you listening to?"

"Cannonball. Needed a fix after this evening. Hey, your girl seems pretty cool."

"Yeah, she is. She said she was waiting for me. I may be in over my head."

Sarah's roommate Anne Rostow was not the only Sig Delt sister waiting for a report on the long evening. After all, Sarah had usually been one of the audience, one of the "spotless." The interrogation revealed she spent a longer time at Bennett's listening to folk music and then stayed up drinking coffee with Paul and his roommates. Her worst transgression seemed to have been missing the Hillel meeting or maybe necking in the pickup truck in front of the house.

Anne had never seen her roommate so smitten. The sisters wanted to know all they could about this new guy in Sarah's life with long hair and no fraternity affiliation. Sarah was purposely vague.

After the friendly interrogation, Sarah stomped out of the room in mock disgust to make a quick call.

The phone rang in Paul's apartment at a quarter to two. Paul knew who it was.

"Hey."

"Hey back," Sarah whispered. "Do guys stay up and review their dates too?"

"No, Mose was just listening to jazz. He's pretty much a night owl. I'm just processing . . . us. Not sure how much sleep I'll get tonight."

Sarah made a concurring murmur as she sat on the hallway carpet in her pajamas twisting the long phone cord with her fingers. "Hey, I have a question about something Mose said to Sally."

"What was that?"

"She said something about being a virgin and Mose said, 'immaculate conception.' Did it mean something? Sally had a look about her."

"She had a baby in high school; gave it up for adoption at birth. She's never seen it since that day. I'll tell you about it if you want to know more."

Sarah was silent on the other end of the phone. Then she whispered, "This was the most special night tonight. All of it. Thank you." Unseen to Paul, she had her chin tucked into her chest and her eyes were wet..

"Yeah, Sarah, for me too."

Saturday, January 21

It was only about 35 minutes from Boulder to Lakewood, to the Garrity house. Paul and Mose arrived just after two. Mose called to let Paul's parents know they were coming, and that if "Dad" could be persuaded to fix an early dinner of enchiladas, then Mose might have some interesting stories to share about Paul. Paul began bringing Mose home as soon as they started playing pickup basketball together as freshmen, and once or twice each month, they ate homecooked meals. Mose never knew his father; he was raised by a single mother in Oxnard, California. He often spent the night on these visits, sleeping in Paul's brother's room.

On this visit, Mose informed Paul's parents that their son had fallen hard for a sorority girl with designs on their son, and that they might want to have that special talk with him before he found himself in a situation that he was unprepared for. Paul feigned complete embarrassment, reassuring his mother that his girlfriend was as naïve as he was. Not allowing Paul off the hook, Mose added that "Sarah's been coming over to the apartment to study."

As they prepared to leave, Paul's dad slipped Mose a ten-dollar bill. He then turned to his son. "Keep it in your pants, son . . . and cut your hair."

Paul arrived early to pick up Sarah, who was already waiting. Public displays of affection were not allowed inside the SDT house; still, Sarah leaned in and hugged Paul. "I missed you today," she whispered.

"Me too. How was your day?" Paul asked while he helped her on with her parka.

"Good. I worked the phones for a couple of hours to raise money for a school in Israel. What did you do today?" As Paul closed the door of the turreted sorority house behind them, Sarah threw her arms around his waist. The silent hug lasted over a minute. Then Sarah whispered, "I really did miss you. I want to hear everything about your day."

On the bench seat of the pickup, they embraced with youthful passion. Eventually, Paul said, "Let's get something before the movie. We've got some time. What do you want to see?' Sarah's dark brown eyes revealed her choice, but she left the movie selection to Paul. He picked "A Man for All Seasons" at the Flatirons Theater, and its impact left them both pensive afterwards in Paul's apartment.

"When we choose principle over all else, our loved ones can sure suffer," said Sarah. "Sir Thomas More's family certainly did."

Paul hesitated. "Family or country? When I told my dad about my opposition to the war last year and that I would be reluctant to serve in the military, he slapped me." Sarah's body tensed as she drew in a breath. "He's old school. His brand of patriotism can't be questioned or challenged. I don't argue anymore when I'm home. Vietnam is an off-limits topic."

Sarah waited to see if Paul wanted to say more. She sensed he would in time, but not tonight. "My family discusses it all the time, especially my dad and me. I'm third generation American from eastern Poland and Lithuania. We've always questioned our leaders. We lost family in the Holocaust. My uncle and his family live in Israel. We're a cynical lot. Sometime, when there's more time, I'll tell you about it. Maybe I'll have my father tell you."

"When will I be meeting them?" Paul asked as he moved a lock of hair from the corner of her mouth.

"Soon, my dear, soon." Sarah took his hand and squeezed it hard. "No more about the movie, okay?" They kissed hard and went to the bedroom.

On the short ride back to the SDT house, Paul asked, "Would you like to go to the basketball game with Mose and me? It starts at one.

You might see another side of me."

"I don't need to see another side of you just now." Paul glanced at her. "Does Sally go?" she asked.

"No, but I still want you to."

"I've got a lot of studying, but maybe we can do that later, can't we?"

"Hello."

"Hi, it's me. I don't know a thing about basketball."

"You sit with some guys who yell a lot, and I'm one of them."

"Oh, is that all? Then I think I'll learn to like the game. Goodnight, my dear."

Sunday, January 22

Paul took Sarah for an early lunch at The Sink. She talked Sally into going with them, and while at The Sink, she persuaded Sally to attend the basketball game too. After her earlier skepticism, Sally liked Paul's new girlfriend. She had mentioned to Mose that Sarah was genuine, but also that she seemed to be a little vulnerable; to what exactly, she was not sure. Mose knew.

Sarah sat between Paul and Sally and enjoyed her first CU basketball game immensely. The physical contact with Paul, the enthusiasm, the camaraderie, and the overall CU spirit made Sarah wonder why she had avoided these games so conscientiously. She understood that being with Paul was the most important ingredient in the mix, but the game was fun. She took it all in and appreciated the mix of guys, and she liked being a part of it. CU won 67-55. They all agreed to meet at the Gondolier for spaghetti dinner at six. Paul and Sarah headed off to Norlin Library to study.

That evening Sarah finished her paper, Paul tried to focus on the Robber Barons, and studying ended around ten when Sally invited everybody on the second floor into her room for snacks. Dan returned from Leadville, so he finally met Sarah.

"Did you get into any trouble for missing mass on Friday?" Mose asked Sarah.

Sarah laughed. "It's not mass, Mose, it was just a weekly service at the synagogue. I've missed it before, just never because I was out dancing with a guy. Usually, when I do attend, I go on Saturday mornings." She looked at Paul and smiled. "Are any of you guys religious?"

"Hey, we're in college, so we don't practice our faiths for four years," said Dan. It was true. Dan and Paul had similar backgrounds: Episcopalians, altar boys as kids, and non-attendance in Boulder, except for three Sundays when Paul had attended St. Aiden's with a girl. "Dating in church," he called it.

Sarah understood. "It happens all the time with my faith. What about you, Sally?"

"Raised Catholic, but when my dad left in junior high, my mom just sort of stopped attending. She worked two jobs and was too tired, I suppose."

"Mose?" asked Sarah.

"Never had one." It was an answer that brought contemplation to the group.

"Anybody searching?" Sarah asked again. Nobody bit. "I am, sort of." She answered her own question. "It's not that I'm looking for religion; it's more like I'm looking for an identity."

"I'm not sure anyone here has one," said Paul, "and that might not be such a bad thing. Right now, if someone asked me what I believe about God—or life—about the only thing I could tell them with any certainty is I'm trying to make sense of a number of things."

"That's certainty?" joked Mose. They all laughed.

"Well, I have to go," said Sarah. "Eleven o'clock curfew. You guys were great today, and I'm glad I finally was able to meet you, Dan."

Paul stood up from the floor and helped Sarah. They all began to stir. Paul and Sarah returned to his apartment to get their coats and her books, then they went downstairs and out to the Ford. It was cold.

"I'm not sure I expressed myself very well tonight," said Paul. "There are lots of things I believe, and I know some of who I am, but it's hard to express sometimes. Of the four of us who live upstairs, I'm the only one with a normal family, and that's a lot of who I am, but it's not what you were asking, I don't think. But I do struggle with the questions of faith and identity."

"Can we talk about it again, Paul?"

"Yeah, I'd like that." Then he said, "I trust you, you know."

"This has been the best week for me, and it's all because of you. You've been very good to me."

"What about tomorrow?" asked Paul.

"Wouldn't miss it. I'll meet you at the same place in the UMC." They arrived at the Sig Delt house. "Paul . . ." Her tone went soft.

"Yeah?"

"It's happened really fast, hasn't it?"

"Does it scare you?" he asked.

"Yeah, some. It just makes me wonder what changed in me that made me so ready for this . . . for you. I don't want you to think I've done this before, for you to think I'm . . . you know."

He took her hand interlocking their fingers. "That thought hadn't occurred to me, but it wouldn't matter." He wanted to say more, but Mrs. Meyer blinked the porch light. For fifteen seconds, neither Paul nor Sarah looked away. Finally, Paul made a slight nod, leaned in for a gentle kiss, and said, "Come on."

Monday, January 23

It was seven a.m. and Dr. Orr was late. Paul smiled, believing finally that his mentor was mortal. Dr. Orr had allowed Paul a glimpse of his private life during these morning meetings, something Paul had never been privy to in his previous educational experiences. As a university teacher, Professor Orr was both the best lecturer and the most demanding task master in the CU History Department. His outstanding reputation was deserved, and it had taken Paul only a few weeks to understand Orr's drive to bring out the best from each student. It was more than professionalism; it was an obsession.

Dr. Orr saw something special in Paul, beyond the uniqueness of each of his students. In some ways, Paul started over as a sophomore, taking intro liberal arts classes, including United States History 101. Dr. Orr pulled him aside after one class in October. "You have some catching up to do, Mr. Garrity, and I'll be both pushing and pulling you. You come talk with me every Monday morning this semester in my office. Curious minds need the morning air. Don't be late." The meetings were continuing for the spring semester. Paul eagerly anticipated each one.

After lunch Sarah headed off to the library, while Paul went back to Hellems for an appointment with Dr. Kennedy about the Vietnam Teach-In. Kennedy was the History Department's expert on Asian affairs. He was enthusiastic about the event and volunteered to take the lead with the faculty in scheduling it. He also felt that the elected student leaders ought to be included, as well as the Student Peace Union and the Young Americans for Freedom. Paul asked whether the Young Dems and Young Reps should take part in the planning. Kennedy scoffed at the idea.

"Neither group has taken an official position. I think you guys and the Freedom Boys should organize the student political activists. Don't let the YAF get away with calling you traitors because you oppose the war. If the war continues unchecked, it's going to devour you all. As it stands now, it just piles on another layer of anxiety. Will you be working with Cohen on this? No? Well, tell him to see me this week, and we'll get a date set, somewhere around the end of February." Kennedy snuffed out one cigarette and lit another.

Tuesday, January 24

Moses Robinson caught the ball on the wing and tripled up. His defender knew, however, that Mose was not going to pass, so he stepped into Mose's hips to take away the initial shot. Using his right foot as his pivot, Mose jab-stepped to the middle before using a wicked crossover to free himself baseline. A second defender slid over to take the charge but was left as a statue when Mose simultaneously jumped and slid into the lane for a hammer dunk. He started laughing and talking almost before he returned to the floor.

"It's an art form, Paul, and I continue to be your professor. But I suppose you're doin' the best you can. Next time, I'll tell you which way I'm goin'." Mose loved to school his buddies. These art lessons, aka pickup basketball games, were given two or three times each week with similar results. Pushing, shoving, talking—and laughter. Two decent players against one gifted athlete enjoying the competition, the game, and their friendship.

Mose showered, talking all the time to his two best friends about their court inadequacies, while preparing to head off to one of the classrooms in the old gym for his two o'clock Theories of Coaching class. Dan thought it ironic that Mose was enrolled in the class given his current problems with his coaches.

"Maybe you'll learn how to deal with misfit players like yourself," he chided.

Dan then headed east to the new engineering building for a science lab.

Paul had no Tuesday/Thursday afternoon classes, so he usually spent the time at the library, but his routine was being transformed by a young woman in search of an identity. He hung his gear in Mose's locker to dry and set out for his third meeting with the preschoolers at the University Hill Lab School across Broadway from the UMC. He knew he was going there to see Sarah, but he had enjoyed his time last week with the children as well.

"Welcome back, Mr. Garrity. I hope you've come to work with Ricky. He's asked for you. Miss Phillips said she thought you'd be back." This was Mrs. Best.

"That would be great, ma'am. Where can I hang my coat?"

"This way." The gray-haired woman led him to an unfamiliar room, an office really, but with children-sized furniture. "Ricky, look who's here to read to you." Ricky did not turn around but remained still while looking out the window. A nurse was sitting silently next to him.

Paul spoke. "Hey, Ricky, can I read you about Rootie Kazootie again?" Ricky turned suddenly and smiled. Paul was stunned. The little boy had sustained some kind of injury to his head. The bruise extended beyond the two bandages that stretched along the left side of his face. Paul bent down on his knees.

Mrs. Best spoke softly, "Ricky had an accident at home over the weekend, but he seems to be getting better." Ricky was holding his new favorite book and held it out to Paul.

Paul looked directly into the little boy's eyes as he addressed Mrs. Best and the nurse. "I think we'll be okay in here for a while." He scooped up Ricky with his left arm and wobbled to the wall. "Yeah, we're going to be just fine. Let us know when his mom gets here." The two ladies left quietly.

The time passed quickly. In addition to reading about the little boy baseball player, Paul showed Ricky how to draw basketball players. Ricky's stick figures were as good as his art teacher's, and Paul asked if he could take the drawings home and put them on his refrigerator.

Mrs. Best put her head in the room. "Time to go, Ricky, your mother is here. Put your coat on."

"Here, let me help you with that, Ricky Kazootie." The little boy laughed. Before he left, Ricky gave Paul a hug, and Paul said, "I'll see you on Thursday . . . two days from now."

Sarah entered the office with tears in her eyes. She went right to Paul and hugged him tightly. He held her, but with some confusion.

"See that mirror behind me? I've been watching you the whole afternoon. What you did with that little boy was incredible." She was talking into his shoulder.

"What happened to him?" There was urgency to his question.

"His mother's boyfriend hit him over the weekend. The police put the guy in jail, but we don't know if he'll make bail or not. I guess Ricky wouldn't respond to anyone yesterday, but he just opened up to you this afternoon. It was something special to watch. Mrs. Best has ushered in all the college aides to watch how you handled him. She let me stay the whole time. You were so gentle and funny."

"Is he going to be alright? You know, the bruises and his emotions?"

"There were no serious physical injuries, just the bad bruise, and the nurse said after watching him with you that everything is going to be fine." Sarah continued to hold on to Paul.

"They're not going to let that guy near him anymore, are they?"

"His mom said she wouldn't. We think she means it." There was uncertainty in her response. Paul took a few moments to contemplate what had just occurred before Mrs. Best returned to the room.

"It looks like we'll be seeing you every Tuesday and Thursday for the remainder of the semester. Go sign up for Sociology Lab 210, and I'll see you get the two credits, even though you'll be starting late." Mrs. Best smiled like she had won a two-on-two basketball game.

The porch light blinked as Paul and Sarah drove up to the SDT house at eleven. On this night Sarah did not want to go home and was willing to risk a curfew violation. He did not allow that to happen.

"Tomorrow's lunch is a long time away," said Sarah. "I was so proud of you today." She kissed him and jumped out of the truck and ran to the door, where she paused, turned, and finger-waved gently.

Mose was returning from listening to the basketball game at another redshirt's apartment at the same time Paul returned. "My guys lost to Oklahoma, 71-66."

"I think you could have found five points for them, Mose. Maybe next season, huh?" Mose shrugged in agreement. Paul slapped him on the back, "Don't take your coat off, Robinson, we've got guard duty."

Wednesday, January 25

Two weeks after Paul met Sarah Phillips, it was snowing again. Paul eagerly anticipated his M-W-F classes. In the morning, he had a double dose of Dr. Orr, first at nine in a US History survey course and again at eleven for History of the Cold War, a class that had become his all-time favorite. Since it only covered the brief period from 1945 to 1965, the events were covered in detail; there were times for questions and current events. Dr. Orr drew the connections between Cold War politics and the civil rights movement, the correlation between the events of the Mideast and Western Europe, and the contradictions surrounding the war in Vietnam and the historical anti-colonialism of America. Always, Dr. Orr's foundational lesson was that these world events would impact each student's life at some point. While not every citizen would know the details of America's past, a substantial portion of the population should, and that group should be vocal and active in guiding America's future in whatever occupation they chose after college. History was not simply an academic endeavor. Knowing the truthful and unfettered history was both honorable and patriotic.

A two-hour break allowed Paul time to get a sandwich and head to Norlin for an hour of reading before his American Lit class. He enjoyed this class too. Never before an avid reader, he was finding that the professor's adage "Everybody likes to read; some just don't know it yet," was holding true for him. A novel every three weeks was taxing his time, but it was opening worlds previously uninhabited for the former math/science student.

This time it was Sarah who was reading the *CU Daily* while she waited in the loggia. She was interested in the Reagan-Kerr controversy swirling in the California University system and about a column by a visiting Jordanian professor who advocated the return of Arab refugees into Israel. Paul startled her.

"Hey, Sars, what are you reading?" He kissed her.

"You're wet, my dear!" She brushed snow from his hair. "Have you read this yet?"

"No, I haven't had time yet. What's it say?" They headed toward the cafeteria.

"More Arab bullshit!" Paul knew his girlfriend was angry, because the only time she cursed was when she was angry. "They all want to destroy Israel, but they dress up their demands for American audiences; make it sound like they're just asking for what's fair, that they're the victims. They don't know what a victim is."

Paul saw a new side to Sarah and was concerned. For the next half hour, Paul asked her about her feelings and thoughts on the Arab-Israeli conflict. He was ahead of her in facts, since his Cold War class had just covered the unit on the creation of a Jewish state in Palestine. Orr's reading assignments provided comments from several viewpoints. Sarah, however, saw only one side, and the issue was personal. Her biases against Arabs were obvious.

"I know, but I don't care about their side. They had their chance in '48 to share the land and chose war instead." She would have no part of the Arab points.

"Sarah, I have to go," Paul interrupted. "I've got that meeting with the Republican guy, the chairman of the YAF. It's just upstairs, but I said I'd meet him at one. Walk me up?"

"Yeah. Sorry about my rampage. I was going to talk to you about something else, but we got sidetracked."

"Do you want to sit in? It shouldn't take too long to set up a meeting with the SPU." Paul was remembering last week's SPU meeting as they walked upstairs.

"Thanks, but I need to go to the language lab and practice my French verbs, especially those for love." She smiled. *Je vous aime, mon cher. M'aimez-vous?*

Paul wasn't sure of his translation. *"Oui,"* he responded tentatively, "if you're asking what I think you are."

Sarah leaned in and kissed him. *"Je suis."*

"I've got some reading for poly sci, and I need to do some research for my Cold War class. Want to go to the library with me?"

"No. You go, and I'll be waiting for you at your apartment when you get back. I have a meeting after dinner with the Pan-Hellenic council, something about building better student-faculty relations. Like I said, there's something I want to talk to you about, but it can wait until tonight."

"Okay."

"Can I get into your apartment?" she asked.

"Yeah, it's usually unlocked. The other guys use it as their kitchen too and put their stuff in the refrigerator. But I'll get you a key anyway."

"My own key to your apartment." She raised her eyebrows, kissed him again, and headed out for the language lab.

Harry Roberts directed the Young Americans for Freedom. A senior from northern Colorado and a conservative Republican to the core, he reminded Paul of his father in some ways. While Paul disagreed with Roberts' politics, he found he enjoyed the man as the meeting progressed, especially his sense of humor. Paul was there only to work out a meeting time between the SPU and YAF, so he sat patiently and listened while sixteen male students conducted a formal meeting, one much more orderly than another led by John Cohen several days earlier. When the time came for "New Business," Roberts turned to Paul.

"I'm here to set up a meeting between our two groups to organize a Vietnam Teach-In. You should've received a letter from our group about it, and I've already talked with Dr. Kennedy, who's agreed to be the overall sponsor. I'm just the messenger boy here," Paul stated.

"How soon?" asked Roberts.

"Probably within the next week or so. Kennedy said he'd like to move on this, you know, have the teach-in around the end of February."

"How about next Monday, up here, at one? Would that work?" asked Roberts, who seemed to be the only YAF member with a voice.

"Yeah, it would. The entire groups or just you and Cohen? I'm not sure that I need to attend, but whatever you think." Paul deferred to the YAF leadership.

Roberts looked to his group for input. There was none, except for some nodding of heads. "Okay then, Monday it is. I'll meet Cohen. Have him bring another 'Spew.'" The conservative members laughed.

"I think that's 'Spoo.' Thanks. I'll pass on the invitation." Paul left to attend his American Lit class.

Two weeks after the bartending experience that brought Sarah and Paul together, they were sitting in a front booth at The Sink sharing a burger. Sarah had a dilemma.

"Every year, my house gives out awards for service." She took a drink from Paul's beer, then put a fry in her mouth.

"What kind of service?" asked Paul, who was eating the last of the burger.

"Just stuff around the house for being helpful, and for CU, and around the community. You know, for some of the stuff I get involved with at the sorority. It's not that big of a deal, really. They're giving out one to a sister in each class. I don't know why I was selected." She seemed honestly embarrassed about the selection.

"From what I've seen, you deserve it. Maybe they asked those kids over at the Lab School to vote." Paul was mixing in some humor, but he certainly wanted Sarah to know he thought it was special. He lifted the beer glass to toast the award.

"Paul, be serious! Anyway, they're giving these out on Saturday night at a dress-up deal, and I want you to go with me," she hesitated, "but I already asked this other guy to escort me before I met you." They were both quiet. "I dated him a couple of times, and I didn't have anyone else, but we weren't a thing or anything, but now I wish I hadn't."

Paul waited, giving her a chance to continue if she wanted. She needed a response. "So, what's the problem?" he asked. "You're getting a special award for doing good things, and I'm really proud of you."

"My problem is I want you to get dressed up and go with me. I want you to be there when I stand up and get my award, and then I want you to give me a kiss when I come back to the table."

"I'd love to go with you, and you know I own at least one tie, unless Mose borrowed it."

Sarah shook her head slightly. "How do I get out of this?"

To Paul, it seemed easy. "You call your friend tonight and say you've changed your mind and are taking another guy. Apologize for breaking his heart and hang up."

Sarah just stared at him. "You don't really understand my dilemma, do you?"

He took her hand and held it. "It's okay if you can't do it. I'll stay home and read my history, and you can call me later." It was true and untrue at the same time.

"Hell! I'd be so upset with myself if you weren't there. Besides, they might need a bartender after dinner."

Hello," answered Paul at eleven-thirty.

"Hey, Paul, I don't have a date for Saturday night anymore, and I was wondering if you would escort me to my own dining room. My treat."

"Who did you say this was?" They laughed like little kids.

Thursday, January 26

"Sars" and "My Dear" liked to study, but Paul's apartment offered a compelling alternative, so on Thursday they went to Norlin Library to work.

"ENTER HERE, THE TIMELESS FELLOWSHIP OF THE HUMAN SPIRIT'"

Paul learned many things about his girlfriend in a short time; one of those was she was a worker. She could go without much sleep to get her studies or service projects completed. Paul's habits were first-rate now too, thanks to some instruction by Dr. Orr, and he truly enjoyed his history assignments. The Cold War class was particularly challenging, and Orr seemed to be giving him special articles on Monday mornings about recent civil rights events to test his political philosophy. If he did not have them read by the following week, well . . . that only happened once, and Orr let it be known that it was not to happen again.

Friday, January 27

Sarah's breathing finally slowed, and she turned back to Paul. "You're really something, you know," she said.

Those eyes, thought Paul. He caressed her face with the back of his fingers. "The philosopher across the hall tells me I shouldn't try to understand all that's happening between us right now, but to just live it and enjoy it."

"That's hard for you, isn't it?" It was her turn to ask rhetorical questions, so Paul stayed quiet. "If it's bewildering to you, you ought to see it from my side. Maybe it would help you understand. You try and analyze everything. You have to know, you think." He waited. "What's it been? Just over two weeks? I've never, and I mean never, felt like this about another person . . . or about myself. This may sound odd, but I love us both so much. Does that make sense?" Her voice was soft, but sure.

"Much more sense than anything I've said to myself. Do you mean that, Sars, about loving me?"

"Paul Garrity," she shook her head ever so slightly, "I've got so much to teach you, don't I! Do you trust me yet?"

"Yes, I do."

"Last Friday, after we first made love—and I cried—I got back to the house, and the sisters wanted to know all about us, about what had happened. I lied to them. But my roommate, Anne—you met her—asked me later, after the lights were out and we were lying in our beds, 'Did you give it up too easily?' And do you know what I said? I said, 'I didn't give it up. I gave it away as a gift to the most special man I've ever met.' And nothing you've done since has made me second guess myself. Whether you end up as the only man in my life, or as just the first man with whom I made love, I'll never regret this. Yes, Paul, I love you."

"When did you realize I felt the same way?"

Sarah smiled broadly. "When I looked out the window of the house after you'd taken me home and you were still parked there twenty minutes later, I knew you were in this as deeply as me." Paul started to speak, but she put her fingers over his lips. "It was my night to say it to you. Your turn is coming, my dear."

Saturday, January 28

When Paul arrived at the Sigma Delta Tau house for Sarah's award, he was wearing a dark blue blazer, purchased at The Regiment, over a light blue shirt with gray slacks. She liked his wide tie. "Very cool!" She received several comments from her sorority sisters about her non-Jewish boyfriend that night, many of whom had never seen him, since they did not reside in the house yet. Sarah seemed nervous, but upbeat, as she steered him into the dining room.

"Paul, I'd like you to meet my parents, Susan and Eugene. Mother, Father, this is Paul, the man I've told you about." Sarah maintained her hold on Paul's arm while he reached out and shook hands. Eugene's hands were softer than Susan's, and both were older than Dick and Diane Garrity. Paul's mind raced. He wondered how he would introduce Sarah to his parents when the time came. He sensed meeting her parents under these conditions was extremely important to her. He liked the atmosphere, since the evening would be largely choreographed.

Sarah's parents had been invited weeks in advance, met at Denver's Stapleton Airport just this afternoon, and driven to Boulder by two SDT sisters. Despite Sarah's earlier denials, this event was "a big deal," and the honorees were highly regarded by "The House" for their service and scholarship.

WELCOME

1967 Sigma Delta Tau House

HOUSE AND COMMUNITY SERVICE AWARDS

Honored Recipients

Freshman	Miss Ronnie Plattner	Mr. and Mrs. Allen Plattner
Sophomore	Miss Sarah Phillips	Dr. and Mrs. Eugene Phillips
Junior	Miss Amanda Glaser	Dr. and Mrs. John Glaser
Senior	Miss Susan Frankin	Mr. and Mrs. Michael Frankin

Sarah wore a long black dress that accentuated her shape and would have been appropriate for any formal affair. Her three-inch heels pushed her close to five-eleven, just a few inches shorter than her date. She wore a small diamond pendant, which stood out against the black gown, with matching earrings. As Paul surveyed the situation—a pretty woman made radiant by her attire, the presence of her parents, and the guest of honor in her own house—he began to feel uneasy, much like an outsider. He laughed under his breath. *Maybe they do need a bartender tonight.*

The mixing lasted about an hour and included drinks, introductions to several invited guests and dignitaries, and vocal music by the CU Buffoons. One of the dignitaries was a Holocaust survivor whose daughter was a pledge in the house. Sarah made the point of telling this to Paul before introducing them, so he could remember the man out of all the people whom he met.

"He spoke to us last fall about his experiences in the camps. He didn't seem bitter, only determined that we should all remember. I asked him about his belief in God, and he said he wondered about God, about what He had been doing during those awful years. He said even now he has days when he doesn't believe in a God, but usually he does. He made me laugh and he made me cry." Paul was surprised at how short the survivor was when he stood next to him. He had not perceived that while Sarah was talking about him.

Sarah was the second of the four Sig Delts to receive her service award. As he watched her and listened to The Survivor list her accomplishments over the past year, he noticed she was standing on the platform in her stocking feet. Again, he suppressed a laugh. Twice she had glanced over to him and smiled, but each smile sent a different message. A complex smile, especially the second one. Susan Phillips noticed.

The award included a wood plaque and a $300 scholarship, plus her name would be engraved on the Service Board in the SDT entrance hallway. It was an important award for the house, and Sarah was a worthy recipient. He was proud he was there as her date, but a bit uncomfortable knowing he was being scrutinized by her mother and the SDT sisters. Sarah remained up front until all four women had been recognized. Upon returning to the table, she received her kiss.

When the mixing ended and Sarah's parents excused themselves to return to the hotel, Paul and Sarah sat on the same sofa that they had at their first meeting. Both admitted to being nervous about her parents meeting Paul and laughed at a few of the awkward moments, especially those with her mother. Paul understood the tension that Sarah had referred to weeks earlier, the smothering aspect of their relationship, but he really appreciated her father's kindness. Sarah frequently reached over to touch Paul's tie or hold his hand or drop her head on his shoulder momentarily, all acceptable within the rules of physical contact inside the walls of the house.

"When the survivor spoke about your accomplishments, he mentioned something about a Readers Network. What's that?" asked Paul.

"Nothing really. Last year when I began working at the Lab School like the freshmen I supervise this year, I enjoyed reading to the little kids, sort of like you do with those three boys. I set up a non-credit reading program in some of Boulder's other elementary schools, enlisting some of my sisters. Now, I'm just the coordinator for it. No biggie."

"How many sorority women do you supervise this year?"

"I don't supervise any of them. They just sign up for a once-a-week session and go."

Paul tilted his chin. "How many?"

"We're in every Boulder elementary school now, and I think someone from every sorority is doing it, but it's still mostly from this house and the Pi Phis. Maybe a hundred volunteers or so. Like I said, no big deal."

Sunday, January 29

Paul was up early working on apartment maintenance, interrupted only by a phone call from Sarah telling him she wished he was going with her on the ride to Vail with her parents, and that she would come over later that evening. He had not realized how tired he was, but for the past week and a half, he and Sarah had been existing on about five hours of sleep per night. They had not neglected their studies, only their rest. CU was playing Missouri at one.

The Buffs rallied behind Pat Frink and Lynn Baker to win in overtime. Afterwards, Paul read a chapter on Progressive reform and wrote a reaction to W.E.B. DuBois' stand vis-à-vis Booker T. Washington. Dr. Orr asked Paul to add a paragraph where he considered how DuBois might have responded to Black Power. Paul moved from the table to the couch to read a few chapters in *The Grapes of Wrath* for American Lit. That's where Mose found him at six to go to dinner; only a few pages had been completed before Paul had fallen asleep.

Sarah called around eight. "Eugene and Susan" boarded the plane for New York just after six, and Sarah and Anne negotiated the icy turnpike back to Boulder in Sarah's Corvair in about an hour.

"I missed you! My mother quizzed me all day about you. Anne was great. She kept saying we weren't serious, that I never get too serious with any of my boyfriends."

Monday, January 30

The previous week had been extremely busy for Paul: classes, campus politics, Ricky on Tuesday and Thursday, an intramural basketball game on Wednesday evening, and always Sarah. "Where are you finding the energy and time?" asked Sally. He just told her he could never remember a time when he was so buzzed. Each activity seemed to have meaning.

He had lunch with Sarah. A slight warming trend for Boulder brought out a new mini skirt. "Just for you! What do you think?" She loved Paul's answer. Paul presented Sarah with her room key attached to a necklace chain, which she thought was goofy but romantic in its own way.

After lunch he joined John Cohen, Harry Roberts, and a second YAF member to take the next step in planning the Vietnam Teach-In. March 1st was the tentative date, but Dr. Kennedy and the CU administration would have to approve. "Make sure they think they're in charge," warned Cohen, "otherwise, they'll put it off." They agreed to meet in a week. "Garrity, you'll run March One past Kennedy, won't you?" Number one SPU grunt.

He was not called on in American Lit, which was a good thing, because he had never returned to the Joad Family's migration on Sunday. He vowed to catch up for Wednesday.

Paul, Dan, and Mose sat with Renee Mattison, a shapely senior from California, for dinner at The Colonial, the large women's rooming house across the street from 1203 where a small group of men from The Hill could buy meal tickets in the downstairs cafeteria. Sarah arrived around seven. He suggested they go to Norlin to catch up. She jokingly protested but knew it was a good idea. He walked her home around 10:30, rather than returning to 1203.

Tuesday, January 31

On Tuesday Paul aced his first exam of the semester in political science. He filled a blue book with a solid analysis of John Marshall's impact on the Supreme Court, but he wrote into his travel time, so he showed up late to Art History.

He was, however, on time for his second art lesson, the art of basketball. Professor Robinson was late, though, something that seldom happened. In the meantime, Dan and Paul out hustled two wannabees. Mose arrived shortly thereafter, and the three of them moved to a side basket.

"They talked about renewing my scholarship for next year." Mose had been expecting the financial aid to be withdrawn. "I guess they're lookin' for a replacement for Baker," he laughed, "as if anyone could."

"Baker who?" asked Dan with a smile.

"What did you tell them?" asked Paul.

"I told 'em I was ready to toe the line, but I also said I didn't like to be yelled at, that I play better, that I learn better, when coaches just talk to me. It just sort of came out."

"And?" His two buddies waited.

"And they said okay. So, I guess I'm back in the fold." He looked up and had a huge grin on his face. "So, I get to kick your asses for another year or two."

It was the best news Paul could hear; his best friend was coming back.

Paul had still not signed up for his new sociology class, but he was not going to miss seeing Ricky. With the warm weather continuing, the kids were playing kickball outside, and Ricky ran up to Paul as soon as he entered the playground and hugged his leg. He examined his little buddy's face closely, poked at it playfully, and asked if there was any more pain. Assured there was not, he joined in the game. Sarah received the second hug of the afternoon, much longer and more involved. "How are you going to run with that thing?" she asked. At 3:30 Paul met Ricky's mother, who also hugged him. *The trifecta*, he thought to himself.

FEBRUARY

Wednesday, February 1

It was snowing again on the first of February. Colorado weather. Sarah's M-W-F schedule meant a busy morning: three classes in three different buildings, but then lunch with Paul. She had been going to the language lab in the afternoons on those days, which usually took care of her French homework requirements. She was looking forward to spending the evening with Paul at 1203, studying, listening to music, small talk with his roomies, and sex. "There! I've said it." And she smiled.

Paul returned to the apartment just as Sally was coming down the stairs for work at the florist shop. "Did you get the mail, Sal?"

"Yeah, it's on the counter. You got another letter from the Pentagon. Looks the same." She brushed snow off his hair and smiled. "Only you would write McNamara about the war."

Paul smiled back. "Pen pals. Form letters, but a response. Drive carefully. It's getting slick."

"By the way, Sarah was by and left you a note. She signed it 'Sars.' I assume you pronounce that with a hard a, short for Sarah."

Paul smiled. "Yeah, sort of my pet name for her, like Mose or Sal."

At dinner Kevin showed up looking for either Paul or Dan. "We need another player for our intramural game tonight against Delta Upsilon. We could win with four, but we'll forfeit if one of you can't play."

"What time?" asked Dan.

"Seven."

"Can't. I'm working with my physics lab partner tonight. Have Paul do it; he's a history major; he'll have time."

"Paul?"

"Yeah, I guess I can, but I'll need to call Sarah and let her know. When'll we be done?"

"I'll get you back by eight-thirty."

They went back to 1203 after dinner to call Sarah but were unable to get through. The sorority line was constantly busy. "Drive me by her house and I'll tell her," said Paul.

"We don't have time, Paul. Have Dan call."

"Yeah, I can do that. If I can't get a hold of her before I leave, then I'll get Mose or Sally to call."

Paul and Kevin headed across campus to play a little hoops. Kevin was a good teammate. He defended, he rebounded, and unlike Mose, he passed. As promised, Paul was returned to 1203 by eight-thirty. Fun game. The Sig Eps won, and Paul scored over twenty.

Sarah was not waiting for Paul nor had she been by. Mose had not gotten in touch with her, so Paul called, only to be told she had gone to the library. He was confused, since he thought that she was going to wait for his call, and then they were going to be together in the apartment. He grabbed his coat and stocking cap off the rack next to the door and headed down the stairs. If she went to the library, she probably drove, so he decided to walk over to Norlin.

He found her at the large oak table in the reading room on the first floor working on proofs for math. Trigonometry did not come easy for her, about the only subject that did not, but she needed six math credits to meet the A & S degree requirements. Algebra last semester had been her only C.

"Hey." Paul pulled up a chair next to her. "How come you're over here?"

"How come you didn't call? Where were you?"

"The Sig Eps needed an extra player for their intramural game, so I played. I tried to call. When I couldn't get you, Dan was supposed to call."

She was not looking at him as he spoke. "Maybe I needed you tonight too," she said while she fidgeted with the key necklace.

Paul touched her arm. "Hey, what's wrong?" Without speaking, Sarah turned to face him. Tears welled up in her eyes.

"This is stupid. Can we go somewhere?" She wiped her eyes with her sleeve, and the two of them gathered up her books. Paul, who had removed only his cap, helped her on with her parka, then took her books. She hooked her arm through his.

Sarah parked the Corvair just up from the SDT house and left it running.

"Bet you didn't know I could be this emotional, did you." She was still crying a little, but she tried to smile.

"I'm sorry. I should've gotten in touch with you before I left."

"You didn't do anything wrong, Paul," and she paused. "I just really wanted to be with you tonight."

"What's so special about tonight? I mean, I was looking forward to being with you too, but Kevin was sort of desperate."

Sarah moved closer to him on the bench seat. "We missed an evening, and lunch doesn't satisfy my new-found sexual desires." She was not joking. "You were all I thought about today. I even gave you a French name at the language lab, so I could practice with you. Pierre Garrity." She finally smiled, and Paul kissed her.

"I can't believe I'm dating someone like you, you know," he said.

"Why?" She shook her head as if his statement was absurd. The passion in them both captured the moment, and Sarah and Pierre made love in the front seat of her 1963 Corvair, just a few feet from the sidewalk that led to the SDT house.

"I wonder if the girls will smell it on me," Sarah mused as she leaned back into Paul's arms. He remained quiet with his head tilted down into her long jet-black hair. To him, she smelled wonderful. "I'm sorry I overreacted tonight. I won't do it again. It's just that . . . I don't know . . . I'm afraid I can't have you forever . . . that this won't last, and I don't want to give you up for even one night. Pretty possessive, huh?"

"Now who's analyzing this relationship?" He stretched his back. "Your parents need to buy you a bigger car," and they both laughed.

"My mother warned me not to get too crazy about you, that I could have fun, but you couldn't really be good for me in the long run. She doesn't think Gentiles can really love us Jews."

"I guess I'll just have to show you. Maybe I'll never be able to convince your mother, but I do love you, Sarah."

She squeezed his arms tightly around her chest. "I knew your day would come to tell me that. Paul . . ."

"Yeah?"

"In some way, no matter what, no matter where, love me forever. Okay?"

"Count on it."

"Hello."

"Hey." Sarah responded on her end of the phone line and then remained quiet.

Finally, Paul spoke. "Can I tell you something I've learned about you?"

"Yeah," she said very softly.

"Despite all your abilities and accomplishments, and even though you have this great desire to achieve, on the inside you're so gentle and tender. And now that all this passion has been unleashed, I think it scares you." He cleared his throat and continued. "Sars, it scares me too. But I'm this big tough guy, and I'm not supposed to show it, but it's there. If you could've looked inside me at your awards dinner, you would've seen it." On separate ends of the phone line, they put their foreheads together.

Sarah sniffled. "Is this the great chapter of my life?" she asked quietly.

"I hope Boulder is just one of the great chapters, but I know there will be others. Trust me on that."

"Pretty serious night, huh."

"Yeah."

"I'm scared about all that's happening, but I'm going to give you my heart and trust that you'll protect it. Kay?"

"I will." Paul paused. "I'll try every day, but I won't be perfect. But Sars, I'll try."

"Thank you for saying I'm beautiful, even though I'm not."

"You're welcome."

Thursday, February 2

Sarah and Paul sat on the floor in his apartment on Thursday evening. A single candle burned in front of them. "Revolver" played on the stereo.

"I'm not even sure why I'm in Boulder. It's the antithesis of Jewishness."

"Maybe you have to not be something before you can really be that thing," Paul said. "My dad thinks that's why I'm a Democrat these days. We aren't always at the center of our own universe."

"I love you at these times. I really do. You make more sense than anyone to me." Sarah was serious and she slid even closer to him on the floor next to the couch. "It's my education, if I understand you right, but it's also that I'm here as a function of someone else?"

"In this case, me. I don't dare think too much about our future. We're only twenty, but my time with you has been so much more than just fun. Every day I'm just buzzed, to use Mose's word, but it's true. This is an adventure, Sars, and we're not just spectators."

"Twenty. We're not missing much, are we?" She held up her wine glass and toasted Paul. "Wherever I am as an old woman, I'm going to thank you for these days . . . and nights." She took a drink, then leaned over and kissed him.

Before it progressed further, Dan knocked once on his way in. "Hey, guys, what's up?" He had been drinking, too. Paul smiled but Sarah's look reflected her desire not to be disturbed. "Don't give me that look. I was living in this apartment a long time before you, Phillips, and I'm not going to let you change my buddy." Sarah and Paul remained mute as Dan walked over and inspected the wine bottle. "Mateus!" He paused in the middle of his act. "Mose and Sally have to see this? Don't you dare move. MOSE! SALLY!" Dan yelled as he stuck his head into the hall. "MOSE. Put whatever you have in your hand down and get in here." Dan looked back at the couple on the floor. "Don't move," he continued without interruption. "MOSE! SALLY!"

Sally appeared first and was joined by Mose, who was wearing a pair of cut-offs and sandals, but no shirt. "What's goin' on, Mountain Man?"

"Come in here. Paul needs our help." Dan ushered his partners into the apartment. "Look at that! Just look!" Still, the couple on the floor had not moved. It was clear that Dan was drunk, the one resident of 1203 who imbibed beyond his limit frequently.

Slowly, Paul raised both arms as if to say, "You caught me. What can I say?"

But it was Sarah who broke them all up when she said, "Daniel, please be a dear and get three more wine stems from the counter and join us." And they did.

Sarah was escorted home by two giggling gentlemen and one wobbly woman that night. Dan had gone to his room to pass out earlier. No one was in any condition to drive. The Corvair could be picked up on Friday.

Friday, February 3

Paul was reading the newspaper when Sarah joined him for lunch at the UMC. "What do you know about an Arab group called al-Fatah? There was a small article in the *Camera* about a raid by this group against a village in northern Israel. It says they're a Palestinian force."

Sarah pulled the paper over in front of her. "It doesn't give the exact location. Just says 'near the Jordanian border.' That's near my uncle's kibbutz!"

"al-Fatah?" Paul repeated as he raised his eyebrows.

"It's a Palestinian group. They don't even have a country, and none of the other Arab countries even want to take them in."

"Is this another Phillips editorial?"

"It's true, Paul. They've been causing trouble for Jordan's king since 1948. I don't know much about them, not as much as I should, but they're just another group of Arabs that wants to destroy Israel." Sarah looked back to the story.

"I guess it's time I started finding out about all this stuff in the Mideast. Wouldn't want to miss out on all this fun you're having."

"Don't joke about this. It's not just my uncle's family; it's all of Israel that's endangered." Sarah was squeezing Paul's forearm as she talked.

"Okay. I'll drop by the bookstore on my way home from class and see what they have on Israel and these Arab groups. No more jokes. I'll become your unbiased expert."

"I'm not sure I want you to spoil all my prejudices about the Arabs. We talk about this all the time at the house, but the Arabs never get their due."

Sarah and Sally cooked dinner in Paul's kitchen as they giggled their way through wine and Sally's Pueblo Italian pasta recipe. "It requires a little bit of vee-no to make it just right," said Sally. Mose and Paul stayed away; Mose in his room listening to Charlie Parker, while Paul sat in the downstairs TV room reading a book on Israel, which he had purchased that afternoon. The girls started late, the sauce took longer to simmer than they planned, and the dinner stretched out until nearly eight. Movie plans were cancelled for the night.

"I'm so stuffed," moaned Mose as he lay out on the couch. "Write the recipe down so I can give it to my future wife," said Paul.

"I think she'll be able to remember it," laughed Sally as she glanced back at Sarah.

"Let's just have a college night where we sit around and talk philosophy until we girls have to go home," suggested Sarah as she rinsed off the plates into the sink.

"I'm not movin' off the couch. Is that a personal philosophy?" said Mose.

Sarah sat across Paul's lap on the big green chair. He kissed her and whispered, "Thank you for dinner," into her ear.

Sally poured herself another glass of wine and sat on the floor with her back against the couch and continued. "Honestly, I love these guys, Dan included. They're like my friends, soul mates, protectors, and brothers all rolled up into one. They kind of adopted me last fall when I was looking for a place to live. I didn't want to live in a dorm after transferring here, being a sophomore and all. Paul was a little concerned about me being the only girl in the apartment, so he gave me an upstairs room at a downstairs price. I know it was so he could watch over me."

Sarah looked puzzled, but Paul rescued her. "There are eight apartments in the building. All four of the upstairs apartments have bathrooms; none of the downstairs rooms have them. They share a common john and they're a little smaller, so the rent is less."

Mose elaborated. "Paul's a carpenter in addition to being a lover. This place was being renovated last year. Nobody lived here. Paul got a job helpin' with the renovations; it was his college job. He got tight with the owner and suggested that each of the upstairs apartments be upgraded and that he could do the work. The downstairs was too far along for changes to be made, but the upstairs—these rooms—was still incomplete. Not only did he help build this mansion, he became the manager of these apartments. He lives here rent free, charges Dan and Sally and me lower rates, and he oversees the entire operation."

"What will I learn next about you?" Sarah kissed his cheek.

Mose shook his head in mock disgust. "He got rooms for me and Dan and another Brackett Hall buddy, but the other dude got a free room on campus, because he works for the athletic department."

"That's how I got the room," said Sally. "We have very little to do with the slugs downstairs. We don't invade their space, and they're not allowed up here."

"How come you transferred to CU?" asked Sarah.

"Everybody knew me at Southern Colorado. Pueblo's my hometown, and I had kind of a reputation for being, well, loooose. I don't know if Paul told you or not, but I got pregnant in high school. It was a big scandal. I was supposed to drop out and stay out of sight, but I refused. I wanted to finish high school and get my diploma, and my mom supported me. I wasn't too apologetic, but I was allowed to stay. I gave the baby, a boy, up for adoption. I graduated and went to SC, but Pueblo's got such a small-town mentality, so after a year, I'd had enough and came up here. I went from being an only child living with a single parent to having three brothers and surrogate parents in Lakewood. Now you know why I'm usually upbeat."

"Was it hard to give up your baby?" asked Sarah. "You don't have to answer that if you don't want to."

"No, it's okay." Sally breathed deeply before answering. "The hardest thing I've ever done." She paused again. "It was the right thing to do. I'm convinced of that, but yeah, for me and my mom." Sally curled her lips inward, almost as if she wanted to say more, but hesitated. She moved her eyes to Mose as if looking for a lifeline.

"Yeah, Paul probably wouldn't have rented her the apartment if she'd have brought along a kid," teased Mose. He had had this difficult discussion with her before and sensed she didn't want to go any further with it tonight.

"We have a pretty good thing up here, even though Mose and Paul always take sides against Dan and me. We all have our idiosyncrasies; we're all a bit different, but we support each other," said Sally.

"Clearly, Sally's had too much wine," interrupted Paul. "Nobody supports me. I'm the butt of everyone's jokes and pranks. Dan mocks my work with the SPU, claims I'm a communist. They think I'm a flake for caring so much about the world out there. Somehow, they got the notion I'm naïve—and you've bought into it."

"Ignore them," urged Sally. "They're beginning to act like children. Mose and I have no father, so to speak. Dan's parents died when he was very little . . .

"But his grandparents are great!" interjected Paul.

"Yes, they are, especially his grandma, but to continue with my thought, only Paul comes from a normal family."

"Dick and Diane would be happy to hear that."

"Would you shut up, Paul!" Sally had the floor. "Your boyfriend, Sarah, nearly flunked out of school last year, so I'm told. I've got this reputation at home, and Mose is partly black. Only Dan knows what he wants to do and is on track to accomplish it."

Sarah looked over to the couch. Mose caught her. "What's the matter, babe? Didn't you know that I was a nee-gro?"

She hadn't but was honest about it. "No, I guess I didn't realize. I just thought you were Greek or Italian."

Mose, Paul, and Sally broke up. Mose finally said, "Yeah, Moses Robinson is a pretty Italian name. Garrity, you've found the perfect girl for yourself."

Sally stood up. "I've really got to pee. When I return, I have a question for you, Sarah."

"Are you guys all jocks?" asked Sarah.

"What do think, Mose? Are we jocks?" Sarah could tell her question was not going to be taken seriously.

"Not me. I don't have an aggressive bone in my body. Too mellow. And not Paul. He reads too much. But Dan? Yeah, maybe Danny Boy is a jock." Mose was talking with his eyes closed.

Sally returned. "Much better. So, Sarah, do you get this much shit at your sorority house?"

"No, they treat me with a little respect there." Paul acted stunned. "But there are some other things I don't get there that I do here." She smiled and pulled Paul's head into her bosom.

"Like spaghetti," added Paul.

"No, I get spaghetti there. It must be something else," she answered with a smile.

"Mose came to CU on a basketball scholarship; Dan on an academic scholarship; and Paul got lost on his way to Fort Collins. I transferred so I could get lost. Why are you here?" asked Sally.

Sarah looked at Paul. "Didn't we have this conversation last night, my dear?" She looked back to Sally. "Probably because it was far away from my parents, my mother in particular, who is pretty suffocating. At least, I thought so at the time. She's always wanted certain things for me, which is good, but as her only child, she was becoming too excessive in her control and advice. So, I think I just bolted."

"Paul's been waitin' for you. You know, don't you, he's had a bit of a crush on you for over a year, but didn't have the nerve to confront you over at Libby. He thought you were probably too good for him. Then you just sort of disappeared until this fall, and he was hooked again." Mose was not saying this to provide information, just to embarrass his best friend.

Turning back to Paul, Sarah asked, "How come none of my friends ever heard of you?"

"Maybe you were asking the wrong friends." Paul had not taken her question seriously yet.

"Did you just hang with the jocks over at the gym, and when you didn't make the team, they sent you to my side of campus?"

"Ouch!" Paul grabbed his chest over his heart. "Actually, you haven't asked your old Libby Hall friends from last year. I dated one of them. She's the one who first told me your name."

"Which one?" Sarah demanded to know.

"Margo Miller. She's a Delta Gamma now."

"You knew who I was last year and didn't talk to me? If you were interested, why didn't you just ask me out?"

"Fear! Plain and simple. I was a late bloomer, wasn't in a fraternity, and generally had no confidence when it came to pretty girls."

Sally spoke up. "I think he met you at exactly the right time."

Mose stirred again.

"How come you don't have a steady girlfriend, Mose?" asked Sarah.

"No social graces," said Paul.

"He's just waiting for me," added Sally.

"Sally's right," kidded Mose, and he leaned over and kissed her cheek.

"Be serious. I really want to know."

"Serious, huh? Okay. How many black girls do you see here at CU? Almost none," said Mose.

"You really aren't that black in appearance, though. Would it matter just to date?" Again, Sarah was simply being open with her curiosity.

"I'm as black as you are Jewish."

"And I'm not dating one of my kind," said Sarah.

"Gotcha there, Mose," added Paul.

"So," cooed Sarah, "how do I casually call Margo to find out about you?"

"Trust me; I was a confused young boy last year."

Saturday, February 4

Dan was in Leadville to work at the florist shop, Sarah had synagogue and Pan-Hellenic, Mose had basketball practice, and Sally worked at the florist shop down on Arapahoe. They often teased Paul about having his weekends off, but they knew. This Saturday he spent the morning cleaning filters, replacing light bulbs, repairing cracks, and refinishing baseboards. While he hated plumbing jobs, he fixed one of the sinks in the first-floor bathroom. Around 1:00, after grabbing a sandwich across the street, he went to the library to read recent newspaper accounts about anti-war protests at other universities, particularly ones on the East Coast, which seemed to be in the vanguard of the movement.

Demonstrations there seemed to focus on the bombing campaign initiated by the Johnson Administration in 1965. The *NY Times* was filled with letters from the anti-war crowd condemning the bombings as "ineffective" and "immoral." In his notes he summarized nearly four hours of reading in four words:

1. Necessary?

2. Effective?

3.Costly!

4.Moral?

One word per hour, he quickly computed with an angry head shake. *Fuck! Indiscriminate killing will be the legacy of the war, something America will look back on with regret and revulsion.* He packed up his notes, put the newspapers back in the rack, and headed out.

At the front desk, he paused to watch the older workers go about their tasks. *Am I just fooling myself about the strength of the anti-war movement? It wouldn't be the first time that I've been naïve about something.* This moment of self-doubt would cause him another late night of pacing.

When he returned to 1203, he had a letter from Sarah's father.

Paul.

It was wonderful to meet you—and thank you for being so kind and gentle with our daughter. As you discovered, her mother can be quite protective, so please don't be alarmed by a couple of her remarks. Paul, community service is important to our family. It gives us meaning, is a way to pay back those who helped us along our journeys and keeps us humble. World events often obfuscate or otherwise overwhelm our personal relationships. Doing local service activities helps to keep us grounded.

Thank you for taking time out of your very busy schedule to share that important evening with us. (Sarah has told us of your many activities and endeavors.)

Sincerely,

Eugene

That evening the group, minus Dan, walked around The Hill, stopping in at the stores, bars, and coffee shops in a mindless tour.

Paul was quiet, something both Sarah and Sally noticed. Mose knew his buddy had moods but also knew they did not last long and were usually rooted in worldly events rather than personal problems, except for an occasional flare-up with his dad. Paul hid his anger about the war from his friends, especially about the bombing campaign, but that anger was escalating daily. Often, he found himself muttering aloud or pacing his room.

After coming out of the Audiophile, Sarah hooked her arm in Paul's. "Care to unload your thoughts on someone?" She squeezed his arm.

"I'm sorry. I just can't keep from thinking about the war. I'm not smart enough to really figure it out. I just have this feeling our time is right on the cusp of something. It just seems like there's something wrong."

Mose interjected a succinct thought. "Yeah, somethin's very wrong. They're killin' people over there."

"Sometimes I think it's just that simple, but it can't be. The bombing though," Paul paused, "not only is it so terribly expensive, but it's just downright brutal, and most of the bombs are dropped on the South, our ally. That makes no sense to me."

At Bennett's, Sally opened the door and motioned for everyone to enter. At the window booth, she leaned across the table and looked directly at Paul. "Does it make any difference that the Vietnamese have never done anything to us? Do you think we really care about those people when everyone refers to them as gooks?"

Sunday, February 5

Roast beef, brown potatoes, and gravy. Sarah had asked, "Is there anything I can do?" and was given an apron by Mrs. Garrity and banished to the kitchen. She was truly at ease and happy—aglow the entire afternoon in her initial meeting with Paul's parents. She had even slapped Mr. Garrity's hand for sampling the carrots still in the roasting pan. Retreating to the TV room in mock pain to rejoin Paul, his only comment was, "She has some spunk."

Sarah never saw two men eat a meal quite like Paul and his father. The plates were literally covered with slices of beef and potatoes, then re-covered with gravy, heavily peppered, with a topping of cooked onions. Portions were small and neatly arranged on Sarah's plate, at least at the beginning of the meal, but for her second helping, she had only meat, potatoes, and gravy.

Diane Garrity asked about Mose and Sally, thinking that they were coming down too, but Paul said Sally had to work, and Mose had to cancel because of basketball demands. "I'll send some leftovers with you for him. I worry he's not eating well."

"Paul tells me your car isn't running all that well. I've got some time next weekend to look at it if you're not using it."

"You don't have to do that, Mr. Garrity."

"Not a problem. We aren't planning to do anything next weekend are we, hon?"

Sarah looked at Paul, but not for help. "Okay, well, it doesn't start at all when it's cold. It shimmies over 50. It's leaking oil, and the heater doesn't seem to get started until I'm already over to Paul's apartment . . . you know, when I go over to study." She had already won them over, but this was frosting.

There was no mention of the war or Paul's brother, as Paul had promised Sarah there wouldn't be. These were taboo subjects in the Garrity household. All Sarah knew was that Ross Garrity was a gifted musician who had run off after high school and become a drug addict.

Sarah was quiet on the way back to Boulder.

"Pretty simple stuff," Paul said. "Probably not quite like dinner in New York when you had your boyfriends over." His right hand rubbed against her left thigh. "Is that a problem, Sars?"

"That you're simple?" She knew that was not the question; it was deeper than that.

"My not being a Jew."

She was slow to respond, not wanting to mislead Paul, but wanting deeply to be as honest as she could. "No, certainly not for now." She straightened her body slightly. "But down the road, maybe." Her words were cautious, but true, according to her feelings. She understood, and she believed he understood, that their age and inexperience would necessitate changes. "Last year I might not have gone out with you had you approached me in the dorm, but I was so into the sorority thing. Maybe even earlier this year. Paul, you're the first non-Jewish boy I've ever dated. I don't know what your thoughts about my past are; I don't think you care too much. You live in the present, and I like that. You don't have any noticeable prejudices, like some of mine, which are so obvious. What am I trying to say?"

The pickup made its first stop at the SDT house so that Sarah could get her books.

When she returned to the truck where Paul was waiting, she asked, "Do you see yourself as a simple fellow?"

"That's not what I said."

"Is that what you meant?"

"No, I just see you as so complex with . . . undercurrents. My struggles seem so ordinary to me."

"Maybe you're just used to them. I see you as a unique, fascinating man who has shaken up my life." She smiled and kissed him.

"I trust that means in a good way."

"In a very good way, because I certainly needed it. I've been so focused on being a sorority girl that I'm missing our world. The best thing, maybe, is I really like me these past few weeks. You've given me such, I don't know, support for whatever it is I'm doing. That's not quite it. I'm just me around you. I'm not acting or explaining. I just am."

"Sally cautions me about you. Not in a bad way, just that I've dived into the deep end, so to speak. You're Jewish and Greek, and I'm not; that none of my friends are. She worries that this will come crashing down. She likes you but just worries about me. I think Mose has told her about my history with dating."

Sarah's face contorted a bit, then she smiled. "Well, Paul Garrity, my history isn't any better . . . and I'm enjoying the deep end."

"Just so you know, Mose thinks we're a pretty good fit."

1203 served several purposes, one of which was a study hall, and in the winter and spring of 1967, the four residents of the second floor took their educations seriously. The addition of the sorority girlfriend did not change that. Sometimes it was just Paul and Sarah in his apartment, but Mose, Sally, and Dan often found space at the table, on the couch, or on the floor listening to the radio or the stereo while they read, solved proofs, or wrote essays. An hour or more would pass without a word being spoken, until someone offered something interesting.

"She killed herself!" Sally blurted out.

"Who?"

"Hedda Gabler. Oh, never mind. You guys haven't read the play." And the students would go silent again.

On this Sunday evening, Sarah did not get the chance to fully follow up with their car talk, but when Paul drove her back to the sorority house, she kidded him that he was stuck with her, that if they broke up, it would be his decision—and probably cause her to go off wandering in a desert for 40 years. "Don't worry, my dear." Her kiss at the door promised him she was not about to go on any desert trek.

Monday, February 6

A portrait of the historian Arnold Toynbee hung on the wall of Professor Orr's office. Paul looked at the old man on the wall on Monday morning as he posed the question to his mentor, "I was reading again this weekend—about Jews—and it made me do some thinking about the destiny of man. Do we have free will or are we powerless to determine our course?"

"Toynbee and Spengler, huh?"

"Yeah, but the book really didn't go into their ideas in any depth, but it made me wonder."

"Why are you reading a history of the Jews?"

"How's this for intellectual motivation. Because I started dating a

Jewish girl recently."

"She seems pretty energetic." Paul looked surprised and Orr took note. "I don't always have lunch in this little office reading over blue books. Occasionally, I'll go over to the UMC for lunch with a colleague."

"She's good for me, Professor, really good for me. She's smart, asks a lot of questions, makes me study, and is different. One minute I wonder what she sees in me, that she'll wake up and realize she could have better. Then, and more often, she gives me this belief in myself that I can pretty much do anything."

"Toynbee, Paul, without a doubt."

Tuesday, February 7

The noon news on KOA reported that the United States was going to begin using chemical defoliants in the DMZ to decrease North Vietnamese infiltration. "Stripping the trees of their leaves will allow the Air Force to monitor the movement of enemy troops into South Vietnam." It was the topic of the moment at The Colonial for lunch.

"I wonder what that'll do to the people who come in contact with the chemicals. Strip off their clothes?" asked Paul. He paused. "I'll bet they've been using for years without us knowing about it."

"Or their skin," answered Sally. "I thought napalm was bad enough."

"There just seems to be such a frustration growing about the progress of the war. It's not just me. It's more than a simple disagreement; it's real anger." Paul pushed his soup away. "I read where they're picketing the Dow Chemical recruiters back east. Mess with those corporations and they'll get you expelled from school. Financial ties and research with war money."

Mose reached across the circular table and took the soup. "It's a shitty war, but what do we do about it now that we're there?" Dan had an answer. "Maybe we didn't know what we were getting into, but we can't just quit and walk away. There's something about honor."

Paul put down his tuna sandwich and stared at Dan. "You sound like my dad." He arose abruptly, leaving his food at the table. Outside, in the middle of Pennsylvania Avenue, he screamed, "FUCK!"

Wednesday, February 8

Paul told Sarah an agreement had been reached and a date set for the Vietnam Teach-In, but only after reading the *Daily* on Wednesday morning did she appreciate how complicated the process had been. Now, his role would shift to publicity, getting the information out to the general student body. Sarah offered to help distribute flyers to the sororities and fraternities so that he could concentrate on his "gofer" assignments. He lightly punched her in the arm. Dr. Kennedy would line up the speakers, and Paul believed he could work more on his own and less with John Cohen.

Thursday, February 9

"Hey, Mose, did you see where Westmoreland wants to continue to draft 11,000 men each month?" said Dan as he walked into Mose's apartment with the *News*.

"Yeah, that's one piece of news I keep track of. Cronkite talks to me each night about it. I keep wonderin' if our deferments will outlast this war, and frankly, I doubt it. Paul! Your anti-war group had better get busy ending this fuckin' thing. PAUL! Did you hear me?"

"Coming, Mose. What're you yelling at me about?" Paul had been in Mose's apartment but had stepped into his own to get an apple. The doors remained open as they usually were. He hopped up on the counter and took a bite.

"I said you need to get this fuckin' war stopped before we graduate." Mose stole the apple, took a large bite, and gave it back.

"What're we afraid of, guys?" said Dan. "We'll have degrees, and they'll make us officers." He paused. "Second lieutenants. What's their life expectancy in Nam?"

"Shit! I come from a family where everyone's served honorably, and what do we get? Viet-fucking-Nam!" Paul was angry again.

"Do I sense some internal conflict, son? Tell Dr. Robinson all about it."

Dan rejected sharing a turn with the apple. "My grandpa served with the AEF in France in WWI, the Great War. Got some kind of medal. My dad fought in World War II. Bronze Star. You're not the only one here with war heroes on your family tree, Paul." Dan and Paul had frequently noted the similarities in their upbringing, from religion to politics to education and athletics, but Paul had moved into the Democratic Party, while Dan had remained a Republican. Mose thought it funny since neither could vote yet.

"Wonder what my dad did?" mused Mose.

"Probably served in a segregated battalion that never saw duty. See how far we've come. Now we draft blacks just like poor white kids," shot back Paul. They all were quiet for a moment. "Sorry, Mose, that wasn't fair of me. I'm not even sure that what I said is statistically accurate."

"The Reverend King seems to think it is," said Mose.

"What'll you do if you get drafted?" Dan asked the question in Paul's direction.

Paul looked at both his mates. "Probably go, I suppose. What about you?"

"Go. I'm not convinced this war is wrong." Dan paused and looked down. Paul and Mose waited for him. "Don't we hate communists?"

"Mose?"

"I got two years to figure it out, maybe three. LBJ and Westmoreland will hopefully have it figured out by then. You guys wanna go to The Sink for a beer?" Mose was already moving to get his coat, a GI coat."

"Let's go. It's been a while since just the three of us shared a pitcher."

The Sink wasn't crowded, so they were able to sit at the counter. It was small talk with beers, and Dan held his tongue about Paul's involvement with the anti-war crowd.

"Where's your girl tonight, Paul?" asked Dan.

"She took Sally shopping over at Crossroads Mall. Then she was going back to her house to study, which is what I should be doing."

"You can't leave here until you come up with the plan for ending the war, Garrity." Mose topped off his glass of beer and held up the empty pitcher for the bartender as a signal for another. "By the way, Paul, my dad was a white dude."

Friday, February 10

Friday arrived with some warmer weather. Sarah gave Paul a special hug when they met for lunch and then surprised him. "Can I go to the basketball game with you guys tomorrow?" Paul smiled as she teased, "I won't get in the way."

"Oh, okay. What about tonight?

"What about this afternoon? I feel like dancing and just having a good time with you. It's been such a busy week, especially for you." Sarah knew the answer and put her arm around his waist as they walked through the wide corridors of the UMC to buy a sandwich.

"What did you and Sally buy at the mall last night? She wouldn't tell me when she got in. Just said 'women's stuff.'"

"Believe her."

They were giddy to be with each other. Taking the previous evening off had caused them to desire one another even more. Sarah and Paul truly liked the other's company, the other's traits and personality, and they were open and uncritical in their relationship. To her sorority sisters, it seemed "too good to be true, too good to last."

"Sally gave me some advice last night, right out of the blue." Paul was interested, and Sarah leaned in and whispered. "She told me to get on the pill. First of all, she said she was surprised I wasn't, after I told her that I wasn't, but then she hugged me when I said I had never needed to be. She just said I do now, and not to let happen to me what happened to her. So, this afternoon, that's where I'm going, but evidently, it takes time, so we have to control ourselves."

"I don't know if I can around you. Haven't so far," he chuckled.

"Then be careful."

Saturday, February 11

It was a happy crowd that left the fieldhouse on Saturday afternoon, as the Buffs breezed by Oklahoma, 71-57, to remain in the hunt for a Big Eight championship. From there, the group of nine walked to The Sink for beers. Three or four conversations were occurring at any one time, and in the dark back room of the bar, it was easy for Dan and Tracey and Paul and Sarah to neck and make small talk.

"Did you get lost on the way home from church this morning?" asked Paul.

"Synagogue, my dear. No, just sidetracked. I started listening to two older gentlemen talk about the existence of God. I was kind of ease-dropping at first, but then I pulled up a chair at their table and asked them if I could listen. I lost track of time because they were so interesting. Neither one of them was sure of God's existence, but they were generally in agreement that He was real. But what was most interesting was what they said about the need for a God to support Judaism. The man who was younger, maybe about 50 or 60, said religion had to have God to be relevant. The older man said it didn't matter, that Judaism had established morality for the world, and that alone was enough to give it relevancy. A person could be a cultural Jew without a definite belief in God."

"I guess I've just always assumed there was God, and it was only young people who debated His existence."

"Have you ever had an emotional experience or feeling that told you there was a God?"

"An epiphany? No never," answered Paul.

"Me either and I thought that meant I could never be a real Jew, but then here's these two old guys near the end of their lives who didn't seem real concerned about it. Maybe I won't go to hell."

"At least not for being an agnostic, but maybe for your other sins." It was a suggestive remark, and Sarah knew it. They kissed. The religious discussion had come to an end.

Sarah pushed Paul's attention to Dan and Tracey. "Think they do it?"

"None of my business, but if they do, I hope they enjoy it as much as we do." Paul's gaze, even in the darkness of The Sink, told of his affection for Sarah.

"That would be impossible," she said.

Sarah was propped up on her right arm exposing her naked breasts to Paul. He continued to explore her body with his hand. They had made love by candlelight, an atmosphere they frequently used in bed. After several minutes of quiet when Sarah kept her eyes closed, she finally spoke.

"Relationships are funny."

"What do you mean?"

"We're so curious about each other and all that's going on around us and to us. We poke and prod to get answers. Tracey and Dan have known each other for several years, so some of the mystery's gone, I bet, but she kind of waits for new things to come to her, like she's afraid of the outside world."

"So, Dan is her protector?"

"Yeah."

Sarah rolled on top of Paul and put her head in the crook of his arm. "Okay. Then there's Sally and Mose. Why aren't they dating each other? They're so compatible, it seems."

"They fight their feelings. There's been a physical attraction between them since they first met last September, but we're all so close, the four of us, we don't want anything to damage this."

"It is really cool up here. You don't lock doors, and you look out for each other. In a sense you all belong to each other."

"Mose and Sally are from broken homes, and they're smart enough to understand what they have here. It even goes farther than that. Whenever Sally goes to Pueblo, she stops by my parents' house to say hi to them, or she'll stop off on the way back. My mom and dad wondered if they were dating too, because of how they are together."

"Will they ever get together?" asked Sarah.

"Maybe, but not for a while. By the way, Sally wants the four of us to go to the Huddle tomorrow to see the We Five."

"That would be fun! They're one of my favorite groups. I saw where they were going to be here, but I forgot. I just can't stay focused on anything but you, my dear." She raised her head and gave him a quick kiss.

"Dinner first then?" proposed Paul.

"Yes, but I'll need to do my studying all day then. And I need to go to the library and the language lab too. Care to join me?"

"That reminds me. My dad wants to look at your car tomorrow, so if you'll drive it over and leave it here, he can use the garage, where it's warm."

"He's too nice. Both your parents are."

"So, what's funny about our relationship?" He shifted a little to take a breath.

"Everything. Here we are naked, and we've been doing this since the first week we were together. I was a virgin, remember. Then it's so . . . all encompassing. You're at the Lab School with me. I go to the games with you. We have lunch together every day. I worry I'll take you away from Dan and Mose and all of this, but instead, I'm drawn into it and accepted . . . mostly. I worry we're going too fast, that our love will burn out, because it's too bright, too hot." She had gotten to the heart of what she wanted to say all along. "My house mom worries about me . . . about our rapid involvement. I've been given a few demerits for our late-night phone calls. I think she suspects us about . . . this."

"Slow down then," Paul said tenderly.

"I don't want to. If I could, I would move in here with you. We haven't spent a whole night together, and I plot ways to sneak out so that we can. I know Anne would help me."

"Let's go skiing together next weekend. Can't you get permission to do that?"

"If we go to Eldora or Loveland, Mrs. Meyer would find out."

"Let's go stay with Dan in Leadville. His grandma'll sign off for you. Say you're staying with them, but we'll get a motel. I'll bet none of your sisters go skiing at Cooper Hill."

Sarah giggled and snuggled up closer to Paul. "Let's do it!"

Sunday, February 12

The We Five performance was fun for them all, but Mose would not admit to it. They not only sang their hits, but they provided some irreverent political comments too. They directed racial barbs at a sixth Five, a black guitarist who traveled with them for concerts, and the audience participated in the singing and satire. Mose told Sally it was all so hokey, and she would owe him an evening of jazz, if ever blues came to Boulder.

"America's all-white town. It's a good thing there's athletes, or this campus would have no color." Mose had brought this criticism up before.

The two couples split up at the top of The Hill, one walking north and the other south. Sarah wished they were all walking north tonight. The warmer than normal February evening and the occasion had allowed her to wear a dress and knee boots, but she needed Paul's arms to keep her warm on the three-block walk to the Sig Delt house.

"Why are you looking at me that way?" she asked when they arrived at the residence.

"It's just you. You and your yellow dress."

She ignored his corny answer. "Thank your dad for working on my car. Tell him that I'm desperately in love with his son."

"I think he already knows." She rewarded him with a passionate kiss. "You're shivering. You better go in."

"What song did you like best tonight?" she asked without breaking their hug.

"Hmm? Well, maybe, it's not my favorite song on their album, but for the way they sang it tonight, I liked 'Somewhere Beyond the Sea.' What about you?" Paul knew she was glad he could answer her question, but she really asked it so she could tell him what song she had liked the most.

"'Make Someone Happy.'"

Monday, February 13

"Good morning, Paul. Coffee?"

"Morning, sir. Yeah, thanks. I'll just hold it next to my body to get warm. Have you ever adjusted to Colorado winters?"

"Oh, yes. I was going to say I sensed a bit of spring this morning on my walk over here, but I guess you missed it."

"It's still winter over on the west side of campus."

Dr. Orr laughed. He had set up these Monday morning meetings as an unofficial independent study because he saw some real insight in the essays of Paul Garrity, and he wanted to push the young man to pursue his talents. Paul was eager to learn, and he was quite capable of the additional reading that had been assigned.

"Did you read any more on Judaism this week?"

"Not much, but Sarah did discuss with me a little about her faith, or lack thereof. It seems like there are quite a few Jews who either don't believe in God or at least don't believe it's important to understand Him."

"Why do you think that is?"

"Beats me. Maybe Christians are the same way, and I'm just not as aware of it, but something seems different. Jews who don't believe can still be avid Jews who attend services and observe holidays."

"What does Sarah believe?" probed Professor Orr.

"Up until recently, I think not much. She's told me how her mom really wants her to be Jewish, and she's tried to run from it. But now I'm not sure if she wants to be Jewish or not, but she wants to know more about it. She's very interested in Israel and the Arabs."

"That's a region waiting for war to break out."

"Soon?"

Orr opened another box of sugar cubes. "I don't know really, but tension between Israel and Syria seems to be escalating, and it's always tense between Israel and Egypt."

"Can't the US manage it?"

"Unfortunately, besides our preoccupation with Vietnam, the Soviet Union appears to be trying to de-stabilize the region, but their motives are a bit unclear."

"Let's see. I've learned the Cold War helped integrate Southern schools and the US Army. Am I about to learn the Cold War affects the price of oil and, more importantly, the moods of my Jewish girlfriend?"

The professor smiled broadly. "I may have to use that example in class to get the other students' attention." Orr reached back for two books. "There are a couple of essays in these *Foreign Affairs* journals that may be of interest to you on this morning's subjects."

"Might help me for class too, huh?"

Dr. Orr was right. This kid had insight.

It was a little warmer, thought Paul, as he waited for Sarah outside of the UMC. With the bright sun, it was pleasant. She was not expecting him outside, so he was able to watch her as she hurried along the east side of Hellems for their rendezvous. It made him feel good to see how quickly she moved just to be with him. He moved at a right angle to cut her off.

"SARAH!" Paul put his one hand on her left hip and kissed her.

"I didn't see you." Her eyes were excited. "Well . . .?"

"It's all arranged from this side. Dan's grandparents are anxious to meet you."

"My mother warned me about boys like you," she smiled.

"No, your mom warned you specifically about me, but not because I might take you to bed, but because I'm a Gentile. I'm not sure she'd be as worried if I was Jewish."

"You're probably right," answered Sarah. "Let's go inside. I'm hungry."

Over soup, Paul and Sarah were giddy. "Do you have an SPU meeting today?" she asked.

"Yeah, but I'm going to be late today." She knew why instinctively. She leaned over and kissed him. Paul stood up. "Come with me. There's someone in here I want you to meet, and I think he wants to meet you, too."

Halfway across the cafeteria, "Dr. Orr, this is Sarah Phillips. Sarah, this is Dr. Orr."

Tuesday, February 14

The *CU Daily's* lead story on Tuesday reported the agreement between the pro-war and anti-war forces for a teach-in on Vietnam to be held on March 1. Four hours were to be allotted for the "instruction," with the Student Peace Union representing the Left. The Young Democrats had not yet taken an official stance on the war.

"Pussies!" cried John Cohen. He had ratcheted up his rhetoric over the weeks since Sarah attended the SPU meeting with Paul, and while his contempt for the Democratic Party was obvious, it was toward the "Establishment" that he directed his most vile epithets. To Paul, Cohen was coming dangerously close to advocating violence against organizations that in any way seemed to support America's war in Vietnam.

"Got a dilemma, don't ya, Garrity," chuckled Dan while he dressed after showering after another beating from Mose on the basketball court.

"Several. Which one are you referring to?" Paul responded, as he tucked his new three-striped Adidas basketball shoes into the locker.

"Your association with an anti-war group that talks about demonstrations, riots, and violence. You think Dr. King's methods can be used to stop the war. Shit, man, LBJ doesn't want to be the first president to lose a war." Dan was baiting his roomie, but both Paul and Mose detected some anger or frustration in his voice. Maybe both.

"You sat there on the couch last night and didn't say anything while we solved the world's problems. Now you bring it up?"

"You didn't solve a thing," Dan said. "It's a good thing Cohen only stayed for a few minutes. What a jerk!" His last sentence belied his casual attitude. "Did you ever think about punching his lights out?"

"Remember?" said Paul, "I'm the non-violent guy."

"Well, you're gonna have to make some tough choices pretty soon," said Mose. "Campuses all across the country are starting to demonstrate, and we've seen how the civil rights movement has turned violent, so I wouldn't be surprised to see the anti-war movement take the same path. You and a dozen others think the method of protest matters, Garrity. The rest of the draft age protestors only want results. They want the war stopped before their name gets called. They don't care how, either." Mose was not kidding now.

"Where do you stand, Mr. Robinson?" Paul was staring directly at Mose.

"You're a persuasive young activist, Garrity, and you keep my rent down, so I'll support you and your idealism . . . for now. Ask me again as we get closer to graduation and the war is still goin' on." Mose tried to mask his seriousness.

"Gotta run, guys. A little boy named Ricky needs me to play with him." With that, Paul headed out of the locker room.

"Tell Sarah we all said hi." Mose then turned to Dan. "That boy has too many irons in the fire."

Dan shook his head. "I'm right about his dilemma, Mose. Not just the non-violent thing, but with his dad and the whole social stigma of being labeled a communist or coward. He needs to drop out of the SPU and go back to working on civil rights. Or join the Peace Corps. Safer." Dan picked up his gym bag and left, leaving Mose alone.

Mose sat back down on the bench in front of his locker contemplating the conversation. He knew Paul wouldn't back away; it wasn't his new path. But Mose also knew that his best friend might pay a price down the road.

Ricky's mother was late for his pickup at the Lab School that afternoon. As it turned out, she was in the hospital after being beaten by her boyfriend. Paul volunteered to take Ricky home with him for the night, and Mrs. McLean could pick Ricky up when she was released the next day.

At 1203 Sally cooked burgers, Mose wrestled with Ricky, they all went for a ride to get ice cream, and Paul read "Rootie Kazootie" to his little buddy, who slept in Paul's bed that night. Nobody studied.

There were no discussions about Vietnam, Israel, or civil rights. Sarah called the SDT house and was given a curfew extension. Dan drove her home a little before one after she kissed her sleeping boyfriend on the forehead. He was curled up next to Ricky.

Wednesday, February 15

Ricky McLean had cereal, a banana, toast with jam, and orange juice for breakfast. Paul and Sally drove him to the Lab School in a pickup. They made one stop along the way to pick up Miss Sarah. That's how Ricky explained it to his mother when she arrived to get him. Paul stayed with Ricky for the remainder of the morning until his mother came. Her bruises were visible through the heavy make-up.

Paul left a phone message for Dr. Orr with the History secretary explaining briefly why he was not in class, but he did meet Sarah at the UMC for lunch. Winter weather returned.

Mose went with the basketball team to Ames, Iowa, for an important game to stay in the hunt for a national tournament bid. The rest of 1203 resumed their study schedule at the apartment. Around nine-thirty, Sally brought over a bowl of popcorn, a six-pack of pop, and Dan.

"They're gonna be okay, you know." Dan said. "They'll get out of town and live with family, away from the asshole. Is he in jail now?"

"He was as of this morning. Let's hope he doesn't make bail this time," said Sarah. The conversation revolved around Ricky and the topic of violence, particularly in the home. Paul remained quiet for the rest of the night.

Thursday, February 16
The surprising CU basketball team won at Iowa State to keep their

post-season hopes alive. Mose returned Friday just before noon, in time to have lunch with Dan and Sally at The Colonial.

Ross Garrity asked to come home, a request that was summarily denied by his father. His mother called Paul "just to talk." Paul sat at the top of the stairs just outside his kitchen while Sarah and Sally studied in his apartment, trying to hear any part of the discussion. Afterwards, Paul confessed there wasn't much to add to his family's drama, that Ross was still in a Los Angeles detox center. It was the one topic Paul kept most private from Sarah and 1203.

Friday, February 17

Room 3. Not 103 or 13, just 3. The Aspen Motel in Leadville only had ten rooms, but they were clean and comfortable, and number 3 had a vase of six red roses.

"This is perfect," Sarah said softly as she wrapped her arms around Paul's waist.

They had dropped Dan off at his house and gone straight to the motel. They would see Dan and Tracey on Saturday and ski and socialize.

"Even though I've made love with you several times at your apartment and a few times in our cars, this is still special, and I want you to know how I feel." Sarah was lying on top of Paul as she whispered these words.

Paul gently moved his fingertips across her naked back while she talked. The bathroom light cast a dull shadow across the room. "I think I do know." They kissed at the end of nearly every sentence, and the tender conversation went on for over an hour as they talked about their first weeks together and the pace with which their love had progressed.

"Any regrets?" he asked tenderly.

"None, except maybe the night you played basketball, and I acted like a little girl and went to the library alone."

"What do you think happened?"

"I was scared, scared I would be taken for granted. I didn't know you tried to call or that Dan or Mose was supposed to call. It's not that I didn't trust you, it's I don't have confidence in myself to keep someone like you." She paused and put her nose to his before adding, "I love our late-night telephone calls. They're so intimate. We reconnect like we've been apart for months. I wish they could be longer than two minutes though."

"Trust. It's an amazing concept, isn't it. It's still hard for me to picture you without confidence. You're always so poised and beautiful and smart."

"Tracey's beautiful, but you've got me believing that I'm up to very pretty. Being in love sure changes one's perspective."

"Yeah, Sars, it does."

Saturday, February 18

Sarah's ski outfit was mostly pink with a slash of yellow, unlike anything either Paul or Dan had ever seen on the slopes. At breakfast Grandpa smiled and covered his eyes, while Grandma complimented her. "You look beautiful in your suit." When Danny cracked that it must be expensive, Sarah struck a pose and replied, "It's what all the rich Jewish girls from the East are wearing this year."

Paul pulled up to the right and sprayed snow on Danny, who was already waiting for his friends where two trails joined before heading to the bottom of Cooper Hill.

"This is a great day!" Paul shouted. Tracey and Sarah arrived a few seconds later, both out of breath. Each girl slid over to her boyfriend for a kiss.

"We got a great break with the weather," said Danny. "After this run, we'll move over and ski blacks, if you girls can handle it." He was addressing his comments to Paul.

"Lead the way, asshole!" They were off again.

After dinner at the florist shop, Sarah and Paul took a walk around the greenhouse. "This is an oasis at 10,000 feet," observed Sarah.

They wandered around the wood paths of the greenhouse, smelling the various plants. A gray cat slept on a water pipe. "I'll call him Mose." Sarah understood and laughed.

Dan bounced out of the house portion of the greenhouse carrying his coat. "I'll be right back. Gotta get the flowers."

Sarah was initiated into the sacred ritual of unpacking cut flowers that arrived from Denver by bus that evening.

"Some of the world's toughest problems are settled out here," said Grandma. "Danny asks the questions, and I have all the answers. So where are you from, Sarah?" asked Grandma Savage.

"New York City."

"What brought you to Colorado?"

"I don't know really. Maybe I was just looking for a boyfriend." She cut the plastic off a bunch of carnations and handed them to that boyfriend.

"What do you want to do after you graduate?"

"Run my own school, my own little kid center. But first, I want to travel."

"Any certain places?"

"I've been to Europe, but I'd like to go back. Maybe take Paul. I also want to see Jerusalem."

"That would be marvelous, to walk in the steps of Jesus, and see the sites the Bible talks about. I've always wanted to go there too, but I don't think I'm going to make it in this life." Grandma checked the tubs against the invoice. "Did anyone see the sweetheart roses?"

"I put them in the refrigerator on the top shelf," answered Tracey.

Paul sat on a stool petting Mose. "Are we done, yet?"

Paul and Sarah drove Tracey home and then returned to the Aspen Motel.

From the beginning there had been an urgency attached to Sarah's lovemaking. Passionate, unrestrained, wide-eyed, and unapologetic. Afterwards, she would calm down and talk with Paul. Not once had either one simply dozed off. Despite the energy of their actions, they wanted to talk, and these discussions frequently lasted longer than the sex. On this Saturday night, coming at the conclusion of such a week of emotions and a day of physical exertion, the lovemaking was tender and measured, and when they had spent themselves, Paul and Sarah quickly fell asleep in each other's arms.

Sunday, February 19

They skied alone for just a half-day, as Danny worked at the greenhouse. Paul let Dan drive back to Boulder, and he and Sarah slept nearly the entire trip.

Paul finished his homework earlier than the others. After opening a can of pop, he settled in on the couch to write the Defense Secretary another letter.

"What're you tellin' him this time, Garrity?" asked Mose.

"Same shit; that we can't guarantee South Vietnam's security forever. They must do it for themselves at some point. That his war is a waste of time."

Mose shifted his weight and continued. "Think he reads 'em?"

"What do you think?"

"Can't hurt. Keep writin'." Mose nodded his approval.

Sarah looked perplexed. "Who are you writing to?"

"Secretary of Defense McNamara. I just keep asking him the same questions, mostly about the bombing and our policy goals."

Sarah's face showed some sense of disbelief. "You're kidding, right?"

Paul got up and went over to her at the table. "Nope." He smiled broadly and kissed the top of her head, then pulled out a chair and sat next to her. Her eyes continued to question him. "Sars, someone needs to keep him grounded. At least that's what I tell myself. He has to be challenged about the bombing. We drop bombs from 30,000 feet, but does he know who's getting killed? How's that going to help win the 'hearts and minds' of the Vietnamese? And the morality issue. Plus, tonight I'm questioning its overall effectiveness. I wanted the pause to continue, but I guess the military got their way."

1203 was aware of Paul's letters. Mose added to Sarah's intrigue. "Paul quit askin' whether the money couldn't be best spent on peaceful purposes here at home. In America. Like on civil rights."

"Yeah, I let King make that argument now," laughed Paul.

"What else?" asked Sarah.

"The contract. The South Vietnamese don't seem to be holding up their end of the bargain. I put something in every letter about that."

Sarah touched Paul's forearm, and her eyes sparkled. "Why McNamara? Why not President Johnson?"

"I own a Ford, and I'm sure he knows that and wouldn't want me to switch to a Chevy. No, slightly better chance they might be read. Besides, McNamara made a comment last year about the right to dissent, so I'm testing him. I usually get a form letter back." Paul stopped and waited for her to catch up.

1203 had been through these questions before with Paul. As if on key, Sally asked, "Have you noticed how tired McNamara looks these days?"

Paul grinned. "Wearing him down, aren't I."

Monday, February 20

"Morning, Paul. Coffee?"

"Good morning, Dr. Orr. Yeah, please. I didn't notice spring in those snowflakes this morning. Did you?"

"I thought they may have contained a bit more moisture than those dry, winter flakes," Orr teased. "You have an opinion on this 'Publish or Perish' issue, Paul?"

"It's not at the top of my agenda these days, but it seems to me if a professor knows his subject and can motivate his students, then he ought to have a place here at CU. Maybe he should be granted tenure." Paul realized he was not well versed on this issue almost as soon as the words were out of his mouth.

"Can a teacher really be effective, over the long run, if he isn't a good scholar himself?" It was a rhetorical question. "Should a professor at a leading university have a responsibility to further the advancement of knowledge in his discipline?"

"Might there be exceptions to the rule?" asked Paul.

"Do you want the exception to drive the policy?"

"I want to be taught by good teachers, not by someone who assigns the class to a graduate student or who thinks the relevant events of US history ended with World War II. I'd like some input in evaluating my professors."

"Ah-ha! So, this all boils down to another issue where the students are demanding more power. Is that your argument?" Dr. Orr had Paul backed into a corner he did not want to occupy.

"Don't worry, sir. When they make me chancellor, you're safe." Paul was bobbing and weaving, but Orr pressed his advantage.

"Suppose the university allows the students to vote yea or nay on every professor. Might they be swayed by an easy grader or by a lax attendance policy, for example? Who, then, is really in charge?"

"Don't you believe student evaluations are valuable though?" *Don't answer the question*, thought Paul, *just pose another question*. He smiled too soon.

"Who designs these evaluations? When are they filled out—on the day of the final exam or on graduation day when CU graduates enter the job market against graduates from Yale or Stanford or Chicago? Is it the purpose of the university professor to be liked, or is his purpose to prepare his charges to be ready to assume their difficult role in this highly competitive society?" Orr hadn't raised his voice, yet his feelings were clear.

"I guess I'll be at the rally on Wednesday morning. Do I have permission to miss your class?"

"I'll be on the dais at the rally. Class will be held in the ballroom. Care to join me on stage?"

"No, sir, not for this one. I haven't done my homework."

Moses Robinson sat at the end of the players' bench in street clothes for CU's game against Oklahoma, a member of the team again, the Prodigal Son. He missed sitting with his guys in the stands. Sarah sat next to Sally and in front of Paul, who analyzed the game with Kevin. Paul kept his hands on Sarah's shoulders throughout the game, except when he would stand or applaud an exceptional play. On this evening there were many, as the Buffs steamrolled OU, 83-73. Pat Frink led the way with 27 points. If Kansas was in line for the automatic bid into the NCAAs, then CU seemed to have the inside track for the NIT invitation, an unthinkable occurrence a few months earlier. Only Nebraska, their last opponent of the regular season, stood in the way. Mose gave a thumbs up sign to Paul as the gang worked its way out of the stands.

Sarah noticed and whispered a question in Paul's ear. "Is he ever going to play?"

"That's the plan, but I honestly don't know. Obviously not this season. He's so good, and he loves the game, but . . . he just lives in his own world. I guess we'll see." There was real concern in Paul's voice. While he was answering her question, he was also watching his best friend leave the court behind the suited players. A part, but not a part. Apart.

"If you want to wait for him, I'll walk back to your place with Sally and wait for you. I can do some trig homework." She was standing one step below Paul, and to her, he seemed so powerful. Yet, she also knew of his vulnerability.

"Maybe I will. He gets lost easily." Paul's laugh was a weak attempt to conceal his feelings for Mose.

On the way home, Mose and Paul stopped to get Mose some tacos at the Mexican fast-food restaurant off south Broadway.

"You gotta good thing going with Sarah. It's all happened pretty fast, you know. You guys gonna ride it through or is it gonna burn out as fast as it started?" asked Mose.

"That's funny. Sarah asked me about the same thing this weekend while we were up skiing. She asked me how I thought our love would end. When I asked her why she thought it wouldn't last forever, she got all serious and said we were both so young and naïve. She emphasized the young part. Twenty."

"She's partly right there . . . about the naïve part." They both smiled.

"Then she said we were just different in our backgrounds and thought the odds were against us." Paul smiled slightly as he spoke.

"The odds are against all college romances, Garrity, but you two fit together. Sally thinks it's Sarah who's lucky, but don't tell Sally I told you that. You've got a way about you though."

"Sally's pretty savvy. I'll bet she knows you and I don't keep too many secrets."

"This is a pretty serious conversation for us, especially since we're missin' Dan and beer." They both laughed. "Well, what did you tell her?" asked Mose. "Something about our young age and inexperience with love, that events could take us in opposite directions. She looked sad, and I mean that—sad. So, I added if we weren't together at graduation, the time would come after that . . . that we'd find each other again, and it would be all right."

"Hmm. Is that what you really think?"

"Hell, I'm so crazy about her, I can't think about the end of all this." Paul shook his head.

"Well, don't worry about it. Everything always turns out for you. Lakewood's Golden Boy. Just like Dan. Let's get out of here. I got homework too. We still on for tomorrow?"

Tuesday, February 21

Dan warned everyone about the Peace Corps recruiters who were set up in the UMC loggia. "Very persuasive. They make you think you can make a huge difference in the world. Just go help refugees in third-world countries. You're their principal target, Paul." Paul avoided them by cutting across to the Lab School without passing through the UMC. Basketball with Mose and Dan had gone overtime, and he wondered if he was avoiding going to work with Sarah's kids because of Ricky's absence. He jaywalked Broadway and entered the huge building just as they were breaking up into play groups. Sarah was waiting for him and had anticipated his anxiety.

"You're working with me today, my dear," and gave him as much of a hug as she could under the watchful eye of Mrs. Best. "You get to see the fairer side. Four girls. We'll be playing foursquare to start out." She took his arm and led him to the far end of the gym, hoping to keep his attention diverted from one missing boy.

Wednesday, February 22

The "Publish or Perish" rally on Wednesday morning was packed. The *CU Daily* estimated over 1,700 students were in attendance, and they were a vocal group, mostly in support of those teachers who seemed to be at odds with the university administrators and regents who believed professors ought to do research and publish their findings. Dr. Orr was articulate in defense of the "publish" position. "At a major university such as CU, more is expected of our students, and to achieve that, more must be demanded of our professors. We must add to our bodies of knowledge as well as transmit that knowledge eloquently to our students. Maybe the equation is framed improperly. It should be 'Teach and Publish—or Perish.' Professors at this university owe our students no less."

Paul attended his American Lit class after the rally before heading back to 1203. Sally was sitting against the porch wall sunning herself in the 55-degree February weather.

"What did you think about Dr. Orr this morning?"

"I can see why you respect him so much," answered Sally. "He really has a presence about him. He kind of turned the crowd around, didn't he."

"Is Sarah here? I don't see her car."

"Yeah, she's back from her hair appointment. You have a surprise waiting for you up in your room." Sally smiled deviously.

"Any hints?"

"No, hon, just go on up."

Paul's door was half open, but he could not see Sarah. "Are you in here?"

From the bathroom she called out, "Close your eyes." He did and she walked over to him. "Okay, you can open them now."

"Wow!" Paul's inflection indicated more curiosity than amazement.

"Do you like it?"

Paul remained silent as he walked around her, touching her new haircut cautiously. Facing her, he pretended to study the results, gently turning her head, first to the right and then to the left. "It's as short as mine."

"Oh, come on! Do you like it, or do I have to go looking for a new boyfriend?"

"Yeah, I do. I really do!" Sarah smiled and threw her arms around his neck. "What's the house going to think?" asked Paul.

"Doesn't matter. It's what I wanted, and only your opinion matters. You're not just being nice, are you? The truth."

"The truth? You could probably shave it all off, and I wouldn't care, but do I like this? Yeah, Sars, I think it looks great, and it fits you."

"If we lock the door, would your roomies think poorly of us?" Sarah pressed in on Paul.

"They already do, but at least we won't be interrupted."

Thursday, February 23

As a result of Wednesday's rally, Paul had no homework on Thursday night, and Sarah finished hers before going to the Lab School, so they drove to Lakewood to have dinner with his parents.

"What's your mom cooking for us tonight?" asked Sarah.

"My mom worries about that, you know. Whether she needs to learn about kosher cooking?"

"She doesn't have to. Did you tell her? Even the house doesn't cook kosher recipes all the time."

"I told her The Sink and Gondolier don't do kosher either. She seemed to accept that. I don't know what we're having tonight."

"Changing the subject, what were you expecting from me when you helped me tend bar at the function on the night we met?"

"Hmm. 'Expecting.' I don't know if I was expecting anything other than getting to meet you. Maybe a date later. I certainly never expected all this. I couldn't have."

"You didn't have a plan for our future, huh?" Sarah asked.

"My buddies from Brackett, and not just Mose and Dan, knew I had a crush on you when I saw you as a freshman. They kept telling me to ask you out, but as I already told you, I couldn't just walk up to you. So, you were just 'out there.' Then, when I saw you last fall, you were even more beautiful than I had remembered."

"Would you cut that out! I'm already sleeping with you."

"Anyway, Kevin was determined to take care of my needs, so he asked around and found out what sorority you belonged to. When the Sig Delts had that function, Kevin met me at the rally and told me. I was just hoping to meet you that night. When I saw you behind the bar working, the idea of helping you just popped into my head. I didn't have the courage to walk up and introduce myself if you would have been a part of the crowd. You were working your ass off."

They were quiet as the Ford pickup turned onto Colfax, a few blocks from Paul's parents' home.

"I'm not a very complicated woman, you know. I'd like to think if you would have introduced yourself to me at Libby and asked me out, I would have said yes."

"Maybe you would have, Sars, but get last year's yearbook and take a look at my picture. It would've been a brief affair."

Sarah laughed again. "I did. I've seen that picture, and you might be right."

"You're not a simple person, Sars. There are forces and feelings simmering beneath the surface in you that I know will erupt, in time."

"Yeah? When?"

"I don't know, but I hope I'm around to experience them with you." Paul laughed this time. "I'm learning a lot from you."

"A good teacher, huh?" She kissed her finger and touched it to his cheek. "You've got it backwards though; you're the force whose time is coming."

"Something like that."

Spaghetti and meatballs. Thick sauce with oregano and basil. And onions. "I like onions," said Dick Garrity emphatically.

Sarah finally got to drive the pickup. They decided to return via Wadsworth Boulevard north to the Turnpike.

"Your mom is so different from mine," said Sarah.

"How so?"

"She's calm for one thing. She listens, and she touches people to make them feel comfortable, not to get their attention. Now I know where you get that habit from. It's reassuring, so wonderful."

"Like this?" Paul placed his hand on the inside of her thigh.

"I was being serious, but don't you dare move it." KIMN was playing "The Ballad of the Green Berets." "You have the perfect family. I think so and so do all your friends. Mose and Sally want to be adopted."

"Things aren't always as they seem. When I was little, my dad and brother were always fighting, yelling mostly."

"Drugs?"

"Now? Yeah, that's why Ross isn't allowed in the house. But back then, I don't think so. It was just anger on Ross's part, and my dad responded in kind. Like I told you, we don't talk about it, but it just destroys my mom. It's one of those things I'm unable to fix."

Sarah drove in silence for a few miles, deep in her own thoughts. *No secrets; I so love this man.* Softly, almost apologetically, she said, "I argued with my parents over the winter break. I yelled."

Paul's response was just as quiet. "What about?"

"My mother never misses an opportunity to push Jewish guys at me, to warn me about how I could lose my faith if I'm not careful. Hell, I don't even have faith. All I've got is a culture." Paul waited. "I screamed at her to give it a rest, to get off my ass—and that's the word I used. So, my dad, 'Eugene, the Peacemaker,' stepped in, and I snapped at him too."

"Did anyone apologize?"

"We all did, but it hasn't changed my mother's behavior."

"I'm the problem this time, aren't I," confessed Paul.

"My mother believes you'll take the Jewishness out of me. My father doesn't seem to worry about it much, but he tells me to be respectful of my mother. But she worries about all my boyfriends, which is why I've never had a serious relationship before you. 'Sarah, the nice girl.'"

"You are, you know," Paul said reassuringly. "Pull up at the overlook and let's talk." The lights of Boulder shone in the valley, and Paul hugged his troubled girlfriend.

"My mother worries about us a lot. Every phone call is a caution. She can't let it go, so I've stopped calling her again."

"Tell her I just plan on dating you for the next two years, but I'll dump your ass after graduation."

"I love you so much, even when you're being stupid. You aren't going to leave me. I won't allow it. What better way to piss off my mom, anyway."

"Then I guess I'll just have to make sure you stay a Jew." It was a half-serious statement by Paul.

"Where is it written I should travel 2,000 miles across the continent to fall in love with a Gentile who would show me how to be a Jew?" She laughed and then pulled Paul's truck back onto the turnpike to Boulder.

Friday, February 24

Mose wanted to check out the newest "Go-Go Girl" at the Honey Bucket for FAC, but that required transportation, so he bribed Paul by offering to buy the beer. Sally shook her head "at boys," but came along for the dancing. They had two stops to make. First, at the Sig Delt house to get Sarah. Three of her sisters jumped into the bed of Paul's truck, while Sarah squeezed in between Paul and Sally. Four in front. The second stop was to get Kevin from the Sig Ep house on Broadway, an easy stop. Kevin brought along two of his brothers, all of whom joined the girls in the bed of the pickup. "The Bucket" was located on the far side of Crossroads Mall, about four miles from 1203. Word got out the party that night after FAC would be at the apartment, and by ten about 30 students crowded into the downstairs den, Mose's apartment, or one of Paul's rooms. Most belonged to one of the two Greek houses that had occupied the bed of the truck, so, except for two younger Sig Eps, the party stayed under control. By midnight most of the partyers had drifted off to the bars on The Hill.

"We got some cleanup, don't we, Garrity," said Mose after the party ended.

"I'll get it tomorrow morning when it's lighter. Go get a couple of jazz albums, and let's kick back in here. We've all had enough beer to become philosophers; we'll solve some more problems." Paul's idea sounded good to the seven remaining students.

"Sars, this is Jeff. Jeff, remember Sarah from last year?" Mose was maneuvering to put Paul on the hook.

"We've met before . . . at the UMC . . . and Jeff doesn't need your help to embarrass Paul," said Sarah. She sat down in Paul's lap at the end of the couch.

"I'm not going to let you follow me around after graduation, Robinson, so what're you going to do with yourself when you're on your own?"

"Did you forget, Garrity? You and I have appointments with The Man in Nam."

"Don't kid about that!" said Sarah. "Do you guys really think you'll end up in Vietnam?"

"One or two of us will," said Jeff.

"Unless we get it stopped," added Kevin.

Sarah slid her bottom lip between her teeth and narrowed her eyes as if questioning the premise. "That doesn't have to happen! It's not written anywhere in stone that . . .. Destiny can't be that cruel. There has to be other paths for all you guys's abilities other than carrying a rifle in a worthless war."

"This is too heavy. We've covered it before." Paul sensed a tenseness in Sarah even before she spoke. "Anyway, I've got a job option in Canada to run an apartment complex in Toronto."

"So, Canada is an option for you, Paul?" asked Jeff.

"Honestly, I don't know."

"Sarah. Sally. What about you guys? You don't have the draft." Kevin was always polite and inclusive.

"I'm living here forever . . . with all you guys," joked Sally. "Seriously, if things wouldn't change too much, and I could get a job working with adults, I'd live in this house for a long time. It's home. I'm comfortable, protected, and accepted for who I am."

She turned the question over to Sarah. "I can no longer plan that far ahead! Three months ago, I was Miss Greek, gung ho. Now my biggest concern is where I'll be spending spring break. Who knows what or where I'll be in two years." It wasn't a question, but a statement of fact, a topic that she had discussed at length with Paul.

"Where will you be over the break?" asked Sally.

"Probably New York," she said without enthusiasm.

"Are you going too, Paul?"

"No. I don't think her mother would accept that yet. But," and Paul smiled and hugged Sarah tighter, "we're working on her."

"You don't sound happy about going home, Sarah," said Kevin who ignored Paul's remarks.

"Since I met this guy, we've spent a part of everyday together. I've rearranged my schedule so I can meet him for lunch or have him walk me home . . . or just do this. Now, in three weeks, I'm supposed to just go home?"

"Can't you stay in Boulder?" asked Sally. "You could even come to Pueblo with me for a few days."

"I've already fought that battle with my parents and lost. I even threatened to miss my plane. That went over well. My mother was hysterical."

Paul concurred. "Her mom knows she'd be with me, and that's unacceptable. If you'll look closely, you'll see that I'm not Jewish," he kidded.

"Not only that, but my mother's brother and his family will be there, and I 'can't miss that,'" mimicked Sarah with air quotes.

"They live in Israel," added Paul.

"You're out of beer," yelled Jeff, who had gone to the bathroom and returned to the fridge, only to find it empty.

"Then it's a good time to go home. Call it a night," yawned Kevin. "Who's driving me home?"

"Just find an empty space around here. Use the couch or go into Dan's room and sack out," said Paul, who did not want to be the chauffeur.

"What about me?" cooed Sarah. "Where do I get to sack out?" The crowd ooed and awed.

"I wish. Grab your coat. I'll go warm up the truck."

"You're taking me home a little early, aren't you?" asked Sarah.

"No, I'm just getting you alone. I've never taken you home early, have I?"

"Once." Sarah paused. "You have something you want to say, huh."

"Yeah." Paul turned right and headed up 13th Street. "When we were talking about where we were going to live tonight . . ."

"Where do you want to live the rest of your life?" asked Sarah.

"Wherever you are." He glanced over at Sarah as he drove.

"Is that a proposal?"

"No, not yet; still a little young. It's more a statement of how I feel about you right now. I don't want you to misunderstand any of my frivolous remarks from earlier tonight." Paul pulled over and parked the truck alongside the neighborhood park a block north of the Sig

Delt house. "We have about a half hour. When I walk you to the door, I want you to be clear about my feelings and intentions toward you."

Sarah liked this side of Paul, when he took control of situations. For an instant she flashed back to the situation with Ricky at the Lab School. "I think I do understand, Paul."

He put two fingers on her lips. "I love you." He let his words sink in. "But I also understand what we have today may be impossible to maintain. We're at a point in our lives, and I don't know the right words, but we're both subject to great changes that could cause us to go separate ways. I don't want it to happen, but it could. If it does, I want you to be free to go." He was interrupted here.

"I'm not going anywhere!"

"Listen," he continued more softly this time. "I think we'll continue to be together. I can't imagine why we wouldn't, except for that Vietnam thing, but the future will decide its own course. I just want you to know I love you tonight, and this love won't burn out. If we go our separate ways, you'll always be able to say there was this guy in Boulder who loved you completely. I want you to know that about me, because that's what I feel from you."

Their eyes were fixed, their faces only inches apart. Sarah's eyes welled up with tears as she spoke. "God. You are a hopeless romantic." She kissed him gently and they rubbed noses. "So, we take it one day at a time huh?"

"Yeah. Take nothing for granted."

She moved towards the passenger door and pulled him over away from the steering wheel. She climbed astride his lap. "What you just said. Can you write it all down, so I can read it to Anne later, or when I'm old and lonely?"

They still had twenty minutes before curfew.

Saturday, February 25

As usual Sarah attended synagogue with her sisters in the morning and Greek council in the afternoon, while Paul attended to the upkeep of 1203 before heading over to the library to study. They agreed to meet around six.

She called around four, but Paul was still at the library. Sally answered the phone. "Usually, when a boy falls in love, he stops studying all together. With Paul it's been exactly the opposite. He doesn't sleep anymore. He just takes you home and then stays up all night reading. His history professor, the one that he likes so well, has him reading a bunch of stuff, I guess." "Tell him I called. Thanks, Sally."

Sarah and Paul had pizza at Bennett's and crossed the street to see *Blow Up* at the Fox. Later at the apartment, they played spades with Mose and Sally. Coke, m&m's, and popcorn—no beer. Mose received a little ribbing about needing so much attention, but mostly the mood was relaxed.

Sunday, February 26

After Sunday's victory the Buffs had to play their next three games on the road before coming home for their finale on March 12. All good things pass quickly, and CU's run for a championship was thrilling for all concerned. Along the way at least two additional students became big fans. Sally and Sarah would savor fond memories of being surrounded by excited young men not afraid of sharing their emotions about this boys' game with two tenderfoots. They first came to be with their guys, but by March both appreciated the athleticism, grace, and toughness of the team that achieved beyond pre-season predictions.

A brief snowball fight broke out on the way home, revealing, however, that none of the athletic skill Sarah and Sally observed over the past two months had been transferred to them. Mose assumed the pose of a scarecrow.

"Okay, I'll stand completely still. Take your best shot." He motioned the girls to move closer. Sarah's toss missed low and to the left, but Sally's snowball grazed his jeans. "Okay, Sal! You get a wish. Name it."

Sally pondered the opportunity, as the group began moving in the direction of the Hill again. As they approached Broadway, she spoke. "You'll grant this one wish, huh?" Mose nodded and smiled. "Then I wish to have all of us stay in Boulder long enough to graduate."

Monday, February 27

Sarah was waiting for Paul outside the UMC at noon. "We got out early." After a kiss, "There's an Arab speaker upstairs at one. Want to go with me?"

"I've got an SPU meeting first, but unless there's something on the agenda I don't know about, it won't take long. I missed one last week. Cohen was hot, but that's more of his personality these days." He changed the subject. "Why am I always so hungry on Mondays?"

"Maybe it has something to do with how much you eat on Sunday night. Do you want me to go to the peace meeting with you?"

"Yeah, then I'll have an excuse to leave early."

The Syrian delegate droned on, it seemed to Sarah, with the same message; *Jews would be welcome in the Arab countries as citizens in Syria or Jordan or Palestine, but not as Israelis. Israel was an illegal nation, created by a guilty world after World War II, under pressure from Zionists who have too much power and influence in Western governments even to this day. Arabs were not anti-Semitic as the Zionists claimed, simply anti-Israel. Anyway, the day would come when the Zionist nation would cease to exist, and when that happened, Jews could live in the Arab world under legal governments.*

Paul could feel the tension in Sarah as she leaned forward in her chair. He wondered if she would be able to contain her anger, an anger that intensified when the Syrian speaker stated the Holocaust had been greatly exaggerated by the Zionists for propaganda purposes. The crowd loudly voiced its strong disagreement with the statement, a crowd that included many Jews from Denver and Denver University.

Sarah groaned and turned to Paul "How can a person deny the Holocaust and maintain he's not anti-Semitic in the same breath?" She turned back to the speaker, who was concluding his remarks.

The United States, as the leader of the free world, needed to re-orient its foreign policy and give up its support of the Zionists. The Cold War was coming to an end, and the Islamic world could be partners with both the Soviet Union and America to bring peace and prosperity to the region. His attempt to field questions from the audience was cut short because there were no questions asked, only statements of outrage from the predominantly Jewish audience. One young woman, who identified herself as Dafna, a senior from DU, ended the session when she stood at her chair near Sarah and Paul and said with dignity and clarity, "Sir, you are free in this country to tell your lies and display your veiled hatred of the Jewish people, but know you only deceive yourself when you say Israel will cease to exist. It's here and it's here to stay!" With that, she turned and walked out, along with the majority of the audience. Sarah studied her as she left the room, then turned back to Paul and heaved a sigh, as if she had been holding her breath.

"She was impressive," Paul said simply. He waited for a response, but Sarah's eyes were set somewhere beyond him. Paul wondered if all Jews were Zionists.

At a minute before eleven, a minute before curfew, at the door of the Sig Delt house, Sarah kissed Paul and asked a favor. "Promise me you'll go home and go to bed. Don't read any of those books Dr. Orr has assigned you on Monday morning and get some sleep. Mid-terms are coming up, you know."

Paul looked puzzled. "Orr hasn't assigned me any readings, except those for class."

Mrs. Meyer stuck her head out the door. "Goodnight, Mr. Garrity. Thank you for getting Sarah home on time."

Tuesday, February 28

On Tuesday Paul asked Sarah if she could get by without him at the Lab School. With the Vietnam Teach-In scheduled for Wednesday, he needed to make sure all the last-minute details were taken care of. "Kennedy and Cohen and Roberts are all busy with the program speakers. I've got to make calls to get students' butts in the chairs. Thanks for contacting all the Greek houses. Kevin and Jeff and I will re-call them today, plus I have to call the dorms and residence halls. I'm going to work out of the SPU office until dinner."

"I'll let you out of class if I can help you after dinner," said Sarah. "We can make some protest signs. Mose can help."

They both laughed.

MARCH

Wednesday, March 1

Dr. Orr planned to spend half of each class discussing the history of Vietnam, not just US involvement, but going back to foreign control by China, France, Japan, and France again. He explained how President Truman decided to take a "Europe first" approach to America's post-World War II foreign policy to blunt the spread of communism into Western Europe. To be successful, the US had to support France's colonial claims in Southeast Asia, in a sense, to deny America's traditional foreign policy of being the leading anti-colonial power. When France proved unable to control Indochina, even using US dollars, America chose to replace the French to prevent the "first domino" from falling. Most of the students in the introductory US history class were unaware of these events. However, the Cold War class, made up of sophomores and upper-class students, came alive with questions, which took up the entire period.

"Why didn't we just refuse France's demands after WWII? They were a defeated nation anyway."

"Could there have been a chance Ho would have linked up to the West, you know, given his rhetoric around independence?"

"Was North Vietnam a satellite of the Soviet Union or China? Or was it just acting on its own?"

"Why doesn't LBJ just turn the Air Force loose on Hanoi instead of dropping everything on the South, on the people who are supposed to be our allies?"

"Can we win?"

"What choices do we have now? It's not 1963, you know."

"Why can't the Vietnamese comprehend what we're trying to do for them?'

Dr. Orr paced the front of the room while these questions were being posed. He did not answer any of them at the time, deflecting them as an expert fencer might a thrusting epee. "These are all excellent questions, questions that will be addressed at this evening's teach-in. I suggest you all attend—and take notes. Try not to get caught up in the gamesmanship of the left and right, who will no doubt try to sway the crowd with signs and chants." He looked suddenly to his right where Paul was seated, catching him off guard. Paul merely smiled and pretended to write something in his notebook, but Dr. Orr was correct. The SPU and the YAF were planning to use the teach-in as a springboard to further political action, and Paul was in the thick of it.

Gofer that he believed he was, Paul decided his part in organizing the teach-in would not be missed for an hour at lunch. He was not sleeping, but he did not want to give up his time with Sarah. She was delighted to see him waiting for her just outside the UMC doors.

"I didn't expect to see you here today, but I'm glad you are!" She kissed him, and they walked arm-in-arm to the cafeteria.

"I won't be able to pick you up tonight. I'll be down here until it's over. I'm going to see my Lit professor after lunch and tell him I won't be in class, and then I'll work straight through." Paul already had dark circles around his eyes.

"A lot of the Sig Delts are coming early, so we can get up-front seats. How many people are you expecting?" She licked her forefinger and pretended to rub the circles off his eyes. "It's going to take soap and sleep," she smiled.

"I'm hoping for as many as attended the Publish or Perish rally, but since we're at night, we may fall short of that, but we'll fill up the ballroom, and it's going to be loud and partisan, I think, but maybe not."

"Did you ever learn about periods in English grammar class, my dear? When this is over, I'm going to put you to bed myself."

"I thought you said I needed some sleep." Paul paused to emphasize the end of a short sentence. "I'll be all right. Maybe I'll ditch classes tomorrow and sleep until noon."

"But you can't miss my class. The kids asked about you on Tuesday. Besides, Mrs. Best has some news for you." Paul started to ask, but Sarah cut him off. "Aa-aa. She made me promise not to tell you, but it's good news."

They walked north to McKenna, the language lab, where she was going to spend the next two hours. "How will I find you tonight?" She squeezed his hand.

"I'll be the guy with the white towel over his arm who's pouring water for the speakers." Paul took a shot to his chest. At five feet-eight with strong features, no one would ever describe Sarah as "delicate." "Just kidding! Just sit with your sisters, and I'll find you."

"Tell Sally I'll save her a spot, and if Mose gets back, him too. Is Dan going?"

"Oh, yeah, Dan wouldn't miss this, unless it was on the weekend. Now go, or else I'll stand here all afternoon with you." He kissed her forehead.

"Gee thanks, dad," she responded sarcastically. Then she put her hand on the back of his neck and gave him a real kiss.

There were plenty of signs, more from the anti-war crowd, and chants, but overall, the students were respectful of the speakers and listened to their reports. By the second hour, the crowd was quiet and intense, with only an occasional individual response from the student crowd. Paul was able to find the Sig Delts and the 1203 house. Mose and Dan had made it.

"You did good, Garrity," Mose said. "This place is packed."

"It seems like I called every one of them just these past two days." It was a weary comment.

"In case no one else bothers, I want to say thank you for all the work you did to put this together. Others will get the credit, but your friends will know. We're proud of you, my dear." Sarah really was proud of her man, and Paul could feel it.

He was surprised when Sally gave him a kiss on the cheek.

"It ain't happenin', Garrity," warned Mose.

The speakers raised all the relevant questions in addition to chronicling the path that America had taken to get to 1967. The Domino Theory and The Cold War, "hearts and minds," the pacification program, chemical warfare and body counts, Operation Rolling Thunder, and Robert McNamara. The bombing came under intense scrutiny. Nothing seemed to be left out. It was all overwhelming to the crowd, and they were left with one final comment by Dr. Whitehead, a political science professor with a reputation for "Socratizing." "It's no longer 1963, my friends; that time has passed. It's spring, 1967. What choices do we have now?" It was after midnight, and the crowd had dwindled to a few hundred. It was time to go.

"I've gotta stick around and see if anything needs to be done. Why don't you guys go on home, and I'll join you there," said Paul.

"Remember when I was a bit frazzled at a sorority function and this guy stepped in to help?" It was a rhetorical question. "I'm staying."

Paul and Sarah walked directly to the Sig Delt house from the teach-in. It had been a tremendous success, and Paul was beginning to wind down. They arrived at Sarah's house around one-thirty, well after curfew, but the sisters who attended the teach-in were not penalized. She was the last to arrive. As always, they embraced at the door.

"Go home and get some sleep. You're no good to me in this condition, and some of my sisters think you're on drugs."

"I'll probably get to bed, and some girl will call and wake me up, so I'll just stay up and wait for her."

"I won't call tonight, I promise." She kissed him and spun him around. "Start walking. It's five blocks north."

"I like it when you order me around. Fewer decisions. Goodnight." Paul walked to the sidewalk and as directed, headed north. Sarah watched him until he was out of sight.

"Hello." Paul had already fallen asleep.

"I lied about not calling. I love you, and I was so proud to be with you. Goodnight."

Thursday, March 2

Paul woke up just in time to shower and drive over to the University Hill Lab School. He parked in the rear where teachers left their cars, and he expected to return to a parking ticket. Sarah's blue Corvair was also parked there. She finished up with her schedule of assignments while he waited patiently. Finally, she scattered the kids, all but two boys, who were told to start reading and wait for her to return. She approached him and took his hand. "Come with me." Outside Mrs. Best's office, she gave him a quick kiss and then knocked on the door.

"Ah, Mr. Garrity, I heard the teach-in went very well. The paper reported over 1,200 students attended. Sarah tells me you were responsible for that." Mrs. Best stood and walked over to the filing cabinet.

"Sarah's been known to manipulate the data. Anyway, I think LBJ put most of those people in the seats. I helped, that's all." Sarah pretended to be hurt. "What do you hear from Ricky?"

"Here's a letter for you." Mrs. Best handed it to him without further comment.

Inside, there were two pieces of paper. The first was a note from Ricky's mother.

Dear Paul,

Ricky and I moved in with my sister and her family and everything is going well. Her husband hired me as a secretary for his construction company, and my sister watches Ricky while I work. He has his own room. He wants you to come see him, but I know that might not be possible, so I'm asking you to send him a picture for his dresser. Thank you again so much for taking care of him at a very difficult time. I will never forget it.

Sincerely,

Sandra McLean

PS. The court ordered my boyfriend never to set foot in Grand Junction, so we are able to relax.

The second piece of paper was a crayon drawing of two boys tossing a basketball between them. One was taller than the other, but both boys were smiling.

Paul was silent as he stared at the figures. He handed both letters to Sarah and sat down. She held them with her left hand as her right hand covered her mouth. When she finished reading them, she sat down next to Paul and laid her head on his shoulder. Mrs. Best walked out of the room. "You two take your time. I'll go back and look after the kids."

"I spend days working on the teach-in, but this seems, I don't know, more important. I just happen to be in the right place at the right time. You were the one who deserves most of the credit." He paused. "Do you have a camera?" He had not looked up until the last question.

Sarah crouched in front of him, still holding the papers. "Why? Do you want to photograph me naked?'

"That too," he said softly with a soft smile and a nod.

"Are you going to be okay?"

"Yeah, I'm fine."

"Good because you've got those two little boys by yourself today. I'm going to Hillel now to listen to a speaker. I'll see you tonight after dinner." She leaned up to give him a kiss.

"Do either of these two kids have a problem I should know about?"

"No. Regular kids. Their parents work for the University."

The Hillel speaker was Theodore Bikel, the folk singer, who spoke about "Jewish Identity and Commitment." Later that day he gave a concert at Macky Auditorium. Sarah brought Paul along.

Friday, March 3

Dr. Orr took questions from his students in both classes about Wednesday night's teach-in. They were excited, and most had attended. Paul knew one suggestion from Orr about going had been much more persuasive than all his phone calls, posters, and *Daily* ads. He wondered if he could ever do that, to command that much respect. Orr's closing comments to the Cold War class tied Vietnam to the Cold War and then to the actions of the students at the University of Colorado. "This war will go a long way in determining the course of the Cold War, and you will determine the course of this war." He paused to allow it to sink in. "Mid-terms in two weeks. Have a good weekend." On his way out, Dr. Orr congratulated Paul on his efforts to get students to attend the teach-in. "Professor Kennedy told me. By the way, do you go anywhere without that pretty, young lady?" He smiled at his tired young charge and put a hand on his shoulder.

"Not if I can help it, I don't."

Sarah took Paul to the Matterhorn, a fancy restaurant about five miles south of Boulder on the east slope of the Flatirons along Colorado 93, for dinner on Friday night. She even drove. "I'll marry you if you throw in your truck as part of the dowry."

"Ooo, I don't know. That's pretty steep," said Paul.

"It's a beautiful view from up here. Boulder seems so peaceful. It's a fantasy land."

Paul turned his head around to see the same view. "Peaceful on the surface, but there's plenty stirring when you're inside." He turned back to her. "CU is this hill from which we are afforded a certain view, a peculiar view. Maybe all universities are. I suppose when we graduate, we'll descend from this hill and have to see things a bit more realistically. Maybe that's the purpose of university life, to see the possible."

Sarah did not respond immediately; she just held her gaze. Paul still had dark rings under his eyes. A hundred thoughts passed through her eyes, but she didn't speak. She knew Paul was catching many of them. Finally, she voiced her last thought. "How about we not go there tonight? How about we leave the serious ideas for another day?"

"Are you going to be able to come back early from spring break? I don't know if I can stand not being with you for over a week." It was a subject they had talked about before.

"I think so. My uncle leaves on Thursday, so I've got my father convinced I'd just be a real pill if I stayed any longer. He'll talk my mother into it." She gave him a devious look. "I re-scheduled my Friday flight to Saturday morning, but nobody else knows that, so I'll need a place to stay on Friday night and a ride to the airport on Saturday morning. Got any suggestions?" She smiled at the gift she had just given him.

Paul was obviously delighted but played along. "Yeah, I do. Mose isn't going home, so he could take you."

"You toad!" Sarah reached up and squeezed his cheeks. "What happens to 1203 over the break? Will anyone be around?"

"Everyone's leaving, except Mose, but I'll be up to do some work on the apartment. I want to have it ready for next fall." Then Paul asked, "If you get back early, do you want to go skiing in Leadville again?"

Saturday, March 4

Mose slept in on Saturday. When he got up, he had a bowl of cereal, and then went to basketball practice. That afternoon, he settled down to read and do some writing, accompanied by his jazz albums. He was a voracious reader, everything from prose to poetry.

Currently, he was involved with Black novelists—Baldwin, Wright, and Ellison—on a recommendation from his English professor. Only Paul knew that Mose wanted to become a junior high teacher after college, either English or math. Paul generally spent the morning working in the garage or repairing the apartment building. Along with Mose, he spent the afternoon reading, but his books tended toward history and philosophy. The new girl also had a predictable Saturday: synagogue in the morning and Greek council meetings in the afternoon.

Around seven, 1203 gathered for pizza. "What a week," said Paul as he collapsed on the couch without dropping his slices. The group bantered, especially Mose and Sally. Sarah could not decide whether they were brother and sister, boyfriend and girlfriend, or husband and wife. "When was the last time Mose paid you a compliment, Sally?"

Paul came to the aid of his buddy. "Just this afternoon he told me what a nice ass you have, Sally."

"Mose!"

"I never said that. I'm gonna kick your ass one of these days, Garrity!" They all laughed, and Paul got up to answer the phone.

"I don't know if I've ever had this much fun in my life," said Sarah, "as when I'm up here with all you guys."

"Except when you're up here just with him," teased Sally.

"That was Kevin. He's coming over . . . with a date. He said since we all had dates, another couple would fit right in, plus, he's broke too. Paul opened a bottle of Coors. "Anyone else?" Sarah took it from him.

"I don't have a date," said Sally.

"You're with me," said Sarah. "Mose is Paul's date."

"So that's how it works," said Mose.

Kevin brought along another pizza and more beer. For the rest of the evening, Paul and Sarah were the brunt of most of the jokes. After Kevin left, Sarah informed the gang the upcoming week would be a mid-term study marathon for them all with no disruptions or distractions, that each of them would ace every exam. Eating—and sex—would be the only distractions. She smiled at Paul.

"For Mose, it's only eating then," kidded Paul.

All of this was to begin at two on Sunday afternoon, long enough to get three hours of studying in before going to the Gondolier, then back at it for another four hours before curfew. Sally said she would go to the store on Sunday morning to stock up on snacks for the week, and everyone would chip in a few dollars. Paul's refrigerator would be ground zero.

Sunday, March 5

Sarah called Mose and Sally into Paul's room at exactly two to join Paul and Anne. "I've got time sheets for everyone to fill out this week," she announced when everyone was present. "Anne will be joining us since her grades have slipped a bit. Her boyfriend hasn't been very good for her study habits." She started shuffling some paper slips on the kitchen table.

"I ain't doin' this shit, Sarah," said Mose defiantly.

"Gotcha, Robinson!" Sarah was so pleased with herself. "What do you think I am—obsessive?" She showed the blank paper slips to Sally and chuckled. "Not that you don't need some guidance. See how well Paul is turning out since I took control of him."

"On your mark, get set, go," and as Paul fired his blank finger into the roof of the apartment, the study marathon began.

Around ten Paul poured himself a glass of water, took a sip, and went over to whisper in his girlfriend's ear. "Is it time for sex now?"

"We can't. We'd have to kick Anne and Mose out. They'd know what we were doing?"

"Like they don't already?"

"Go back to the Cold War," Sarah ordered.

"Very cold." Paul kissed her on the cheek.

March 6--March 10

The tone at 1203 was serious all week. Each day was indistinguishable from the previous day. Paul came under abuse due to the fact he was dating a drill sergeant. Everyone went to class, or work, or practice, or attended meetings; they ate on schedule at The Colonial. But when the obligations and basic needs were met, each student cracked a book and prepared for the next mid-term exam. Nobody's tests seemed to be bunched up on the same day, except Paul's double shot of Dr. Orr on Wednesday. In preparation he pulled an all-nighter on Tuesday, but then crashed on Wednesday afternoon, missing his American Lit class. His test for that class was on Friday, and it was the final test for any of the gang at 1203. The week became a fog in his otherwise clear memory of these days.

The celebration as a reward for a week's worth of concentrated study began around 4:00 at Tulagi's. It seemed as if every Greek at CU had the same idea. Tulagi's was packed. Sally hugged Sarah when she arrived. "Your study week was really a good idea, especially now that it's over, but from what I'm hearing, we all did very well on our tests. Mose even made a 'C' on his stat exam! He's pumped!" This FAC, coming on the heels of midterms, was like one giant fraternity function, with each house staking its claim to a couple of booths. The beer flowed, the Moonrakers rocked, and the students danced. It was loud and fun, and it was the prelude to spring break, which was just a week away.

Paul rolled onto his back and blew out heavily. He and Sarah stayed quiet for a few minutes and listened to "Pet Sounds," all the while holding hands as they regained control of their bodies.

"What do you think Sally thinks when Mose is with someone else?" She paused. "I know it doesn't happen much, but I worry for Sally."

"She dates more than he does, and I think they each accept it, but I don't know what each feels about the other . . . in that way. Last fall, Mose and me found out she was drinking alone in her room a lot, especially on the weekends. Out of loneliness. That's when he started spending time with her, but I know it was to be her friend; it was never sexual." He rolled to his side, so he could see his girl. She turned to him. "You and I have been so involved that I haven't worried about their relationship. We're just one big happy family."

"Except it's not always happy, huh." Sarah instinctively knew his entire thought.

"Not me. I'm on cloud nine these days, but, yeah, I worry about my roomies, and about you."

She smiled and touched his nose. "Why me? I've got you." She wasn't concerned yet.

"I worry about all the people I love."

"That's a cop-out, you know. What do you really mean?" she pressed.

"This is our time, Sars, and our place." He let the words sink in. "And I don't know if any of it is transferable. As long as we're here, together, it's perfect, but I do worry for you, for us, when the time comes that we don't have this place." He breathed in heavily and exhaled slowly. "I only know you here and now, but even in this, I see you changing, growing, for sure, but I don't know where you're heading. So, sometimes I worry for you."

"You can always come with me. Open invitation." She smiled.

"All my friends here, my parents, and the other guy who lives inside of me, they all push me to you, tell me how right you are for me. All those people out there," he motioned in the air above their heads, "your parents especially, and that 4,000-year-old history, they're all pulling you away from me. They warn you about me, that I'm not your future, or at least not your best future."

"I'll bet you've never used that phrase with any other girl, have you." She smiled slightly.

"Which one?"

"That a 4,000-year history is pushing you away." She turned around and slid her naked back into his naked chest and pulled his arms tightly around her. "You know me better than I know myself."

"No, I don't."

"Well, then, my dear, your pull is just going to have to be stronger than their push."

Saturday, March 11

Dan and Sally were on the road by seven. Paul and Mose slept in, trying to recover from the recent marathon. At synagogue Sarah barely heard the words of Rabbi Michelson when he spoke of the impending crisis for Jews in Israel. Her thoughts were focused on a generous young man whose love was giving her a confidence she had never known, whose love was finally setting her free to choose for herself opportunities previously not available. In one week, she would be flying back to New York and would be apart from Paul for the first time since they met. She would feel the pull of those Jewish forces.

Around noon Mose offered to buy burgers at The Sink. He was extremely upset that the CU basketball team had not been selected for the NIT playoffs. Sunday's game would be the team's last of the season. On the way home, Mose suggested the evening's plan. "How 'bout if we get Sarah and drive to Denver and go to a jazz club?"

"I wouldn't know where to go. Do you?"

"Yeah, I can get us there. All black section of Denver, near Five Points. It'll be fun."

"Will they let Sarah and me in?" asked Paul seriously.

"You'll be with a black guy. I'll take care of ya." Mose put his lanky arm around Paul. "Just like I always do."

Paul pushed him away. "Shit! Who takes care of who?"

El Chapultepec, on 20th and Market, was dark and smoky. Mose tipped the doorman two dollars, said something to him at close quarters, and they shared a laugh. The doorman pointed to a booth at the end of the club, away from the door, and motioned to the waitress, who strolled over.

"They're cool. Just serve 'em sodas. No booze." He gave her one of the dollars and stuffed the other in his shirt pocket.

From the table Mose and his two companions could not be seen from the front door. He turned his chair around and straddled it, so he could give full attention to the jazz trio playing just a few feet away. He nodded to them, and they acknowledged him in return. Paul and Sarah sat across the table from Mose, but still facing the musicians. It was obvious from their mannerisms they were unsure of the proper behavior in the black club. The waitress brought three club sodas and set them on the table. As Paul reached for his wallet, she shook her head, "No charge," and smiled.

"This is almost better than riding in a pickup truck for the first time," said Sarah into Paul's ear. He smiled and put his arm around the back of her chair. "I keep having these new experiences with you."

"Have you ever been in a situation where you're the minority?" asked Paul.

Sarah drew her head back slightly and cocked her left eyebrow. He did not understand. Finally, she said, "In case you haven't noticed, I'm Jewish." She put her finger on her nose. "This often makes me a minority. Every public prayer invokes Jesus Christ, my dear." She smiled, but she was giving him a lesson about herself too.

"Sorry, I just meant," he paused. "I guess I better not try to explain myself out of this one, huh."

She put her hand on this thigh, leaned in, and kissed him, then motioned for him to pay attention to the band. She picked up her soda and took a drink. Mose was riveted to the three men on the one-step stage, who all understood that the tall, slender boy had some knowledge and experience in jazz clubs. He was comfortable. He fit.

At the break the chubby, whiskered drummer strolled the length of the club talking with the patrons, before working his way back to where Mose sat. He pulled up a chair. "Where you kids from?" he asked in a gravelly voice that perfectly matched his visage.

"Boulder, sir. CU," answered Mose with none of the cool he normally showed.

The drummer looked at Paul and Sarah. "First time?"

"Pretty obvious, huh?" said Paul.

"My name's Roy, but mostly people call me 'Sticks.' We're glad you're here. What're your names?"

"Mose."

"Sarah, sir."

"Paul."

"Mose? Short for . . .?"

"Moses, but I like to think it's after Mose Allison."

"You black, son?" Sticks asked. He reached out and rubbed Mose's head. "I'll be damned."

"He doesn't look black," offered Sarah, who immediately wished she hadn't, as she looked to Mose as if to apologize.

"No, no he doesn't, but then . . . you don't look particularly Jewish either in this light." Sticks stood up with a smile and extended his hand to each kid. "You're welcome here anytime."

They stayed into the next set. About half an hour later, Sarah caught Paul concentrating on her more than the jazz trio. "Why are you looking at me like that?"

"I was watching you listening to the music. Your face is always so expressive, so reflective of the situation. I just love studying it." He reached over and touched her cheek with the back of his fingers. She moved her hand to his, squeezed it, and kissed it.

"I keep having these new and wonderful experiences and feelings with you. From our first date, you've made me your girl, haven't you?"

Paul smiled. "Whatever chemistry we share, you've always responded so positively to everything I've tried to do for you. You amaze me still."

"I wonder what . . . no, I'm not going to wonder tonight. I'm simply going to accept all this. I'm going to keep giving you my dark brown eyes and sexy bod and passion without questions." She kissed him on the lips. "We've got to go. Do you think we can get Mose out of this place?"

Next to the truck, as they waited for Paul to unlock the doors, Sarah grabbed Mose's ears and gave him a big kiss. "That was wonderful! I owe you."

"That was cool, wasn't it? Sticks was great! You looked stunned when he said you didn't look Jewish. Pretty sharp guy." Mose thumped his hands on the dashboard in staccato strokes when he got in.

Sarah fell asleep before the pickup had reached the toll booth at the Broomfield exit. Paul eased the truck to a stop to pay his quarter, hoping not to wake her. She stirred but seemed to relax again as the pickup increased speed again.

"She doesn't do things half-way, does she," Mose said. "You are one lucky guy, Garrity, but I've gotta admire you for pickin' her out when nobody else did. What'd you see in her anyway?"

"Pretty obvious, isn't it?"

"Yeah, she's pretty and stylish, but it takes gettin' to know her before she's beautiful."

"Maybe I always thought she was. Did you ever consider that, big guy?" The lights of Boulder appeared suddenly as they reached the overlook.

"Well, she loves your ass. You make a dumb remark over a beer about her hair gettin' awfully long, so she gets it cut shorter than yours. She doesn't care what her sorority sisters think; she just wants to get a rise out of you."

"And I love her short hair. Makes her kind of tough looking." Paul began to decelerate as he passed the new Williams Towers. "You're right though, Mose, I am a lucky guy." He turned off the turnpike, and after a left and a right, started down Broadway toward the Sigma Delta Tau house. Ten minutes to curfew.

At the door Sarah was just beginning to wake up. "I had the best time. I always do."

"Sleep in tomorrow. Call me when you wake up. Okay?"

"By the way, my dear, I'm the lucky one, and I'm glad you like my hair. I wasn't sure about that one," she said. The porch light blinked.

Sunday, March 12

Lynn Baker used the high screen from Karl Tate to get into the lane. As the Nebraska defender slid off his man to help, Bake used a left-hand push pass to get the ball to Pat Frink, who drained the eighteen-foot jump shot. The basket gave CU its first lead of the second half. After that a parade to the free throw line secured the win. The final score was 64-57, giving the overachieving Buffs two victories over the NIT-bound Cornhuskers on the season. The crowd stood in appreciation, but the team's celebration was muted. For basketball purists the ending of the careers of the seniors on such a note was sad. It had been their time, but for reasons out of their control, that time ended too soon. 1203 stood and applauded as the team walked off the court for the last time together. Even the novice, Sarah Phillips, recognized the unique relationship that existed among the basketball team. Even though Mose hadn't played, she thought she understood him a bit better and maybe his motives. He walked off the court with Lynn Baker's arm around his shoulder, the star and the promise. Sarah's body shivered; she slide her arm around Paul's waist.

Paul's parents drove up to take the kids out to dinner after the game. Mose arrived late to the Harvest House, spending time with the team and listening to the coach's final words. All five ordered steaks and baked potatoes, except for Mose, who had fries, and the conversation was light. Mrs. Garrity remarked how everyone seemed ready for spring break and made Moses promise to spend a few days with them in Lakewood. He promised he would. On the way home, Paul, Sarah, and Mose noticed the abundance of flashing police and ambulance lights at the Kittredge residence halls.

Monday, March 13

"Good morning, Paul. Winter seems to go on forever around here, doesn't it?"

"Morning, Dr. Orr. I don't know what the correct answer is. Remember, I missed the first indications of spring, and now you want me to predict more weeks of winter? That's the job for that beaver that's looking for his shadow, isn't it?" Paul poured himself a cup of coffee.

"Groundhog. Can't something be two things at once?"

"People usually are. Sarah said something to me the other day about that. We were having one of those college philosophy discussions with a couple of our friends, and she said, 'I believe in each of us, several people exist—some good, and some not so good.' It sure set off the discussion for the next hour or so."

Dr. Orr handed Paul a box of sugar cubes. "Is it one person who is in transition from one developmental stage to another, or is it multiple people?"

"That was my position. Sort of like a metamorphosis, that individuals grow and change, but some of the old person remains, I guess."

"Did Sarah accept that?"

"Not at first. We all thought if you really wanted to, you could decide to be someone else and become that new person. Click off one switch and click on another. But after more talk and more beer, we thought maybe it was all part of normal development, even though for some, it could be pretty dramatic."

"Funny how beer seems to clear things up sometimes." Orr was enjoying his young charge. "What affects that transformation?"

"Our families, our friends, our environment. Our teachers." He acknowledged his professor's influence. "Might just be hormones. Sarah said she knew she was metamorphosing right now. My friends agreed to that emphatically. I think the word she used was 'shedding.'" He smiled as he recalled the conversation.

"Sounds like a productive evening. I miss those college talks." The mentor reached around to a small table behind him and grabbed some papers. He looked at them briefly and then handed them to Paul. "You can be proud of these scores. You earned the highest mark on each midterm. You blew the curve away on the Cold War exam. I'm proud of you, but now I'll expect even more." He smiled as if he had just won another round.

Paul beamed. "Well, sir, I'm not the same student I was last year. Does that prove or disprove what I just said?"

Paul was so intent on the lead story in the *Daily* that he did not see Sarah approach him at lunch.

"Oh, hi." He kissed her. "You're wet."

"What's so interesting in the paper that you're not on the lookout for me?" She grabbed his paper with her free hand. "My God!"

"That explains the lights at Kittredge last night." They stood in silence and read the story. Paul finished first and put his hand on Sarah's neck, waiting for her. "Let's go grab a table."

"You go to your meeting, and I'll wait for you here. Then, I'll walk you to class." The news was troubling Sarah, and it seemed as though she wanted to digest it on her own for a while.

"The SPU needs to decide what we want to do for the World Affairs Conference. Cohen wants something splashy. You know how he is." He paused. "Will you be okay?"

"Oh, yeah. I'm just not in the mood for a political tirade. Just don't be long. I don't get to spend enough time with you as it is." She grabbed his sleeve and pulled him closer for a kiss.

"We have a great opportunity here, and we better not blow it! We have to be ready on the first day of the conference to push the anti-war message. Some of the speakers will be on our side, and we'll need to pack their sessions." Cohen was ranting to seventeen SPU members like they were 70. "Flyers, newspaper ads, and, I think, a booth by the fountain to get out our anti-war literature." He took a breath.

"Where do we get a booth?" asked one of the regulars.

"We build it ourselves . . . on the Sunday before the conference starts."

Oh, shit, thought Paul. *That means me.* He raised his hand to speak. "Where do we get the money for the materials?"

"We all pitch in. If we're really committed to the cause, we should put our money where our mouths are."

"Tell you what, Cohen. You buy the wood, and I'll build it. Just tell me how big, and I'll have the plans to you the next day. Gotta go. Call me." Paul was developing a dislike for Cohen, but he knew that the SPU was the only committed anti-war organization at CU. The Democrats sure weren't.

Paul bought Sarah's dinner at The Colonial that evening, and they sat with Mose, Sally, and Dan.

"Was it a new-born baby or a fetus?" asked Sally.

"It was a baby but probably born just hours before they found it. Evidently, it died from neglect," answered Paul.

"What are you thinking, Sally?" asked Sarah.

"About the mother." She paused. "I'll bet she had no one to talk to throughout her whole pregnancy, no one to share this with." She spoke with compassion. "I don't know anything about her, but I can relate. If she's living in a dorm, that probably means she's a teenager, a freshman, no more than nineteen. I was eighteen, but I was living at home, and my mom was there for me every step of the way. We talked about the options, and I had some: abortion, keep the baby, give it up for adoption. She supported me." Sarah reached out and took Sally's hand. She was speaking with glazed eyes. The hand brought her back to the group.

"What about the father?" asked Dan.

"Don't think badly about me, but . . . I didn't know which one he was. Obviously, none of them stepped forward, but how could I expect any of them to step up and take responsibility for a baby that, by odds, wasn't theirs. I was the one who was irresponsible. More like out of control," said Sally.

"Let's get out of here and go back to Paul's. This doesn't concern anyone here." Mose was looking out for his good friend.

"You guys go. Dan and I'll put the trays away," said Paul. "We'll be right over."

"Why not abortion?" asked Mose quietly. He was holding Sally's hand.

"We almost did, my mom and me, but I would've had to go to Mexico. The news got out to my school, so I couldn't conceal it. That's kind of self-serving, but it's true. Then my principal called me into his office and told me I needed to drop out of school and get my GED.

That pissed me off, and I got stubborn."

"Nooo, not you," kidded Mose.

"Why did you give him up, not keep him?" asked Sarah.

"What would you do?" said Sally almost as a challenge.

Sarah looked at Paul. "I'd know who the father was, and I know he'd be there for me. If we didn't get an abortion, then I'm pretty sure we would keep it." She never looked at Sally but kept her eyes directly on Paul.

"If I would've had Paul . . . or you Mose, or you Dan . . . maybe I would've kept the child. I wish any one of you would've been there, but you weren't. It seemed as though it was me versus the world. I would've gone to Mexico, probably, to get the abortion. I'm glad I made the decision I did." Sally received a hug from Mose, who was sitting on the arm of the couch next to her.

"Do you ever wonder about him?" It was the first time Paul had spoken on the subject.

"Oh, yeah, every day," replied Sally. "But I have to have faith his new family loves him, because they wanted him. I believe he's doing good." Everyone was quiet. Finally, Sally cleared her throat. "Let's not end on this. It was not about me tonight; it's about a girl in the dorm who desperately needs someone and about a dead baby, who needed someone last night. If I'm not mistaken, each one of you could've had this happen to them."

"Except Mose. He's a virgin," interjected Dan.

"As I was saying, we need to get more involved with these issues here on campus. There needs to be a system in place to help pregnant girls, some kind of organization of support. I'm going to see what I can do." Everyone nodded. "One more thing, thanks for being here for me all year. I was so scared last fall, and you guys . . ." Sally didn't have to finish her thought.

Sarah and Paul tried to study after the rest of 1203 had gone back to their rooms, but they were in no mood for French, sociology, or US history.

"Let's just cuddle and listen to music. Pick something, okay."

Paul put Johnny Mathis on his stereo and joined her on the couch. "How's that?"

"Perfect." She laid down and put her head in his lap. He responded by running his fingers through her hair and along her neck. "It wouldn't have to be a pregnancy, would it?"

"Nope. You're stuck with me . . . for as long as you want me." Paul knew what was coming, at least in tone.

"Thanks for catching me when I fell off the train."

"You keep implying it was a fall, Sars, but I'm not sure you didn't just take off, and you're bringing me along for this wonderful adventure."

"What's the difference?" she asked.

Paul hesitated with his response and then gave a non-answer. "You see more when you're flying as opposed to falling."

"You're so full of shit sometimes." She turned slightly so she could see him directly. "Sometimes, you pretend you don't worry about what will happen to us in the future, that you're just going to enjoy each moment. Well, my dear, I don't believe that. You worry about us just as much as I do. I don't know what's going to happen to us either, but I worry." Her voice was rising, and her eyes burrowed in on his. "If we can't be together because some force pulls us apart, then I guess I can accept that. But I don't want some phony, stupid, emotional reason to come between us. And when I thank you for catching me, why can't you just say 'you're welcome' and let it go at that?" She sat up quickly, stood, and then sat on his lap with her legs straddling his. She gave him a hard look, then buried her face into his shoulder and put her arms around his neck. His arms automatically wrapped themselves around her back. He knew enough to stay quiet, to let her finish. "One of my sorority sisters got pregnant last fall. She dropped out and had an abortion. Her boyfriend paid for it, or at least his parents did. He's still in school, but she isn't. She's back in Illinois." Sarah pulled back and looked at Paul. "I was late with my period a couple of weeks ago, just as I was starting the pill, and . . . I didn't care, because I knew you wouldn't desert me, and because I . . . you . . . we love each other so much." Tears welled up in her eyes, and she grabbed the hair over his ears. "It started again. I only told Sally, and she told me to tell you. If

I would have missed another one, then I would have told you." Sarah wiped her nose on Paul's shoulder and then returned to the spot where she could look into his eyes.

"Thank me again for catching you," he said softly.

"Thank you for catching me when I fell from the train."

"You're welcome." They leaned forward so that their foreheads touched. Her hands relaxed and fell to his chest.

"Take me to bed."

Tuesday, March 14

Paul was looking out his back window when Sarah drove up and parked her Corvair behind his truck. He reached over and opened his door so she could walk right in, which she always did anyway. The others usually knocked once as a warning or a courtesy before entering. Open house at all hours. He put his apple juice glass in the sink and wiped his hands just as she came in.

"I could get used to coming over every morning, maybe even getting you out of bed," she said.

"If you weren't so Greek, you could just live over here with me, but then we might never get out of bed." They gave each other a kiss. "We'd flunk out."

"I brought in this newspaper. When did you subscribe to the *Boulder Camera*?"

"Today's the first day it's been delivered. With all that's going on, I need something more than just the *Daily*. Now I'll have to get up earlier to read it. Mostly I want news on Vietnam that's up to date. Every once in a while, Dr. Orr talks about it in class, and I'm not current. I hate that. I'm ready," he said pulling on his hooded sweatshirt. "Is it cold out?"

"Not really. We'll have a nice walk." Outside, they headed east on Pennsylvania and crossed Broadway. "That was a pretty heavy conversation last night, wasn't it."

"Which one? Sally's or ours?" responded Paul.

"I guess I was referring to Sally's, but they both were. I'm sorry I got angry with you." She took his arm and bumped her head against his shoulder.

"It was my fault, so don't apologize. I stayed up after you called thinking about what you said. You're very perceptive, you know." He paused and changed subjects. "I'm not playing basketball today, so can we have a long lunch? We don't have to go to the UMC, since we'll have a couple of hours before we need to go play with the kids."

"Yeah, I'll meet you in front of Guggenheim. Have you noticed the extra pounds I've put on since we've been having lunch together? I'm getting fat!"

"No, you're not!" They arrived at the north entrance to Hellems. "I've got to go. See you at noon." They kissed and Paul hustled off to class. Sarah's French class wasn't until 10:00, so she walked back to 1203 to work on her trig problems. She had stayed awake the night before too, probably having some of the same thoughts as Paul had.

LBJ flew to Guam to meet with his generals, at the same time the air war over Hanoi was intensified. US casualties mounted as the number of American deaths in Vietnam approached 8,000. The debate was becoming more bitter in Washington and on college campuses, even though Paul felt CU was dragging its feet.

"Is it going to take the overhaul of the draft system to get us interested? I swear, unless we all lose our undergraduate exemptions over the weekend, CU students will continue to be ignorant about all the crap going on over there!" Paul was reading his new newspaper but commenting out loud to Sarah.

"I'm just going to have this leftover pizza. How old is it?" She smelled it, decided it was okay, and took a bite. "Do you want this lunch meat?"

"Stop the bombing and just see if Ho will come to the peace table!" He was now talking directly to the President, who just as obviously was not listening.

Sarah decided to answer her own question. "Lunchmeat? Sure,

Sarah, I'd love some. And a glass of milk too, please, if it's not too much trouble." She was teasing him. "By the way, my dear, I have a Greek meeting tonight at seven, and I don't know how long it will last." She wondered if he had heard her.

Paul looked up from his paper. "Your Greek meetings are on Saturday mornings, I thought. Why the change?"

She was pleased her schedule was more important to him than the President's. "Elections for Pan-Hellenic officers." She brought a ham and cheese sandwich over to the table for him, then went back for the milk and potato chips.

"Wasn't this a full bag yesterday?" asked Paul looking into the sack. "Maybe you do need to watch your weight." He patted her tummy.

"In January I wanted to become an officer on the Pan-Hellenic Council in the worst way, but now I don't care. I'd rather be with you and Mose and Sally. Your problems seem real, and . . . God, I don't believe I'm going to say this, it's okay for me to be Jewish around you guys.

"It's not okay in your sorority?"

"In mine, yes, but among the whole system, it's just not mentioned. Remember what I said about prayers ending in 'Jesus Christ.' Well, all the Greek meetings invoke his help. 'In this we ask in the name of Our Lord Jesus Christ. Amen.'" She put a handful of chips on her plate.

"Mose is going to have to change your nickname to Pudge." Paul gave her a mock smile.

"What name has he given me now?"

"Spike. Sometimes Butch." He rubbed his hand in Butch's hair. "He's so clever."

"Hello."

"Hi. We're done here. I'll come over for about a half hour. Do you want anything to eat?"

"No, we bought pizza. There's some left, so, I just need to see you. Did you win?"

"No. I didn't put my name in the hat."

"On purpose?"

"Yep. I'll be there in a few minutes."

Wednesday, March 15

The usual crowd of students at the UMC seemed to be jazzed over the imminent arrival of warmer weather and spring break. Paul and Sarah were a part of this. "We'll have to be a bit devious on Friday to get me out of the house without Mrs. Meyer suspecting anything. Also, I'm going to bring my skis over tonight and store them in the garage for next weekend."

"Am I still picking you up at three to go to the 'airport'?" asked Paul.

"Yeah. I'm going to be dressed up like I'm getting on the plane. I'll change back over at your place. What're we doing about dinner?"

"Oh, I forgot. Sally's cooking us all dinner, a little send off. Even Dan is staying until it's done. She wants us to eat around 5:00 so he can get away. She's not going to go back to Pueblo until Saturday morning. We can catch an early movie if you want."

"Maybe I can help her cook." She pushed her fries over to Paul.

"We learned a little about Israel and the Suez Canal crisis today in Orr's class. You really ought to be taking that class. Maybe you could just sit in."

"Did you forget, my dear? Number one, I have sociology then, and two, you're supposed to learn it and be my teacher. You guys in history take too many notes anyway."

"Remember our pact for the next two nights. Homework only, so we don't have any over the break. At least this time, you only have to monitor me, instead of the whole floor." Paul smiled as he remembered the grief Sarah received during midterms.

"Don't let Dan call me the 'homework Nazi' again. Not a good term for a Jewish girl, even in jest."

Thursday, March 16

The students began pouring out of the Hellems classroom building around ten-thirty as warnings of a possible bomb were relayed from classroom to classroom. Paul and Sarah instinctively knew where to find each other. "Do you think there's any possibility there could be a bomb?" she asked skeptically.

"I'm not worried about it, but there're some crazies around who might decide it would be a great way to protest the war. The rhetoric is heating up, even here in Boulder. If you're an administrator, I think you'd have to honor the call and evacuate." Paul looked at his watch and smiled, "We don't have class until this afternoon. What do you want to do?" "It's Mrs. Meyer's day off. Let's go pack up the stuff I'll be storing with you. It won't take long, and then we can hang out at the apartment until we have to come back."

Holding hands, they worked their way through the crowd of students around the north side of Hellems and back toward The Hill. Only a few of the students seemed to be in a hurry to get anywhere else. Paul and Sarah dropped their books off at his apartment and then climbed into his truck to drive to the Sig Delt house. The red and white pickup was a familiar sight in front of the house, but Paul seldom entered it. If they arrived with any time remaining before the curfew light flickered, they sat in the truck and talked and touched. Anne Rostow had once observed, "You guys don't give away any time, do you," and it was true.

After packing her ski clothes, Sarah and Paul climbed into the pickup and headed for the apartment, but instead of stopping, Paul continued west on Pennsylvania. "Let me show you something." Paul turned back to Broadway and drove south past Baseline, then onto a narrow street with small houses, where he pulled over to the curb in front of a white frame house with yellow trim.

"What's this?" asked Sarah.

"It's Ricky's house . . . was Ricky's house. Remember the day I sat with him after he'd been beaten? After I took you home that night, Mose and I came over here and guarded the house. Kind of macho stupid as I look back, but it's something I needed to do. Mose and I talked and kept each other awake. We never went to bed that night." Sarah waited. "I was kind of looking for Ricky this afternoon, hoping he'd stop in." He smiled. "We can go now."

They rode in silence for a few minutes before Sarah spoke. "What would you have done if the guy would have shown up at the house?" she asked.

"I would have tried to beat the shit out of him."

"Why'd you take Mose along?"

"Company," he smiled. "Not really. I think he would have kept me from doing something dumb."

Sarah smiled. "Tough guy, huh? You had me fooled."

Friday, March 17

Dr. Orr planned to leave his Cold War class with an intriguing question to ponder over the break, even though he knew only a handful of his students would grapple with it. Paul would be among this group. "Since the United States and the Soviet Union were on the same side in denouncing the aggression of Britain, France and Israel against Egypt over the Suez Canal, and since America had chosen to take no action against the Soviets for its aggression against Hungary, why didn't the Cold War come to an end in 1956?"

"If we say that it did, can we stop coming to this class after spring break?" asked one clever coed.

"No, Miss Colgate, because that would be an inaccurate conclusion. We'll start up with this after the break. Give it some thought and write your thoughts out next Sunday night so we can discuss it. Have a nice break." With that, Paul's Spring break began, since he had no plans of going to his afternoon Art History class. He said goodbye to Professor Orr and hurried off to meet Sarah.

Sarah was stunning in her traveling outfit, a tan lightweight turtleneck sweater over a brown miniskirt. Paul was carrying out his role too, by wearing a sweater rather than a sweatshirt. The 70-degree weather would make the drive to Denver quick and easy for those CU students who were flying to exotic locations or home to family for the break.

"You look lovely," complimented Mrs. Meyer as Sarah descended the stairs with her suitcase. "You drive carefully, Mr. Garrity. I want all my girls to arrive safely at their destinations this week."

"I will, ma'am. What will you do this week?"

"I'll be spending time with my family in Fort Collins. I get to be a full-time grandmother. I'm looking forward to it. Thank you for asking." She gave Sarah a polite hug and a kiss on the cheek as she left. "Tell your parents I said hello when you see them tomorrow."

In the truck Sarah cocked her head and looked back to the doorway where Mrs. Meyer still stood. "She knows."

"There's a special Shabbat at the Hillel House tonight." Sarah washed while Paul dried the dishes and put them away where they belonged, as if it mattered much to him. "It commemorates the Warsaw Ghetto uprising, sort of. Did you ever hear of that?"

"Yeah, Orr gave me a novel to read a while back, *Mila 18,* and it's all about the Jewish resistance there. Great book." Paul turned to see Sarah staring right at him. "What?"

"When have you found time to do all that reading?" "After you're back at the sorority house. Sars, I'm sorry, but I've kind of been keeping a secret from you. I'm trying to learn more about Judaism and Israel's history. Orr's been helping me. You know, suggesting some books. When I first met you, I knew next to nothing about Jews, and I want to understand all about you. You've told me I need to be your teacher about Israel, and I know you were mostly kidding, but I figured I couldn't understand Israel without knowing about Judaism and about the Holocaust." He waited for her reaction. She shook the suds off her hands and reached for the dish towel he was holding. She never took her eyes off him, and he could not read her feelings.

"This isn't a part of your class, is it?" Sarah asked.

"No."

She put the towel on the counter, took his hand, and led him to the couch. "Why the secrecy?"

"I guess I didn't want to tell you I was going to learn all about your faith, and then not have the time to do it and fall short. I didn't want to disappoint you."

"Oh, Paul, you couldn't . . . you've been . . ." she searched for the words. "I've spent a part of every day with you since January, and I have never been disappointed in you."

Paul felt a little more relaxed. "I was going to tell you after the break when you got back from New York. I'm going to do some more reading this week while you're gone. It's how I'll feel you."

"Do I disappoint you I'm not very Jewish?"

"But you are. I see it in you every day. Well, almost every day, especially since I'm becoming more aware of your faith. You're more Jewish than I am Christian, and I think I'm a Christian. Sort of, anyway."

Sarah pondered his words. Eventually, she smiled and continued. "Anyway, tonight's service at the synagogue is a pre-Purim commemoration. Purim is not one of our high holidays, but I've always liked it even though I don't know if I've ever understood it fully. Some Jews give gifts on Purim, and I have one for you. I was going to give it to you tomorrow, just as I was getting on the plane. You know, for that dramatic effect. Wait here." She got up and went to her purse and pulled out a gift-wrapped box. When she returned, she straddled his lap and handed him the present. "Open it."

It was a baseball-sized glass orb with strains of yellow colors running through it. Paul turned it in his hands, then held it up to the light. "It's beautiful. Does it have meaning beyond its beauty?"

"It's supposed to be a symbol of our world, yours and mine, because it's been so intertwined. I looked all over for something special, something other than a shirt or sweater, and when I saw this in the jewelry store at Crossroads, I knew it was what I wanted for you. Do you really like it?" Sarah held her breath.

"How could I not like it!" It was a statement and not a question.

Paul pulled her into his body where he held her for several minutes. "It's going to be really hard putting you on that plane tomorrow, you know."

"Oh God, you don't know how hard!" She pulled away to where she could see him again. "I have another gift for you, but I know you'll like this one." She got up again and retrieved a manila envelope. She returned and assumed the same position. "Here."

Paul undid the clasp and removed a photograph, a six-by-eight black and white studio shot of Sarah.

"He got my good side." She was truly proud of this portrait.

"Haven't I told you since the beginning? You . . . are . . . beautiful!" Even though he said it quietly, he said it with tremendous emotion. They hugged again."

"Paul?"

"Yeah?"

"Do I . . . do I have meaning beyond my beauty?"

"Yeah, Sars, you do." He drew his arms around her even more tightly and wondered to himself why he had been chosen.

Saturday, March 18

Just after eight the next morning, Paul knocked on Sally's door. "Hey, Sal, sorry to get you out of bed, but I need a favor. Will you drop Mose off at my parents' house when you leave?"

"Yeah, I can do that. When are you taking Sarah to the airport?"

"We're going to leave here pretty soon. Hey, thanks again for the dinner. It was so good. Stay and talk to my parents for a little while. You know they would love to have you stay for lunch."

"Will you be there by noon?" asked Sally.

"I should be. Sarah's plane is scheduled for about eleven. If she refuses to get on, I'll bring her with me."

"Don't joke. She told me last week she might do exactly that. If she misses the plane, she'll get into a bundle of trouble, so make sure you put her on it."

"I will. Promise. See you at Dick and Diane's."

Sarah and Paul held onto each other until the final boarding announcement was made. "United Air Lines, Flight 517, non-stop to New York is in the final boarding stage. All passengers should be on board."

"Call me at my parents' when you get home."

"I will. I love you."

"I have something for you too. You can open it on the plane. Come on, you've gotta go." He put his forehead on hers, their favorite pose. "I love you too, you know."

Sarah was the last passenger to board the plane.

Sars,

I sat down and counted our time together. What a wild time it's been! Now we're going to be apart for six days, well, almost six days. I guess I can let your parents have you for a week. (Do I have a choice?) Anyway, here's my poor attempt to try to tell you how I feel about you and what these days have meant to me. As you will see, I'm no poet. Maybe I should have built you something out of wood.

Limited in my experience and imagination,
I have been overwhelmed by her attention,
By her love.
My breath has been taken away,
By a woman so remarkable and interesting
Yet so modest and giving
Who chose me as her partner,
And as her lover.
My time with this wonderful woman
Has been the best period in my life.
She is all that I think about and

All that I feel.
I love you.
Maybe you shouldn't consider this a poem, simply a note from a 20-year-old love-struck college boy.
Paul
PS. I warned you about this. It's not very good poetry. See you on Friday.

PART II

SPRING BREAK

Saturday, March 18

In Washington Secretary McNamara pushed the second button on his speaker phone. In a nearby office the Assistant Secretary John McNaughton picked up his phone.

"John, the General has asked for 200,000 more troops."

"Mr. Secretary, if you oppose this, the reaction will become intense, especially from the Joint Chiefs."

"I'm aware of that, John. Come over. We need to get a response to this."

In Colorado at the Garrity house, Mose, Paul, and Paul's dad were out on the driveway shooting hoops when the phone rang. Paul's mother called him in.

"Sarah!"

"Hey, Paul, I snuck off the plane after you left, and I'm at the airport. Come and get me." There was a moment of silence on the Lakewood end.

"What?"

"Just kidding. I'm at home. Everything went well, except I miss you already."

"I am gullible, aren't I?"

"Yes." She giggled on the other end.

When she arrived at JFK, Sarah was met not only by her parents but by her uncle, Sarah's mother's younger brother, and his family, the Mandels, who lived on a kibbutz in Israel. It had been nearly fourteen years since she had last seen them. Now the Mandels had four children instead of two: Hannah was eighteen and had similar features to Sarah, John was fifteen, and there were Robert and Judith, thirteen and eleven. During their stay, Hannah was sharing Sarah's bedroom, which was convenient, but also part of Susan Phillips' plan to have her daughter exposed to the personal side of Israel.

"We're going out to dinner later to my parents' favorite restaurant over in Brooklyn, in the neighborhood where we used to live. We know the owners, and Uncle Abraham wants to see them again and the old house. Roots, I guess."

"You'll feel that way about 1203 in twenty years," said Paul, "when we go back to CU reunions."

Sarah smiled in New York. "I'd like that." There was a short pause. "Will you be staying in Lakewood tonight?"

"Yeah. Mose and I thought we'd spend the weekend here and head back to Boulder on Monday, so call here tomorrow, okay?"

"Paul . . ."

"Yeah?"

"I'm going to be okay this week."

"I know."

"I'll talk to you later. Warn your parents."

Sunday, March 19

Paul went to church with his parents on Sunday morning, the early service. For the remainder of the day, he read: newspapers, Cold War notes, his textbooks. Mose kidded him about getting away from school, but Paul ignored him. He dabbled with poetry for Sarah but got nowhere. Mostly, he waited for her call, which came just after dinner.

Sarah described a stay-at-home day where she got to know her extended family and began to learn about life on a kibbutz in northern Israel, near the Lebanon-Syrian border. There were pictures of the kibbutz, of Tel Aviv, and of Jerusalem, at least the parts where Jews were allowed to visit. Susan Phillips brought out pictures of when she and her younger brother were children at the old house in Brooklyn.

"They asked me questions about you. I guess my mother had told them, but Uncle Abraham and Aunt Marilyn weren't critical at all. In fact, they teased my mother about being so smothering.

"How'd she take it?"

"Well, I felt more at ease around her than I have in a long time."

"That's a good thing."

"A very good thing. When we ate dinner, my mother said a prayer, and she even included you in our thoughts. I think my uncle's having an effect on her."

"Maybe I will be welcome in the Phillips' house someday."

"It won't matter!"

"Family always matters."

"Yeah . . . and that's why it's so important that I'm free to choose my own."

Paul hung up the kitchen wall phone, but he didn't rejoin the household immediately. *Family always matters.* His thoughts turned to the mothers—Sarah's, Mose's, his, Dan's grandmother. Paul smiled thinking of Grandma Savage, a whirlwind of activity despite her age, all the while asking questions about the times, gentle curiosity packaged in a tiny body. Wise. Mose's mom: a single mother working service jobs her entire life to raise a local athletic star. Always in the shadows. Paul wondered if she was always tired. Sarah's smothering, seemingly stereotypical Jewish mother. Again, Paul smiled. Maybe it was her controlling behavior that pushed Sarah out of the East to the foot of the Rockies—to him. Sarah almost enrolled at Rutgers University, close to home with a strong Jewish student body—her mother's choice—but Sarah bolted.

Paul opened the refrigerator and poured himself a glass of juice. A half-dozen photographs graced the fridge door, all of him at various stages of his life. None of his brother. Not allowed. Paul knew how the divide between his father and brother tormented his mother, and now, his own politics were adding to her stress. Caught in the middle again. Paul put his glass in the dishwasher, walked to the living room where his parents and Mose sat, each reading. Paul plopped on the couch next to his mother and kissed her on the cheek without saying anything.

Monday, March 20

When Sarah called on Monday morning, Paul had already left for Boulder, but Mose remained in Lakewood to be pampered for a few more days. Mose realized immediately that Sarah was missing Paul more than she had expected to. "Get it out, Sarah."

"I just miss him so much. I'm trying, but he's just taken over my .. ." Sarah paused, "my whole life. Even here; he's even here, but he's not."

"Do you want to explain that to me?" Mose asked.

"I was hoping you'd explain it to me. Have you ever been this much in love, Mose?"

"No, babe, I haven't, but how about you just enjoy it instead of worryin' about it?"

"I'll call him in Boulder."

Paul was changing from a tee shirt into a flannel work shirt before cleaning up the garage when Sarah's call came.

"Mose just told me that you really missed me. Do you know how that makes me feel?" she asked.

"Like I'm pretty dependent on you, maybe?"

"I miss you, Paul."

"I'm glad you called, Sars. What do you have planned for today?"

"All of us girls are going shopping in a little bit. There seems to be a few things Hannah can't get on the kibbutz, and my mother and I definitely know where to find things in this city. Hannah's great, Paul! She lives on Kibbutz Shamir, and it gets shelled regularly by the Syrians. Her boyfriend is in the army and is stationed on the border with Egypt, so she doesn't get to see him much. Her parents think he's too old for her—he's 23—so they give her some grief, sort of like my mother gives me."

"Does anyone get hurt by the shelling?"

"I guess not. Uncle Abraham says it just kills the chickens sometimes. Hannah doesn't seem to worry about it. She wants me to come visit them next summer. What would you think about that?"

"Could I go with you? To protect you from the shelling?"

"Would you worry about me?"

"Very much."

"Well, don't, because I've decided I'm spending the summer with you in Boulder. Carpenter's assistant."

"You could stay in Dan's room."

"Bullshit."

"Hey, potty mouth, I got a hold of Dan earlier, and he set up the motel for us on Friday and Saturday. Same room."

"Paul . . ."

"Yeah?"

"Are you okay? Tell me the truth."

"Yeah, Sars, I am. I miss you, but it's only a few more days, and you're calling me every day. What about you? The truth."

"I need to go. My mother's calling. I'll call again tonight. I'm going to buy you something. Bye for now."

Tuesday, March 21

Paul spoke with a half-dozen people on the phone on Tuesday. John Cohen called to confirm that Paul was still set to build the booth for the SPU during the World Affairs Conference. Paul told Cohen he would get the materials a week ahead of time when Cohen got him the money. Mose's mother called, and Paul gave her the number in Lakewood. He took two calls from students looking for rooms over the summer. Dan called just to check in and to invite him up for a day of skiing, which Paul declined. He was enjoying the time away from school to catch up on his apartment chores. His mother called just to chat. He fixed two TV dinners early and had settled into the green chair to read when Sarah called.

"It's me. I don't know when your birthday is."

"October 13. What made you think of that?"

"When I bought you a present yesterday, I thought maybe it could be a birthday present. And I thought there's still so much we don't know about each other."

"You shouldn't buy me presents. That's one thing you need to know about me," said Paul.

"What about the two I gave you last week?"

"Those were different. Those are things I'll have for the rest of my life, things you thought about for a long time before you got them."

"How long do I have to think about something before I can get it for you?" asked Sarah.

"You know what I mean."

"Yeah. You mean you're not a good present-buyer, and so I shouldn't buy you any. Just chalk it up to a woman's prerogative. I promise I won't buy you too many, but I'll buy you a few when I see something special, or when I need to for me, or when you just need a new shirt. All you have to do is write me a poem whenever I give you something. Okay?"

"I wrote that poem before you gave me the glass ball and the picture."

Sarah was quiet for a moment, and their words became very soft. "I'm sorry. That's how we've always shown our affection in my family, with gifts."

"You don't have to with me."

"I should know by now. I guess my lack of self-confidence still comes out every now and then."

"Where does that come from? Is there anything I'm doing?"

"Oh, no, nothing has made me feel better about myself than you. Before you . . . I just thought of myself as that . . . that plain looking, nice Jewish girl who needed someone to set me up, like with Cohen." She paused. "You've made me feel pretty. And confident. Confident enough so I didn't have to be a Greek officer."

"Sars, you don't have to tell me this."

"I want to. I want to remove every last little defense I have when I'm around you. I'm almost there, and it feels so good. But just being back here, it shows me sometimes I'm still scared, and that I need to do something to earn your love. I won that service award as a cover-up. I did so many of those things to prove myself."

"That doesn't diminish them, Sars."

"No, it doesn't. I just want you to know me, and part of that is to know who I was. You've taken me so far, Paul."

"Maybe your words would be my words if our roles were reversed. You come to 1203, and Mose tells you about my freshman year, but with humor. I tell you about having a crush on you last year, but not having the confidence to talk to you, and we laugh. You're every bit as good for me as I am for you. I guess we're the perfect match."

"I think we are," said Sarah.

"Remember when you asked me what I was expecting when we first met at the function? What were you expecting after we talked, and you said you'd meet me for lunch the next day?"

Sarah smiled on her end of the conversation. "I guess just a college boyfriend, one who wasn't Jewish, so I could be a little bit of a rebel." She paused and Paul waited. "Kind of corny, huh."

Paul laughed hard. "So, I'm the reward for your rebellion? Talk about the old adage about the right time, right place."

Sarah laughed too. "I've got to get off the phone for evening family time, and my birthday is May 10. I'm older than you."

Wednesday, March 22

After pouring himself a scotch, Assistant Secretary of Defense John McNaughton joined his boss on the leather sofa in McNamara's office. Both men remained quiet while they sipped their drinks and contemplated Westmoreland's most recent request for troops. Finally, McNamara spoke.

"Got another letter from the kid in Colorado again, John."

"Same stuff?"

He handed the letter to his assistant. "Here. These damn college students never let up. They've gotten in the way from the beginning." McNamara waited while McNaughton scanned the two-page letter.

"Ever consider calling him for a talk, Mr. Secretary?" McNaughton asked with a hint of sarcasm.

"Could you imagine what the President and the Chiefs might say if I told them who my special adviser on this was?" He smiled. "No, John, you get the blame."

Sarah's call on Wednesday night was short. Paul could barely understand her words, but he understood the problem.

"Somebody wants to talk to you, Paul. Hang on."

"Hello. Paul?"

"Hi. Who's this?"

"Hannah, Sarah's cousin."

"Are you as drunk as Sarah?"

"Pretty much."

Thursday, March 23

Their final phone call before reuniting on Friday was short, as Sarah's mother had limited her phone time because of her drinking episode.

"Hi. My uncle's family got off okay. They have a stopover in Paris, so they won't get home until tomorrow. I really enjoyed seeing them again."

"You and Hannah hit it off, didn't you?"

"We're going to start exchanging letters. Pen pals. We're both in trouble for last night. My mother's so mad; she hasn't spoken to me all day."

"Will she . . . before you leave tomorrow?"

"I don't know. How was your day?"

"Let's see. Mose and Sally got back. Lawrence Sitler, one of the downstairs renters, was in a freak accident at his home earlier this week and won't be back for the rest of the semester. Do you know which one he is?"

"The short, skinny guy who never changes his clothes?"

"That's him."

"How bad?"

"Not good. His dad said he had a broken collar bone and leg."

"Can I have his room?"

"No, you're in with me. Anyway, I called Jeff Swanson to see if he wanted it, and he might move in. I'll have to clean it though next week."

"Do you want me to help?"

"That's asking too much. Dan called to make sure everything was still on.

"I'm all packed. I get in around ten-thirty."

"I'll be there."

"Come alone."

Friday, March 24

What a difference a week had made. Last on the plane—first off. Tears and reluctance to laughter and anticipation. Gentle touches to bear hugs. Sarah bounded out of first-class seating and jumped into the arms of the first young man she saw. Fortunately, it was Paul.

"I'm so happy to see you!" she said into his ear as she lifted her feet off the ground, and then she giggle-squealed.

At that, Paul's smile turned into a laugh. "Sars, you feel so good!" and they hugged for several moments, her arms around his neck and his arms around her waist, with her mini-skirted legs swinging side to side.

There were stares, but none of disapproval, only those of accep-tance or envy, because it was obvious to the deplaning passengers that these two young people were ecstatic to be reunited. Finally, after all the remaining passengers had proceeded down the concourse, Sarah dropped her feet, pulled her head back, and kissed her boyfriend—not a closed-eyed, mouth-open passionate kiss, but a cheerful, "happy to be back with you" kiss. A kiss, however, promising more later on.

"We can't stay here all day. Sally and Mose want to see you and go to lunch, and Dan is expecting us for dinner this evening."

They chatted as they walked arm in arm to the baggage claim.

The drive to Leadville was quick and easy and beautiful; a clear blue sky over snow covered mountains. They checked into the Aspen Motel just before four.

"Grandma Savage is too nice, a dozen red roses this time."

"Read the card," said Paul.

It was a small florist's card that said simply, "I love you. Paul." Sarah turned to see Paul holding the phone.

"Grandma Savage. Hey, this is Paul. What time is dinner? Okay. We'll be there about six. Yeah. No problems whatsoever. She thought you put them in here. She did. Okay, I will. Bye."

Sarah hadn't moved while he was on the phone. She just stared and waited. He hung up and smiled. She put the card down next to the flowers and walked slowly over to him. "It's been a week," and she began to unbutton her blouse.

Over dinner at Danny's house, they caught up on a week's worth of events. Laughter was the order of the night.

"Are you guys gonna want breakfast before you head up to ski?" asked Danny.

"You make it sound like you're not going," said Paul.

"I'm not. It's Easter and I'm working. All those lilies out there need to be delivered before Sunday. Grandma and Tracey will foil and bow them and write the cards. Robyn and I will deliver."

"I deliver. He just drives." Robyn corrected Danny.

"So, you're on your own tomorrow, guys."

"Hello."

"Sally, it's Paul."

"Hey, what's up?"

"Do you have to work tomorrow?"

"No, I'm off until Tuesday afternoon. Why?"

Saturday, March 25

At eight-forty on Saturday morning, four CU college students entered Savage's Greenhouse through the back entrance. Sally worked the bench, Mose replaced Robyn as Danny's runner, and Paul and Sarah did gofer work, either moving plants or delivering singles to remote addresses. The shelves were barren by nine-thirty, leaving only the church arrangements to be completed.

Mose, Paul, and Sarah watched as Grandma, Danny, Tracey, and Sally tied a variety of flowers and greens together into beautiful sprays and bouquets that would adorn the altars of Leadville's seven Christian churches on Easter Sunday. These were finished and delivered by six, just in time for dinner, ala Sarah Phillips.

"You guys have been too much," said Danny with sincerity.

"Goodness gracious! We couldn't have done it without your help," added Grandma Savage. "Well, I'm exhausted. I'm going to bed, so I'll be ready for church tomorrow morning. Anybody want to go with me?" Grandma smiled, not expecting any takers.

"No thanks," said Mose. "I'll just take the top bunk."

"Mose!" Sally backhanded him across the chest, but they all laughed.

The gang looked from one to the other then focused on Sarah. She smiled and shook her head, as if in disbelief. "I hope your God likes jeans, because that's all I've got."

"What time?"

"Early. Seven, but the early service is short. Then we'll all go skiing. My grandma's paying," said Dan.

"I'll loan you a dress, Sarah," offered Tracey. "You, too, Sally."

Sally put her hands alongside her hips, a mock display that she would never fit into anything Tracey owned.

"Goodnight, Mrs. Savage. I have a date with UCLA and Dayton on the tube." Mose gave her a big hug. Six-feet-five versus four-eleven. Dayton had about the same disadvantage.

"We did a good thing today, my dear. You don't regret missing skiing, do you?"

Sarah repositioned her naked body against Paul's in room 3 of the Aspen Motel.

"Not at all. What amazes me is they would've worked as late as necessary to get everything done for tomorrow."

"I watched Tracey a lot. You know what I noticed?"

"No, what?" answered Paul.

"She watched us. Me, you, Sally, Mose, and Dan. How we interact. The way we talk to each other, the way we touch, the way we tease. It was like she'd never seen such a relationship. You were right about her. She's sharp, she sees things, takes them in. She got up from the work bench once and went around the corner just to watch Mose and Robyn wrestle. I couldn't tell from her face whether she was envious of Robyn or guarding her. Except for with Dan, she still lives on the periphery, like she doesn't know where she fits in."

"I know this other girl who's pretty sharp, too. She sees things others don't. Thinks about them, tries to understand. Asks why. Keeps a lot inside." Paul kissed Sarah's cheek.

"Sometimes," Sarah said quietly, "that girl lives on the periphery too." She paused, and Paul waited. "I'm trying to . . . to be less . . . cautious, less tentative." She paused again and then smiled to herself. "A work in progress."

Sunday, March 26

Neither Sarah nor Sally borrowed a dress for the Easter service, but being a part of the "Seven o'clock crowd" diminished their apprehension about their attire. Paul and Danny had assured them that no one, including God, would be insulted for wearing jeans. Early attendees in the Episcopal Church had a reputation for being less formal and less devout. Sally did, however, borrow a tan sweater from Sarah, who was always over-packed. They sat midway along the right side of St. George's Church on West Fourth, not quite close enough for Grandma, but a compromise for the visitors. Mose politely refused the invitation and slept in. Grandpa had not gone to church in over a decade.

The communion service was short and simple, unlike the eleven o'clock service would be. No singing and only a short sermon for Easter. Grandma, Danny, and Paul received communion, and Robyn joined them at the altar for a blessing. The three young ladies sat quietly in the pew, one of them taking in every detail of her Christian adventure.

Sarah noted the beauty of the old church with its elaborate organ and colorful stained-glass windows. She watched the congregation genuflect before taking their seats, and she tried to keep up with the pattern of kneeling, standing, sitting, and kneeling that went on throughout the 45-minute service. The ritual most intriguing to her was the prayers said by the priest that transformed bread and wine into the body and blood of Christ that then were consumed by the parishioners.

Only when the service ended and the priest greeted each person at the church entrance did either Sarah or Sally speak. The priest shook each girl's hand and thanked them for coming.

"It was a last-minute decision," responded Sally, "so I apologize for my casual attire." The priest waved off her statement.

"Thank you, sir. I enjoyed your sermon," replied Sarah to her greeting. "Your gown is beautiful." While the priest only said thank you,

Paul could barely contain a laugh, which he only suppressed until they got into the truck.

Paul, Sarah, Danny, and Tracey skied Cooper Hill for about four hours before they had to leave. Paul and Sarah made every ride up the ski lift together and were often out of sight of their partners for several runs at a time.

They drove back to Boulder in tandem, with Dan in the lead. Unlike the last time when all of them had been tired and Sarah had slept, this time Paul and Sarah were relaxed and refreshed and talked nearly continuously. Where US 6 came out of the tunnels of Clear Creek Canyon on the west side of Golden, the three vehicles split, with only the Ford truck proceeding east to the Garrity house.

"Do you ever feel the need for church these days?" she asked.

"No, there's no unseen force drawing me in. I mean, I was comfortable this morning. The service was the same as my Lakewood church, St. Paul's, but I'm more comfortable sleeping in on Sundays or reading the paper with a cup of coffee."

"There's sure a lot of kneeling in your service."

"You don't?" asked Paul.

"None. We stand and bow occasionally or sit."

"What else about a Christian service surprised you?"

"The wafer and wine that represents the body and blood of Jesus. Seems bizarre to me."

"I'm not in touch with that either. The whole spiritual nature of Christianity has thus far eluded me. Like I think I told you before, I've never had an epiphany, I guess," admitted Paul.

"That's a good way to put it. Epiphany. Neither have I. Do you have to believe to get into Heaven?"

"Yeah. Christians have to accept Christ to enter into Heaven. I'm still a kid, but it seems to me God would want a good person who lived a moral life to live with Him, that He wouldn't turn someone like that away."

"It would seem like it." Sarah grew quiet trying to process it all.

"You know Jews don't believe Jesus is the Messiah, don't you?"

"Yeah." Now it was Paul's turn. Sarah waited. "Sometimes, I don't believe He is either. I don't reject those teachings; it's just mostly I don't know."

"What would it take?"

"To believe?"

"Yeah."

"I don't know. A burning bush? Growing older maybe? I probably don't think about it enough right now, just sort of too busy with other stuff." Paul turned onto 20th Street and into the driveway of his Lakewood home. He honked.

"No dinner, okay. Your mom will want to feed us."

They were back on the road fifteen minutes later with a plate of chocolate chip cookies, a twenty-dollar bill, a new nineteen-inch black and white television, and an unopened package—an Easter present for Sarah.

"Ironic isn't it that I'm the one getting an Easter present. Any guesses before I open it?"

"My mom got it, so it could be totally useless." Paul had flashbacks to bowties, mittens, and a symphonic rendition of Beatle songs. "Open it."

Sarah carefully unwrapped the paper and then the box. It held a pair of navy blue, knee-length stockings that were quite stylish. "These are cool." She admired them for a moment before returning them to the box. "She likes me a lot, you know."

Paul drove directly to the Sig Delt house. Sarah would drive to 1203 later, but she needed to check in and see what news there was from her sisters.

"You need to attend synagogue with me sometime." She smiled in victory. "Help me with my suitcase."

That evening the gang sat around Paul's apartment snacking on fruit slices, popcorn, and pop. Only Dan drank beer. Sarah had returned from dinner at her sorority house. All of them were relaxed and ready for the final assault on the semester. The three boys were slugging each other in their arms to see who would give up first.

"Don't you think at some point, you're all going get tired of each other?" teased Sally. Mose, Dan, and Paul looked at each other in mock bewilderment, as if to say, "impossible."

Settling down, philosophy 101 began anew. Paul said the stretch to the end of the semester would be more difficult than the first part had been. "Maybe not more difficult, but certainly more intense."

"How can my classes get any harder?" asked Mose.

"I wasn't really talking about our classes, but I think even those will get more demanding. What I meant was the things happening in the world now."

"Oh, God, that means I'll need another beer tonight," said Dan.

"What things, Paul?" asked Sally.

"The war. The anti-war movement. Campus politics. The whole pile of shit, I think."

"Israel's situation?" asked Sarah.

"Yeah, that too," answered Paul.

"I think I'll just concentrate on my little part of the world over on campus and ignore everything until it goes away," smiled Sally.

The discussion went on for another hour until Sally did her best imitation of a house mother and sent the boys back to their respective rooms and dismissed herself, so Paul and Sarah could have the last hour before curfew to themselves.

Lying in bed Sarah spoke. "Are we entering the second phase of our relationship now after spring break? You know, after we had to spend a week apart and reflect?"

"What's the second phase? What would it entail?"

"Calmer. More secure. No emotional outbursts." She had a smile on her face.

"I like your displays of emotion. I wish I showed more emotion like you," said Paul.

"I know when things get to you. You don't have to act out to show them, you know."

"Still, by staying in control, sometimes I think I back off, and there're some things that really matter to me."

"Like the war?"

"Yeah."

"Like civil rights or children getting punched?"

"Yeah, of course."

"You showed your feelings on those things."

"Not nearly enough."

"Like me."

"Not nearly enough."

"You're so easy. I so adore you," said Sarah softly. "Does it ever bother you that Dan mocks your stance on Vietnam?

"A little. He's a good friend. His views are like most of the other students here. America is at war, and we need to support our country's efforts."

"Well, it bothers me. He doesn't listen to the sounds around him."

PART III

SECOND NINE WEEKS, SPRING SEMESTER, 1967

Monday, March 27

Two months remained in the semester. Paul knocked lightly on Dr. Orr's slightly ajar door before entering.

"Good morning, Paul. There's coffee. How was your break?"

"Good. Productive. How was yours?" He slid into the student chair opposite Dr. Orr.

"Relaxing. My wife and I spent the week in northern California visiting our parents. Just returned Saturday."

Paul smiled and sipped his coffee. "I imagined you staying here through the break, grading papers, preparing for next week's lectures, or writing. I even came by once to talk."

"Sorry, but I do have another life. What did you want to talk about?"

"Vietnam. We're not winning, are we?" Paul asked tentatively.

"What's winning mean? What would victory look like?'

"I don't know. Keeping South Vietnam free. Defeating the Cong. Bringing our troops home, I guess. It just seems to be getting out of control." Paul paused but wasn't done. "Even if we won, I wonder if it would matter much."

"It's going to get worse, I fear. This idea of strategic-limited war will never sit well with this country, and yet, a long-protracted war may be the best solution in light of the Cold War alternatives."

A long-protracted war. Paul considered that for a moment. "What does it mean for me and my classmates? Can I expect a draft notice along with my diploma in a couple of years? Am I fighting windmills here?"

Dr. Orr swiveled in his chair and reached for a donut. "You worry about your non-college peers, don't you?" He motioned to Paul to take a donut.

Paul nodded his head. "Yeah, I do. There's a basic unfairness to this war. I have certain, I don't know, advantages just by being here that they don't. I'm not really at risk."

Dr. Orr disagreed silently, knowing that time and events were collapsing and that many college students would be swept up in the war. "I don't know what Congress will do with the draft, but I think they're moving towards fewer exemptions, to be sure. I hope you can enjoy your university experience without having it hang over your head on a daily basis though."

"Mostly, I'm fine." Paul flashed a reflective smile.

"How's that girl of yours?"

"Good. She went home to see her parents too."

"Does she worry about the war as much as you do?"

"No, her concern is Israel. She told me we each have two countries right now. Mine are the United States and Vietnam, and hers are the United States and Israel, and in none of them are things as they should be. As much as Vietnam causes me stress, I think Israel presses down on her, but without . . . structure. More omnipresently, I guess. Does that make sense?"

Dr. Orr nodded. What Paul said made sense; the war did not.

The evening's homework bantering quieted, and the gang put in two hours of solid studying before Sally spoke on a more serious matter.

"I went over and signed up for the Clearing House this morning," she said.

"What's Clearing House?" asked Mose.

"Community service through the university," answered Sally. "They're going to let me design a program for pregnant girls."

"Hey, all right! That's terrific!" said Paul.

Mose smiled at Sally and nodded. "I'm proud of you."

"Me too," added Sarah. "It's a needed program, and you're just the right person to do it."

Sally beamed. "All the stuff you guys do kind of inspired me."

Sarah looked down for just a moment and then looked over to Paul, who was leaning against the counter. "I resigned from Pan-Hellenic," she said.

"What? Why?" asked Paul. "You really liked that."

Sarah walked past Sally and kissed her on the cheek on her way over to Paul. She slid her arms around him. "I was a fill-in anyway."

"What do you mean?"

"The Pan-Hellenic council is made up of the presidents of each sorority house, seniors mostly. Ours got sick last fall and needed a sub, so the SDT lapdog volunteered, like always." Sarah's response was half demeaning. "Lauren, our president, never asked to come back, so I kept going, but I was kind of ignored at meetings. I thought I was part of it all, but I wasn't. And now that I have you and you guys, I realized I didn't need it."

Tuesday, March 28

Mose decided not to go out for track despite Lynn Baker's urgings, but he promised to stay in shape by doing some daily workouts, including jogging. When Mose began to enjoy his runs, it surprised his roomies, since running seemed like work. "I've always liked solitude," he explained, and he would use the time after his last class and before dinner to run the neighborhoods west of The Hill. What started out as fifteen minutes every other day quickly turned into 45 minutes daily.

"Not on Friday afternoons though," warned Sally.

Sarah chewed on a pizza crust while she mused to Paul. "Maybe if the Egyptian economy continues to be in ruins, and if they continue to feud with Jordan, then, well, maybe Israel will be safe." Her interpretation of the *Camera's* headlines seemed inaccurate to Paul, but he held his reply for fear of worrying her more about her promised land. To him, it seemed just the opposite. Arab problems might make them lash out at Israel as a scapegoat. It certainly would not be the first time Jews had been used for that purpose. He had met Sarah at the UMC after playing basketball with Mose and Dan before their scheduled sociology lab with the pre-school kids.

"How long does it take for a letter to travel from Israel to Boulder?" he asked.

"About two weeks from the kibbutz, sometimes longer. Lots of times, letters never arrive. They get lost . . . somewhere in the desert." She laughed. "Why do you ask?"

"You mentioned you and Hannah were going to write each other, and I was wondering what her take was on the various events."

"For anything serious, my uncle and father talk on the phone. My father has contacts, both in New York and in Israel, so incidents are relayed to him rather quickly. He stays informed."

"Those are the secret contacts he won't tell you about?" replied Paul.

"Uh-huh."

"Does he ever share information with you?"

"I never was really interested, but I think he would if I asked."

"Why is Jordan angry at Egypt anyway? We haven't covered that in Dr. Orr's class."

"I'm not real sure, but it has something to do with King Hussein believing Nasser is all talk. He criticizes other Arab countries for their inaction against Israel, but then he does nothing. He's the big cheese, you know." It was obvious she did not think too highly of Nasser.

Paul changed the subject. "What time do we need to go over to the Lab School?"

"Probably now. I need to check the sheets for the week, since I didn't do it before the break."

"You're not going to give this up, are you, the overseeing of us big students?"

"No way! This is my career." She was not kidding. "Come on, let's go." She helped him to his feet.

Wednesday, March 29

With all that was going on in Boulder and around the world, the biggest issue at 1203 on Wednesday was the news that the NCAA had adopted a resolution to outlaw the dunk in college basketball, clearly a rule aimed at Lew Alcindor and UCLA.

"You just lost your whole game, Robinson. We can't allow you to use it in our Tuesday-Thursday games. You know, bad habits. You'll have to develop other parts of your game." Dan was having a field day at Mose's expense.

"That's crap! The whites who run the NCAA can't stand to see blacks dunkin' on their boys, so they outlaw it. Racism, pure and simple!" Mose continued to fume.

"You don't really believe that, do you?" asked Paul.

"Yeah, I do!"

"Then," asked Dan, "who do we get to change the rule? If Reverend King does it, it won't be changed for another ten years, but if we get the Black Panthers on it, it'll be changed before next season. Those guys will scare the shit out of the men who changed the rule."

"Actually, it's kind of an interesting hypothetical problem for blacks," said Sarah. "How do blacks get little things changed when decisions are made for them by whites?"

"Always been the problem, Butch," said Mose. "How do the Jews do it?"

"Oh, we Jews have always been good at fitting in here in America. Haven't you observed me here at Boulder these past few months?" She struck a pose.

"So then," asked Mose, "you're partly to blame for this no dunking rule?"

Thursday, March 30

The temperature in Boulder on Thursday reached 77 degrees, and it brought out the bare shoulders and shorts. Many of the students had practiced for the warmer weather a week earlier in Florida, Texas, or Mexico. It also brought out the pamphleteers and protesters to the fountain just outside the north doors of the University Memorial Center. The war was not the only issue, but just one in a cornucopia of topics, as special interest groups positioned themselves for the World Affairs Conference, a week away.

Paul sat with Cohen and a handful of anti-war advocates who were being wooed by the SPU for membership. The reports of increased casualties that splashed the headlines in all the newspapers were making the task easier . . . that and the reports the draft would be altered to make young men more vulnerable. Paul enjoyed Cohen's arguments when he was not posturing.

Lunch with Sarah was shortened to twenty minutes because she was meeting with Mrs. Best at twelve-thirty. She promised to meet Paul at one on the steps of the chemistry building, where, earlier, a discussion about the slow pace of school integration in five deep Southern states was taking place. Sarah came up to Paul a few minutes early and listened to his and Cohen's remarks patiently. She was still thrilled by the precision of Paul's arguments and the calmness of his presentation.

"Are you ready to go?" he asked after he finished. "Are they still talking about school desegregation over there?"

"I think so. Are you done?"

"Yeah." He picked up his notebook and put his left arm around Sarah. "Get me some money soon, so I can get the wood," he yelled to Cohen as he left.

As they walked around the north side of the fountain to a slightly quieter spot, Sarah complimented him. "You sure were persuasive when you made your little speech to the crowd just then."

"I don't think so. It's just not that convincing."

"Can you make it more effective somehow?"

"Haven't been able to so far."

"You will!"

"Thanks," he squeezed her, "but I doubt it. It's like America is racing down the tracks, out of control, and the engineer is more worried about the panicked passengers than the destruction of his train. All the while the passengers scream louder, and the engineer becomes more distracted by them."

"Then you need to quiet the panic so the engineer will listen. You can do it."

"I'm just a passenger myself on the last car, and nobody's listening to me."

At two-fifteen Sarah pulled Paul away, so they could get to the Lab School on time. "You could listen to this stuff all afternoon, couldn't you?"

"I could. It's the issue that turned me to the dark side." Sarah looked puzzled. Paul smiled. "Made me a Democrat ... disappointed my dad."

"You're kidding, aren't you?"

"We don't talk politics much anymore. To him, a Democrat is just one step from a socialist, and two from a commie. It disappoints him. He just handles it well in front of company."

"Wow," she said softly. "He's such a nice person to me." She went inside her head for a moment. "I'm a Democrat; my whole family is; most Jews are since The New Deal. I guess I'll keep that to myself when we're around your father."

"When's Sarah coming over?" asked Sally after dinner at the Colonial. "She was going to help me with some sociology."

"You're not struggling with that class, are you?" asked Paul.

"No, but she knows how to write case studies, and I haven't done much of that. God, I read a couple of hers, and they're so good!"

"She edits some of my essays, and she knows what she's doing. She's even stopped laughing, so I must be getting better."

"So, when's she getting here?"

"I expect her anytime. Hey, how's the Clearing House thing going?"

"I went over to the health clinic this morning and talked to a couple of people, a doctor and a counselor, about procedures. What I learned mostly dealt with confidentiality and laws. It's a big problem, and there isn't a real program to help the girls. They were really excited about talking with me. I hope I'm not in over my head," said Sally.

"Who's in over her head?"

"Hey, Sarah," said Sally. "I didn't hear you come up the stairs."

Paul got up from the kitchen table and met Sarah near the door where she was hanging up her jacket and baseball cap. "Cute," he said, touching the cap. As always, they hugged and kissed.

"Don't you guys ever wear out?" joked Sally.

"Haven't so far, Sal," smiled Sarah.

Mose and Dan came over to study later, Mose about eight and Dan at eight thirty.

"You just reading?" Dan asked Paul, who was trying to make sense of some recent Supreme Court cases for his political science class. "I need the table for these linear equations."

Paul cleared his space and dumped his pile on the floor in front of the couch. "You just want to sit next to the girls."

"Eat mine!" replied Dan. The girls giggled.

After about twenty minutes of studying, broken only by the quiet discussion of writing techniques between Sally and Sarah, Mose farted. Intentionally.

"Shit, Robinson," complained Paul, who bailed out quickly. "What was that for?"

"Look at us. The perfect college kids. Every night we study. We go to all our classes." He paused for effect. "What's wrong with us?" No one spoke, expecting Mose to continue.

Finally, Dan put his pencil in his calculus book and closed it. "I thought that's what we were paying tuition to do, sort of the expectation, isn't it?"

"Jesus, dickheads, we're sophomores! We're too serious. We're missin' somethin.'"

"Speak for yourself, Mose. I'm not missing anything," said Sarah. She got up and went to the refrigerator where she retrieved five cans of beer. "Studying's over." She set three on the table and tossed one to Paul and one to Mose.

Sally took hers and went to the couch where Mose sat. She smiled and waved the smell away. "It sounds like you're complaining, and I don't agree. Seems to me I'm living with some guys who have everything going for them at the moment. Maybe I'm a pessimist, or maybe it's just my life, but I don't expect this to last forever. Sarah's right. Speak for yourself." Sally's voice was confident. Nodding in the direction of Sarah and Paul, "Those two are having the time of their life, and we're all happy for them. Dan's got a goal and a deadline and is working his ass off to achieve it. He doesn't have time to worry about what he might be missing, and I'm so grateful for all I have right now that I could burst. I've never been happier or more proud of myself than I am these days." Her eyes bored in on Mose. "If you're missing something, whose fault is that? Don't project your boredom or inactivity on us. If you're not satisfied, then do something about it." She was done, but she remained fixed, hovering over Mose.

"I didn't mean it quite like that, Sal."

Sally didn't allow him to go further. "Like hell, you didn't. You're a great guy, but every once in a while, you just go off and feel sorry for yourself. This has been coming since your mom called you last week."

Mose's face reacted defensively to Sally's last statement. "You don't know that. You don't know shit!" He rose quickly and pushed past Sally toward the door.

"Mose . . ." said Sarah.

His door slammed behind him.

The remaining four students were stunned. "What the fuck was that all about?" asked Dan.

"I need to go too," said Sally softly as she began to cry.

Paul and Sarah stopped her. "No, you don't, Sally. It'll be okay." They held her as her body began to tremble.

"Sometimes he feels so isolated, so lonely, and I should've just kept quiet and listened. He doesn't know how to tell people." Sally was not able to keep it together. Paul led the girls to the couch and sat them down.

"Come on, Dan." He leaned down. "He'll be okay, Sal. We'll go talk to him." Then he whispered something into Sarah's ear.

They knocked once and entered 2B. Mose had put a jazz collaboration on his stereo and was sitting in the dimly lit room staring at the opposite wall.

Paul walked over to him and handed him his beer, then took a seat on the brown hassock. None of them spoke, but it wasn't an uncomfortable silence. Finally, Mose regained control of his eyes.

"How's Sally? She okay?"

"She was crying when we left, but Sarah'll watch over her."

"D'you tell her?" asked Mose.

"You know I didn't. I haven't even told dickhead here."

Dan waited to be let in on the secret. He was patient, accepting the bond between Paul and Mose without feeling hurt by it.

"How'd she know then?"

"She doesn't. She just read you. I've noticed it too, but I was watching for it."

Mose looked over to Dan. "My mom has cancer. It's not good."

When Dan had walked in, he had taken a seat on the countertop. He looked down only for a moment. "Shit, Mose, I'm sorry." He pushed himself off the counter and left the room. He returned quickly with the two young women. "Tell her what you just told me."

Mose explained the circumstances of his mom's illness and then buried his face into Sally's shoulder as she hugged his head. Dan motioned to Paul and Sarah. "We'll be in Paul's room if you need anything." In the hall Dan said goodnight to Paul and Sarah and went to his apartment.

Paul and Sarah spent the last half hour in the apartment in quiet contemplation of the news. The lights were out with only a candle burning on the back windowsill providing light. She sat in his lap with her head on his shoulder.

"Shouldn't he go back and be with his mother?

"She told him there wasn't anything he could do right now, so he could wait until summer."

"Can he? Will she be alive?"

"I think so, but I advised him to go see her now too."

"Is he going to?"

"He says he doesn't have the money, and his mom won't send any for a trip."

"That's sad." She tilted her head so she could see Paul's face. "You kept his secret all week. You never let on."

"He asked me not to."

"I'm glad you didn't." She turned his face with her right hand and tenderly kissed his lips. "Can I help you pay for his plane ticket?"

"Hello, Sars."

"Hello. Have you talked with Mose or Sally since I left?"

"No. I think she'll spend the night."

"Will they. . .?"

"I have no idea, Sars."

"Sally was right about me having the time of my life."

"Me too. Tell me again why so many Jewish guys missed the opportunity."

"Too busy reading the Torah, I guess."

"Must have made them blind."

They were quiet for a moment, not wanting to hang up the phone. Then Paul asked, "What was the new word you made up today?"

"Landa. It means I love and adore you," said Sarah.

"I like it. A lot. Landa."

Friday, March 31

Paul was using lunch at the UMC Grille to complete his reading for American Lit, since the event of the previous night had kept him from finishing his homework.

"We need to go dancing this afternoon," said Sarah as she put aside the *Daily*.

He rolled his hand over to grasp hers, which she had put on his earlier. "Yeah, it's been a busy week, and I haven't been alone with you enough."

"Alone? At the Tule?"

"You know what I mean." He took the last piece of her pizza, holding it up for her to claim one last time before he ate it.

"How's Mose?"

"Hurting. He was a little embarrassed about last night."

"He doesn't need to be." She waited for a response but only received a stare. "What about Sally?"

"She's fine. She just worries about him. I talked with her this morning before I left for class. She'll be okay. Both of them will."

"I don't understand why those two are reluctant to be a pair."

"Maybe at base level they're not sexually attracted."

Sarah wondered. "Do you know," she paused, "I was sexually attracted to you almost immediately. I mean, I liked you the first night . . . thought you were handsome. And you were really cool at the SPU meeting, but you just seemed . . . hot." She blushed until she realized she had made Paul more uncomfortable.

"I think maybe you were looking for a guy to jump on, and I showed up at the right time."

"Maybe, but it doesn't matter." Her look told Paul everything he needed to know.

The Kandy Store Prophets were the FAC band at Tulagi's. King Louie was in Gunnison at Western State College playing at the Last Chance, but it did not matter to Paul and Sarah. They danced and sweated and nuzzled.

"Are Mose and Sally coming?' she yelled on the dance floor.

"No. If we see them, it'll be later. Mose went to Lakewood to see my parents, and Sally's working late. She might come over, but I think she's pretty tired. She said to come get her if we went to get something to eat." Paul was yelling into Sarah's ear.

"Is Mose going to tell your parents?"

"Yeah. He wanted to go alone, to be by himself for a while. He's coming back tonight if they'll let him. He's going to fly to California on Sunday. Do you want to go to the airport with us?"

"Yes, of course."

Several of Sarah's friends from the SDT house were at Tulagi's too. Anne, Gretchen, the recruit, and seven other sisters shared the usual table. The buzz concerned reports that Arab guerrillas were attacking villages in northern Israel, and it was more serious than the previous Syrian raids. Information was sketchy. Sarah had not heard any of it until after six.

"Hello."

"Father! Is it true? Is Israel under attack?"

"No, Sarah. It was a single raid by Palestinians near the Jordan River. It seems as if they were trying to destroy a water pump, at least that's the information I have now. We'll know more tomorrow, but it's nothing to worry about."

"Are Hannah and Uncle and the family okay?" There was some desperation in her voice.

"Yes, yes. They're several miles from the attack. They're safe."

"Well?" asked Paul when Sarah hung up. Paul had only been able to hear one side of the conversation while he sat on the counter.

"Not so bad. Just a simple attack by the Fedayeen. My uncle's family is okay."

"You okay?"

Sarah took a deep breath, then another. "Now I am. I don't know why I panicked. It just seemed personal all of a sudden. Hannah . . ."

"You're shaking." He pulled her into a hug.

"What's the note say?"

When they had arrived at 1203 to call back to New York, a note had been tacked to Paul's door.

"It's from Sally. Mose's staying down at my parent's tonight. If we go get something to eat, she wants to go, but we'll have to wake her."

The phone ring startled them both, but particularly Sarah.

"Hello."

"Paul. It's me. Did Sally tell ya?"

"Yeah, roomie, I just got her note. How's my mom treating you?"

"Too good. I'll be back before noon. Thanks for the truck. Hope you won't be needin' it."

"Nope. We can use Sarah's if we go somewhere."

"Thanks for everything. Look in on Sally for me."

Sarah took the phone. "Mose! Hey, it's Sarah."

"Hi, Butch."

"Hey, I love you, you know."

The silence made Sarah realize Mose probably did not hear that phrase very often. Finally, "Thanks. See ya tomorrow."

Sarah handed the phone back to Paul who said goodbye and hung up. "You've got a wonderful family, my dear." She smiled before putting her head into his shoulder.

Paul held her for a moment. "I've got two wonderful families."

Sarah reflected. "Two?"

"In a sense," said Paul.

"I like that. Let's go get your sister Sally and eat. I'm starving!"

At Bennett's they shared a pizza before returning to 1203.

"I'm going to bed. I didn't get much sleep last night. God, being a bitch is tiresome," said Sally.

Sarah gave Sally a hug, then turned to Paul. "I'll be back in a few minutes. I'm going to tuck Sally in."

From nine until twelve forty-five, Paul and Sarah were finally alone. All of it was spent naked in Paul's bed. Since Mose had the truck, they drove back to the SDT house in her car, and Paul walked home alone.

APRIL

Saturday, April 1

Sarah swung by the apartment before synagogue on Saturday morning only to find Paul still in bed. She resisted the temptation but did tease him. "There's a story about the raid in the paper. The Palestinians are messing with the water supply. It's supposed to be a really nice day, and I'm free. I'll be back for lunch. I brought a change of clothes." She kissed him and left, not allowing him time to argue.

Paul got up, fixed coffee, and sat down with the *Boulder Camera*.

They tired of throwing the football, mostly because Sarah "threw like a girl" and could not catch, but it brought much laughter and some exercise. The walk took them over the stone bridge at Varsity Pond and to the Norlin quad, where they found a sunny spot to eat the snacks Sarah had packed for the picnic.

"Hannah wants to get married when she graduates this summer and before she goes into the army. So does her boyfriend." She said it without looking up from her pbj and chips.

"She's pretty young. Do Israeli kids marry young?"

"No, not really. She said most of her friends don't want to get married at all, just move out and live with their boyfriends, but Hannah can't do that. Her boyfriend is a career soldier, not just a reservist, so living together under those conditions wouldn't work."

"How long's her army training?"

"I'm not sure. A couple of months or so. She's not looking to make a career of it." They were quiet for a moment because both knew where the conversation was heading.

"Did you put mayo on this?' he asked.

"Yeah. What about us?" This time she looked at Paul, but he was slow to return the look. Finally, though, he raised his head and answered her query.

"I've thought about us, as in being married. We've only been together for a few months, but it's been intense. I think there're some issues." He was speaking slowly, measuring his words. "We're pretty young still, but as this continues, and I expect it to, then at some point, you'll have to decide how to respond to my question. Not yet though."

She liked his answer but did not show it in her face. Instead, she proceeded. "What issues?"

"Do you want the big ones or the little ones first?" He smiled.

"Ease me into it." She put a chip into her mouth.

"Well, you're rich and I'm not. I mean, you grew up rich, an only kid, so you had a lot of material things. Might be a while before you get them again."

"You're right, that's a little thing," she said. "What else?"

"Where would we live?"

She cut him off. "Not an issue; it'll work itself out. We'll probably spend time in several places so you can get your advanced degrees, and then we'll settle in when you become a professor. I can teach and help with child centers nearly anywhere."

"Hey, I'm not arguing against you on this. I'm just telling you my concerns. Okay?"

"I'm sorry. Is my emotional unstableness an issue?" She laughed.

"No, it isn't. Big issues. Ready?" She nodded. "It would be an interfaith marriage, and while neither of us is particularly devout at the moment, that's likely to change."

"How so?"

"How do we raise our kids? What about your mother? What's that word you said? 'Goy?' I picked up it wasn't a term of love or endearment."

"I didn't say it. She did!"

"That's my point."

"We have a lot going for us, too, though."

Paul leaned over and kissed her on the lips. "We have that, and it's not infatuation. Sally said it best the other day. She said, 'You two are so good for each other.' We are. Our love is fun, we love being together, and we haven't limited each other in any way."

"You left out the sex." She smiled.

"Oh, we'll have some sex one of these days, and even if it's not too good, we'll work through it."

Sarah dived on him, and when she had him pinned, she said, "You're a toad, you know."

"Now that's a term of endearment."

"What else? Any more big issues?"

"The biggest. Would it be okay if, well, if Mose could still live with us?"

Sarah joined Mose, Sally, and Paul for dinner at The Colonial, her first meal there since buying a dinner pass. It became available when Lawrence Sitler dropped his slot after the accident. Jeff Swanson was going to take Sitler's room at 1203 but did not need the meal pass since he continued to eat at Baker Hall for free.

"When's Jeff moving over?" asked Sally.

"As soon as I get it cleaned up. Lawrence's dad has taken all his stuff. Seemed like a nice guy. Hard to see how he raised a son like Lawrence, who's such a jerk-off."

Sarah laughed. "Jerk-off? What kind of word is that?"

"It's Yiddish for fool. I thought you said you went to Hebrew school back in New York?" said Paul.

"Anybody have any ideas for tonight?" asked Sarah.

"Kevin and his new date are going up to Estes Park tonight and asked if we wanted to go. A place called the Rock Inn, and we decided it could be fun," said Paul.

"You didn't tell me," said Sally.

"A surprise," smiled Mose, "if you can get a date." Sally slapped his arm.

Renee Mattison walked by with two of her senior buddies. "Hi, Moses."

The Rock Inn was a stone building located on the extreme west edge of Estes Park. It was a bar that tended to be filled with college students from Fort Collins and Greeley, many of them cowboys. Happily for the gang, the band was Avanti. The usual game of "Name Kevin's Date" was more difficult since his partner was attractive and personable. They settled on "The Fox," but it was a compliment. Sally and Mose danced with several different partners, and all six had a fun evening. No politics, no personal problems. On the way out, just before midnight, Sarah pointed to a bumper sticker on a car in the parking lot.

WIN OR GET OUT

Sunday, April 2

Sally said goodbye to Mose in Boulder and let Paul and Sarah drive him to Stapleton Airport. He would fly to Los Angeles and then catch a bus to Oxnard where his mom lived, where Mose grew up.

"I'll pay you back for the ticket, you know," said Mose at the concourse gate.

"Okay. Maybe I'll put you to work on the upstairs apartment."

"This summer?"

"Yeah. Give our best to your mom. Call me mid-week. Did you get Dean Elliott to take care of your classes?"

"Yeah, everything's taken care of."

"Did you pack your running shoes?'

"Garrity, you don't wear shoes on the beach!"

"You do in New York," chimed in Sarah. Mose smiled. "Take care, Mose. Hug your mother."

"She's going to be okay, Mose," said Paul. "See you next weekend."

Monday, April 3

"Good morning, Paul. Coffee's hot."

"Morning, Dr. Orr."

"That was an excellent essay you wrote about the missile gap. I was particularly pleased with some of the questions you raised regarding why the Soviet Union chose to act as though the missile gap was a reality even when they knew it was a myth." He handed Paul his graded essay. "You still have some grammatical deficiencies to overcome, but even those are becoming fewer and less serious. I've noted them where they occur."

Paul shook his head as he skimmed through the comments. "How many times did I misspell Khrushchev?"

"If you think an 'h' might be there, include it. If this had been a take home essay, I would have dinged you harder for being sloppy."

"I didn't know the answers to my questions. I guess that's why I like your essays. I can speculate."

"Why do you suppose Khrushchev gambled with the missile gap myth?"

"I would guess he was having trouble with the Russian hardliners who clearly wanted a tougher stand, and maybe because China was pushing for a more aggressive ideological position against capitalism." He paused and smiled again. "At least that's what some of the documents indicated that you had us read last week."

"The articles didn't mention the Chinese pressure. That's good thinking on your part. Any applications elsewhere?" Dr. Orr was good at using his lessons to draw connections to other situations, especially for the immediate concerns of college students.

Paul thought for a moment. "Maybe people respond to what they believe is real rather than what is actually true. Myth versus reality. It's kind of scary to think of all the actions taken because we believe something is true when, in fact, it isn't, both in national policies and in our own lives." He sipped his coffee. "But I guess we have to sometimes."

"Why? Why not just wait until we can marshal more facts?" asked Dr. Orr.

"Wouldn't that just paralyze us? I'm not talking about being reckless, which is how I believe the US is acting in Vietnam, but don't people need to be decisive when they have a certain amount of information?"

"What about here at school? Can you bring this generalization down to a more specific, or personal, event happening in your own environment?"

Paul again was slow to answer. He was not sure his mentor wanted to hear about his and Sarah's behaviors. The History secretary interrupted them before Paul could answer.

"Dr. Orr, the two gentlemen from Connecticut are here."

"Well, Paul, I've got an appointment to discuss this Publish or Perish thing with these two men." He turned to his secretary. "Tell them I'll be right there." Turning back to Paul, he continued. "You're really doing good work in my two classes. You make me work harder in order to challenge you. Keep it up. You'll have graduate students lecturing in your two classes this morning. Try not to intimidate them, okay."

Tuesday, April 4

Dr. King's April 4 speech was his most passionate plea to end the war, by linking civil rights with the anti-war efforts. At about the same time King was challenging the morality of America's actions in Vietnam, three middle-aged women were hard at work in apartment 1C removing the stains and smells of Lawrence Sitler. Paul let the women in around eight before heading off to class. They assured him the place would be spotless by one. He paid them upfront.

After working with the pre-school kids, Sarah went back to the SDT house to sleep, while Paul drove to Lakewood for his mom's birthday dinner. Diane Garrity asked Dick not to make a big deal out of her 45th, but having Paul home was the perfect gift.

"How's Moses?" asked Mrs. Garrity.

"How's his mother?" added Mr. Garrity.

"I haven't heard from him yet, maybe tonight. I'll call you if I hear anything." They ate and chatted and laughed.

"Your brother called." The conversation stopped momentarily. "To wish me a happy birthday. He's still in Los Angeles."

"Anything new?"

Diane Garrity's response was barely audible. "No."

"Well, at least he remembered."

Paul's dad tossed his fork onto his plate and left the table.

The winds blew down the Front Range at near hurricane force that evening. Paul navigated the return trip up Wadsworth to the turnpike, avoiding Highway 93 because of the high wind warnings. He was thankful the predicted snow had not come. His mom liked her presents: the desktop bookshelf, the scarf from Sarah, and the book of poems from Sally/Dan/Mose. Sally had been kind enough to sign the boys' names to the card. She had also sent along a bouquet of pink sweetheart roses, Mrs. Garrity's favorite. Paul smiled. The evening had gone well, except for the brief moment when Ross' name was mentioned. Family secrets, he thought to himself. So much is going on. He closed his tired eyes and shook his head.

Sarah took the call at the end of the hall on the second floor of the SDT house, the same phone she used each night after curfew. "Hello."

"Sarah, this is Dan. Hey, I'm gonna come over and get you. Paul's been in an accident. He's at Memorial Hospital, and we'll go over there." Sally stood next to Dan as he spoke calmly and in control, she thought.

"How bad is he? Tell me the truth!"

"He was in the emergency room, but I talked to the nurse, and she said he'd be okay. We'll go see," Dan said.

"Let me talk to her," whispered Sally.

"Sarah, it's Sally. It's going to be okay."

"Why didn't he call me? He's hurt bad, isn't he?"

"No, no! They tried to call you, but the line was busy, so the nurse called over here." Sally could not tell if her reply had eased Sarah's apprehension. "Get your coat, and we'll be by in five minutes."

"Hurry, Sally! Please hurry!"

In five minutes, Sarah applied lipstick and eye shadow, brushed her hair, put on a warm sweater, and changed into low heels. All the time, she kept thinking Paul wouldn't care how she looked—and prayed he would be able to see her and touch her. "Please God, please God, make him all right." She told Anne and Mrs. Meyer what she knew and promised to call as soon as possible with news, then rushed out the front door to meet Dan and Sally.

An elderly night nurse obviously experienced at dealing with panicked family and friends coming to the emergency room rose from her desk and escorted the three students through the metal double doors into a large emergency room. Individual beds, workstations really, were separated by curtains. A small boy cried in the station nearest the main nursing center. Paul was in the fourth station sitting on the gurney without his shirt while a nurse worked to clean the blood out of his hair. The trio stood politely at the edge of the station at first, until Paul heard them and looked up. He smiled almost sheepishly and then motioned with his index finger for Sarah to come to him. She was crying.

"I'm going to be fine, Sars," he whispered into her ear as they wrapped each other in their arms. The nurse pulled the cloth away and said she would return in a few minutes and then motioned for Dan and Sally to approach the patient.

"Not quite so hard, Sars. I'm a little tender."

"What happened?" asked Dan. Sally put her finger up to the cut on his forehead.

"They think I fell asleep and drove off the turnpike into a fence. Luckily, it was a fence with bushes behind it. My truck's in bad shape though."

"What's the damage to you?"

"Didn't break anything, but I'm going to be sore, and I've got some stitches." He paused and pointed with his finger. "Here in my head and on my shoulder, but they're going to release me tonight, I think."

"Did you get a hold of your parents?"

"Yeah, I told them to stay home, but my dad wouldn't have any of that, so I think they're on their way up. They liked your presents."

Paul returned his attention completely to Sarah, who had not noticeably relaxed her hold or held her tears. "Hey, look at me." She ignored his command, so he ducked his head down towards hers. "The doctor thinks I may have a concussion, so someone needs to watch me all night. Will you do that for me?"

The nurse returned to complete the cleanup. "I think you'll have to work around this obstacle," said Paul. The nurse smiled, indicating that she could.

Dan finally found the secret to remove Sarah from Paul's body. He recommended she call her house to let them know where she was and when they might expect her home. She used the phone at the front desk to speak directly with Mrs. Meyer, who told her to stay with Paul all night if she needed to. Mrs. Meyer liked Paul from the beginning and while she enforced the sorority rules strictly and watched over her girls closely, she sensed Sarah had fallen in love with him long before the sisters did.

When Sarah and Sally returned to Paul's station, they found him being re-examined by the doctor, who was especially concerned about a possible concussion. As he looked into Paul's eyes, he spoke quietly about procedures that Paul was to follow over the next few days. Satisfied with Paul's condition, he took Dan into the central area to repeat his instructions. Sarah and Sally helped Paul get dressed as the nurse put the final dressings in place.

Paul's parents were sitting in the waiting room when the four came through the double doors.

"Why didn't you come in?" asked Paul.

Dick Garrity pointed to the sign over the doors. NO VISITORS BEYOND THESE DOORS. MEDICAL PERSONNEL ONLY. "Am I the only one who follows the rules these days?"

Dan stepped forward and put his arms around the parents' shoulders, a la Moses Robinson. "You see, Sally and I had to go with Sarah because no sign was going to keep her out." He was definitely in charge. "Your boy is fine, some cuts and bruises, but no broken bones and nothing permanent. Let's go home." It was twelve-thirty.

Paul dozed off on the couch with his head resting on a pillow. The doctor told Dan he did not believe Paul had a severe head injury, possibly a minor concussion, but probably not even that. Around two in the morning, Dick and Diane drove home, and Dan and Sally returned to their respective rooms. They all knew their son/friend was in good hands.

Sarah whispered to her boyfriend as he slept. "You scared me, my dear. You scared me like I've never been scared before. Don't ever do that again. I don't know what I would do without you now. I couldn't go back to who I was because I'm not that person anymore. You're beautiful, you know, even with the big bump on your head and the bruise on your chin. If you could hear me right now, I would use the word handsome, but you can't, so I can describe you like I want. So, you're beautiful. I love you so much. I should've gone with you today. You wouldn't have fallen asleep with me there. I'm sorry I let you get hurt."

Sarah had not said many words all night. Now she was letting her feelings out. As she spoke softly to her first real love, tears dripped off her cheeks. She stroked the contours of Paul's face, while those tears fell onto the bandage on his forehead.

"I've never had anyone before. You're the first, and I'm so blessed. Did I say 'blessed?' Okay, then fortunate. I imagined you before I ever met you, but you're better than I imagined. So much better. What was it like when your truck hit the fence? Did it hurt? Did you worry about dying? Did you think of me? I'm sorry the house line was busy. I was going to meet you over here anyway, but I got behind, and I started talking with Gretchen. She wants me to get more involved with the house again. I'm sorry. Dr. Orr will wonder where you are tomorrow morning. No, you can't go to his classes, not even the Cold War class that's your favorite. I'll go see him, and tell him, and get your assignments. You'll need to rest. Rest. If you need me, I'll be right here. Just moan. Get it, just moan. How come you're not laughing, my dear? That was funny." Sarah paused to wipe the tears from her cheeks.

"Goodnight, my love. My Paul. My beautiful Paul. Thank you for being there for me. 'Sars.' I love that name."

The bedroom light cast a soft hue over the two bodies, the sleeping young man on the couch and his lover, who sat on the floor with her head on the cushion next to her man's shoulder. Her right hand lay gently over his chest collecting his heartbeats.

Two hours earlier Dan had called Mose. He stood in the hall outside of Paul's apartment so as not to disturb him. Dan wondered which should come first, questions about Mrs. Robinson's health or a report on Paul. He decided on the former. Mose told him his mother was doing well, that her spirits were excellent, and she would begin treatment immediately. He seemed more optimistic than he had just three days earlier.

"Oh, by the way," said Dan casually, "the answers to your questions about Paul are the same. He's doing well and his spirits are excellent."

"What the hell you talkin' about, Savage?"

"Our boy wrecked his truck tonight." Dan and Mose talked for another ten minutes about the details of both events. Dan laughed on his end of the phone twice.

"Someone will pick you up on Sunday. Call if anything changes." Mose said something on his end, and Dan responded. "No, he's asleep on his couch, and Sarah won't move an inch away from him."

Dan was wrong. Later that night Sarah called her parents. It was nearly six in New York. "Thank you, Daddy. It means a lot to me."

Wednesday, April 5

Sarah contacted all of Paul's professors and three of her own by mid-morning. As expected, Dr. Orr was the most concerned and the most helpful.

"Paul's coat is a little large on you though." He gave her a hug before she left. "I'll call him later in the week. Tell him I'll see him Monday."

As she walked back to 1203, she wondered what the two men talked about each Monday morning. Whatever it was, she knew Paul held Dr. Orr in the highest esteem, and despite the fact she received the highest grades throughout her schooling, she had never developed a relationship of that significance with a teacher.

She returned to the apartment only briefly. Paul was sleeping again, and his mother had driven up earlier and was washing dishes. Sarah spoke to Dan about the pickup, and he said he would take care of it. He had already made arrangements to have it towed to a repair shop on North Broadway. Dan offered to drive her back to the Sig Delt house, but with the weather approaching 70 degrees, she declined in order to walk and calm down. As she walked past the park a block from the house, she realized how skuzzy she must look. It had been nearly twenty hours since she had taken a brush of any kind to anything on her body. *Thank God for baseball caps*, she thought.

Many of her sisters were coming down to eat lunch when she arrived at the house, and immediately they wanted information about Paul. "I should have called Anne earlier to let her know some of the details," she said as the girls crowded around her. "He's going to be fine. He has big cuts on his forehead and his shoulder, a dark bruise under his chin where it hit the steering wheel, and another on his shoulder. He also has a concussion, but probably not a bad one, and he's sore all over." She was too tired to cry. "I'm sorry I didn't call last night, but all my attention was with Paul." "So nothing's changed then," yelled one of her sisters, which brought a laugh.

"Hush, Sylvia," said Mrs. Meyer.

"As you can see, I didn't get much sleep last night," said Sarah.

"So," said Anne, "nothing's changed then." The house laughed again, more in relief after a night of uncertainty for one of their own. Many of the girls moved to hug Sarah and say a few words of encouragement.

"Okay, let's move on. Go to lunch and leave Sarah alone for a while." Mrs. Meyer waved her hands and approached Sarah.

"Thank you, Mom. I'm going to take a shower and a nap."

Anne hugged her roommate from behind. "I'll take care of her, Mrs. Meyer. It'll be good for some of us to look after her for once. She's taken care of us this past year." Now Sarah turned around and let Anne hold her. The tears returned.

Sarah and Paul watched television all evening, periodically dozing off, and alternately massaging each other.

"I'm staying over again tonight," but before she said another word, he began to smile that male smile. "No, we aren't going to do that. Rest! Remember? Anyway, Mrs. Meyer and I talked, and I convinced her you needed me for one more night."

"How long did you sleep last night?"

"Long enough. I took a long nap this afternoon. I guess Anne guarded the hall to keep all the girls quiet."

"I'm lucky."

"Only in the sense it could have been much worse. Dan said the truck is a mess, windows broken out, front end dented up, but at least it didn't roll over. The bushes held you up."

"No, I mean I'm lucky to have you and Dan and Sally and my parents, but especially you." With some effort he shifted his body on the couch. "It's funny. I don't think I was ever unconscious, and all I thought about was getting the blood stopped so you wouldn't see me like that. I remember asking the guy who first looked in on me if he had a towel, so I could wipe my face. I wasn't worried that I was hurt. I just didn't want you to see all the blood."

"Didn't it hurt right away?"

I don't think so, at least I didn't notice it, until they laid me down in the ambulance and drove off."

"You made the paper. It said you were given a ticket for careless driving, and the truck sustained $900 worth of damage."

"He should've ticketed me for an illegal right turn."

"John Cohen called. He seemed legitimately concerned. I told him you'd call back tomorrow or Friday."

"Oh, I have to build the booth this weekend."

"We'll see."

"Bedtime, my dear. I'll just sit here until you fall asleep. Don't be getting any desires during the night either." Sarah sat down on the bed and watched Paul fall asleep. She kissed him softly on the lips, "*You don't need to get any desires; I have enough for both of us.*"

Thursday, April 6

Paul was moving more easily than he expected he would. Less pain. Only when he raised his arms over his head did he wince, but basic movements returned to near normal.

"Any headaches?"

"No."

"Soreness?"

"My shoulders still."

"Ribs?"

"No."

"Watch my finger." The doctor moved it from right to left, then up and down. He seemed satisfied. "Any questions?"

"Do I still need the night nurse?"

The doctor smiled. "Milk it for as long as you can."

"I think her house mother's already suspicious."

"You can put your shirt on. I'd say you can do whatever your body allows. We'll re-dress your cuts, and I want you to change the bandages on Sunday. Come back next Thursday, and I'll remove those stitches."

"Thanks, Doc."

"One more thing. I heard your anti-war remarks at the fountain last week. I hadn't considered what the effects of chemical warfare and carpet bombing might have on our moral position." He took the stethoscope from around his neck and laid it on the counter. "Take care of yourself. The movement needs you."

Paul worked light duty at the Lab School, but he knew the reward would be substantial. He was free to watch Sarah work her magic with the kids. Mose was right. Maybe she was not the prettiest girl on campus, but she became more beautiful in her element, one of which was the Lab School.

"What a great day this has been!"

"You were going to tell me about Hannah's letter," said Paul. "You were pretty excited."

Sarah rolled onto her side to look directly into Paul's eyes. "Her letter was funny but pointed. She called herself a Sabra, which means a native-born Israeli and comes from the Hebrew word for cactus, so she can be direct, almost rude in her interactions with others."

"Was she that way in New York?"

"Not to me, but, yeah, a little. Anyway, she's looking forward to her military service. She boasted she was going to kick some Arab ass. Because of where she lives, she said mostly she wanted to fight with the Syrians. I guess her farm was hit by a few artillery shells while they were gone. Missed their tractor, though."

"That's kind of scary, isn't it?"

"To me it is, but Hannah just takes it in stride. She seems so brave, so confident, so alive. I really admire her courage. I'll let you read it sometime."

"You talked to your parents too?"

"My father. Susan's still a little angry with her only daughter. Anyway, he asked about you and sends his best wishes. We've been talking. I'm trying to make him see how I feel, and that it's okay. He's been great about it. I think my parents will accept you over time."

"I hope so. I'm trying to treat their daughter well."

"I know you think family matters, and it does, but in the end, I'm going to do what I want to. I'm going to be the one who decides what's best for me. It may not be the wisest course, but it will be my course."

"Pretty brave, Sars."

"I couldn't have said that two months ago."

"There are a lot of things you couldn't have said two months ago."

Sarah yelled into the hall. "Sally, Mose is on the phone!" She returned to Mose. "He's back to normal, said he would be ready to play basketball with you next week, although the doctor may have something to say about that with the stitches and all. I think he's still planning on building the booth for the SPU on Sunday. When he's not busy, he gets antsy. Here's Sally."

"Hey, babe, how's your mom?"

Sarah signaled she was leaving to find Paul and headed downstairs. He was not in the den, so she went across the street to The Colonial. She found him in the dining room sitting with Katie Drumheller and her boyfriend. Katie was a Sig Delt who had tired of the Greek life and lived at The Colonial. Her boyfriend, Terry Something, belonged to the SPU. Paul gave Terry some cash and a list. Sarah walked over to the table and put her arm around Paul's shoulders.

"Hi, Sars."

"Hi. Hi, Katie. Terry"

Katie joked, "I didn't know you were such an abusive woman. Try not to leave scars next time."

"Mose is on the phone, but Sally will get the info. His mom's feeling better. What're you buying?"

"Terry's going to buy the materials for the SPU booth for me and deliver them to the fountain on Sunday morning. Did Mose say when his plane gets in?"

"Late afternoon. Dan said Tracey and Robyn are coming down, so he would be willing to help on Sunday. If you're still working on the booth, Sally and I can go pick Mose up. You shouldn't be driving anyway. Oh, I forgot, you don't have your truck." They all laughed, even Paul.

Friday, April 7

Sarah bounded up the stairs a few minutes after eight in the morning on Friday. She was a knockout in her navy mini-skirt, navy stockings, teal turtleneck, and sweater vest—an outfit designed first to impress Paul, and then to show the CU student body just who Paul was dating. Her makeup was a bit overdone, again for effect, and the whole package had the desired impact on Paul. She modeled for him as he stood motionless by the sink.

"All this only took an hour and a half," she said coyly. "I checked the weather report last night to make sure it wasn't going to rain today and had Anne and Gretchen do my hair. Mrs. Meyer complimented me on my outfit, but she asked me what the occasion was." Sarah placed her hand on his chest. "Slow your heart down, my dear," she kidded. "And," she paused for emphasis, "I had Gretchen take a roll of pictures for you."

"I was going to go to class this morning, but we might just stay here so that I can look at you."

"No, we're going, but we're going to leave here shortly, so we can take the long way." She finally eased up and gave him a hug, but no kiss. "How's your head?" She checked his bandage.

"No headache. Even my shoulders feel pretty good." They grasped each other's hands. "Sars, you're more than beautiful. What did I do to deserve this?"

"This sounds, I don't know, goofy, but you lived, and what you said about the wreck, that your first thought was about me. Do you remember what you did when we came into the emergency room?"

"I smiled?"

"Yeah, but you didn't look at Sally or Dan. You fixed your eyes on me and kept them there, and then you motioned for me to come to you, like there were only two people in the room. This is your reward for that moment. I only hope I look as good right now for you as you did for me in the hospital." There was a bit of apprehension in her voice.

"Hold very still." He let go with his hands and put them gently on her cheeks. Then he kissed her so softly on her lips so as not to smear her lipstick. She held still, except that she closed her eyes and spread her fingers on each hand. "Go show yourself to Sally, and I'll put on a sweater. Then we'll go."

"Good to see you, Mr. Garrity, but are you sure you should be here this morning?" greeted Dr. Orr.

Paul nodded his head. "Yeah, I'm feeling pretty good—and pretty lucky."

"Sarah must have taken good care of you." It wasn't meant to be suggestive, but Paul took it that way.

"She did."

"Did you get your reading completed?"

"I did, but not the question. Can I turn it in Monday?"

"No problem. What about the Cold War readings?"

"Those too, but I answered those questions. I'll need to get the notes, but other than that, I'm all caught up."

"How many stitches?"

"Eight here," he pointed to his head, "and 21 in my shoulder."

"That bruise on your jaw looks nasty."

"They said I hit it on the steering wheel while my head was moving toward the dash."

"Not wearing a seatbelt, huh."

"No."

"Don't ever let it happen again."

"No, sir, I won't."

"Let's go to work."

Paul waited outside Sarah's ten o'clock French class in Hellems Annex, something he seldom did. She walked him to his Cold War class, knowing she could afford to be late for her sociology lecture more than he could walk in late to Professor Orr's class. Students, quite simply, were not late to any of Orr's classes. Sarah's weather report had been correct, and by lunchtime the temperature in Boulder was approaching 60 degrees. She found Paul sitting on the steps that led to the Mary Rippon Theatre waiting for her, watching her as she walked towards him on the west side of the fountain. He was not the only guy watching her. He stood as she approached and kissed her when she hugged him.

"How did it go?"

"Fine. Just like normal. Orr gave five pages of notes in each class and still found time to challenge our weak interpretations of the readings. Want some lunch?"

"Yeah, I didn't have breakfast. Let's get a paper. My professor said the Colorado Legislature passed the abortion bill."

"Sally will be happy."

That afternoon, as they prepared to go dancing at Tulagi's, they shared the newspaper. Sarah read rapidly through the story on page one. "Air, Ground Battles Raging Near Tel Aviv." She was looking for any mention of Kibbutz Shamir but found none.

"Whose report is accurate?" She turned to page two, trying to get some clarification. "Why can't they just leave them alone to work their fields?" It was more of a plea than a question.

Paul stood next to her with his hand on her neck. "Israel's figures are always much more accurate, but Cronkite's on at five-thirty, and Huntley-Brinkley after that. Maybe they'll tell us more." He tried to be calm and reassuring, but he knew she was not going to accept it. She knew what he was trying to do. He assumed the jets were Israeli and Syrian, since the Palestinians had no air force. Those farmers who tilled the soil and watched the air battles saw them through different eyes.

"We should go to Tulagi's, so I won't think about this."

"No, let's wait for the news, and then you can call your dad. He would've called if your uncle's family was in danger, but it won't hurt to call."

Sarah turned back to the front page and then slapped her right hand down on the paper. "Shit!" She turned and bumped into Paul. She was not looking for a hug but accepted it anyway. "This is going to be a long fifteen minutes. Do you think it will be the lead story?"

"First or second. Let's share a beer, and I'll tell you what Orr had to say about this last week."

Sarah turned on the TV and sat at the table. Paul brought over a beer, changed the station to Channel 7 and sat down with her. "Orr said he believed a war could happen, but Israel would win quickly and easily. He thought the UN wouldn't allow it to get out of control."

"But if Egypt and Syria and Iraq all strike at Israel, what then?"

"That happened in '48. Dr. Orr didn't give specifics; he just said the Israeli Air Force would be too much for the Arabs. He's not usually wrong."

Walter Cronkite led off with the Israeli-Syrian fighting. The action was not around Tel Aviv but centered west and north of the Sea of Galilee. CBS reporters verified Israeli statistics, which were extremely low. Still, there were casualties, including one death in Israel. Vietnam, Adam Clayton Powell, Hubert Humphrey's European tour, and Colorado's abortion legislation were the following stories. On a packed news day, the Arab-Israeli fighting was deemed the most important. The NBC Huntley-Brinkley Report had a similar news line. "Good night, David." Sarah dialed the phone.

"No shelling at Shamir from what I could ascertain. Everyone's safe." Dr. Phillips seemed relieved and confident at the same time. "Is it over?"

"Sarah, it's never over, but we'll hope things calm down for a while."

"Will there be war?"

Dr. Phillips paused before answering. "If it comes, Israel will be ready."

"Thanks. Is mother there?"

"Right here. She wants to say something to you."

"Hello, dear, how is Paul feeling?" asked Sarah's mother. "Much better. He went back to classes today."

"Sarah, your father has been talking with me, and maybe I've been too judgmental. I'll try to be nicer, and maybe I'll understand you better."

"I will too. I'm sorry for my attitude."

"I love you, dear. Give Paul our best."

"I will, Mother." As she hung up the phone, Paul noticed tears in her eyes. "Let's go dancing."

"You okay?" he asked.

"Better now. I did it again, didn't I?"

"Did what?"

"Lost it emotionally."

Saturday, April 8

Norlin Library was quiet and not crowded, perfect for some serious studying, and for over two hours, Sarah and Paul sat quietly at an oak table on the first floor working on American Literature and French. Occasionally, one would reach over to touch the other without the need for recognition. Around three-thirty he asked if she wanted a short break, maybe a fifteen-minute walk outside, since the weather was so nice.

"How's the French coming?"

"*Bon!*" she smiled. "*Si je me suis sauve a Paris cet ete, iriez-vous avec moi?*"

"*Oui*, even though I have no idea what you just asked me."

"You said yes even though you don't know what I'm getting you into?"

"Have I ever said no to you yet?"

"But what if it was trouble?"

"Hard to imagine either you or me getting into serious trouble. We're both pretty safe and conservative in our lifestyles."

"So, if I planned something without your knowing about it, you'd go along just because I asked you to?"

Paul stopped walking and took Sarah's left hand. "Yeah."

She smiled and a 'humph' came from her throat. "I'll have to work on this one, but it'll be fun." She stood on her toes and kissed him. "Let's head back." They were in no real hurry, and their hand holding shifted to body holding. She reached up along the path to one naked tree and felt for buds. "I thought of something else about what was said at synagogue this morning."

"What was that?"

"People were talking about fundraising, about what we could do here in America to help, and I told them about trees." Paul waited, as Sarah looked back in time. "As a kid, I donated money every week to plant trees in Israel, somehow to turn the desert into forests, back to the 'land of milk and honey.' Some of the others had done that, too. Then a woman told about giving $19.48 every month to the UJA, and some others said they had done that. My mother still does. I think for the first time since I came to Boulder, I felt an attachment to the other Jews there. I mean, there's an attachment because we're all Jews, but it was more. I don't know . . . something."

"Sort of like when we sit around at my apartment and drink beer and eat pizza with Mose, Sally, and Dan." Paul smiled.

"You're kidding, but yeah, sort of like that . . . like I finally belonged a little."

Another hour of studying, a light dinner—cold cuts at The Colonial—and Sarah headed to the Sig Delt house to get ready for the function at the Greenbrier with the Phi Sigs.

"Kind of dress up, okay?"

"Tie?"

"Yes, of course. I should have bought you that herringbone jacket."

"What time are you coming back?"

"Eight. Okay?"

"I'll be ready."

Paul went upstairs to get his checkbook, and then hustled off to

Kinsley and Company. The herringbone jacket turned out to be one of his better presents to Sarah. The Phi Sigs were the counterpart of the Sig Delts. The chief topic was the outbreak of hostilities between Syria and Israel. Surprisingly, thought Paul, he knew more about the events leading up to the fighting and about the politics involved than most of the other students did. He stayed quiet, however, during their harangues and allowed them to vent their frustrations to each other.

The finger food was good, the alcohol was plentiful, and the music was provided by Great Lips, one of the more original groups who never gained a strong following under that name. As always for Paul and Sarah, the dancing was the best part.

"Not a lot of people are talking about Vietnam or civil rights tonight."

"That's okay, Sars. Saturday should be a politics free day. We should have at least one a week."

"It's not political talk. Tonight, it's just war talk. It's the beer talking in all those guys."

"What about the Mideast?" asked Paul.

"You don't want Israel to go to war with the Arabs?"

"It's me, Sars, remember, your non-Jew boyfriend. I oppose the war in Vietnam. I admire King's non-violent methods to get rights. Wars in the Cold War just kill people and create bigger problems down the road."

"But the Jews keep getting shelled. They can't live with that, can they?"

"No, they can't, and I don't pretend to know what they should do. I have only two connections to Israel. One is a grade in my Cold War class, and the other is with this girl I love. One is teaching me to think and the other teaches me to feel." Paul took a last drink from his plastic cup, then tossed it into a trash can two steps away.

"Did you ever smoke?" she asked waiving her hand in front of her face.

"No, not really. Mose got some cigars last year after finals to celebrate, but that's the only time. Why?"

"No reason. Just watching all my sisters."

"Did you?"

"Yeah, I tried it in high school and again last year but couldn't do it. I think I told you I moved because of a roommate who smoked."

"You did."

"Hannah smokes. She said most of her friends smoke. I wonder what it's really like over there."

"I suspect that you'll find out one of these days, won't you."

"Next year in Jerusalem," she replied.

"What does that mean?"

"It's something Jews say to one another at special times."

"Sort of like 'See ya later, alligator.'"

"You're so dumb sometimes. Let's dance." Sarah wrapped both arms around Paul's neck and pulled him into her body.

Paul kissed his girlfriend at the door of the Sig Delt house and straightened her up. "I'll be by in the morning to pick you up so we can build the SPU booth. You won't be the only sister who's a little loose tonight. Anne was fired up too. Are you sober enough to get to your room?"

"I'll call you in ten minutes. Don't wreck my car on the way home." She thought that was very profound.

There was no call that Saturday night.

Sunday, April 9

Paul's plan for the SPU booth was a triangle with a 120-degree angle in the front allowing for both stability and greater access. Four peace workers could stand inside the booth without being crowded. There, they could pass out anti-war literature and discuss politics to interested students. A plywood roof would slope front to back, with a two-foot overhang to protect the counter. Paul spent the entire $28 on lumber. Nails, screws, and hinges were salvaged from the buckets in the 1203 garage.

He arose early, partly to pack Sarah's Corvair with tools, partly to read the Sunday *Camera*, but mostly because he was excited about building the booth. Dan teased him about spending four years to get a liberal arts degree only to spend the rest of his life as a carpenter. There were times, he thought, when working with his hands, quietly in his own shop, apart from politics, seemed ideal. Dan the florist and Paul the woodworker, but with college degrees.

The newspaper provided him with additional motivation to get started. Two front page articles focused on the war 9,000 miles away. A Viet Cong attack on an American outpost was described in one story, while the other told about the cost of fighting the conflict.

"Two thousand dollars per minute just for the munitions," he said aloud. "What a waste!" An editorial stated that the US bombing killed five times more civilians than did Viet Cong atrocities. *The bombing*, he wondered. *Was it really accomplishing what Curtis LeMay and the Air Force claimed*? He was convinced it wasn't, and his opposition to the war was intensifying daily. No longer was his opposition based on how the war interfered with civil rights or The Great Society programs. It had become personal to Paul. Killing with chemicals, killing from the sky, free-fire zones, the body count! He saw the war becoming a permanent condition that went against his vision of what America stood for . . . *whatever that is*! "Shit!"

"I smell coffee." Sally poked her head in and smiled.

"Hey, Sal. Grab a cup. Did you get any sleep last night?"

Paul and Sally drank coffee and read the paper, commenting on various stories. They could hear some stirrings around nine. He was able to get hold of Terry who promised to meet him in the parking lot east of the UMC at ten. Terry had two other SPUers who were going to help unload the lumber.

"You gonna get Sarah?"

"Not if she's not up when I leave. She said she'd call when she got up. She needs to sleep after last night." The reference to her drinking was obvious. They both laughed.

"I admire what you two have so much. You just have fun. I hope that's in my future."

Paul poured out his cold coffee, set the cup down in the sink, and went over and gave Sally a hug. "It is."

Dan and Tracey walked in. Robyn was still asleep.

They decided to erect the booth on the north side of the fountain to take advantage of the sun. Students walking out of the UMC would see a "Peace Now" banner hanging from the roof of the booth.

"Those people in Washington are out of their fucking minds, Garrity." Cohen had been ranting since he arrived. "LBJ is obsessed!"

"Did you see the paper this morning?" asked Paul.

"They're so optimistic in public, but they're shitting their pants in private," said Cohen. "They don't know how to get out now." Paul's shoulders were still sore, but he climbed the ladder to mark the plywood, listening to Cohen's rant silently. "They don't get it. Sure, there's communism, but the driving force is nationalism. To the VC, the US is just another foreign occupier. China, France, Japan, France again, now us." Cohen and Terry carried the plywood to the blocks to be cut to specifications.

"It's not only about that. I think the whole war is the enemy of the poverty programs here at home too," said Paul.

"The war will destroy your precious Great Society, Garrity. There just isn't enough money for both, and guess which one LBJ will sacrifice?" It was a rhetorical question.

"It's a stalemate," said Terry. "A stalemate with body bags."

The workforce doubled in size with the arrival of Dan, Tracey, Sally, Robyn, and Sarah.

"I'm helping you under protest," called out Dan. "It won't make a difference."

"Careful. The siders are just tacked together for now, so we could check the measurements of the roof."

Sarah walked up to him and gave him a hug. "Good morning, my dear. You let me sleep in. How are you holding up?" Paul shook his head that he was fine and then gave Dan a few directions, knowing Dan was as capable of building the booth as he was. The two teams worked, told jokes, and argued politics for the next hour and a half, while they completed the booth. Robyn and Tracey colored the banners.

Sarah pulled Paul aside during that time to point out the two Leadville sisters on their knees working together. "Is thirteen too young to be an anti-war activist?" she asked.

A little after one, it was done. Two banners hung from the overhang. "Peace Now" and "Student Peace Union." Cohen was pleased.

"We can all go get Mose," said Paul.

"Oh, I forgot to tell you," said Sally. "Your parents called this morning after you left. They're going to pick him up and take us all to dinner."

"Where're we going?" asked Sarah.

Sally looked at Dan and smiled. Dan looked at Sarah.

"We're taking Paul's parents to The Sink," said Dan.

Mose was all smiles when he returned. It was a reunion of sorts, and the good news was his mother was feeling well and optimistic about her cancer. He received the lowdown on Paul's accident, with a "Sorry I missed it" response.

They toasted Mose's return with beer and cokes and then dug into the burgers so famous at The Sink. Tracey, Dan, and Robyn needed to leave so the girls could get on the road to Leadville in order to get home before it got too late. The forecast was for dry roads, and Tracey promised to call when they were safely home.

"Mr. Garrity, you ought to see the booth Paul built before you go home," said Tracey.

"It's no big deal, Tracey, and you need to get on the road before it gets too late," said Paul.

"It's probably too dark anyway," added Sally.

Tracey looked confused but did not pursue it.

"Any word on the truck?" asked Dick Garrity.

"Dan's been taking care of it. He said it should be repaired in another week. I'm sorry about it all, Dad."

"You just fell asleep. No alcohol involved. We're just thankful you weren't hurt worse."

"I just feel pretty stupid about the whole thing."

Mom Diane came to the rescue again. "Dear, there's nothing to be ashamed of. We're proud of you."

Dan stayed only for about an hour in Paul's apartment after the Garritys left. He had homework. Mose said he would start back up on Monday, and the others had finished most of theirs on Saturday, although Paul needed about an hour for his US History essay.

"What was that about not going to see the booth?" asked Sarah. "I felt a little tension."

"My dad's not a big fan of my anti-war stance, remember?"

"Trust me, Sarah," added Mose, "you don't want to see his dad angry. I joked about Vietnam last fall, and he called me a 'commie.' He stared me down worse than any coach ever did."

"The war poisons families," said Sally gently.

"My dad's a veteran, Sars. World War II. Europe. He believes our generation is a bunch of cowards. Last thing he needs to see are those banners you hung on the booth."

"So, it turned out pretty good, huh," said Mose.

"Come down tomorrow morning and I'll give you a flyer, from one communist to another," joked Paul.

Monday, April 10

"Good morning, Paul. Little wet outside this morning. Always seems to happen for the World Affairs Conference. How are you feeling?"

"Everything's fine. I'll get the stitches out later this week. I have that essay for you."

"There are some interesting speakers this week. Have you seen the schedule?"

"Yeah. Is it still okay to miss your class if I'm attending a session?"

"Yes, I encourage it."

"I just don't want to get behind."

"I'm only going to review this week. Remember what I said last week, no new reading or homework. I really want you to attend as many sessions as you can this week."

"Did you see the SPU booth by the chemistry building when you came in?"

"No. Anti-war booth?"

"Yeah. I sort of built it yesterday with some of my friends, so we could have a central location to pass out literature."

"I suggest you see Norman Thomas this morning at eleven. His topic will pertain to the Cold War."

"He's the socialist, isn't he?" asked Paul.

"Yes, he is. Are you?"

Paul smiled. "Only in my dad's mind. I don't know enough about economics to know, but I don't call myself one. I don't think so."

Dr. Orr paused and looked at Toynbee's portrait. Without looking back at Paul, he said, "Paul, I wasn't quite honest with you last week, and I want to apologize." Paul waited. Dr. Orr swiveled back in his chair. "The men were not here to hear about the Publish or Perish controversy. They came to interview me for a job . . . at Yale." He paused again. "I'm on their short list, and those gentlemen are history professors at Yale, checking me out to see if I would fit in. They can be quite flattering."

Paul thought about what to say carefully. "I suspect you made quite an impression on them."

"Well, they're still interested."

"What's next?"

"I'll fly out this weekend for another quick visit."

"Just so I know, in case you get the job and I have to transfer, what's the tuition at Yale?" Paul smiled.

"Quite a bit more than here, I assure you."

They talked for a few more minutes before their time was up. As

Paul rose to leave, he turned back. "You wouldn't think of turning it down if it was offered, would you?"

Dr. Orr picked up a pen and played with it for a moment. "It hasn't been offered to me."

"It will be." Paul turned and was out the door before Professor Orr could reply, heading to the SPU booth. Dr. Orr put the top back on the pen, held it under his lower lip, and considered how good he had it at CU.

Paul ducked out of Norman Thomas's keynote address early to meet Sarah for lunch. Thomas was pushing for a foreign policy of disarmament, unilaterally if necessary, to prevent total human annihilation. Paul opposed the war in Vietnam but thought Thomas's solution was childishly naïve. Sarah found him at the booth a few minutes before noon handing out pamphlets critical of Operation Rolling Thunder. Interest was increasing in the SPU position, but there had been several hecklers, some of whom had been vulgar in their remarks. Paul left the booth to Terry and two others so he could give Sarah a hug and a kiss. The earth shook!

"What was that?" she asked with wide eyes.

For six seconds the ground heaved, causing students to cry out and wonder. The booth seemed to hiccup, and stacks of leaflets were tossed to the ground.

"I think we've just experienced an earthquake, but I'm not sure." He held tight to Sarah. "Boulder's not in an earthquake zone, is it?"

She still had wide eyes and was staring over the piazza. "That was quite a kiss!"

A buzz began over the area, which soon became quite crowded as students filed out of the two major classroom buildings that surrounded the fountain pavilion. Like many things occurring in Paul's life, he was not able to explain the April 10th earthquake.

At dinner 1203 was excited about the day's events. It seemed as though nearly every student eating at The Colonial had been on campus when the earthquake hit. The half-dozen aftershocks kept people alert, to be sure. The talk eventually settled on comments about the various World Affairs sessions. Over 100 such sessions were scheduled for the week on topics ranging from nuclear energy to magic, from geodesic domes to wigwams, from Buddhism to Zionism. It was an "intellectual smorgasbord," just as its sponsors proclaimed. The CU World Affairs Conference was the largest and most intellectually exciting gathering at any US university during the spring of 1967.

Dan was going to a physics seminar on quantum mechanics, Sally to a session on institutional racism in American law schools, and Paul and Sarah were going to hear a presentation at the Old Main Chapel entitled "The Arab and Oil." Only Mose had no plans to participate. "I have lots of catching up to do."

"How's the anti-war movement going?" asked Mose.

"The booth's been a gathering point. Despite the rain, people came by and asked questions. We signed up over 75 students for SPU membership, and we ran out of literature. Sarah was there when a couple of Young Republicans got into a screaming match with Cohen." Paul tilted his head. "It was pretty cool!"

"Male testosterone and lots of cuss words, but it was fun. People were interested and excited. I'm going back tomorrow after lunch to pass out leaflets," said Sarah. "Sally, come with me."

Tuesday, April 11

The phone rang again at two forty-five that night. It was John Cohen. "Garrity! They blew up the booth!"

It took Paul just fifteen minutes to dress and run down to the Memorial Center. When he arrived, he found Cohen out of control, yelling to the crowd of male students from nearby dorms who had quickly gathered at the sound of the explosion. "The police said it happened about one-thirty. They're not sure what kind of explosive was used or who did it, but you can bet it was those fucking YRs!"

Paul was amazed at how completely the booth was demolished. Pieces of lumber were found as far away as the southeast steps into Hellems. Not a single board was intact. Two windows had been blown out in the chem building behind where the booth had stood. A custodian, working late, had seen three boys running around the west side of the UMC after the blast.

"We'll rebuild it!" stated Cohen.

"No, we won't. Even if we could get it up in the next day or two, the university won't let us. But I think they'll give us a table just inside the UMC now. We just got a ton of free propaganda for the cause." Paul was surprisingly at ease with the events.

The *CU Daily* and the *Boulder Camera* photographers were already on the scene to document the crime. Debris was being collected and stacked at the original site, as a handful of policemen tried to collect evidence. They asked Cohen who he believed might be responsible for bombing the anti-war structure.

"President Johnson and the CIA!"

Paul paused for one last look at the destruction now littering the fountain area. He noticed the remains of the "Peace Now" banner that were caught on the lower limbs of a pine tree, visible only because a spotlight shone on a nearby set of steps. He pulled up his collar, turned, and headed home. *Peace*, he thought. *Not now. Not at this time.* It was not raining, but the air was damp in anticipation. He passed a sign at the west edge of campus that displayed the week's World Affairs Conference schedule. *So busy, so much going on here. Does any of it really relate to my life?*

There were no cars on The Hill, and not much sound either. As Paul passed in front of The Regiment, he stopped. It was four-twenty. He turned back and headed south on 13th to the Sig Delt house, four blocks away. When he arrived, he stood motionless, just looking at the building. Sarah's room was on the far side, a soph's location. He wished he could just walk in, go upstairs to her room, sit on her bed, and tell her about the bomb blast. He blew into his hands. *I should be angry at someone*, he thought, but his expression in the darkness displayed calmness. She would be stressed. He wondered how long he had stood there under the streetlight. Paul turned and walked home.

Sarah returned from showering to find Anne in her pajamas standing by the door. "Call Paul now. He said it's important." Sarah exchanged her towel for a terry cloth robe, then used the towel to dry her hair.

"Hey. I was in the shower. What's up?"

"You will never believe what happened last night!" Paul stretched out each word. "Somebody blew up my booth!"

"What? No!"

"I got a call from Cohen about 2:30. Somebody bombed the booth all to hell. There were pieces all over the fountain area. The cops had all the lights turned on over there, and they were looking for clues."

"Was anybody hurt?"

"No, and except for the booth, there wasn't much damage. A few broken and cracked windows."

"God! I'm sorry. You know, I wish I would've taken some pictures, especially yesterday when so many students were gathered around asking questions or arguing with you and Cohen. It was so cool, and now there'll be no evidence that it ever existed." Her voice was tinged with sadness.

"We'll simply move into the UMC loggia and keep putting out our message. We might even get more of an audience because of the crappy weather."

"I suppose, but, you know, we built it. Think they'll find out who did it.?"

"I'm not sure the cops want to. They sort of agreed with the bombers, that the commie, hippie, anti-war booth needed to be blown up. A couple of cops thought it was pretty funny."

The bombing was the big news on campus on Tuesday. While Cohen had been enraged at the event, he was politically savvy enough to see the propaganda value of it. He told the CU custodians that if they would stack the debris near its original site, the SPU would haul it away. For two days he stood in the rain to decry the lengths fascists would go to prevent free speech; that the destruction of the SPU booth was simply a metaphor for the destruction of basic rights, all resulting from an unjust war being waged in Asia. Paul had to admire his dedication and intensity, but he wondered to Sarah how he was able to pass any class when he never seemed to attend one.

Along with their roomies at 1203, Paul and Sarah attended a four o'clock World Affairs Conference session in Guggenheim entitled "Not for Me," given by a conscientious objector. In addition to providing information on how to be a legal CO, the speaker maintained it was not enough to simply be against the Vietnam War. One had to act. Mose, who had not planned on attending any session, found it interesting.

"He makes it sound easy. I wonder if it really is?" "Just drop out after this semester, Mose, and enroll in a seminary. You'd make a wonderful priest." Dan had not been impressed. He had been toying with the idea of joining the Army after graduation for a variety of reasons. However, his relationship with Tracey seemed to be an obstacle. No one doubted that if he did not marry her this coming summer, they certainly would tie the knot after graduation.

"He should've called his talk 'The Fastest Way to Destroy a Family,'" said Paul.

Sarah and Paul wanted to eat and get to their homework in order to attend another WAC presentation at eight. The Jordanian ambassador to the US was speaking about a new direction for American foreign policy regarding the Middle East.

"Bring your rubber boots," warned Sarah.

"Now, now, Sars. Let's give the man a chance."

Ambassador Shrebeilat was sharply critical of Israel, especially the

Zionists, and stated that they had entirely too much influence on US politics. He maintained the Arabs were being asked to resolve Europe's age-old problems and to assuage its guilt over the Holocaust, an event that was not nearly as destructive as the Zionists were saying. The crowd was active and participatory throughout the session.

"And THAT is Israel's friendliest neighbor," stated Sarah sarcastically upon exiting Macky Auditorium. She was angry at what she believed were blatant lies and outright misrepresentations of facts. "How can he say those things knowing there are dozens of Jews sitting in the audience, and almost no Jordanians?"

"He's not speaking to you. He's trying to convince me and all the other Gentiles who are unaware of the events over there. He can say pretty much what he wants, so long as he has the microphone, and he can outshout the hecklers."

"You don't believe what he's saying, do you?" Sarah stopped and turned on Paul.

"Some of what he says is true. There are lots of Arabs who've been living in refugee camps since '48, whose lives have been pretty difficult to this day. A lot of Palestinians have been forced to relocate. His take on the Holocaust is scary, though. But you did notice he received quite a bit of applause for presenting a seemingly rational alternative to America's present course. Remember, he holds oil out there as both a threat and an enticement."

"Israel isn't making war against the Arabs. They're protecting their land, and they have every right to do so! Jordan's farmers don't have to put armor on their tractors! They don't have to put barbed wire around their villages! They don't have to worry about the safety of their children each night! They don't have to deal with centuries of hate and murder by people who should know better!" Sarah had arrived at that place again, and Paul knew she was getting there quicker and more often these days. And, as he always did at these moments, he held her and stayed quiet. He knew that his recent research needed to be expanded to include information about those Arabs who had been displaced. The Palestinians seemed to have been forgotten in the clamor of international politics.

Wednesday, April 12

The *Boulder Camera* had a picture of the booth, or what was left of it, on the front page. The *CU Daily* ran an editorial about the bombing in its Wednesday issue. The editor Bob Ewegen was quite critical of the perpetrators, calling them "night crawlers" and "sub-cretinous" in describing their actions. Cohen, whom Paul was talking to before Sarah arrived at the UMC for lunch, was ecstatic, believing it had political opportunities. Paul told Cohen he would come back after lunch to man the table.

The Grille was a beehive of activity at midweek of the World Affairs Conference, and many of the patrons were not CU students, but visitors from surrounding areas. Even that, to Paul, was interesting, noting he was not used to a cosmopolitan atmosphere as Sarah was.

"Are you up for another round of the Arab-Israel conflict, my dear?"

"Of course. I saw it on the schedule, and Dr. Orr recommended it to our Cold War class this morning. Besides, it's not by an Arab, so his statements shouldn't get you so mad. By the way I bumped my shoulder coming out of Orr's class. It hurt, but not very long."

"That's good news. I'm going to go to the language lab for a while, but I'll meet you back at the table just before two. You're obviously not going to class then?"

"No. All my professors have been pretty cool about excusing me to attend these sessions. Come on, you can walk me back."

"Oil and the Arabs." Dr. Michael Conner, UMC Forum Room, two pm, Wednesday. Conner was a political science professor from Indiana. His key points were that the abundance of wealth would project those Arab states possessing it into prominent international roles for the remainder of the century. Rapid population growth was leading to a large group of unemployed young males, a potentially explosive group since Arab economies were not improving. Conner was concerned these young men could be manipulated by Arab leaders who opposed US interests in the region. His conclusion was that Middle East oil had spawned a group of corrupt Arab leaders who would use the issue of Israel to mislead a generation of young Arabs about the true nature of their problems, which would lead to problems for the United States and Europe.

Sarah was quiet as they left the UMC. "I don't know if I should be pleased with his conclusions or not. He's pretty pessimistic about Israel's predicament."

"It sort of goes along with what Dr. Orr has been saying in my Cold War class. He thinks Israel will be dependent on US protection to a large extent. The problem with that is we could become dependent on Arab oil."

"What does he think will be the result?"

"He never tells us. He leaves it for us to draw conclusions on essay tests."

"So, what's your conclusion?"

"That the Vietnam War distracts us from our real problems, both at home and abroad."

Sarah's mood seemed energized when she arrived at 1203 after dinner. "Uncle Abraham says the northern border areas are demanding vengeance for the Syrian attacks."

"The kibbutzes have a lot of political clout, don't they?"

"Kibbutzim, and, yes, they do. They've been the proving ground for young Jews. You can't be a true Israeli unless you spent time on a kibbutz."

"Is your uncle calling for a military response?"

"Yeah, he is. His whole family seemed pretty militant when they were back over the break. I got the feeling he'd take his own rifle out and shoot someone if he could."

"Hannah?"

"The whole family! Israeli Jews are different. For them, this conflict is about survival. It's hard for us to feel that here in America, especially in Boulder where every Jew is safe and comfortable."

"Or Greek."

"Then all three." She smiled and gave Paul a kiss. "I asked my father if I could go to Israel this summer." She let that sink in.

Finally, Paul responded. "Remember what I said about me being your bodyguard?"

Sarah gave him a deep stare and saw his concern. She stood, pulled him up with her, and led him to the couch. *Si je me suis sauve a Israel cet ete, iriez-vous avec moi?* Her stare remained the same.

He knew what she was asking this time, but he did not know the right answer, and for the first time since he had met Sarah Phillips, he felt insecure. He had an undefined sense that something bigger was in the pot. "I guess I could sell the truck," he joked.

She sensed his uncertainty. "If I went, I'd only go for two or three weeks. I wouldn't need a bodyguard. Just another poem until I got back."

"Hello."
"Hi. I don't know what I did to deserve you."
"Sex."
"You're still a toad. Goodnight."
"Goodnight, Sars."

Thursday, April 13

Hard rain. The pre-school kids were forced back inside after several weeks of good weather, unseasonably warm weather. Mrs. Best thought it was good to give the kids a little more structure again. Summer would come soon enough. Paul and Sarah looked at each other when she made the remark, but each knew she spoke the truth.

The *Boulder Camera* was filled with disheartening news on all fronts. Upstairs at 1203, they read the stories together.

"Boy, we're really wearing them down in the Mekong Delta, aren't we," said Paul. "If Westmoreland or Maxwell Taylor would just come here and see all I'm doing to end the war, they'd see how futile their efforts are."

"You're doing what you can."

"Lot of good that's doing."

"Don't be so pessimistic. Momentum against the war is building because of people like you." She leaned her head against his shoulder and then pointed to another story on the front page. "See. Even Dr. King has become more outspoken against the war."

"He and I need to go have a few beers. He's got to be the most frustrated man in America. All the good that's been achieved in the past few years is threatened by this war, and he knows it's happening."

"You don't sound like the session on Dr. King tonight will make you feel better. I know the speaker is going to criticize him for losing touch with the movement and probably for his recent statements about the war," she said.

"Mose and I are going. Dan refuses. You up for it?"

"I don't know. Maybe I'll go home and study. I haven't done much of that this week."

"Look at this story." Paul straightened out the fold of the paper. On page 21, the headline read, "Israel Port Suddenly Becomes Jobless Nightmare." They read in silence the rather lengthy story.

"You can't expect the economic boom to go on forever, or immigration either. This guy paints such a pessimistic picture."

"Do you know anything about what this guy is saying?" Paul asked.

"Not the specifics."

"What about the brain drain?"

"I don't know." She paused. "Why would so many of the brightest Jews be leaving Israel?"

Paul thought he knew what it meant, but he just shook his head.

"Hello, my dear."

"Hey, it's snowing. What're you doing?"

"Studying. How was the session? Did you throw anything?"

"No, but I did challenge him at the end."

"What did he say?" asked Sarah.

"I politely asked him what the alternative was, and when he said, 'Malcolm X,' I said he was dead. He said what he meant was Black Power, then Mose jumped in and asked if those were the only two choices. I was proud of him. The guy never had a chance to answer. People started talking, or should I say yelling out their comments, so the narrator guy just ended the session."

"I missed the fun." On her end, Sarah's tone changed.

"Yeah, you did, and it was fun. Mose and I went over to The Sink and had a pitcher. We haven't really talked all week."

"He's a great friend, isn't he?"

"Yeah, next to you."

"Are you drunk?"

"No," answered Paul realizing Sarah was serious now.

"I hate it when I don't share these times with you."

"When has this happened before? Isn't this the first time?"

"No. All those things you did before I met you count for me, you know. And your crash."

"Oh, that was a fun time."

"You know what I mean," said Sarah.

"You were there for me."

Friday, April 14

The World Affairs Conference ended with a whimper; it seemed to Paul. He attended no sessions on the last day. Between the building and bombing of the booth, working at the SPU table in the student center each day, the seven sessions he attended, and his regular class schedule, he thought he might be tired, but when he walked out of his American Lit class at three, he felt alert and excited. Not having seen Sarah the night before only deepened his expectations for FAC. With the temperature near 60 as predicted, he knew that she would be wearing something enticing to Tulagi's. After a week of damp, gloomy days, the Friday sunshine perked up the entire student body. King Louie read the mood perfectly, and Tulagi's rocked. Sarah did not disappoint.

After some pizza at Bennett's, the gang went to see *Georgy Girl* before heading down to the Scotch Pub to listen to some "old folks" music, as Mose called it. However, it allowed them time to talk and laugh, and they began to make plans for the summer.

Back at 1203 around midnight, Mose and Sally called it a night, and Sarah and Paul went to bed too. Lovemaking was intense after a day apart, but the ensuing conversation was gentle. Paul told Sarah that Tracey had invited them all to her high school graduation in May, and Dan was leaning toward a summer wedding.

"So, they'll beat us to the altar?" Sarah asked.

Paul smiled and pulled Sarah closer into his body.

Saturday, April 15

On their way down to Lakewood for a late dinner with his parents, Paul pointed out the spot on the turnpike where he crashed his truck.

"I know." Sarah's mood was pensive. "I drove out to find it last weekend. Of all the places you could have crashed, this was the best."

"Why'd you do that?" he asked.

"I don't know, just something I needed to do. The fence messed up the truck—and you—and the bushes just sort of caught you and held you." She looked straight ahead at the spot where the crash had occurred. "Protected you for me."

Sunday, April 16

Mose strolled into Paul's apartment about nine on Sunday morning and went to the cupboard for a mug. He poured himself some coffee and took a seat across the table from Paul.

"These past two weeks have been hectic, haven't they," said Paul. "Did you talk with your mom last night?"

"Yeah. Says she's doin' fine, and her spirits seem good. Funny, Garrity. She seems like she has more energy and enthusiasm now than she has in years. I would've thought it was just the opposite. Still wish I could do more for her."

"Remember when you said she was proud of you for just going to college? I suspect she'll be even prouder when you graduate."

"Graduate. We're only two years away. Two and a half, maybe. I've gotta tell ya, Garrity, I didn't come here to graduate. Only came to play ball. That's all I could do. I didn't even think about school much, or graduation, and now it really matters."

"Kind of amazing, isn't it. All of us are on schedule, except me and I'm only a semester behind. I can catch up this summer." He paused to consider what he had just said. "We're doing all right, aren't we."

"Sarah comin' over?"

"No schedule. She'll call. I'm sure we'll do some studying later on. She said she wanted to do a little research for her house this morning. She volunteered to become their, what did she call it, liaison for information about Israel right now. The whole thing over there with Syria has her upset."

Mose smiled. "Kind of impulsive, huh. Keeps you jumpin.'"

"Just kind of impulsive?" Paul responded.

"You gonna marry her soon, Garrity?"

Paul smiled this time. "Not for a while, big guy. We're too young."

"Maybe, but where're you gonna find anyone better? She's pretty cool . . . and she loves your young ass."

Paul leaned across the table and popped Mose on the forehead. "We've thought about it and kidded about it, but now's not the time. We'd have to live in married student housing. Not sure they'd let you be my roommate there." They both laughed. "Anyway, Sarah's so talented and has things she wants to accomplish, and she needs her degree for that. We're doing just great as it is; no need to change that." He paused and smiled. "There's that other thing too."

"What? Her being Jewish?"

"No, her having Jewish parents who don't approve of me. Especially her mother."

"It's not their decision!" said Mose.

"No, but it's still a concern. She's an only child to older parents. Besides, if we wait, I can keep working on them from a distance. Her dad seems to be getting used to me, and I think her mom may come around. There's time. We couldn't spend any more time together anyway."

"What's her mom's beef?"

"Just the Jewish thing, I think. She thinks I'll keep her daughter from becoming a real Jew. Hell, Sarah's moving in that direction more now. Maybe not religiously, but at least culturally."

"Well, you have my approval."

"Thanks. That's what I was really waiting for. What about you and Sally?"

Mose shook his head. "It's not that kind a thing. Even if it was, don't you think she's a little too good for me?"

"Shit, Mose. Sarah's family is rich. She's a Greek, and she's super smart. I'm not the guy who should be telling you someone's too good for you."

"You're right, you aren't." They both laughed. "Sally's a great friend, and I love her, but not like that. She'll find someone good. I think it's good for her, after her problems, that she's in a place where she doesn't have to hook up, where she can sort of use me as an excuse for a boyfriend and have time. This place has been great for her, and she's told me that." Mose slid his chair out so he could cross his legs.

"Are you going to have to go home this summer to be with your mom?" asked Paul.

"I thought so when I first found out, but being home a whole week was too much. I'd rather stay here and get a job and work on my game. Are you hiring?"

"Probably. I talked to Mr. Noonan about hiring someone, and he said I could. He might go as high as four dollars an hour. You know, of course, being your boss would ruin our friendship."

"Shit. We can't stand each other as it is. We have nothin' in common. I don't care about politics, and you can't shoot."

"Be careful. I'm healthy again."

"Why don't I call a couple of the guys, and we'll go play some hoops around noon. I'll let you be on my side, so you can win for once."

"How about you quit talking trash, and we get Sally and go get some breakfast?"

After studying for two hours, Paul and Sarah left the library for the Gondolier around six to join the gang. They were back at the library by seven-fifteen, Sarah with her sociology and Paul with his US history. His class chronology had begun to meld with the Cold War material, making preparation for both courses easier. Winston Churchill's admonition about history being learned more by rereading was certainly true for Paul. Around ninw Sarah had enough of the library for one day and convinced Paul to take her back to 1203. There, they found Dan, Mose, and Sally sitting around his table eating popcorn and drinking pops.

"Enough for us?"

"Dan brought back some Jiffy Pop, so we can make some more," said Sally. "We're just trying to locate ourselves in the universe."

"My grandma tries to make sense of the war in Vietnam; asks me questions all the time. She was saying her generation had The Great War, and my dad had World War II and Korea, but she didn't know if our generation really wanted to identify with Vietnam. I didn't have a good reply," said Dan updating Paul and Sarah on the gist of the conversation.

"Sadly, I think we're stuck with it . . . and with our pathetic support of it," said Paul.

"Or our opposition," said Mose.

"That's what he meant," said Sally.

"Yeah. It's the high school kids who are going off to fight the war, not us. We're just the draft dodgers, the protesters," said Paul. "It's not a shared experience, is it."

"Us girls too?" asked Sarah.

"I don't know," Paul responded.

"You never thought of us, did you, you chauvinist," teased Sarah.

"I guess I didn't. So, what will define our women?" "Our men?" asked Sally.

"Our clothes," stated Sarah. "Just kidding. It won't be miniskirts or hoop earrings. I'll decide, but it has to be something other than Vietnam or our men. Maybe it can be something positive, Sally."

"Civil Rights," said Mose.

"I wish," added Paul, "but us whites were pretty reluctant to grant you anything, Mose. *Your people*," Paul looked directly at Mose, "accomplished everything on your own, with just a little help from the Supreme Court and LBJ."

"My people." Mose held out his arms.

"What do I tell my grandma?"

"Tell her we're not done yet," said Sarah. "Paul and I have a lot to accomplish still."

"And that's just tonight," teased Sally.

"Hello, Sars."

"Hi. You make me ask myself big questions, you know."

"Like what?"

"Like where I fit in in this universe."

"You've been pondering that since I met you. You're the one who's causing me to see a bigger picture. You and Orr."

"It's still okay if I go with you tomorrow morning to see him?" asked Sarah.

"Yeah, especially since you need his help."

"I'm excited about doing this."

"I know. It'll help you with one of your big questions."

"Maybe. You're still my biggest question."

"Maybe you could sneak out tonight, and we could work on an answer."

"For three months I've wanted to do that, and you haven't allowed it. Why the change now, love?"

"I haven't. Just kidding, you know. Sars, I'm not your biggest question. I'm pretty much a simple guy who loves you."

"I know, and that's why I'm so concerned."

"I'm confused."

"So am I. It's late. I love you. Landa."

"Goodnight, Sars."

Monday, April 17

As was frequently the case, Sarah captivated those around her almost to the exclusion of Paul or others in her company. So it was on Monday morning with Dr. Orr, who was able to provide her with several options for obtaining information about the events unfolding in Israel. Paul drank coffee and listened. He knew some of Orr's suggestions would now be on his reading list.

"Your best sources are still primary in nature, and I would encourage you to get in touch with New York's senators and congressmen. Both senators are Jewish, Javits and Ribicoff, and I would guess around ten or twelve of your representatives are too. If you could convince one of them to speak to you on the phone every week or so, you'd really have something. Their positions should allow them to have contact with leaders in Israel."

"I'll bet my father could help me there." She turned to Paul. "Thanks, you were right."

"We've taken my allotted half hour, so we need to let Dr. Orr go. I'll walk you to class. Thanks for your help, Dr. Orr. I'll see you in class."

"Thank you so much, Professor Orr. This will be a great help!" "You're welcome, Miss Phillips." She stood and shook his hand, which caused Paul to smile. "Stop back in and see me in about twenty minutes, Paul."

"He's so smart. Each time I've seen him, he's really impressed me. It's easy to see why you've adopted him as your mentor." She had a sparkle in her eyes. "I'm sorry I took up all the time this morning, but it was nice of him to ask you back."

Paul's thoughts were elsewhere. "Yeah. See you at lunch?"

He knocked on the half-open door and waited.

"Come in, Paul." Orr was standing and held the door open for Paul. "That's a delightful girl you have there. Quite charming, I must say."

"She does that to a lot of people. I still haven't gotten over it." He smiled, knowing that the small talk was over.

"I don't want this information out just yet, but I wanted to talk to you." Orr paused and returned to his desk chair and waved for Paul to have his customary seat. "When I was growing up, my family attended the Catholic Church each Sunday, a small congregation, very close knit in our little town." Orr was storytelling his own experience, and Paul knew there would be a lesson attached. "Our priest, Father Stewart, was young and enthusiastic, great in CYO, and had really attached himself to our town in the few years he was there. When I was in high school, I remember him asking our prayers for 'someone in need of guidance.' This went on for several weeks, as I remember, and people wondered who he was referring to. As it turned out, it was for him that he was seeking guidance. He had been given the option to move to a larger church in San Francisco, but his heart strings were tugging him to stay." Dr. Orr paused.

"Sort of like CU and Yale?" Paul was bailing out his mentor. "What an opportunity. Did your priest go?"

"Yes. Yes, he did. Explained to the congregation one Sunday what had been offered and how he struggled and what his decision was. He said God had directed him. God hasn't talked to me. I've had to make the decision on my own and with my wife's counsel. When Father Stewart left, I let my religious discipline slip. He was such an influence on my young life."

"What happened to him?"

"Became a bishop and moved again." He knew Paul knew where he was going, but still, he wanted to say it. "I've accepted Yale's offer. This will be my last semester at 'Dear Old CU,' but I have some unfinished work." He swallowed hard and continued. "I have been trying to guide you in a certain direction, allowing you to discover it on your own, but guiding, nevertheless. Paul, you have a historian's mind and pen, and I want to encourage you to pursue this field. It will be your choice, but that's my recommendation." He paused again, this time to allow Paul time to absorb his guidance and comment.

"I've already made my choice," Paul answered, "if that little war in Asia doesn't interfere, but don't worry. When you leave, I won't slip away."

"I'm glad to hear you say that. We'll have five or six more weeks to work together." He looked at his watch. "Don't you have a nine o'clock class to prepare for?"

"Yes, sir."

In both of Orr's history classes, Paul sat in the second row near the wall to the right of the podium. To get to his desk in each of the lecture rooms, 205 and 227, he had to pass in front of Dr. Orr, both coming and going. While his mentor was not usually there when Paul arrived, he always was when he left, which allowed them the opportunity to speak to one another for a few moments. Paul was seldom in a hurry for class to end.

On this Monday he did not know quite what to say to his professor, so he asked about the Vienna summit conference between Kennedy and Khrushchev and then left to meet Sarah. By twelve-thirty she still had not arrived, so he went into the Grille for a burger and sat at their usual table, pretending to read, but keeping an eye out for Sarah. By one she had still not come, the first time since they had begun this particular dance that she had not met him. He still had a chapter to review for American Lit, so he headed off to Norlin to finish it. But he wondered.

Paul returned to 1203 about three-thirty and found Sarah's note. "I have the surprise. Call me." Paul took a pop from the refrigerator and dialed the Sig Delt number.

"I'm sorry I missed you for lunch, but I was making plans. Can you clear your calendar for Friday and this weekend?" asked Sarah.

"I have my classes and Dan mentioned something about all of us going to Leadville with him, but we hadn't decided on anything for sure. What do you have?"

"Can you talk to Dr. Orr and miss his classes?" she persisted.

"Yeah, I can." He paused. "You sound excited about this surprise."

"I am! I'll tell you about it tonight. See you then." She hung up before he could respond.

Dr. Orr sprint-walked the two-and-a-half miles to his home south of the UMC. So much had come to him so easily, he thought, and he had never faced such a difficult decision. To leave this university, the Flatirons and its trails, and so many wonderful students, like Paul Garrity. He knew that his decision was correct, but he still wondered if he would have the same kind of impact on his students in New Haven as he did in Boulder. Would those students be as talented as advertised? Would these three dozen or so students who were so strongly attached to him continue to produce excellent results? Had he had enough time with Paul Garrity to make a difference? He wondered if he would ever realize the answer.

Mose was sweating heavily when he returned to 1203 from his afternoon run. Paul knew which of his friends was ascending the stairs by the sounds of the footsteps.

"How far today, Mose?" asked Paul.

"About eight, just over 55 minutes." He exhaled loudly. "Feels good. Maybe the best shape of my life."

"Go shower. I'll wait for you, and we'll go get some dinner."

"Dan?"

"I'll get him. Hurry up, I'm starved." Paul picked up his Cold War book as Mose went to his apartment. He was reading about Berlin and the Wall, but he could not stop thinking about the article in the *Camera* about that other divided city. Jerusalem. Grandma Savage and Sarah had talked about their desires to visit this holy city, this focal point in the Middle East conflict, the city Grandma Savage would never see, but Sarah would most likely tour this summer. The *Camera* story maintained there could be no solution to the conflict without a resolution to the problem of Jerusalem, and the article implied no solution seemed available at this time.

"I'm ready. Did you get Dan?"

None of the guys noticed the Blue Bomb parked in the driveway when they returned from dinner. They had stayed a few extra minutes at The Colonial watching 'The Dating Game" before returning for the regimen of study. Sally and Sarah watched them from Sally's window as they crossed Pennsylvania and headed back. Mose held Dan in a headlock for much of the short walk in response to Dan's remark about Renee Mattison.

"We're in Sally's room," yelled Sarah as the three boys pushed each other up the stairs. Sally's apartment was the smallest of the four on the second floor, one living/bedroom and a bathroom. Paul found Sarah and gave her a two-handed hug and a kiss, while Dan and Mose sandwiched Sally on her small couch. She noticed that Dan's ears were still red.

"Cozy?" she asked.

Mose put his arm around Sally. "What's up? Did you girls get any dinner?"

"A little. Ready for your surprise, Paul?" Sally already knew what it was and thought it was pretty cool—and very Sarah-ish.

Sarah had been holding her hands behind her back and produced two plane tickets. "Where do you think we're going, my dear?" Sarah was noticeably excited.

"Paris?" he replied remembering a previous challenge.

"We only have three days. Guess again."

"This weekend?"

"Yes. Guess."

Paul really had no idea, but he played along. "Help me out here guys. Where's she taking me?"

"San Francisco," guessed Mose.

"Aspen," added Dan.

Sarah shook her head on both responses. "America's greatest city."

"Oxnard," guessed Mose again with a smirk.

"New York!" stated Paul. "You're going to ask your mom for permission to . . ." He stopped himself and smiled.

"You'll have to do that on your own when the time comes. New York, yes, but to meet a Jewish congressman who's going to become my contact person for Israeli updates. My dad set it up. Wired me the money this morning for tickets."

"And why am I going?" asked Paul.

Sally did not allow Sarah to answer. "Because she loves you, dummy, and because you deserve to go too, after staying up late every night reading about the Jews and Israel."

"You're my expert on Mideast affairs. I told my father you're the force behind my newfound interest in Israel. He was anxious to have you come."

"Who's the congressman?"

"Hello."

"Hi. Tell me the truth. Are you excited to go?"

"Very! I'm also nervous. I've never been to New York or met a real congressman or been an expert on anything. And your mom."

"But you still want to go?"

"Yes, very much. I wish you'd let me pay for my own ticket though. I can do that."

"No! This is for me. Another jump for me, but I need you to catch me, except I won't need the net. You'll love my city, even for just a weekend, and my parents, both of them, are excited to treat you for being so good for me."

"What've you been telling them?"

"Only the truth." Each end of the line was silent for a moment. "Paul . . ."

"Yeah?"

"What are you thinking?"

"It won't make sense," he said.

"Try me."

"I've been in a car wreck, the booth was bombed, Ricky, Orr's leaving. So much has happened this semester, and yet, it's you. Every day, it's you!"

"It's me what?" Sarah's voice was so quiet.

"It's you that's been . . . the most important thing in my life. Not an hour passes when I don't smile about you. That's corny, huh?"

"No, that's beautiful."

"Come get me for breakfast tomorrow, okay?"

"I will. Paul?"

"Yeah?"

"You said Dr. Orr's leaving?"

"Yeah but keep that between you and me for now. I'll tell you tomorrow."

"Keep smiling about me, my dear."

"Count on it. I love you, Sars."

Tuesday, April 18

At breakfast on Tuesday morning, Paul, Sarah, Sally, and Dan were joined by Junior Owens, one of the 1203 downstairs tenants, who was checking on his room for the fall term. An engineering major, he had few table manners. He was the first person whom Sally met when she inquired about the vacancy the previous summer, which almost kept her from pursuing the room any further. He lived in the room directly below Sally's, and she often smelled the aroma from his marijuana habit. Still, he paid his rent on time, was quiet, and, surprisingly, scrubbed the first-floor bathroom once a week without any require-ment to do so. After getting the answers he wanted, Junior rose to leave. "See you guys. When you going out with me, Sally?"

"I'll check with Mose," she smiled sweetly.

Junior knew that was a rejection, but it did not bother him. He took his tray and left.

"Mose protects you even in absentia," said Dan.

Paul shook his head. "Piece a work, isn't he." He sipped his coffee. "Are you and Mose still going to Leadville this weekend?"

Sally nodded. "Yeah. We're going to explain our generation to Grandma S. By the way, I forgot to tell you. Cohen wants you to meet him at twelve-thirty. Said you'd understand."

"He called this morning. I thought it was you," Paul said nodding at Sarah. "We're going to see where we stand after last week; maybe our membership will hit double figures. The bombing helped us, I think."

"Which bombing?" asked Sarah, "the booth or Rolling Thunder?"

"Both, but I was referring to the booth."

Sarah went with Paul to his meeting with Cohen. With the weather unseasonably warm, they decided to sit on the patio on the south side of the UMC.

"I thought I'd see you last Saturday at the courthouse for the protest. There were about 300 people there." Cohen had jumped right into politics after a quick greeting.

"The paper said about only a hundred or so. We had dinner with my parents. Must've been quite the rallies in New York and San Fran though." Paul had talked about them with the 1203 gang on Sunday with enthusiasm, but he was subdued with Cohen.

"Do you think King was right when he called for blacks and us whites to boycott the war, to become conscientious objectors?" Cohen surprised both Paul and Sarah by asking for their opinions.

Sarah had strong feelings about this on Sunday when they had discussed it. "Yes, I do. The war is morally wrong. Because America's reputation is to only fight for what's right doesn't change it. Dr. King is right to oppose it and tell us to do the same thing."

Paul remained silent. Cohen had little patience for silence; he would fill the vacuum. "I thought you'd be overjoyed at King's stance. It's the same as yours, Garrity."

"I was," he finally answered, "on Sunday. But the NAACP absolutely repudiated his stance, called it a 'serious tactical mistake.'" He spoke in measured terms.

Sarah jumped in. "But he's right!"

Paul was still measured. "He is, but is this going to help either group, or will it just alienate us from mainstream America even more? I mean, the Civil Rights Movement won some victories, but I don't see Congress moving to help anymore."

Cohen cut him off. "Congress hasn't passed anything in over a year for the blacks. The Fair Housing Bill is dead now. All the emotion and all the money goes to that fucking war! Why NOT join the student anti-war movement?" It was Sarah's turn again. "Blacks have to be made aware the war hurts them more than anything else. That's all King is saying. The issues are already joined!"

"The war's spinning out of control, and it's only going to get worse. Cohen, you're trying to get it stopped, but it's not. Secretary Rusk has already said the protesters aren't going to affect our fighting in Vietnam. If the Congress is lukewarm on civil rights now, think how they'll feel when it's joined by the anti-war movement. LBJ has been the best thing for civil rights since Lincoln, and now King is doing his best to piss him off."

"All I can say is anything we do to put pressure on those in charge of the war is a good thing!" Cohen was all about the impact of events on each day.

They continued to discuss the two movements while they set a date for the next SPU meeting. Because Paul would be gone for the weekend, they decided to hold off until the following Wednesday. They would need lots of flyers, and Paul volunteered to call some students who had signed up during the World Affairs Conference.

"Don't go getting discouraged on me, Garrity," Cohen kidded as they left. "If LBJ doesn't get it pretty soon, we'll dump his ass and find a candidate who will."

"Let's just go to the Lab School now. We can study over there until two." Sarah took Paul's arm and squeezed it. "Why does Cohen always have to be a jerk at the end?"

Paul laughed slightly. "It's just his nature. What got into you? You've never expressed yourself so forcefully about Vietnam until Sunday and today."

"You! I've been selfish about our discussions. Always Israel, but you're so patient with me. The war does matter, and I need to get involved, at least to some degree."

"For America all this is connected. Vietnam, civil rights, Israel. I just think that 1967 will be a year to remember, to study." He took her shoulders and stared at her. Then he looked beyond her. "I just wish I understood it all."

"Someday, you will, my dear. Someday you will. You'll make a difference."

At that moment, Paul wasn't so sure.

Mose had Monday's *Camera* at dinner. "How do you take in all this shit, Garrity? Vietnam bombing, school integration, Muhammad Ali's draft status, hippies, King's prediction about summer race riots, and I haven't even got to the sports page." He laughed.

"That's all I should read. What time's the game tonight? Philly's about to take your Warriors down," teased Paul.

"Care to bet a beer?"

"You're on, big skinny."

"Hello."

"Who won?"

"San Fran. Rick Barry went for 54. Mose is still dancing and taunting me."

"Let's go dancing tomorrow night. I need to feel you."

Paul was quiet. "You don't need to go dancing to have me do that, you know."

"We just get so busy, and even though I'm with you, I'm not." She paused. "I just want to dance and not think about the world or my sociology. Can we do that?"

"Yeah, I need it too. How about if we have dinner together away from everyone else?"

"I'd like that. Do you have any more studying to do?"
"Some of everything, but I think I can get it done by one-thirty. What about you?"

"Just bio. I'm going to write down some questions for my interview with the congressman."

"What's his name?"

"Rosenthal. He knows my father."

"No surprise there."

"Paul?"

"Yeah?"

"This weekend is going to be special. I'll make sure of it. You won't be disappointed."

"I never have been."

Wednesday, April 19

Paul went to see Dr. Orr the next morning, arriving at his Hellems office at seven-ten.

"Morning, Paul. What brings you in this morning?" Orr pointed to the coffee maker.

"Just came in to talk you out of going to that little school back east. It would be a real career stopper. Where would you go from there?" Paul smiled at his little joke.

"I don't know. Nebraska, maybe." They shared a laugh. "Sit. I don't have anyone coming in for a while."

"I need to miss classes on Friday. I'm going to New York to meet a congressman."

"Sarah doesn't waste time, does she? Connections?"

"I've always thought her father knew people. He's a doctor, but he just seems in the loop. Anyway, we're flying out tomorrow night and meeting with the congressman on Friday."

"What's his name?"

"Benjamin Rosenthal. His district is on the northside, whatever that is. I'll be back on Sunday night."

"Have you ever been to New York?"

"No."

"Take it all in. Walk Manhattan. Sample the neighborhood foods. Go to the Statue of Liberty and read the inscription, the entire inscription."

"You've been."

"Twice. It's the most amazing city. You'll like it."

"Then it's okay for Friday?"

"I'll call on someone else to answer my questions. Give the rest of the class an opportunity to impress me."

Sarah laughed at Paul's choice for a dinner date: Furr's cafeteria. From there, they went back to The Hill to Tulagi's where the Moonrakers were playing. They shared a single beer, danced nearly every dance, and left around nine-thirty to go make love.

"Hello, Sars"

"Perfect evening, my dear."

"So, the planets are aligned again, huh?"

"Are you packed? We need to leave by four, right after our lab class."

"I'm ready. Will your mom be okay?"

"She'll be on her best behavior, I promise. Don't worry."

"I have a present for her."

"What is it?"

"It's a surprise for you too."

"A poem?"

"No. Those are only for you."

"What? Tell me!"

"See you at noon tomorrow."

"Landa, Paul Garrity. Your last name is Garrity, isn't it?"

Thursday, April 20

Paul wore his new jacket and tie, covered by a trench coat. Sarah was stunning in a green pants suit. They arrived with the gang in tow at Stapleton Airport in plenty of time for their four-hour flight to New York.

Sarah hugged both Dan and Mose before taking Paul's hand to board the United jet. Dan and Mose watched out the window until the jet taxied away from the terminal.

"He's scared shitless," said Mose with a smile. "He's never flown."

"They're the perfect couple," noted Dan.

"Yeah, maybe, but why would you say so? What about you and Tracey?"

"She's too dependent on me. Her world would collapse if I wasn't there for her. Those two are always happy. He thinks he's lucky to have her, and she thinks she's the lucky one. They support one another. Completely comfortable together." Dan paused. "Remember how nervous he always was when he was with a girl? None of that now, and I get a sense she was the same way."

"Lots of sex too." They laughed and turned away from the windows and headed down the concourse.

It was first class and Sarah insisted Paul take the window seat. His fear lasted only until the plane was airborne, and then it changed to intrigue as the jet banked to the north exposing the Front Range to the left side, Paul's side, of the plane.

Friday, April 21

"Good morning, Sarah and Paul. Such a handsome couple!" Congressman Rosenthal shook Sarah's hand first and then Paul's. He had a firm grip to go along with his irrepressible, but genuine smile. He was into his third term as a representative from upper Manhattan, and his office was filled with memorabilia from his time in the United States Congress.

"Good morning, sir," said Sarah.

"Good morning, Congressman," said Paul, who stood a step behind Sarah.

"Come in. Come in. I understand you arrived very late last night." The congressman's voice filled the high-ceilinged, but warm office. Most of the dark hardwood floor was covered by rugs. A huge mahogany desk was the centerpiece, although an elongated table that seated eight balanced out the room. Paul stayed quiet, believing it was Sarah's role to carry the conversation during the initial stages. He had promised her that he would ask relevant questions if the meeting extended beyond a simple introduction.

"Yes, sir, around midnight. My father was there to get us, but we didn't get to bed until about two."

"About the time you college students normally get to bed then." Rosenthal laughed slightly at his little joke, but he was not far off the mark. "Your father and I have known each other for many, many years . . . from the old neighborhood in Brooklyn. He was the smart one; I was the big talker. He ends up being a doctor, and I become a politician, so I can keep talking." He motioned for Sarah and Paul to be seated at his desk. "Would you like something to drink?"

"Coffee, thank you, for both of us." Sarah showed no nervousness. Her sorority training was kicking in.

Rosenthal removed three China coffee cups with saucers from the cupboard and placed them on the desk. From a drawer he took three spoons. Each had a different design, which indicated to Paul they had been gifts. He wondered how many different spoons were in the drawer. The coffee was poured from a silver pot. "Sugar or cream?"

"Cream, please," answered Sarah.

"Sugar," replied Paul.

"Your father tells me you will be serving as your sorority's source for information on the events going on in Israel these days. How did you get the job?"

"I volunteered. I'm a little embarrassed to admit I haven't kept up on the events of recent months, but since I've been dating Paul, he's made me more aware of the world outside of Boulder."

"And what's your connection with all of this, Paul?"

"I'm a history major and my favorite class this semester is about the Cold War. I have an inspiring teacher. Meeting Sarah has personalized much of the material for me."

"He's sort of been my mentor, sir," added Sarah.

"Your mentor, huh." Rosenthal smiled and raised his left eyebrow before finally taking a seat behind his desk. "Well, what is it I can do for you, Sarah?"

"I need a resource person who has contacts with Israel, someone who knows what's going on there on a daily basis. I want someone who knows what the newspapers don't tell us, and I want to be able to call that person whenever I have a question." She placed her right hand on Paul's left thigh as she spoke, out of sight of the congressman.

"Don't you have an uncle who lives in Israel?"

"Yes, but Uncle Abraham doesn't have a phone on the kibbutz, at least not one that can be used frequently for overseas calls. Besides, he wouldn't tell me everything. He'd filter the bad news so as not to alarm me. I have four cousins. I'm corresponding with his oldest daughter, but letters from the kibbutz take two to three weeks to arrive."

Rosenthal looked over to Paul. "Do you think conditions in the Mideast warrant such attention? I mean, there is always tension between Israel and its Arab neighbors. Are these days any different?" Paul realized he was being tested. He wondered if Rosenthal would be as tough as Dr. Orr. He also wondered how Sarah was going to react. "Sir, it does seem like conditions are changing over there. The Soviet Union seems to be pushing the Arabs toward a more dangerous policy, especially Syria and Egypt. I don't know why. Maybe because they feel the US is too caught up in Vietnam to offer much support to Israel. Maybe it's because they see an Israel that has lost a bit of momentum and can't respond. Either way, the border raids and the Egyptian rhetoric seem to be increasing to levels that make it difficult for Israel to ignore."

Sarah continued to stare at Paul, as Paul maintained his contact with Rosenthal. The congressman turned to Sarah. "Is Paul pro-Israel?"

It was a strange question for her, one she had not contemplated. "I haven't asked. As I said, he's trying to have me see the whole picture." Rosenthal's tone changed, and he lost his smile. He turned back to Paul. "These border raids, how do you know?"

"Sarah's cousin's letters, the newspaper, talks with my CU professor."

"What should Israel do?"

Paul shifted on his chair. "It can't allow them to continue."

"What role should America play?"

"Should, or will, play?"

Rosenthal nodded and smiled slightly. "Should." "LBJ should let it be known, maybe not publicly, but at least through diplomatic channels, that the US will protect Israel's security. Maybe he already has done so. I have no way of knowing."

"Will that be enough?"

"If he was forceful enough, but . . ." Paul did not finish his thought.

"So, what will happen?"

Paul glanced at Sarah and slid his hand on top of hers. "There's a good chance for war, I think." Sarah tensed.

"I hope you're wrong, Paul." Rosenthal's eyes shifted. "A liaison often needs to conceal certain pieces of information or at least soften the delivery. In your case, your sorority sisters might not all be in the same place you are. Do you understand?"

Sarah turned to the congressman. "Is Paul correct?"

"He is correct that tension has increased, and the Soviet Union seems to be pushing the Arabs to be more reckless. We hope those who favor peaceful solutions can prevent another war, however. I'm optimistic the current state of affairs, sort of an armed tension, will continue without flaring up into a wider war." He turned to Paul. "Back to the second question. What would the United States do if war broke out?"

"I'm pretty pessimistic about the actions of our government these days, sir. You would have a better handle on that than me."

"You think Israel might have to fight a war alone?"

"It might."

"Sarah." Rosenthal turned back to her abruptly. "I'll do what I can for you. I do have communications with certain officials in Israel and with some of its diplomats here in New York and DC. I'll give you my telephone numbers for this office and for my office in Washington. I'll instruct my secretaries about what you need and what you want, but I may not be able to take your calls immediately. You cannot use my name as your source, not that it matters much, but Israel uses me as a link to the President, and some of that information is sensitive. I'll pass on information but you and Paul will have to determine what it means and how much you will need to pass on to your sorority sisters. Understand?" Rosenthal was leaning across his desk now.

"Yes, sir. Thank you so much."

The trio continued to talk for another ten minutes, but on a lighter note. Families, college, basketball—Rosenthal had played in college—all were discussed. He described the many artifacts and pictures that adorned his office, including one of him with John Kennedy. As Paul and Sarah prepared to leave, Rosenthal added, "Have you ever been to Israel, Sarah?" "No, but I plan to visit there soon, maybe even this summer."

"Will you be going with her, Paul?"

"No, I'll be going to summer school and managing an apartment."

Sarah jumped into Paul's arms when they exited the revolving doors onto 57th Street. "That was fun, and you were wonderful!" She kissed him. "He is a talker, isn't he?"

"He's really a nice man. I thought we might get five minutes, but we spent a half hour in there. There were some distinguished looking men waiting to see him."

"Are you ready to see my part of New York?" She was excited at the idea of showing Paul her neighborhoods. "We don't have to be back home until about seven. My mother has a special dinner planned."

"Are we eating in or going out?"

"In, but it'll be catered. Today, you're going to see Midtown and Upper Manhattan. I'm going to take you to the Empire State Building. The view is spectacular, and then we'll walk back, taking everything in. Tomorrow we'll see Lower Manhattan and take a boat to the Statue of Liberty. My parents want to go with us, but then they'll leave us alone to walk the neighborhoods."

"What about synagogue tomorrow?"

"I'll go with my parents, and then we'll come back and pick you up around noon."

"Could I go with you?"

"Hello, Eugene, this is Ben. Your Sarah has grown up to be a beautiful woman. She and her boyfriend just left."

"Thank you for seeing them on such short notice. Will you be able to help?"

"Yes, I think so. I'll pass along to her the same news I've been giving you over the past few months. Can she handle it?"

"I'm sure she can. How did you find Paul?"

"That one is perceptive. He has a handle on what is occurring in Israel at this moment. I found him to be very interesting. Your daughter is quite taken with him, I'd say."

"She is. It worries Susan, but I have to tell you, I like him very much."

"He's as aware of the events over there as any Jewish boy I know. Are they planning to get married?"

"I don't know, Ben, but they have become mates for now, that's for sure."

"I watched them closely while they were here. He's very kind and gentle to her. Very protective. When I asked him if there would be war, he didn't want to answer for fear of scaring Sarah. She could do worse."

"Thanks again, Ben. I'll be in touch."

"Shalom."

"Well, Paul, what did you like best today?" asked Mrs. Phillips. The lamb-based dinner had been the best he had ever experienced, and the wine was taking its toll. The conversation focused on the Phillips's family history and the current events of the Middle East. Sarah had been right; there were no questions about their relationship, or hints either parent disapproved of it. Paul could not figure out whether Mrs. Phillips was accepting him or whether she was simply keeping her feelings in check. Regardless, he was relieved to the point where he had become comfortable in the Phillips's presence.

"That's a hard question. I saw so much that I just have never seen in my entire life, sort of like a kid in a candy store. Maybe, though, it was the art museums."

"You visited more than one?"

"Yes, ma'am. Sarah took me into both the Metropolitan and the Guggenheim. I was amazed at the European painters."

"Paul was really taken by the Impressionists at the Met and by the Picassos at the Guggenheim. We didn't have time to stay long enough to see it all. I just knew he would like those exhibits."

"What else did you see, Paul?" asked Eugene.

"Just the whole aura of New York. The skyscrapers, the shops, the various groups of people, the subway. It's obviously so different from Denver. Even the smells."

"Mother, Paul wants to attend services with us tomorrow."

"Planning to convert?" Mrs. Phillips' question caught the others off guard momentarily, but she smiled and winked. "I'm only teasing. We would be happy to have you as our guest. Eugene can loan you a kipah."

Paul did not understand the term, and it showed in his face.

"A skullcap," said Sarah as she put her hand on his forearm for reassurance. She was most pleased by her mother's response, and she reached in the opposite direction and took her mother's hand. "Paul, my parents have a surprise for you tomorrow." Paul looked over to Dr.

Phillips, who was relaxed. Sarah continued, "Tell him, Mother."

"We are going to take you to the theater," she said.

Paul wanted to ask what had changed, but he knew somehow it was the wrong question at the wrong time. "I have a gift for you, from my family. My dad's had it for over twenty years and has been uncomfortable with it. It's in my suitcase. If you'll excuse me for just a minute."

A week earlier at a kibbutz in the Hula Valley in extreme northeastern Israel, an Israeli farmer, while mending a fence, was wounded by Arabs operating out of Syria. On the evening of April 20, that same Arab unit crossed over the border a few miles to the north and staked out a position on a hill that overlooked Kibbutz Shamir. From there they watched the movements of the men and women as they completed their chores and prepared for Shabbat.

"John! Robert! The sun is down, and you need to be at the house," the man called as he stood at the door of the greenhouse. Abraham Mandel turned to the east, in the direction of the Golan, in the direction of the noise he thought he heard.

Dinner in New York ended around nine. Sarah and Paul took a cab to the Empire State Building to see the city at night. They did not return until two-thirty.

Saturday, April 22

"You didn't understand much of that, did you?" asked Sarah as they exited the synagogue. It was more of a statement than a question, and she said it in a manner to comfort him and relieve him of any apprehension.

"No, not much, but I'm still glad I came. How long do I wear this cap?" Paul removed it from his head when she held out her hand, then ruffled his own hair. "I expected more Hebrew."

"We don't use it much in the Reform services."

"Don't girls get to go up and read the prayers?"

"No."

"That was longer than any Christian service I ever attended."

Susan and Eugene caught up with them after speaking with Rabbi Silver. "Do you see what we Jews have to endure, Paul?" joked Dr. Phillips.

"We'll need to hurry just now," warned Mrs. Phillips. "Our boat reservations are for 1:00."

"The Grand Lady will wait for us," said Eugene.

For Paul the Statue of Liberty was everything Dr. Orr said it would be. He and Sarah began their trek around Lower Manhattan around three-thirty, starting at Battery Park.

"Be back by seven, dear. Our reservations are for eight-thirty." Sarah's parents took a cab home.

"Chinatown and Greenwich Village first, my dear. One out of every seven people you'll see today will be a Jew. On this island I'm among my people." She looked straight ahead. "And with you here, I'm complete." She hooked her arm in his, kissed him on the cheek, and started pulling him up Broadway.

Sunday, April 23

It was crowded around the Garrity dinner table on Sunday evening when Paul and Sarah returned from New York.

"Mr. Garrity, tell me about how you came into possession of the shofar. My parents were touched." Sarah wiped a touch of gravy from the corner of her mouth.

"It was just one of those war souvenirs soldiers pick up. The war was almost over, and my unit had just captured Leipzig. Late April if I remember right. Anyway, we were using a house to sleep in, a bombed-out place mostly, but warmer than the ground. Pass me another piece of roast beef there, Dan." Everyone continued to eat as Mr. Garrity recounted a single wartime event, but nobody spoke. "Some of the guys were clearing out a single room, and the horn was under some rubble, so I took it. It was an interesting piece, with the carvings. I knew it was Jewish from the Star of David." He paused, looking at his plate and not at the people seated around the table. "We weren't supposed to take bootie, but we all kept something. Knives, pistols, artifacts of all kinds. I just put it away when I came home with a couple of other trinkets. I hadn't even thought about it until you and Paul were dating. When Paul told me you guys were going to New York, I decided your parents should have it." He ended his account with a matter-of-fact statement.

"I hope you don't mind, but my parents are going to give it to the rabbi at our synagogue. A shofar has special significance at some of our holidays."

"No, not at all. It was never mine to decide anyway, even though I had it for all these years. It needs to be where it belongs." He looked around the table. "Hey, there's a lot more food. Mose, if you're going to bang with Kansas next season, you've got to put some meat on those bones."

"Dad, Mose is too pretty to bang," said Paul.

"After dinner, on the driveway, Garrity. You and Dan."

"Sally and I have winners," said Sarah.

Sarah and the four residents of 1203 gathered for a few hours of study on Sunday night, but unlike most nights, there was no immediacy to their work. They relaxed and joked among themselves, and they generally made it difficult for Paul to catch up on his work and recent events.

"Your history professor's younger than I thought he'd be," noted Mose as he handed Paul the lecture notes from Dr. Orr's two Friday classes. "Seemed like a nice guy though."

"Nice until you haven't done the readings for class, then he becomes your worst nightmare," said Paul.

Dan, who had been subdued most of the day, finally spoke. "Leadville had its first Vietnam death this week. The guy was just a year older than me. Graduated in '64."

"Did you know him?" asked Paul.

"Yeah, pretty well."

"We're sorry. What about? I mean specifically," said Sally.

"About me here in college with a deferment and him without the chance to go to college after high school. Worked in the mines for a year before he got drafted. His dad worked there all his life." Dan had his hands folded, and he was not looking at anyone in the room.

Paul bent the corner of his history text to mark his spot and then closed it. "It really isn't a fair war, is it?"

"My grandparents aren't rich, but they saved enough to send me here. It's always been assumed that I'd go to college and get my degree. But for someone like Bernie, the guy who was killed, he was headed for the mines." Dan paused. "I talked to him last fall. He was kind of looking forward to going into the Army, almost like an adventure, a way just to get out of Leadville. He wasn't worried or anything, and now he's coming back for good." Dan paused. "At least his body is."

"What's fair?" There was a bit of anger in Mose's question, and a hint of despair. No one spoke for a few moments.

"Fair is when at least a few college kids serve as grunts in the rice paddies," said Dan. He raised his eyes and looked at all three of his friends, ending with Sally.

Her eyes narrowed when she spoke. "Don't even think about it!" she said. "It's a stupid war, and you won't solve anything. You have Tracey and your grandparents and your future."

"Calm down, Sal. I'm not going anywhere." Dan was trying to reassure her.

Mose saw her anxiety and stepped in. "Hey, babe, we all have a date with graduation, so we'll be stayin' around here for at least a few more years. By then Paul will have figured out how to end the war."

"Yeah, I'll call McNamara tomorrow," said Paul.

Sally would have none of it. "I'm not kidding, Dan, and this is not a joke. You're not going!"

Sarah stayed mostly quiet, allowing Sally to make the argument to Dan about military service in a controversial war. Sarah's thoughts turned to Tracey. *What do wives or lovers do when their soldiers don't come back from war?*

Monday, April 24

"Good morning, Paul. How was your trip?"

Paul removed his coat and put it on the back of the chair. "Fabulous! What an amazing city! We walked all over Manhattan, went to the Statue of Liberty, and rode up to the top of the Empire State Building twice. I went to a synagogue, met Congressman Rosenthal, and saw the United Nations."

Orr could feel Paul's excitement. "What did the congressman have to say?"

"He promised to tell Sarah everything he knew. I'm not sure that he'll tell her everything, but she'll be able to call him whenever she feels the need. Her dad said he'd pay the phone bill."

"What was he like?"

"The congressman or Sarah's dad?"

"The congressman."

Paul laughed. "He was the exact image I had of him before I ever saw him. Very Jewish looking. Short, very well dressed, non-stop talker, but funny. And he was polite."

"Did you get any idea of his connections?"

"He had pictures in his office with him standing with each of the last three presidents, one with Ben-Gurion, another with Eshkol, and a group picture with some other congressmen while in Israel. It was curious because Sarah's father arranged the meeting. I have this feeling he's privy to all the information coming out of Israel too."

"Did you sleep? When I've been in New York, it seems as though I never slept."

"The place just starts going after ten. We didn't eat dinner until after eight either night." Paul and Dr. Orr exchanged experiences about New York for the minutes that remained of their morning meeting before the professor noticed the time.

"Ready for class?"

"Yeah. Thanks for the notes. Yours are more complete than the ones I take in class," said Paul.

Paul completed his Cold War exam early and knew he did well. He chose to answer the essay about the Sino-Soviet border conflict and what it meant to a united communist front. He had a few extra minutes to wait at the UMC before Sarah arrived, time to read the newspaper. The *CU Daily's* lead story was the continuing bombing in North Vietnam.

"Every day!" Paul muttered under his breath. "Every damn day!" In the Senate J. William Fulbright was critical of the war, but General Westmoreland was complaining the protestors back home were hampering the war effort by giving encouragement to the communists. "The general says that publicly. I wonder what he says privately." Paul hoped there was greater coverage on both stories in the *Camera*. Philly lost the fifth game of the NBA playoffs but still led three games to two. He wondered if tonight's game was on TV.

"Hey, lover, sorry I'm late." Sarah gave him an extra strong hug and a kiss that made the surrounding students take note. "How did you do on your test?"

"Good, I think. Dr. Orr gave us a choice of questions to answer instead of just one. He avoided any Middle East questions, so I wouldn't set the curve."

She took his arm, and they walked to the Grille. "Passover starts today. The house is having a Seder tonight, and I want you to go with me."

"Okay. What time?"

"It starts at sundown, but you should probably be there around five-thirty. It'll be kind of long because of the ceremony. I also know your NBA game is on tonight."

"It's okay. I'll at least catch the second half."

"You must love me," she smiled.

"Yeah, I must."

"The game's on tonight and you're going to a religious dinner with Sarah? You must really love that girl," kidded Mose.

"Yeah, I do," said Paul as he knotted his tie and headed over to the SDT house for the Passover Seder.

<u><Let all who are hungry come and eat.></u>

The SDT sisters and their guests entered the dining room and took their seats around an elaborately laid out table. Paul was amazed at the ritual involved with the meal and with the various foods being served. Periodically, questions were asked, and many of the sisters rose to respond. Paul understood the history of Passover, the exodus from Egypt to escape slavery, and he knew the readings from the *Haggadah* were meant to teach Jewish values. There were several glasses of wine.

<u><Do you separate yourself from the community?></u>

Sarah whispered to Paul that there would be another Seder tomorrow at the Hillel House for the community and the sisters were invited. The ceremony continued and a young boy got up from his chair and opened a side door of the dining hall.

<u><Next year in Jerusalem.></u>

The Seder ended with laughter and hugs and handshakes. Paul wondered if the dinner had been more elaborate because the sisters were away from home and needed a reminder. Throughout the evening, he watched Sarah, as he usually did, to get more clues to her essence, into her, dare he say, her soul. Tonight, she seemed more into the community of Passover rather than into the religious aspects.

There was still half an hour until tipoff.

Paul sat on the kitchen counter making SPU calls while the Warriors battled Philly. "Hello, this is Paul Garrity," he said reading off a card. "I talked to you during the World Affairs Conference about ending the war in Vietnam. The Student Peace Union will be holding a meeting on Wednesday at twelve-thirty in the UMC, room 206. You expressed interest in joining our group, so I hope you can attend. Do you have any questions?" He stopped calling when the fourth quarter began. The 76ers held on to win 125-122 for the NBA title.

"You owe us a pitcher," boasted Dan to Mose.

Sarah called about fifteen minutes after the game ended. "Hello," answered Paul.

"Hi. How's the calling going?" asked Sarah.

"I got a hold of over half the students who signed the petition. Most of them said they'd be there."

"I reminded the house about the meeting. I think you can count on a handful to show up. Who won the game?"

"Philly. Dan's all over Mose. Sally's trying to calm them both down."

"Busy day, huh?"

"Yeah. I haven't even read the paper, and I wanted to see what it said about Westmoreland's speech."

"You won't like it."

"It's our fault we're losing, huh," Paul said with a hint of anger.

"That's what he says."

"Shit!"

"What did you think about the Seder?"

"It was cool, really, even though the food was strange. I haven't had much time to contemplate the ritual though. I'll have some questions about it, you know."

"You always have questions. The Seder is all about questions. I think being a Jew is to ask questions. By the way, this is the longest we've gone without doing it since we first did it. Five days."

"But who's counting? We'll have some catching up to do."

"I'll be over after breakfast."

"Sars . . ."

"Yeah?"

"How have I done these past few days being a Jew?" Paul chuckled on his end.

"You've been the best Jewish boyfriend I've ever had, but you can go back to being a non-practicing Christian tomorrow."

"That's an easier role for me."

Tuesday, April 25

Art History. While Paul enjoyed learning something that was unknown to him prior to taking the class, it was still something foreign to him. Cubism. The Cezanne phase? Modifications and assimilations? Professor Augenstein was passionate about his art, which Paul liked, but the professor's description of Paris at the turn of the century made the lesson come to life. Another wonderful teacher.

A university professor. From Lakewood. Paul straightened up and tossed his head back. *Maybe . . . and Mose's assistant basketball coach too.*

The rain turned to snow by three-thirty when the last of the children left. Something was bothering Sarah, but she was separated from Paul during the afternoon, plus the kids demanded her attention, so he was not able to get it out of her. In his truck she showed him the letter.

"I talked with Congressman Rosenthal at noon, and he said skirmishes between the Jews up north and the Syrians occur almost weekly, but they're not much of a threat to peace. He said President Johnson was monitoring the events and felt comfortable Israel was secure. But I get this letter from Hannah today, after I talked with Rosenthal, and she paints an entirely different picture," said Sarah.

"Her letter was written in early April, just after that air battle with Syria. Do you think that has anything to do with her tone?" asked Paul.

"Probably, but I think more of it is the ongoing attacks. She told me a little about it over spring break but tried to stay optimistic. Her letter, let me see it. Here. <*We all want to go to war with the Arabs, expecialy Syria.*> The public is anxious to go to war. It's Eshkol who's holding us back, and it's LBJ who's pulling his strings!"

"That's pretty harsh." He took the letter from her hand. "Is Hannah afraid?" he asked.

"She's sabra, but she worries about her little brother and sister, and she can't talk with Martin as often as she'd like."

"If they fight Syria, they'll have to fight Egypt."

"I wish I could bring them back to America!"

"Then who fights?" Paul asked as he reached over and took her hand.

Paul finally had the time to read the newspapers, first Monday's and then Tuesday's. *What a couple Sarah and I are*, he thought. *We both have these crusades, when we should just be enjoying college and each other.*

Sally walked in. "Hey, babe, I just got your note. Can I use your phone?" Sally patted him on the top of his head. "Did you see where Governor Love signed the abortion bill? I guess that letter I wrote him made the difference." Paul seemed to be in another zone, so she called Planned Parenthood.

Mose strolled in wearing his coat. "Let's go eat. I'm starved." He put his arm around Sally and pretended to listen in on her conversation.

Paul mouthed the words "Planned Parenthood."

Mose leaned into the mouthpiece and said, "I'm not the father."

Sally slapped at him and turned away. "Never mind, just one of the little boys who lives around here." She listened. "I can come in tomorrow." She listened again. "I will. Thank you. Goodbye." She hung up the wall phone and spun around with a smile. "I got it!"

The four residents of the second floor of 1203 were sprawled out studying when Sarah arrived at nine. She joined Paul on the couch and pulled out her sociology text. She read for only about ten minutes before closing the book and laying her head on his lap. "Wake me in twenty minutes." Paul stroked her head and then left his hand on her shoulder.

A few minutes later, Sally got up and got a blanket from the bedroom and covered Sarah. "What you said the other day, Paul, you're right. She's exhausted and fragile. What're you going to do?"

Paul stroked her hair again gently, and without looking up said in a whisper, "Ride it out, Sally, and look out for her. She'll get through it." He paused. "I'm not sure about the fragile part though."

Wednesday, April 26

Cohen was wired, so much so that Sarah suspected he had taken something, but Paul did not think Cohen used anything stronger than marijuana, although he smoked a lot of that. No, he was just on a power rush.

"Hey, Cohen, great turnout!"

"Hey, Garrity. Sarah. I've counted over 60 so far, and they're still filing in. Come up front with me."

"No, I'll stand here at the door and greet them and then lock the doors. It's your baby."

Cohen moved to the front of the room, which had a single riser and a podium. He got right to the point and was blunt. "The war in Vietnam is wrong! LBJ and Wastemoreland must be stopped, and only we can do it! You and me!" The applause started early along with the cheers. "We're children of privilege, and so far, we've been exempt from the fighting, but our time is coming! More importantly, America's reckoning is coming! We're fighting for the soul of America!" He had a supportive audience, and he had connected early.

Sarah leaned over to Paul's ear. "I never thought I'd say this, but he's doing well. Did you coach him?"

"Actually, we did talk on the phone last night about what he was going to say. We only expected about 30 or 40 people. Maybe CU is finally waking up."

Cohen was yelling now. "The bombing goes on every day, 77 tons in March! The totals will be higher for April, and those bombs, 3,000 pounds per minute, are killing women and children, people who have never carried a gun and who will never threaten us here in America, here in Boulder! But the war machine tells us they're communists, so we have to kill 'em! For how long?" The room erupted. "We must end this immoral war now! We must do our part here in Boulder! We can't be bystanders to this crime!" Cohen could no longer be heard above the crowd.

Paul wondered what those close to him would think if they attended this meeting. Dan Savage. His high school baseball coach. His dad. The anti-war protest in Boulder, Colorado, was at a crossroads on April 26, 1967, and Paul thought he knew which direction it was heading. It made him very uncomfortable.

"How was the meetin', Che?" Mose was sunning himself on the porch when Paul arrived home just after four.

"Scary," said Paul. "John Cohen screaming in front of about 70 students, telling them the time for peaceful protest was over."

"They didn't take him seriously, did they?" asked Mose.

"That's what was scary. They did."

Another study evening. Dan helped Sarah with her trig at the table, while Paul reviewed some of the important foreign policy decisions concerning the Mideast. Sally read Tuesday's *Camera* about the governor's signing of the abortion bill, then started on Wednesday's edition.

"How long can the government keep the truth about President

Kennedy's murder covered up? Says here that Garrison guy in New Orleans can prove it was the CIA."

"LBJ had to have helped, along with the military." Mose finally stirred from his meditative state. "Nobody in government thought Kennedy was tough enough to handle the Soviet Union."

"Too many coincidences for just Oswald to have done it," said Sally.

"Think we'll ever find out?" Paul asked.

"Nobody can keep that secret hidden forever in America," said Sally again.

"We'll never know for sure," said Dan. "It might as well be Oswald by himself. Some secrets stay secret."

"Hello, Sars."

"Hi, lover. There's a lot going on in our world, isn't there."

"The world's world or the 1203 world?"

"Both. They aren't inseparable."

"FAC this Friday?"

"Yeah, good plan. You know I love dancing with you."

"It's a date then."

"It was good to be with you again, you know, naked."

"Yeah. Very good!"

"Goodnight, my dear. Will you be going to bed soon?"

"Probably stay up for a while. Got some thinking to do. Sleep tight, Sars"

It wasn't Vietnam that Paul was thinking about or the JFK assassination or Israel's war plans. Dr. Orr had alluded to the forgotten people in any war, the civilians who were caught in the middle. He was referring to the Vietnamese, but as a sidebar, he included the Arabs of the West Bank and Gaza—the Palestinians. Paul thought it curious that his professor had named them. "Palestinians." Sarah, Rosenthal, and the newspapers always said "Arabs" and lumped them together with Egyptians, Syrians, Jordanians, and Lebanese. Again referring to the Vietnamese, Dr. Orr asked the class, "Who protects these people?"

Paul sat down at his table and made a rough sketch of Israel and its Arab neighbors. He drew arrows from each Arab capital extending them into Israel. Syria's arrow passed through the Golan Heights, Egypt's through the Sinai, Jordan's through the West Bank. Israel was surrounded, but so were the Palestinians. If those arrows were reversed, Israel's forces would have to pass through the lands inhabited by Palestinians. *Do the Palestinians have an army? Who is their leader?* Understandably, the media's focus was on Israel's plight, but was there something Paul was missing, invisible civilians caught in the middle who had no protector?

Paul dropped his pen onto his crude map and stretched out his shoulders. *Go to bed, dummy. This is way too complex for this late.*

Thursday, April 27

The temperature hit 70 degrees on Thursday, and the students' clothing reflected the warmer weather. Sarah shielded her eyes from the glare of Paul's ultra-white legs when she met him at lunch, but his were not the only ones. Hundreds of others were in shorts. Mose extended his afternoon run to 75 minutes and altered his route to take him along Canyon Boulevard west into the foothills. Dan cut his afternoon lab short to watch the Buffs baseball team take on Oklahoma State. Paul and Sarah supervised an hour and a half kickball game at the Lab School. Only Sally missed out on the warm afternoon, spending an hour at Planned Parenthood and three hours at her job at the florist shop.

That evening all five seemed to have been refreshed from their activities as they settled in for a group study session. Each had sufficient homework to stay busy, even Mose, who usually seemed to have the least amount of homework. Still, he carried a 2.4 gpa and had never failed a class at CU.

"Tracey's coming down here this weekend," said Dan.

"What about her little sister?" asked Sally.

"Nope, quiet weekend in Leadville—no weddings, no funerals. Tracey isn't needed, and since our weather is supposed to hit 80 this weekend, she decided to come down here."

"You haven't given any more thought to dropping out and joining the Army, have you?" It was obvious Sally had not forgotten Sunday's discussion.

Sarah looked from Sally to Dan. "What's this?"

"Nothing!" said Dan. "We were just talking about how Vietnam is unfair, and Sally made the giant leap that I was ready to grab a rifle and head to Nam."

"You aren't, are you?" asked Sarah.

"Leave it alone, Sally. We'll all do what we have to." Dan stared straight into Sally's eyes. "When you're called, you answer."

She was not convinced. "It's not so far-fetched, you know."

"I ain't surrenderin' my draft deferment," said Mose. "In fact, I'm thinking about having 2-S tattooed on my chest over my heart."

Friday, April 28

It seemed to Sarah that she fell in love with Paul all over again every FAC. He was always energized and touchy, and his attention was completely focused on her. There was no Vietnam or Galilee or Mississippi at Tulagi's. There was only Sarah in his thoughts.

After FAC and a quick burger on The Hill, they walked back to 1203 for the drive over to the Timber Tavern. Mose picked up a date: a tall, dark-haired freshman who was at the Tule with her dorm mates from Farrand Hall. Sarah quickly made her feel like she was one of the group. Being from Salida, just 50 or so miles south of Leadville, she shared some common acquaintances with Tracey.

The jazz group Super Boogie was playing at the Tavern, a club which tended to attract an older crowd, as opposed to the bars on The Hill or the Honey Bucket. Mose knew two of the four members of the band, so he briefly chatted with them while the guitarist went off on his own for a four-minute solo.

"Are you guys couples, or did you sort of hook up like Mose and me?" asked Marti.

It was Tracey who answered her. "Danny and I are planning to get married soon and those two should be." Neither Paul nor Sarah flinched, but under the table their hands squeezed each other's thighs.

"When?" asked Marti.

"We haven't set a date. They'll probably wait until they graduate. Everyone here is a sophomore except me. I'm still a high school babe."

"Isn't beer wonderful," said Dan. "Three hours at the Tule and she'll tell anyone everything." He gave her a kiss.

Mose returned with a pitcher and six glasses. "First one's on the house."

The group of six quickly broke up into three separate couples with their own agendas. Tracey caught Danny up on the events in Leadville, especially with her little sister. Mose and Marti, which had "a nice ring," according to Paul, made small talk to find common ground, and Paul and Sarah went off to slow dance in a corner, one of their favorite activities. Sarah believed they communicated better in that position.

"We haven't discussed marriage in over a month," whispered Sarah while they danced.

"Doesn't mean I haven't thought about it though."

"After graduation sound about right to you?" she teased.

"Can we wait that long?"

Saturday, April 29

Sally answered Paul's phone on Saturday morning while she was drinking coffee and reading the paper. It was Sarah. "He's out in the garage working on something for the apartments. Do you want me to get him?"

"No, I'm stopping by on the way to services. How'd your date go last night?" asked Sarah.

"Really well. He was a gentleman, and the show was pretty good."

"What did you see?"

"*Hurry Sundown*. Then we went over to Bennett's afterwards to listen to Achilles and Frank. I think we'll go out again. He asked me for tonight, but I told him to call me this afternoon. I didn't know if you guys had anything planned for tonight."

"Paul's parents want to take us all to dinner, including you. Bring your new beau. What's his name?" asked Sarah.

"James. Do Paul's parents think I'll be with Mose?"

"I think Mose might bring Marti, so it won't matter. Just call James and bring him. This will be a first. The first time all of us have a date. It'll be fun!"

"Okay. See you soon." Sally hung up the phone and wondered about her relationship with Mose. Maybe it was a good thing they each were dating another.

The two new additions at the dinner party had different personalities. James Martin was a quiet gentleman, just as Sally had described him. He was tall, not quite as tall as Mose, but taller than either Dan or Paul, big boned like a football guard, and blondish, and he had impeccable manners. Quick to smile but hesitant to speak except when addressed, James was reserved and attentive to Sally. He was a junior, majoring in music, and hoped to be a band director at a high school in a few years. "A suburban school, where they have money enough for lessons and uniforms."

Marti Wilson chewed gum during dinner and asked lots of questions. Her laugh could be heard throughout The Lamp Post, a rather upscale restaurant on Arapahoe and 28th, and there were plenty of opportunities to laugh. Each time she did, she would cover her mouth and turn either towards Mose or Tracey. Despite some youthful quirks, the 1203 gang warmed up to her. Mose seemed amused by her behavior and by the goofy remarks about him and his date from Dan and Paul. Diane Garrity went out of her way to make James and Marti feel welcome.

James had not said much during the meal. Finally, during a lull he asked Mose about Ali's decision to refuse induction on religious purposes, claiming to be a Black Muslim preacher. Paul's eyes went quickly to his dad who had already dropped his head slightly and set his jaw. Paul swung to Mose, hoping to head him off, but he had turned towards James. Paul knew if Mose said what he really thought, all hell could break loose.

"Ali has every right to refuse to be drafted. Not only is he a minister, but he's a black man, a proud black man. He's the Olympic champion and the heavyweight champ. Why the hell does America need for him to go to Vietnam?" Mose wanted to say more, but Mr. Garrity broke in.

"He's a goddamn coward, that's what he is! America's been good to him. Doesn't matter who you are or what you've done. When your country's at war, you serve!" Dick Garrity was smoldering, holding this issue inside too long. He was not only speaking about Ali. "Cassius Clay!" he said with contempt, "and every other man who's called should go." The table was silent, and Paul thought the issue might pass. He was wrong.

"I agree with Mose," said Marti. "It's a free country and you shouldn't have to go if you don't want to." Paul cringed.

"You're damn right it's a free country, and how do you think it got that way?" Mr. Garrity's eyes bored in on Marti as he leaned forward over his plate of meatloaf. "Because men fought. Little boys stayed home."

"Dad!" Paul interrupted. "That's enough. We all disagree with you at this table, and this'll do nothing except ruin dinner. Let's just drop it!" Again, the table grew silent.

"I agree with you, Mr. Garrity." Dan's voice was quiet but assured. "Lots of men have disagreed with every war America has ever fought, but it doesn't matter. Maybe you'll get lucky and not get called, but if you're drafted, you go. It's that way for poor people in America, and it ought to be that simple for famous people and college students like us." Dan lifted his head and seemed to be directing his words to Paul and Mose. He swallowed hard and continued. "Oppose the war, protest it, march at rallies. You have those rights. But when the time comes, you stand up like a man and do your duty." This was the position Dan had been grappling with for over a year, but now he spoke with conviction, as if he had made his decision. He ended his words with his eyes on Paul.

Beneath the table, Sarah's hand squeezed Paul's thigh. *Not here*, she thought. *Not now.*

"You think this is easy?" Paul was hurt. He turned to his dad. "You fought against Hitler and fascism. Granddad went to World War I. I'm a former Boy Scout. But this is Vietnam. It makes no sense, and it makes no difference!" His voice was rising. "We continue to fight because someone made a bad decision, and LBJ doesn't want to be the first president to lose a war!" He looked directly at his father. "You can't stand Johnson, yet you support his war. I liked what he was doing, but I hate his war. Where's the sense in all this?"

Dick Garrity seemed to have heard nothing from his son. "Your country is at war, son, so you fight. If you don't, you're a coward." His words stunned Paul, whose eyes stayed fixed on his dad's.

"Paul is no coward, Mr. Garrity, and neither he nor Mose is a boy." Sarah was fighting tears. "And if you think they are, well, you're just plain wrong."

Marti raised her hand like she was a student in class and then spoke softly. "This sounds like the fights we used to have over dinner at my house, between my dad and my brother. They'd yell at each other about the bombing or the draft or something, and neither one would give in. Nothing my mom or I said could stop them. Now my brother never comes home anymore. Sad. I miss him."

Nobody apologized, not even Mrs. Garrity, who knew better than to broach the subject again, and only James and Dan thanked Mr. Garrity for dinner. They left just as they had come, in three cars: Paul's parents back to Lakewood, Dan and Tracey with Sally and James, and Mose, Marti, Sarah, and Paul, who was driving Sarah's Corvair. He had been wounded.

As he turned off Canyon Boulevard south onto Broadway, Paul finally broke the silence. "You okay, Marti?" he said softly.

"Yeah, what the hell was that all about?" she asked.

Mose answered for Paul. "Vietnam. World War II fathers and their Vietnam-era sons. Mostly me not remembering when to shut the fuck up."

"Wasn't your fault, Mose. He was ready to blow for some reason. James's question just lit the fuse."

"God, did it!" said Marti. "He scared me."

"We probably should go talk to Dan," said Paul. "He'll think he's to blame."

"He is partly to blame," said Sarah. "Sally's going to need to talk too. She just adores your parents, but I know she's on your side." Sarah turned in her seat so she could see Mose. "The three of you are her heroes."

"Some hero. A coward," muttered Paul.

"Fuck, Garrity! I don't wanna hear that shit!" Mose put his hand on Paul's shoulder. "If you believed in what America was doing in Vietnam, you'd give up your deferment and go."

"He's right, my dear. If you thought you could make a difference, you'd go."

Dan and Sally were sitting in Paul's room waiting for him. Sally went to Paul and hugged him tightly without saying anything. Dan stood behind her.

"Sorry, man, I really am." Dan's eyes met Paul's.

They drank coffee and pop and discussed what had just happened and the subject that they had talked about for a year and a half. But this night there was no bluster or positioning. It was emotional, but without loud voices or swear words. Mostly Paul and Dan spoke, each expressing his fears and convictions.

"It's just not good foreign policy. If you can get away from all the talk about morality or military tactics and just concentrate on the decision to stop communism in that area of the world, I believe it will turn out as a bad decision." Paul held his Coke in both hands.

"Was the help we gave to Europe after the war bad? Was it wrong to support South Korea? It's a new type of war with new strategies. Who's to say which countries we defend against communism? I'm certainly not going to make the call."

"Vietnam's no threat to us. Even if there was some proof, which I haven't seen, the domino theory just seems like our attempt to prevent China from having its sphere of influence. We have one, why can't they?"

"Because we've learned since Lenin that communism is expansive. The lessons of appeasement from Munich and Hitler." Dan surprised the group with his details.

"I can see the time before this war is over when maybe 20,000 US soldiers have been killed, and nothing will have changed. We can't give them stability forever, and we can't expect Ho and the NVA to ever give up." Paul was not thinking about his dad's accusations.

"Why not?" challenged Dan. "Bring enough pressure to bear, and they'll negotiate. But we need soldiers on the ground to maintain the South." Dan paused because he was remembering Paul's dad.

James spoke quietly. "There's so much out there to prove each of your sides. It's tough to know who's telling the truth. I don't think the US is inherently bad for wanting to protect that part of the world from communism, but I sometimes wonder if that's our true motive. What if this war is just being waged to make money for the munition's makers?"

"Some people will always get rich during war. It happens, but when did we stop trusting our leaders?" It was a serious question, but then Dan laughed. "Hell, Paul, you're the guy who believes in big government with the Great Society. Doesn't that imply you trust those guys?"

Around twelve-thirty Sarah called Mrs. Meyer and was granted an extension of the curfew. When she hung up the phone, she did not return to her place beside Paul on the green chair but sat on the floor against the wall next to Sally.

"All of your reasons against the war make sense to me," continued Dan, "but you could be wrong. I know you've thought about that."

Paul swallowed hard. "Believe me, I know. My opposition to the war has more to do with helping people in America rather than the Vietnamese, even though I do think the bombing campaign is immoral. And if I'm wrong, all my apologies will sound hollow. People will think I was just scared to go or whatever they want. I can live with that. But what if America is wrong? Who will we apologize to?"

Mose stood. "I've gotta get Marti home. Sarah, can I drop you off too?"

"No, I'm staying for a while longer." She noticed the looks of concern. "That's who I was just talking to. My housemother said it was okay."

James stood to say goodbye to Marti, and he apologized to Mose for opening Pandora's Box at dinner. Mose would have none of it. As he led Marti out the door and down the steps, he ordered the gang to lighten up the conversation before he got back.

James left shortly thereafter, and Dan explained to Paul that when he said, "stand up like a man," it was just a figure of speech. Paul understood and tried to brush it aside.

"No," Dan persisted, "I'm sorry."

Before he could continue, Paul cut him off. "I know you think I'm smart and wonderful and brave, so leave it there. Just drop it, okay?"

Dan nodded and pulled Tracey off the couch. "All right. Been a long night. We'll get out of here, so you guys can lighten up for a while." His left hand took hold of Tracey's right, and he led her to the door. With his right he shook Paul's hand. "As long as you believe it, don't back down," and then he nodded.

As she passed Paul, Tracey leaned in and kissed him on the cheek and whispered in his ear. "That part about 'smart and wonderful and brave.' I think it's true. It's very hard to stand against your own father."

Sarah rang the doorbell of the SDT house at two in the morning.
"Will you be okay?"
"I've got you, don't I?" said Paul.
"Forever and ever."
"Then I'll be good."
"I love you."
Mrs. Meyer opened the door in her housecoat and smiled.

Sunday, April 30

Diane Garrity called early to ask Paul to drive down and attend church with her.

Sarah noticed just after noon that Paul was holding something in, that he wasn't focused on his work. He wasn't turning pages in his history text or amending his class notes. She rose from the table and stood over him at the couch.

"What?" he asked looking up.

She reached down and removed the book from his lap, then straddled his thighs. She stared into his eyes, leaned in to kiss his forehead, and then put a finger where she kissed him. "What's going on in there that you're keeping so secret?" She waited for him.

"I didn't get any sleep last night and . . ." he paused and looked down. Before returning to Sarah's eyes, he placed his hands on her thighs. "I drove home this morning and went to church with my mom. Then we went to breakfast to talk about what went on last night. My dad and I hurt her last night. Bad. I hadn't even thought about her in all of this, but she just broke down at breakfast. My dad rants about Ross a lot, and now she has me to worry about. She said she couldn't handle it if he and I were in mortal combat over politics. She didn't think my dad would let it go on his own. Basically, she was pleading with me to somehow make peace with him." Paul breathed out slowly.

In a moment Sarah took his hands and kneaded their fingers together. "Do you remember what Marti said as she was leaving last night, about the breakup of her family over Vietnam? You can't allow this to happen to yours."

"I'm not sure my dad will listen to anything I have to say."

Sarah jerked his hands. "You have to make him listen! You can do this." She set her jaw and challenged Paul with her eyes. "What happened at dinner happens all over the country. Your damn war is a man's war that hurts families. Your mother is just saying what mothers are saying all over America, and you have to make peace with the family. Otherwise, it will fester in our hearts for years to come, and we may never heal."

Sally walked in after a single knock carrying a notebook and a small stack of three-by-five cards. "Oh, God. Are you two moving towards sex already?"

Sarah smiled and then peeled off of Paul. "You know I'm always moving in that direction, Sal, but Paul is so focused on his history that I get nowhere." She handed Paul his textbook and went back to the table.

"Hello."

"Hi. Your line was busy."

"It was Marti and Mose. We may have some competition for the phone."

"I think not. This is our special time. You're the landlord. Install another phone for Mose."

"What'd you think about tonight?" asked Paul.

"Dinner or making love?"

"Dinner. I always know how you feel about the sex. You don't hide your feelings about that," said Paul.

"I hope I never do." She laughed. "Dinner was fun! A lot better than last night! Marti's kind of gullible, huh."

"Yeah. It takes a little pressure off me though. What about James?"

"I like him, especially for Sally. He's so nice to her. What did you think?"

"Sally was in to talk after you left. She said she hasn't had sex since she's been in Boulder, and she wanted to go slow with James. She hoped he'd be patient with her," said Paul.

"Did you tell her that not everybody jumps into bed on the first date like we did?" Sarah smiled on her end.

"Yeah, something like that."

"But she likes him, doesn't she?" asked Sarah.

"Yeah. She complimented you . . . said she hopes she can act like you towards whoever she falls in love with."

"What did she mean? How do I act?"

"She didn't elaborate, but she's always thought you were pretty cool," said Paul.

"I like having people think we're getting married. What Sally said touched me. You were really quiet for the rest of the evening, but very touchy."

"Yeah."

"Yeah, what?"

"Yeah, I was quiet and touchy."

"What else?" asked Sarah.

"Taking care of you . . . for a lifetime . . . would be an awesome responsibility. I look at the picture of you on my dresser, where you're looking directly at me from behind your hair and I'm humbled. You're not like Tracey or Sally or my mom, and I don't know if simple love is enough. You have this will, something that's been awakened in you, and you've just scratched the surface of what's to come. It's power-ful." Paul paused. "No, you're not going to graduate and become a housewife."

"It's because of you, you know."

"No, well, yeah, I've played a part, maybe even speeded up the process. But it's something else."

"I want you with me." Sarah's voice was soft.

"It might happen, but . . ."

"Shhh." Neither spoke, but Paul could feel Sarah's tears on the other end of the phone. After several moments passed, Sarah spoke very quietly. "It could happen though?"

"Yeah, Sars, it could," he said.

"I've felt it too. It scares me a little."

"It's part of what makes you so intriguing to me, and I won't be a part of holding you back in any way."

"So, I can't just be a passenger on the train? I've got to get off?"

"Yeah."

"You're not afraid of what I'm becoming, are you?"

"I worry because you'll have some bumps and difficult times, and you can be so sensitive, but I believe in you."

"You're so good to me," Sarah said with a sniffle.

"No shit. I try."

"You're a toad, you know, but I love you so much."

"And I you."

"Goodnight, my dear."

"Goodnight, Sars.

MAY

Monday, May 1

"Good morning, Paul. What happened to summer?"

Paul slipped his coat over the back of the chair, stuffed his stocking cap into one sleeve, and took a step over to the coffee pot. "We were playing softball in tee-shirts yesterday, and now they're predicting snow again for tonight. As my granddad always says, 'Ah, springtime in Colorado.'" Paul dropped two sugar cubes into his cup and sat down.

"So where does our war in Vietnam fit into the whole Cold War package? I know you are working with the SPU to protest it, but does it have a place in the wider area of our foreign policy?"

Paul smiled and thought about the previous two days before answering Dr. Orr. "There are the arguments for containment and the domino theory, that America can't allow communism to spread unchecked. First, there was containment of Soviet expansion, but clearly this is not a Soviet driven war. Are we containing Chinese expansion? I have a hard time believing the Vietnamese aren't more concerned about Chinese imperialism over the long run than US control. Both the Soviet Union and China have interests in Indochina and are supplying Vietnam with weapons, but I still think the war is Vietnamese driven and always has been. It's an anti-colonial war at heart. As for the domino theory, with Vietnam being the first domino, I think that's overblown. So, what if Southeast Asia is controlled by the communists, if that's their sphere of influence so to speak? I don't believe it has a chance to spread into Australia or Japan or west into India."

"If it's this clear to college students, why can't the President and his advisors see it?" Dr. Orr's sarcasm was seldom subtle. He smiled.

Paul laughed. "Damned if I know. Because they won't take my calls or answer my letters?" Dr. Orr laughed at that. Paul continued.

"Money, I think. The military-industrial complex. The economy depends upon it." Paul paused. "That's the SPU talking. I'm not an economist. I'd be delighted to be proven wrong on any of this."

"What if America just pulled out today? The President sees the light and brings the soldiers home. What message is sent to our allies?"

"Maybe that they better take care of their own house first, or that the US can admit to a mistake in a far corner of the globe, and we have more important regions to spend our money on, and there are more pressing issues at home."

"Such as civil rights?" asked Dr. Orr.

"Civil rights, the war on poverty, inner-city education. Yeah."

"How could Johnson and Humphrey be so right about the problems at home, so concerned about the issues addressed in the Great Society, and be willing to sacrifice them for this war 10,000 miles away?"

"I honestly don't know the answer to those questions," said Paul. "They inherited the war and can't let it go."

"I hope to grow old in Connecticut. Promise me you'll keep in touch over the years so we can see how this turns out, to see who's right, you or the President."

"Do you think we need to be fighting this war in Vietnam, Dr. Orr?"

"Paul, do we have to have a victory over there? Could we fight to a draw as we did in Korea and still achieve our Cold War aims?"

Paul smiled. "All I know is that I only have three more weeks to get you to answer just one of my questions in a definitive manner, without asking me a question in return."

"Ah, my young scholar, hope springs eternal."

Paul and Sarah walked directly to 1203 at noon so she could call Congressman Rosenthal. He took her call immediately.

"We're still seeing some raids in the northern areas, but there have been no casualties. The animosity among the Arab leaders works to our advantage, by that I mean Israel's advantage. King Hussein is being ostracized by the Egyptians and the feud works to prevent any war."

"But the continuing raids? My cousin said the farmers want a war, especially against Syria, to punish them for these raids."

"There will be no war. Egypt is too busy in Yemen, and Syria won't act without Egypt, despite the Soviet pressure. That won't happen. The raids are inconvenient, but they will not bring about a war," Rosenthal sounded convinced.

"Are the kibbutzniks safe?"

"Yes, Sarah. Certainly, there are risks, but these are brave men and women who have chosen their lifestyles. Each kibbutz is fenced in and has a security force. They know how to protect themselves."

Paul was listening to only one side of the conversation and trying to discern the answers from the expressions on Sarah's face. He wrote out a question for the congressman and slid it across the counter to Sarah. "Congressman, if war breaks out, and I know you're saying it won't, but if it did, could Israel be assured of American support?"

"America is a good friend, Sarah. If Israel is attacked by its neighbors, we will support her. Is there anything else?"

"No, sir. Thank you so much for taking my call. I know how busy you must be."

"You're so welcome. Say hello to Paul for me. Shalom."

Sarah hung up the phone slowly. Paul waited as she processed the information. He was always patient with her, especially regarding her views on Israel. He did not hold all of the same views, more like a blank slate about the Arab-Israeli conflict, but he had not tried to persuade her to a more balanced position.

"He doesn't trust me to hear the hard truth. He sugarcoats it."

"Why do you think he does that?" replied Paul.

"I don't know. Maybe it's because I'm a girl and must be protected." She looked past Paul. "I need to go over there to see what it's really like."

Tuesday, May 2

The children at the Lab School seemed subdued to Paul on Tuesday afternoon. Maybe it was because of the weather. All the university students enrolled in the course were there, no doubt to be sure they had the requisite number of appearances for credit. As a result, Paul was not needed, so he mostly hung around with Sarah. Mrs. Best once told him that Sarah ran her class with such efficiency that she did not need supervision, unlike the M-W section which required Mrs. Best's constant monitoring. "She could step into a school now and run it." Paul could envision the day when Sarah ran her own daycare center, a children's home for boys and girls from both sides of the track.

"Ready to go? I've got a bunch of homework tonight." Sarah took his hand and led him out the back door to his truck. "Goodbye, Mrs. Best. See you on Thursday."

That evening Paul read the *Camera* and watched Huntley-Brinkley while finishing off some leftover pizza. Sarah was coming over after seven to take him to Norlin for uninterrupted study. The news was the same. Heavy bombing of Hanoi, intense fighting for Hill 881 near the DMZ, Governor Romney criticizing the dissenters for driving a wedge between society, and Senator Hatfield maintaining dissent was not treason. "Coercing the public is the action of a tyrant." Paul knew he loved America, but he also believed it needed to be criticized for its current behavior. Every US war had its dissenters, its peaceniks. "Hell," he said under his breath, "Lincoln opposed the Mexican War."

The lead story in the *Camera* was about narcotics raids in Boulder in the Williams Village dorms and a local rooming house which resulted in five arrests. Paul knew the cops could raid the first floor of 1203 with similar results. The phone rang.

"Hello."

"Hello, Paul?"

"Yes?"

"Paul, this is Eugene Phillips. I'm trying to get in touch with Sarah."

"She's not here, sir, but I expect to see her later this evening. Can I take a message or have her call you?"

"Yes, if you would please."

"It'll be about seven or a little later."
"That would be fine. Thank you, Paul."
"Goodbye, Dr. Phillips."

When Paul returned from class, he noticed Sarah's Corvair illegally parked. He bounded up the stairs with his poly-sci book in one hand and a six-pack of beer in the other. "Sars! You need to move your car."

She was sitting at the table writing in a journal she had started as a record of the events in Israel. She quickly arose and hugged him tightly. "They shot at Uncle Abraham and the boys!"

"What? When?"

"The Syrians shot at my uncle about ten days ago. No one was hit, but they could have been." She was shaking. "They could have been killed. This has to stop." Sarah's body tensed.

"That's what your dad wanted to talk to you about? What are you going to do?"

"My father said he would keep me informed from now on, that I wouldn't need to talk to Rosenthal anymore. He'll tell me the truth without a filter."

Wednesday, May 3

May of 1967 would turn out to be Boulder's wettest May in history. The city received a trace of snow in the morning before warming to nearly 50 degrees in the afternoon. Sarah met Paul for lunch at the UMC wearing her customary jeans and jean jacket.

"I think I understand something, my dear." She leaned in for a kiss, putting her left hand on the back of his neck.

"It's about time. I'm getting a little tired carrying the load." He smiled, not letting her go.

"I'll bet Congressman Rosenthal keeps my father well informed because my father raises so much money for Israel and for his re-election campaign. He's always known about things in Israel as soon as they happened. I assumed my uncle kept him up to date, but he couldn't have, at least not right away. Only by knowing someone with government contacts could he have had the information so rapidly. And why would Rosenthal be so open with the news? Certainly not just because they were boyhood friends, but because my father provides big chunks of money."

"And you're now going to charm your dad for information, aren't you." Paul already saw Sarah's gears in motion.

"Boulder's an outpost. It's not New York or Washington, but my Jews at the house are going to be well-informed," she said. "But you've got to help me make sense of the events. Kay?"

Paul finally smiled back, took a step forward, and kissed her gently.

In Paul's room that evening, the mood was quiet, studious. The only interruption came when Dan and Sally wanted Mose to explain the Black Panthers' motives for taking guns into the Sacramento courthouse.

"Did I mention they were loaded?" Mose shook his head. "Those dudes aren't bluffing."

Thursday, May 4

Sarah was waiting for Paul in the hallway just outside of his Art History class in Hellems. "Lunch is on me—at The Sink. Don't give me that look. I aced the quiz in trig and got out early. It was over the exact stuff Dan helped me with last night."

"Are we drinking?" kidded Paul.

"No. Too early."

They hustled down the stairs and out the north doors, then headed west to The Hill. It was drizzling again. They paused at the window of the Audiophile to read the announcement for the release of the Beatles new album. "Next one for your collection." There was also a flyer for the Glenn Yarbrough concert on May 11 at Macky Auditorium. "I've already got tickets for us through the house. You'll have to sit in the Jewish section, though, because we bought a block of 30," kidded Sarah.

When they arrived at The Sink, the front booths were filled, but Paul asked a couple of guys to slide down at the counter so two stools would open up.

"Two burgers." Sarah removed her raincoat and gave it to Paul who hung it up by the door. "Funny," she said. "I really like this front part of The Sink, but I hate the back room, all the smoke and darkness." She let it go there and squeezed Paul's hand.

"Okay, I've been patient enough. What gives?" asked Paul.

"I talked with my father this morning, and he said I could spend the summer out here with you even if I don't go to school. I've been working on him for over a month. Pretty cool, huh!"

Paul rubbed his forehead. "Your mom? Does she know where you plan on living?" Then he smiled broadly and clenched his fist as he displayed his happiness at her plans for being with him throughout the summer.

The cook brought two cokes. "Burgers'll be up in a sec."

Sarah placed both hands on Paul's knees, which brought her body closer to his. "It's not without conditions, my dear. I have to go home for a couple of weeks when school's over, and I'll go home for a couple more weeks in late August, early September. But that's not all. I think my father wants to send me over for eight or ten days to visit my uncle. I want you to go with me."

The burgers arrived. They loaded them up with special sauce.

Paul had to ask again. "What does your mom say?"

"My father says he'll take care of her, and, yes, he knows where I'll be staying." She smiled. "In Dan's apartment." They both laughed at her joke. "He'll be sending the rent money to you at the end of this month for three months."

"He's got to know . . ."

"He does, but it's part of the ruse for my mother. It's a game, and we all know it, but it has to be played. All that matters is I'll be with you." They stared at each other for a brief moment and smiled. "Eat your burger, okay."

It was Mose who answered the phone just before midnight.

"Mose, it's Sarah. How come you answered? "Where's Paul?"

"He's downstairs talking with Cohen, somethin' about him getting arrested, so Paul's tryin' to get him out of it. You know Paul. He'll work out some kind a deal somehow."

"Mose, how's he doing . . . with his dad and all?"

"He hasn't talked much about it, but the same, I think. They've talked on the phone a couple of times about it, and I think that's helped."

"God, it must be so hard! We've talked a little bit. He just says it'll be okay. I don't know if I'm any help for him at all."

"You still don't get it, do you?" Sarah was quiet on her end. "Sarah. You don't have to do anything special for this. Just by being his woman, you do all that needs to be done. He knows that, whatever happens, he'll have you and me and Sally. "

"I know, but . . ."

Mose cut her off. "I'm not sure you do know. Yeah, he's hurtin', but he's gonna be okay. We're his family now, and that includes you." He paused, then confidently, "Yeah, Sarah, especially you."

Cohen took a deep drag from his Salem, tilted his head back, and blew two smoke rings toward the TV room's ceiling. "They were actually nice to me, Garrity. Polite even." He reached over to the ash tray on the coffee table and flicked his cigarette. "I thought I was gonna be arrested for drugs or something, but it never came up. Just asked about the Union and what we were planning. Wanted to know if we were a part of SDS." A thought occurred to him, and he smiled. "They asked about you too, you know."

Paul seemed surprised. "Me? Why me?"

"They see you as a leader, Garrity; had pictures of you building the booth. One even showed you hugging Sarah. Pretty radical stuff." Cohen laughed.

Paul thought for a moment before responding. "We're not SDS."

"They don't see a difference. We're all anti-draft, anti-war, anti-American communist sympathizers. Little anarchists."

"Shit, John! We're not anti-American!" Paul's attitude shifted from amusement about Cohen's predicament to anger. "It doesn't sound as if those guys were just Boulder cops." He was talking more to himself than to Cohen. "Anti-American. No way!"

Cohen remained irreverent. "What are we for then?"

Paul shook his head and smiled again. "Good question."

"Wanna smoke a joint?"

Paul grunted and shook his head no. "You're just trying to corrupt me, Cohen."

Both young men were quiet for a few minutes. Cohen finished his cigarette, while Paul contemplated what he had just said about who Cohen's interviewers were.

Cohen finally spoke. "Your mind is rolling again, Garrity. What is it?

"Are we focusing too much on the university and losing sight of the bigger picture?"

"What's the bigger picture, dude?"

"The war. The draft." Paul paused. "The government."

"Wake up, Garrity. ROTC and the research grants are the government. It's all bound together."

"Where's the dividing line?" Paul asked.

"Maybe there isn't one."

Paul let Cohen's statement sink in. "Gotta be for me." He got up from the couch and ran his left hand through his hair.

"Garrity . . ."

"Yeah."

"They want me to be a rat."

"A what?"

"An informant on the group. That's when they mentioned they knew I used drugs, almost like a threat. You might want to mention that to some of your renters."

Friday, May 5

One of the things Sarah liked most about 1203 was the quiet, spacious rooms on the second floor, especially compared to the cramped rooms and density of the SDT house. Often, she would bring her books over to Paul's apartment when he was not there and study alone. She could smell his presence. This place was not the sorority house, and it was not New York. It was a corner of Boulder she would always remember, the part of The Hill that she loved.

On this afternoon while Paul was at his lit class, she curled up in his puke green chair and covered herself with the orange and brown blanket to wait for him to return. Four inches of snow muted the sounds from The Hill, and she quickly fell asleep. She did not awaken when Paul returned at three forty-five. He hung up his coat after putting his books on the counter, got a slice of pizza from the fridge, and went out into the hall so as not to disturb her.

The landing at the top of the stairs leading into apartments 2A and 2B, Paul's and Mose's apartments, was a popular gathering spot. Mose climbed the stairs after his run and found Paul sitting on the landing reading the *Camera*.

"You really are committed, Robinson. You just might be an all-conference player next year after all."

Mose dusted the snowflakes from his head. "Surprises me too. You guys got anything planned for later?"

"Nothing specific yet. We'll do something, but I won't know until Sarah wakes up and tells me. She's in her regular spot for now."

"Your bed?"

"Funny. The chair. You seeing Marti tonight?"

"Yeah. Can I use your truck to go get her?"

Paul put his hand on Mose's shoulder to help himself up. "Just bring her back here. Take a shower first, for Marti's sake, and for the sake of my truck. When are you going to get her?"

"I've gotta call. What about FAC?"

"Or a movie. We'll all just go eat across the street and then decide, I guess."

Sally came out of her apartment just as Mose was entering his.

"Hey, Mose."

"Hey, Sal."

"Paul, do you want the rest of my pop?"

Paul took the can and the two of them went into her room to allow Sarah more quiet time to sleep. He stretched out on the floor to read the paper while Sally cleaned. After thirteen days and the aid of B-52s, the Marines finally captured Hill 881 in the Khe Sanh Valley, but at the cost of over 160 dead. He resisted the urge to shout an obscenity. He wondered what kinds of kids had died, where they were from, and if any of them had girlfriends like Sarah. He knew a few must have, and he shuddered. On page 6, he found a small account of a minor skirmish between Syrian commandos and Israeli farmers near the Lebanese border. He wondered if they were really Syrians and how close they were to Sarah's family's kibbutz. Thank God no injuries had been sustained. Sally was walking around her apartment with a rag and a can of Pledge, stepping over his mess as if he was not there.

"Hey, mom, do you have any chips?" he teased.

"Careful. I'll have you cleaning the toilet." She put the Pledge in the closet and tossed the rag into a wicker basket. "Better go wake up Sleeping Beauty, so we can all go to FAC."

Saturday, May 6

Mrs. Meyer had been the SDT housemother for seven years. Before, she taught at an elementary school in Denver, but when her husband took a job in Boulder, she gave up teaching and found her new position through a flyer at the Hillel house. Being a Reform Jew herself, the housemother position for a group of Jewish girls who had varying beliefs allowed her, as she called it, "to keep the faith." Her husband died about six months after he had taken his job.

Sarah Phillips was like so many of her freshmen pledges of the past, more into the sorority aspects than the Jewish practices. Sarah would accept any role for the house, take any action necessary to represent the house, and be an enthusiastic supporter of the SDTs at all functions. She was a sorority girl, a Greek, and never gave much thought to being a Jewish sorority girl. As a pledge she volunteered for all the grunt work around the house: server, secretary, janitor. Her college world revolved around the house activities, and she paid scant attention to her Jewish beliefs. Living in the dorm for her freshman year, amid the Gentiles, it was easy to do.

Her metamorphosis started as a sophomore when she moved into the house. Sarah began to attend synagogue again, sporadically in the fall, but more regularly as winter arrived. Mrs. Meyer teased many of the girls about the rebirth of their faith but was happy when most of them moved back to a belief resembling that of their pre-college days. On this first Saturday in May, Sarah headed off to synagogue with a handful of her sisters in the Blue Bomb.

Paul let himself into Dan's room to take advantage of the warm sun in the south-facing window. While trying to understand Sarah's faith, he was learning more about his own, or at least about Christianity. This morning's book was a study about how the two religions differed. "Sometimes," he had told Sarah, "I could be a Jew. They don't seem to ask much of their God, and He doesn't seem to ask much of them. That can't be right though."

Sarah stopped by after services with three of her SDT sisters to plan the rest of the weekend. She found Paul in Dan's room.

"We're all going to Denver tonight to initiate Marti and James."

Sarah smiled. "That was fun. Can I pay?"

"If you want." Paul changed the subject. "Are you getting any more answers from the synagogue these days?"

She shook her head. "Not really. The world is still confusing, I can't feel my soul, and I don't feel guilty about having sex so much." She smiled with her last remark and walked into a hug putting her arms around his neck. For a few moments, they said nothing.

Finally, without letting go of the hug, Paul spoke. "In high school I went to church and never thought about religion. Now I don't go to church, and I think about God a lot." He paused. "I probably make religion more complicated than it really is."

"Where do you find the time? Vietnam. Israel. Religion. Me!"

"My mind races, but it always begins and ends with you." He pulled back and gave her a serious look. "You better get your sisters back."

She cocked an eyebrow and pursed her lips. "I love you so much." Her right hand slid off his shoulder and brushed his hair back off his forehead, and then she used her index finger to touch his slightly pointed nose. "Do you want to invite your parents along for another night of fun?"

"Funny." Paul shook his head. "No."

As it turned out, James could not hold his liquor. At some non-descript bar on east Colfax where IDs were not checked, he and Mose started drinking shots. Something about jazz versus classical music that made no sense to the other four students. Paul and Sarah stopped drinking, realizing they would be needed to drive back to Boulder. Marti got pretty drunk too, while Mose and Sally were giggly. James rode up front with Paul and Sarah and fell asleep before his Chevy Impala was as far north as Stapleton Airport. He was joined in dreamland by Mose, Marti, and Sally by the time Paul pulled onto the turnpike.

"Look in the back seat and tell me which one is Mose's date," said Paul after surveying the trio in the rearview mirror.

Sarah looked back and smiled. Mose had an arm around each girl, but his head was resting on Sally's head. "You two were both looking out for Sally again . . . just like her brothers. It's sweet." She kissed him on the shoulder. "I think Marti may have been in this condition before, but I'm not so sure about James. God, he's so out of it."

"Think he's a virgin?" asked Paul.

"Maybe. Do you think Sally has told him about her past?"

"I know she hasn't. She told me she wouldn't until it got real serious, then she'd take her chances. He doesn't need to know."

"You've never told me about your old girlfriends."

"Oh, if we ever get serious, I might." He glanced over at his girlfriend.

"Yeah, I suppose we have some time then." They rode in silence for a few miles, with Sarah sitting as close to him as she could.

"Would it matter?" Paul finally asked.

"No, but you're a guy and supposed to be experienced." She was serious. "What if I had Sally's past?"

"You don't."

"Yeah, but would it matter if I did?"

Paul had never wondered about Sarah's previous boyfriends. He had become so enamored by her from the very beginning, it never seemed important. He pulled the Chevy off onto the shoulder and rolled to a stop. Sarah looked puzzled. He put the transmission into neutral and turned to her. "No, Sars, it wouldn't matter," he said taking her hands into his and looking at her intently.

"What wouldn't matter?" asked Mose from the back seat.

Paul and Sarah both smiled. "It wouldn't matter to Paul if I was less than I am. He'd still love me."

"Yeah, Phillips, he would. But you're not less than you are," Mose responded.

Paul started the car back toward Boulder. "Go back to sleep, big skinny. You're making too much sense." Paul put his arm around Sarah and pulled her tightly into his body and drove the rest of the way home with one hand.

Sunday, May 7

One of the benefits for Paul of living at 1203 instead of the dorms had been the solitude of Sunday mornings. Mose always slept late, and Dan was usually in Leadville. Sally stayed in her room doing who knew what. What made it even better this spring was Sarah's company. Since spring break, she had been coming over around nine. She made no demands, and the conversation revolved around the paper. She remarked she did not feel as comfortable coming over on Saturday mornings because he worked on the apartment, and she had been taught work was not to be done on Saturdays. Sally once observed that while they had become so devoted to each other so quickly, they observed a respect for each other's zone. When pressed, she could not define what "zone" meant, but they understood it to mean personal space. Even though Sarah knew, she remarked that Paul was adept at "penetrating my personal space."

This Sunday, due to a guest sleeping on the couch, Paul and Sarah were quieter than usual, and Sally came over even before Sarah to check on the condition of James. Sally did not think the quiet was necessary. "Look at him. You couldn't wake him even if you put on The Doors."

Sarah reflected for a moment. "We should have put him in your bed and had you sleep on the couch. Then when he woke up, you could smile sweetly and thank him for the wonderful evening."

"Come on, Sars. Grab your coffee and paper. We're going over to Dan's room so Sally can wake him up in her own way. No hurry, Sally," said Paul.

In Dan's room Paul turned on the radio, permanently set to 95 KIMN, and stretched out on the floor in the sun. Sarah sat in a high-backed orange chair on the west wall. They were quiet for a time. Finally, Sarah finished the paper and joined Paul on the floor. She made it impossible for him to continue reading.

"One of the things I love about us is we can be quiet together. But something I love even more is we usually aren't." She rolled onto his back and wrapped her arms around his neck and laid the side of her face on his shoulder.

"I don't believe in fate, and yet when I think about us, I wonder." He put his hands under his chin and turned his head to one side. "We didn't start out slowly. It's as if, from the time we met, we were united. I was ready for you, and you were ready for me."

She kissed him on the neck and settled back into her previous spot. "Does that mean we were meant for each other, or does that mean we were both so desperate we only had one option?" She smiled as she asked the question.

"Definitely destiny. It's not the same as fate, is it?" Paul was teasing.

"I've always thought fate implied a negative ending, whereas destiny was like a triumph, a good thing that had to happen."

"Then destiny, for sure," said Paul.

She hugged him tighter and allowed for that thought to be imprinted forever in her memory. When it was, she relaxed the hug and continued. "What will you do next year without Dr. Orr?"

"Let's see. I'll sleep in later on Mondays, and I'll have less homework, more time for you, and there'll be fewer all-nighters." Paul smiled. "There are some other really good professors here I'll get to work with and like."

"You'll miss him, won't you?"

"Yeah, enormously. It's been such a great match, and he's prepared me well."

"Ever have a teacher like him before?" she asked.

"I've always been one of those students who teachers like, who tell me how much they liked working with me all year, but, no, I've never had one like him. Not even close. Do you know he went over to the registrar's office and made himself my advisor without even asking me? He reworked my schedule for this spring, so I would be with him this semester too."

"He challenges you, doesn't he?"

"I was scared of him first semester."

"Not now?"

"Not as much. Now, I'm just in awe of him."

"Did you ask him to stay?" Sarah asked.

"Of course not. Not go to Yale? He knows how much I want him to be here, but that's just a great opportunity for him. He has to go! It's his destiny."

"Am I getting heavy?"

Sunday evening studies commenced with the realization that finals were only two weeks off. Sarah marched into Mose's room with a five-by-seven note card and a stern look. "Time card. Fill it out each day, and I'll sign it. You'll thank me for this come June 1969." Then she bent over and kissed him on top of his head and left. Mose never turned it in to her to sign, but he did fill it out each night.

Sarah drove herself back to the SDT house early on Sunday evening to call home and then pass any information about Israel's situation to her sisters.

"Hello, Sars. Any news?"

"About the same." From the sound of her voice, Paul could tell Sarah was tired. "My father wants me to call Rosenthal in the morning. He said he talked to him about shielding me from the hard news, and Rosenthal said he'd tell me straight up what he knew."

"That's good. I missed you tonight. Dan's going to go to summer school for the first session."

"The five-week session?"

"Yeah, the one that starts on June 19. Anyway, even though you wanted his room, you'll have to stay with me during that time."

"Damn! Hey, when did Mose get off the phone?"
"He only talked for about fifteen more minutes. Seems strange to see him acting this way."

"He has a melancholy side, you know. Ever ask him about it?" said Sarah.

"Oh, yeah, we talk about it nightly."

"You toad. No, really, he does."

"I'll give him a hug."

"Save them for me. Thanks for a really wonderful day."
"We didn't do much."

"We talked and touched all day."

"Kind of what we do best. By the way, on Tuesday night I'm going to hear some Episcopal priest rip on my church. Want to go?"

"Might be interesting. Yeah, I'll go. Remember, we're going to see Glenn Yarbrough on Thursday." She had made a list of events for the week and was checking them off.

"I went to see his concert last year," said Paul.

"Oh! Who with, my dear?"

"Mose."

"You're such a liar! Who did you go with?"

"A Pi Phi from Denton, Texas, but she was out of my league at the time. One of my three-week girlfriends."

"Was she pretty?"

Paul didn't know what the right answer was to this question but tried anyway. "Gorgeous, but she was simply preparing me for you."

Sarah seemed to accept that. "Back when you were little, huh. Well, I'm glad you grew up, so you were ready for a Sig Delt."

"Me too."

Monday, May 8

"Good morning, Dr. Orr."

"Morning, Paul."

Paul poured himself a half cup of coffee and settled into his chair. "Does the bombing ever bother you?" he asked.

The professor looked up from his notes. "All the time, Paul. Why do you ask?"

"Because every day I read about it or hear about it on TV. Every day! Do you really think it's helpful, or are we just terrorizing the North Vietnamese?" Paul asked.

"Could we fight the war without bombing the North?" Orr paused. "Could the President face the country and tell the people our troops are getting the best protection without the bombing?"

"It's all or nothing, isn't it?"

"Paul, at this point, more of your countrymen would like to see the President hit North Vietnam even harder."

Earlier that morning in Washington, Robert McNamara passed the signed documents to his secretary commissioning a confidential Pentagon study on the US involvement in Vietnam. Alone in his office, he added a few last-minute notes to his preliminary report to the President opposing General Westmoreland's request for a major buildup of troops for Vietnam. He slid the report into his leather briefcase and headed out for his meeting at the White House with LBJ. He was fairly certain what the President's response would be to his recommendations to reduce the bombings and offer diplomatic concessions to the North Vietnamese.

With temperatures reaching the high 70s, Paul and Sarah chose to walk to The Hill for lunch. They bought lunch from a street vendor across the street from The Sink and ate them on the bench in front of The Spoke, where the sun was bright and hot.

"I'm afraid for the semester to end," admitted Sarah staring straight ahead. "Things happen."

"You have a melancholy side too, you know." He touched his hot dog to her cheek, leaving a mustard stain, then licked it off."

"That's gross!" She wiped her cheek with her napkin. "I am kind of moody, but not so much this semester. I haven't had a reason to be." She smiled.

"You care deeply about some things, but I like that in you." He took her bag of chips and bit it open. "I thought we made a deal not to worry about our relationship."

"I don't, except . . ." she paused, and Paul waited, "except when I get off the phone late at night, and I realize how much I love you and how inexperienced I am at loving a man."

"Come on, let's walk. I've got to get my lit notebook." He took her paper tray and threw it away. "Keep talking."

"I didn't come to CU to get a husband. So many of my sisters did and will drop out as soon as they get one, but I'm here to get my degree and run a school."

"I'm not sure I'm following you. You're doing everything right to accomplish that goal. What's the fear?" They walked casually toward 1203. There was plenty of time before Paul had to be back on campus.

"My mother has a college degree and does volunteer work. Your mother has a degree in English and has never worked. I worry I won't follow through."

"Because of me?"

"Can I have both?" she asked as they reached 1203. Paul opened the door for her and followed her upstairs. "Hey, Mose, we've already eaten."

"Okay, I'll go over by myself. Hey, Garrity, she's psychic." Mose walked down the stairs and across the street to the Colonial for lunch.

Paul put his history books on the table and glanced at the mail Mose had brought in. "You got an Israel letter, Sars. How come it's addressed here?"

"I liked the idea." She took it and went to the couch to read it.

< . . . *and I worry expecialy for my brothers because they have stand guard duty late in the evening. Robert is thirteen. Security always been a chief concern, expecialy at night, but now have we armed men with us during the day. There are incidents almost dayly, and no farm is closer to the Syrian border then ours. Martin write that he believe Egypt is planning something in Sinai, but Papa does not think Nasser risk it just now. Still, there is ominous feeling in the air. We are small and vulnerable nation, and there are no guarantes as are in America.*

Martin is well and we are planning to live together when I finish my hitch. He will be off active duty then. Give Paul hug for me. If he is wonderful as you write, then hang on to him.

Even though I don't write often as you, please continue to send letters. I will try to do better. Judith wants me to say hello for her. I worry about her most. She is not handaling tension so well. Shalom, Sarah.

Hannah

P.S. I look forward to your visit this summer. I teach you how to wring neck off of a chicken and fire a rifle. >

Sarah laid her head back on the couch and closed her eyes. She handed the letter over to Paul but remained motionless in every other part of her body. As he read the letter, she finally got up and got an address book from her purse. She found a telephone number and dialed it, as Paul continued with the letter.

Rosenthal told her of a recent attack by Syrians that destroyed a farm truck on a kibbutz just north of the Galilee. He admitted the situation had worsened and Israeli Foreign Minister Abba Eban was seeking to get certain guarantees from the United States regarding military aid, aid LBJ was reluctant to promise. It was the US position that there would be no war.

After Paul left to attend his lit class, she called her father to tell him about Hannah's most recent letter. Dr. Phillips wondered whether Sarah should be visiting her cousin this summer with tension so high.

Tuesday, May 9

Dan went with Sarah and Paul to Macky Auditorium on Tuesday night to listen to Reverend James A. Pike present his non-conformist opinions about the changing role of the Christian Church. Dan brought along a spiral notebook to jot down the priest's most important points, so he could discuss the presentation with his grandma later. "She read an article about him in the *Post* and can't believe a priest would say all of those things."

"Is your grandma real religious?" asked Sarah.

"Yeah, she is. At least she goes to church every Sunday. We only have one drawing of Christ, but no crosses or praying hands."

"That's more of a Catholic thing to me," said Paul. "Are you really going to take notes?"

"This place is packed. I guess CU students aren't completely pagan."

"Our seats for the Glenn Yarbrough concert are better than these. We're in about row seven, in the middle," said Sarah pointing to the spot.

The Episcopal priest talked and answered questions for the better part of two hours, and he certainly was controversial. Those in attendance learned speakers in Macky expected to be cheered or booed throughout their speech. Pike opened the dialogue by stating the Christian Church was a dying institution because it was irrelevant to the modern world. It had disconnected from a congregation needing a closer affinity in an unfeeling, industrial society. Dan began writing in his notebook as rapidly as he could. Several times he leaned over to Paul and asked him to repeat what Pike had just said.

Over the course of the evening, the priest denied the Virgin birth, the Trinity, the divinity of Jesus, and the perfection of the Bible. "How can he call himself a Christian if he doesn't believe in those things?" whispered Dan. Reverend Pike expressed his support for the Civil Rights Movement and was especially impressed with the non-violent nature of Dr. King's methods. "True Christian spirit," he said. Pike was in direct opposition to the war in Vietnam, "for obvious reasons."

"Does this guy believe in anything?" asked Dan.

As if on cue, Father Pike answered him. "After my lengthy diatribe against the modern Christian Church, some of you are probably wondering if there is indeed anything I do hold sacred. As an ordained minister in the Episcopal Church, there are several ideas I believe in." He paused for a drink of water and ran his index finger around his white collar. "I believe in a loving, eternal God. I believe in life after death, this idea of everlasting life. And I believe in living a life based on Christian charity. My faith revolves around these three principles." The priest paused and sipped some water. "Now, may I take your questions?"

From Macky Auditorium Paul, Sarah, and Dan stopped in at Bennett's for a beer and to review the Reverend Pike's statements. Dan Savage appeared stunned; a condition Sarah had never observed in him.

"That's how he looks whenever Mose schools him on the basketball court. Notice the blank stare," teased Paul.

"I wonder how the Episcopal Church can continue to allow him to minister given his absence of basic beliefs they hold sacred," said Dan.

"Don't you mean *we* hold sacred?" asked Paul.

"Your ideas have always seemed strange to me," noted Sarah.

"Because Jews rejected them, we've been ostracized or tortured for centuries. Jesus not the Messiah?" she said in mock horror. "That has to hurt."

"It's fundamental to Christianity," said Dan. "Jesus is the Christ; God made Man. All that. I'm hardly an expert, but I did learn some things in Sunday school."

"Don't Jewish people have divisions within their faith?" asked Paul more as a statement.

"Oh, yes, from ultra-Orthodox to secular. We have groups who won't speak with one another. And surprise! Not all Jews are Zionists either. Sometimes I think certain Jews hate other Jews worse than they hate Arabs."

"It's such a good thing all Christians love one another," said Paul.

"Come on boys, walk me home. My sisters will be interested in hearing about the Reverend Pike's blasphemous statements. We Jews love to make fun of Christians and your theology."

Wednesday, May 10

Twenty-one long-stemmed red roses greeted Sarah when she awoke on her birthday. "From Paul and the gang at 1203. We love you, Sars."

Sarah dressed up. She was wearing a plaid miniskirt with knee-length stockings and brown buckle shoes when she met Paul at the UMC. She rewarded him for the flowers with a public display of affection worthy of a weekend detention. Fortunately, Mrs. Meyer was nowhere near to punish her.

"They are absolutely fabulous! Where were they hidden last night?" asked Sarah with her arms still around his neck.

"In the garage. Mrs. Meyer let Sally and me in this morning just before six. Happy Birthday!"

Their second embrace was interrupted by Dr. Orr. "I can't stand around and wait until you're done. I have a lunch meeting, but I wanted to give you this, Miss Phillips." He handed her a card and a little box. "Have a happy birthday, Sarah." He turned and walked off.

Sarah looked at Paul in disbelief, handed him the card and box, and then ran to catch up with Dr. Orr. Paul watched as she overtook him near the steps of Hellems. They exchanged a few words. He glanced over in Paul's direction, and then Sarah hugged the professor.

Mose's present to Sarah was a Cannonball Adderley album. Sally gave her a pair of three-inch hoop earrings. Dan's present was a glass vase Tracey brought from the greenhouse. Dr. Orr's box contained a lapel pin designed like the Israeli flag. Paul's gift was wrapped in gold paper with a silver bow, and Sarah opened it last. Inside was an eight-by-ten pencil drawing of her standing arm-in-arm with Paul at the SDT house, a re-creation of a photo taken at Sarah's awards presentation back in January. She still had long hair. The drawing was framed in wood, a frame made by Paul in the garage out back.

"Who did this?"

"I paid a girl I know over in the art department to draw it. It came out pretty good, I think." Tears welled up in Sarah's eyes, but Sally came to the rescue.

"Come on guys, we're going to the Tule to celebrate with a beer and a song. You're my date, Dan."

"Thank you all. Everything's so special!" Sarah hugged each one, including Marti.

Sarah put her arm around Paul's waist and called out to the others. "We'll be right behind you!" Then she turned to Paul. "The drawing is so special, something I'll have forever." She kissed him tenderly.

In that world far apart from Boulder, United States' B-52s continued to pound Hanoi, Haiphong, and the DMZ, while anti-war demonstrators maintained their silent vigil at the Pentagon. General Westmoreland insisted that the pacification programs were working and called for more US troops. Negroes in Mississippi, protesting a police incident, rioted at Jackson State College. Al-Fatah staged another raid in the Hula Valley of Israel. The JFK probe continued in New Orleans as District Attorney James Garrison sought to link several agencies to the President's assassination. Muhammad Ali criticized the war to 2,500 students in Chicago. The only political topic discussed that night at Tulagi's was the application by a twelve-year old girl for an abortion, to be Colorado's first recipient of an abortion under Colorado's liberalized law. Sally was adamant this was exactly why such a law had been needed, but asked rhetorically, "When will abortion be allowed for the 28-year-old housewife who simply doesn't want any more children?"

Sarah thanked Paul for making sure King Louie and the Laymen played for her birthday. They left earlier than their mates to return to 1203 so she could thank him for everything. Sally and Marti had been asked to ensure no one return to the apartment before ten forty-five.

"Hello?"

"Hi, it's me again. Have you ever heard of a black concert pianist named Philippa Schuyler?"

"No, why?"

"She was killed in Vietnam today. Helicopter crash. I went to one of her concerts in New York a few years back. So gifted." Sarah's voice trailed off, and Paul waited. "You know you made this the best birthday ever, don't you?"

"I hope so."

"I love us. Goodnight, my dear."

Thursday, May 11

Paul left early, even before breakfast, without telling anyone where he was going. He did not return to the apartment for the rest of the day. He met Cohen at the UMC for coffee and to discuss their upcoming meeting. "Do you have an agenda for today's meeting, or are we going to wing it again?"

"Nothin's written out," said Cohen.

"Maybe that's our problem. No organization. Just anger."

"Fuck you, Garrity."

After the SPU meeting, Paul left the UMC and walked across Broadway to the Lab School. The rain was not heavy, but it would keep the kids inside. Sarah was talking with four coeds about their assignments. Her smile was still radiant, he thought. Maybe he ought to celebrate her birthday once a week. He hung up his coat and brushed the raindrops from his hair. After today there would be just one week left of babysitting the little kids.

"Floater again, babe. Hang on a sec until I get the others assigned, then you can help me with the records." Sarah turned back to another small group of coeds, and Paul wandered back to Mrs. Best's office to wait.

The concert hall, aka Macky Auditorium, was packed with fraternity boys in coats and ties and sorority girls in dresses, plus a number of non-Greeks, who were not so expensively dressed. The best seats were occupied by the Greeks who pre-purchased blocks of tickets in the lower level closest to the stage. Most of those in attendance had seen Glenn Yarbrough before and could sing along with the crooner. "Stanyon Street" was still the crowd's favorite, a Rod McKuen poem put to music. The concert was, at its base level, a lovers' concert, and Paul and Sarah were swept up in the atmosphere. When it ended, they walked as one across campus to Bennett's, where they had a pre-arranged rendezvous with Anne and her date and with Sally and James. Later, when they returned to 1203, they found Dan and Mose in Paul's apartment drinking beer and listening to the radio. It was obviously not their first brew.

"Did you young 'uns have a good time tonight?" asked Mose with a hint of sarcasm and the obvious cadence of a man who was drunk.

"Yes, we did, thank you," responded Sally, who refused to bite the cheese.

"This isn't just a casual gathering. Somebody has some news here, and my guess is that it isn't Mose," said Paul as he helped Sarah with her coat, while James took Sally's, and they laid them over the arm of the couch. Paul's tie was already loose, but he removed his sports jacket. "What's up, Savage?" he asked..

"I got engaged today," Dan said, slowly lifting his beer in a solitary toast to himself.

"To who?" asked Paul. Dan smiled back and flipped him the finger. Both Sarah and Sally went over and hugged him. Sally gave him a big kiss on the mouth.

"Jeez, Sally, if I'd have known, I might have waited." The gang listened as Dan gave them the details.

"A toast," said Paul lifting his beer. "To our roomie, the first to go. May you have a long and happy marriage."

Mose started to speak but was cut off by Sally. The others chugged their beer, while Sarah took a sip of her wine and looked over toward Paul.

"Hello."

"I'm a little bit jealous of Tracey, you know."

"Because she got Dan, and you're stuck with me?"

"No, turd face."

"Sars?"

"Yeah?"

"Would you say yes?"

"You won't know until you ask."

There was a long silence while they contemplated that next step. Then Sarah spoke quietly, "In a heartbeat, my dear." She waited for a silly response.

"You know my reluctance isn't about you . . . or even us. It's me and our age."

At the SDT house, Sarah sat down on the hall carpet. "What do you mean?" she said softly.

"Sometimes I barely know myself. I've been here for two years, and I've gone through so many changes. Majors, politics, body style, everything. The only time I've been consistent is since I've been with you." He was quiet for a moment, and Sarah waited for him. "I know I've got such a long way to go still, Sars."

Sarah spoke tenderly. "Paul, I love you, even though I don't know the Paul who existed before us. Doesn't matter." She was searching for the path to him tonight. "Sally and I talk, but she didn't know you before this year either, so she only sees you as you are now. Mose and Dan don't tell me much except when they're teasing you, but Mose said he thinks you're lonely at some level, that you live in solitude sometimes. I know you stay up late at night and read or write or listen to music. Sally says sometimes you pace and talk to yourself." Paul closed his door and sat down against the wall but said nothing. Sarah continued. "College is supposed to be a journey. Hey, I'm not telling you anything you haven't told me. Just allow me to be a passenger on your train too. You're always there for me. I want to always be there for you. I don't want you to protect me from you. From everything else, yeah, but not from you."

Rubbing his head with one hand, he replied. "I could change into something you wouldn't like."

"I doubt it, and if you didn't change, you'd be boring." She laughed a little.

"I'm not lonely, you know."

They remained quiet for a few minutes before Sarah spoke. "You don't trust Dan, do you?"

"It's not so much that; I just don't confide in him like I do Mose. Dan has his own views, and I've learned to ignore most of what he says."

"You didn't always?"

"No, but you and Mose and Sally believe in me. That's a pretty powerful coalition of support."

Friday, May 12

Sarah's father's message was not positive. Al-Fatah raids across Israel's northern borders were occurring daily. Even though these raids and the shelling from the Golan Heights had been criticized by United Nations Secretary General U Thant, there did not seem to be an international outrage against the actions. Privately, according to some of Dr. Phillips' most trusted sources, the Israeli cabinet was beginning to plan for a retaliatory response against Syria, an action that could lead to a general war in the region. Another reason her father called was to tell her Hannah had left the kibbutz to meet with her boyfriend in Tel Aviv for a few days together, just in case war did break out and things occurred. Sarah skipped both biology and French to meet Paul at ten, between his two history classes with Orr. She was visibly upset and needed to be reassured.

"I imagine Hannah's dad is really mad."

"No, he understands. He believes war may come, and Hannah should be allowed to see Martin. He had a three-day pass from his unit."

"Come on," said Paul. "Let's go get some coffee." He wrapped his arm around Sarah's shoulder.

"How can I be so high one day and so low the next?" she asked as they left Hellems. She did not expect an answer, and Paul left the sociologist to her own conclusions.

They both went to their eleven o'clock class, but Paul was late, since he stayed with Sarah until her professor arrived. Dr. Orr gave his charge a look of concern when he arrived but said nothing. Paul was never late. After class Paul apologized and briefly explained his reasons. Dr. Orr noted the region had the potential for a flare-up, but he did not believe it would escalate beyond border skirmishes, a few dogfights in the skies, and heated words in Arab newspapers, at least for the moment. "Egypt and Jordan are not apt to be enthusiastic about coming to the aid of Syria just now, and Syria cannot stand alone against Israel."

"What about the Russians?" asked Paul.

"They have to be aware of Syria's current behavior, but I don't think the Soviets would be pushing Syria to act at this time."

Paul shook his head as he tried to figure out the situation. He noticed Sarah at the door of the classroom. He motioned for her to come in.

"Thank you for the Israeli pin. It was very thoughtful of you," said Sarah to Dr. Orr.

"You're welcome. Paul tells me you're a bit worried over the recent happenings in Israel. There's some cause for concern, but events will have to get much worse before anything will happen."

Paul was pondering a tangential historical event. "If Stalin was so important in lining up support for a Jewish state in Palestine in '46 and '47, what changed?" he asked Dr. Orr.

"That would be a splendid question for your final exam."

Sarah was reading the *Camera* when Paul returned to 1203 after basketball with Mose. He pulled his wet sweatshirt over his head and laid it over the wooden chair. She had put herself back together on the outside but remained upset about continued raids against Jews half a world away.

"How can I help?" he asked her while bending over for a kiss.

"Tell me about your basketball game. Tell me about your lit class. Tell me about college life, without any mention of Israel or Arabs or Vietnam. Give me back my birthday. I choose Wednesday to live over and over again. Help me to live this life, my life, not the life of situations I can't change or control." She pushed the paper aside and rolled her face onto his outstretched arm.

Paul maneuvered himself into such a position where he was sitting next to her, and her body rested on his. Then he spoke gently.

"I shot the ball pretty well. Not Mose-well, but good for me. You know, I never was much of a scorer in high school. More of a defensive role player. That's me, the consummate role player. But this afternoon Mose was helping me get open shots, and I was putting them in. You have to cover Mose, or else he'll burn you. So, when my man came off me to help, I would just drift to the open spot where Mose would find me. Mose made me laugh once when he asked me how it felt to be him. It was just three-on-three half court, but it was fun. We held the court for the entire hour." He stroked her head and ran his fingers through her not so butch haircut anymore. "In class a couple of girls gave their poetry presentation, original poetry. It was pretty good. They tried to recreate the feelings of people living during the Depression. One of the girls, Erin, said it was very hard for her because she'd never been poor. Our professor appreciated her honesty." Sarah's body relaxed and her breathing was steady. Paul knew this rhythm well. The movement of his hand through her hair continued. "Years from now I wonder if I'll remember these days with much clarity. I mean, I'll certainly remember Mose and Dan and Sally, but will I be able to see their faces? There was this one guy in the dorms. His name was Rick, and he went skiing up at Breckenridge over Christmas last year, a year-and-a-half ago, and he died. Fell and punctured an organ with his ski pole, I think. Funny kid, but none of us ever saw him again. It was as if he dropped out of school at the semester and never came back to see us. His stuff was moved out of the dorm before we got back from the break. I wonder if I'll remember him when I'm 64." Sarah was still motionless, except for her breathing. "I've always liked The Sink. And Bennett's. I don't think I've ever been in either place by myself, always with friends. That's probably why I like them so much. Had my first legal beer in Bennett's—with Mose. We had several, if I remember correctly. He said we sat with a girl while we were there, but I sure don't remember her. I met this other girl last year. Her, I remember. It was at the Libby cafeteria during the first week I was here at CU. I was sitting by myself at lunch, when she came over with her tray and asked if I was saving seats. My hair was shorter and pretty goofy then. I told her I wasn't, so she sat down with a couple of her friends. I remember one of her friends was named Susan. Anyway, she introduced herself and thanked me for sharing my table. Then she and her friends talked among themselves. She was wearing this god-awful pea green rain slicker, but I thought she was so pretty and nice."

Sarah kept her head resting against his body where they could not see each other's face. But she finally spoke softly. "That wasn't an ugly coat. It was very stylish."

"No," Paul corrected her. "It was ugly. That girl seldom came into the cafeteria. Must not have liked the food. I'll bet she didn't put on the freshman fifteen."

"She didn't. She lost weight, which was good for her, and she got her braces off in October."

"There must have been other girls I met, but I just can't remember. Kind of funny how that works. Probably every guy at CU meets someone during his first few weeks at school, someone who just blows him away, but I wonder how many get to meet her again. Regular guys of no particular note who were notable in high school, but who get lost among so many young notables here at CU. Guys who have to find their way again over the next few years." He stopped massaging her head and just held her body. It was so warm. "A few of them do, I guess, but some are sure luckier than others."

"I don't remember that lunchroom encounter, but I remember the girl you just spoke of." Sarah sniffled. "She came to CU just to learn and be a part of the whole college scene, just to have a good time. She was a little afraid, though. Didn't know where she fit in either, so she just kind of got swept along. She studied hard. After all, she was her high school's salutatorian and head girl. She joined a sorority and stayed active and had fun, I think. But something was missing, so when she went home to New York over semester break her sophomore year, she made a decision to not be afraid of her shadow. She ended up falling for a bartender. Fell in love so hard. Best thing she ever did, but very courageous, given her previous fears. Funny how that works."

"Lucky bartender."

"Yeah, he was lucky too. I know The Hill to you is The Sink and the bookstore and the energy, but for me, it's Tulagi's. Always will be. Dancing with you nearly every Friday." She paused. "That first Friday that led to this, the first time we made love." She paused again and Paul waited. "The beginning of our journey." Sarah finally stirred. "I've really got to pee. Then, let's leave a note for the gang that we're going to The Hill for dinner and then to dance."

Saturday, May 13

Paul worked the drawings all Saturday morning. He went through three cups of coffee and was still no farther along with a plan for remodeling the third floor when Mose came in around ten. He stood over Paul and stared at the blueprint for a few minutes. "The paper's on the couch. Some guy named H. Rap Brown replaced Stokely Carmichael at SNCC. Know anything about him?"

Mose picked up the paper and found the article. "No, but I bet he's every bit as radical as Stokely. That's SNCC's path now. Black Power, and they're moving to be more militant rather than less." He turned back to the front page. "Our little war keeps chuggin' along, doesn't it. Just waitin' for us."

They remained silent for a few minutes after Mose's last comment. Then Paul rolled up the blueprint, got up for a final cup of coffee, and returned to the table. "Two years will be here before we know it, big guy, and I can't stop it." Paul looked directly at Mose. "I'm not going to do the SPU thing anymore."

"You're dropping out of the peace movement, Garrity? I can't believe that!"

"It won't work. We won't make a difference this way."

"What way?"

"Protests. Marches. You know." Paul's voice trailed off and they were quiet again.

"So, what're gonna do?"

"I don't know. It's just so frustrating."

"You've gotta do somethin.'" Mose was joking and serious at the same time. "I'm countin' on you to get this mess ended before I graduate. I ain't goin' to Nam!"

"The Viet Cong aren't going to give up, you know, and, like Dan says, we won't either. At least for a while. So, no matter what I do about it here in Boulder, the war's going to go on for a few more years. It won't end like Dan thinks, either. It's a fucking mess."

Mose looked into his empty cup and started toward the sink, but he stopped just behind Paul. He turned slightly and backhanded his buddy lightly on the back. "If you're drafted, will you go?"

"The alternatives suck too and would destroy my family, especially my mom. I think I'll get back to the civil rights thing."

The girls cooked dinner. It was not elaborate, but it was plentiful. Salad, garlic bread, red wine, and Marti's special spaghetti recipe: tomato sauce with cheese, hamburger, onions, and butter. "Now don't give this away!" she warned with a laugh. They didn't need more. It was the company that always made the meal, as Marti and James were discovering.

"Did everyone remember that tomorrow is Mothers' Day?" asked Sarah. To her delight they all had. She and Paul were having an afternoon dinner with his parents. Sally had made a corsage for Diane Garrity at work and put it in the refrigerator to keep fresh.

Sunday, May 14

The dinner at Paul's parents' house was a semi-relaxed affair, despite the political bantering between Paul and his father, which had been placed off limits since the Ali flareup. Paul's talk with his dad after the public explosion had been a good idea, and a measure of calm had descended upon the family. For how long Paul did not know. The huge pro-war rally held in New York City on Saturday was discussed.

"It wasn't a pro-war rally, Dad," said Paul keeping his voice restrained. "It was a support the troops rally. There's a big difference."

"The troops fight the war, son. If you support the soldiers, you support the war effort. All these people, nearly a quarter of a million, are telling the President they support his actions in Southeast Asia to stop communism. This is a country where when the President declares war, we stand behind him."

"The President can't declare war. Only the Congress can, and it hasn't, and won't!" The volume was beginning to build.

"It's the modern era, Paul. I doubt if you'll ever see the Congress declare war again. They'll just sign the checks."

"How can you support LBJ? You're a Republican, for God's sake. You hated him when he was passing the civil rights bills and welfare programs."

"Not about civil rights. Besides, war isn't a political issue. It's neither Republican nor Democrat. War should unite the nation."

"Not this war! It's going to tear us apart." Paul's level was higher than his father's.

Sarah moved to end the debate. "Paul, if you'll get everyone something to drink, I think we can eat. Mr. Garrity, you can cut the meat now."

Mrs. Garrity sided with Sarah. "I think we can all agree that we love our country and are lucky to be living here."

Paul understood, rose from the couch, and offered a hand to his dad. "Come on, Pop. Let's eat."

Monday, May 15

"Good morning, Dr. Orr. Another rainy day. Did you walk in?"

"Morning, Paul. Yes, I did." The professor was standing on a chair attempting to clear three small boxes, a globe, and a model plane from the top of the eight-foot-high bookshelf behind his desk.

"Why the plane?"

"It was a gift from a student during my first year here. It was supposed to symbolize that I had given her wings."

"What's she doing now?" asked Paul.

"Last I heard, she was a housewife pregnant with her third child." He flew the plane in for a landing on his desk. "Grounded now, I guess."

"Do you receive lots of gifts from your students?"

"No. Thank you cards, but not gifts. This plane just happened to be my first here at CU, and it's been on top of the shelf ever since."

Paul sat down in the corner chair with his coffee. "Has it gone by fast? Your time here."

Orr stepped back onto the chair and reached up for the globe. He said nothing at first. He stepped off the chair and handed the globe to Paul. "My dad gave me this when I graduated from high school. Told me this was the world I was going to change. His world. It was going to change, but he was telling me I was going to have a hand in it. That was 1947." Paul studied the globe while Orr continued. "I came here in 1959, and it seems like yesterday. Has it passed quickly? In the beat of a heart."

A few minutes of silence passed while Paul studied the globe. French Indochina. No Pakistan. Palestine instead of Israel. The Belgian Congo. "I always thought the Belgian Congo was orange," mused Paul.

"What color is it there?"

"Yellow. Faded yellow."

"This is really amazing . . . in just twenty years!" Dr. Orr was leaning over his desk now. "Africa has had a revolution. Colonial Africa is mostly a thing of the past. Take a look at the Mideast. I suspect the need for oil will force more changes in the region very quickly."

"And Israel?" asked Paul.

"Paul, I think Sarah's fears are well-founded. It's an unstable region with high volatility. The Palestinian people were forced to pay the price for Europe's crime, and they'll never accept the UN's decision to take part of their land. The Arab governments need a scapegoat to obscure their own decadence. Israel is convenient."

"How soon?"

"I'm a historian, not a seer, but the recent skirmishes along the Syrian border don't bode well. These may not lead to war now, especially since Egypt is preoccupied in Yemen, and Jordan is at odds with both Egypt and Syria, but the time is coming."

"There seems to be more of these skirmishes between Israel and Syria." Even if Paul did not have the experience, he had his facts, which Dr. Orr noticed.

"I have real sympathy for the Palestinians, and I see no ready solution to their predicament. They don't have a voice, certainly not here in America. Our perspective is all one-sided, pro-Israel. We just don't know about the Palestinians, so we lump them all together as just Arabs. Invisible. These next few weeks will be critical. Watch the actions taken by Egypt and the reaction of the UN to those moves."

Paul was keeping up. "How will the United States react?"

"I honestly don't know. I can't get a feel for LBJ's commitment to Israel. If it weren't for Vietnam, I think his response would be more predictable, but the war changes the scenario."

Paul handed the globe back to his mentor. "Cool gift." He removed a piece of paper from his pocket and looked over his scribbling. The student had another question. "It's confusing to me from what I read, that somehow the Holy Land has been taken over . . . wrong word maybe . . . colonized by the Jews with the approval of the international community." Paul paused and Dr. Orr waited while his charge organized his thoughts. "Why would, why did they ignore the Palestinians? I mean . . . I know some of the rationale after the Holocaust, of course, but why before, especially from the end of World War I up to World War II? Especially the British; why did they commit so many troops to put down the revolt in the thirties? What was in it for them?" Paul shuttered his head. Still. Dr. Orr stayed silent, and Paul eventually smiled. "I know what you're going to say. 'Are there any other applications for this event?'" He paused again. "I'm just trying to make sense of it all." He didn't expect an answer. "Are you going to assign any homework this weekend?"

"Nothing new in either class. I'll review some of the more difficult issues in preparation for the exams. Some of your fellow students could use the time to finish their readings. I don't suppose you do."

"No, sir." Paul stood and turned to go but stopped and turned back. "Did you just answer some of my questions without posing one back?"

After sharing a sandwich and a banana with Sarah, Paul went back to Norlin Library to prepare for his American Lit class, while she went to the language lab in McKenna. His lit average was at 88 percent, and the professor did not round up. He had a short essay on Wednesday and his final to find two full points. He had decided not to tell Sarah about his conversation concerning Israel. She could worry about it over the summer when it would not interfere with her studies. Still, he did not want to treat her as Congressman Rosenthal had done by trying to protect her from the hard facts.

She met him in front of Old Main when his class ended, and they walked back to 1203 past the pond. The rain had stopped again, and the sun was trying to break out.

Upstairs at 1203 Paul resumed work on his literature essay, and Sarah scanned the *Camera*. She found what she was looking for in the front section under "World News," a brief account of the military parade for Israel's independence day.

"I wonder why it was small?" she asked almost to herself.

Paul heard her. "What's small?"

"It says here Israel toned down its military parade, but it doesn't say why."

Paul measured his words. "Maybe the economic problems caused them to keep it small."

"Maybe they didn't want to alarm their Arab neighbors who would use it as an excuse to write about Zionist military aims."

Paul let it die and turned back to his essay. The questions that he had asked Dr. Orr would not be asked to Sarah.

"Hello, Sars."

"Hi, lover. I got another letter from Hannah. It's from the last day of Passover. She told me she was going to meet Martin in Tel Aviv for the weekend. She's angry over the Arab raids and worried for her family."

"You already knew she'd gone, though. And where their farm is . . ."

"Yeah. Sort of on the front line, if anything happens."

"They'll be okay."

"Promise?"

"I do."

"And if you're wrong?"

"Then I'll get out of your life so you can marry a Jew."

"That's not funny. I already know who I'm going to marry. I just need to grow up more and become more stable and confident, so he'll have me."

"And what do I need to do now?"

"Dig in and hang on." She pursed her lips as if to tell Paul that the serious response was coming. A moment passed. Sarah spoke with her eyes first and then, "Keep holding my hand and my heart."

Tuesday, May 16

Tuesday's routine was in place for most of the day. After babysitting the kids at the Lab School, Paul walked Sarah back to the SDT house. "Talked to Cohen this afternoon. He said the guy who spoke about the Vietnam War at the World Affairs Conference got elected as president of the Young Republicans."

She did not know who Paul was talking about. "None of those guys were students at the Teach-In."

"I'm sorry. This guy, Hank Brown, I think, spoke in favor of the war over at Old Main just before the teach-in. He's a grad student at the law school and was in the Air Force in Nam."

"What's Cohen think?"

"We both thought it was interesting how the war was sort of started by the Democrats, but it's the Republicans who're lining up in favor of it, while Democrats are becoming more and more opposed to it."

"I've noticed. I've also noticed the largest group of doves in Boulder have the least input in all these affairs."

Paul looked confused. "Who would that be?"

"Women! You guys at the SPU ought to enlist all the girls at CU to help your cause, but you won't. You're still a bunch of chauvinists at heart."

"Even me?"

"Even you. Not as bad as most . . . Cohen's the worst, but, yeah, even you."

"I've asked you to all of the meetings and taken you to the rallies," argued Paul.

"Yeah, because you know me and want to get laid. But women as a group are left out. You still have an image of us as followers or helpers. You're partially right about us. Lots of women buy into your stereotype, but it's changing."

Paul kept silent this time, pondering what she had just said.

"I've got to get ready, my dear. I'll come over when I'm done to study."

"What's the dinner about?"

"I'm introducing this semester's service winner from the sophomore class. I didn't win it this time."

"You spent too much time with me," said Paul with a smile.

"No. Just the right amount of time. I got my priorities in line. Life is all about choices, my dear."

Sarah changed into jeans and a black CU sweatshirt and hurried over to 1203. Her make-up was untouched, and she still wore her diamond pendant around her neck. She raced up the stairs and burst into Paul's apartment. "Syria and Egypt are putting their armies on alert! My father just called!" She was distraught.

Paul rose from the table and took hold of her shoulders. "Why? What else do you know?" Mose came in from his apartment when he heard Sarah's voice. Marti was right behind.

"They're saying Israel is planning an attack within the next few days, but they're not!" She had taken her hands and put them across Paul's elbows.

"How did your father get the news so fast? Was it Rosenthal who told him?"

"No. An aide to Abba Eban called him. He said Israel is going to need more money if war breaks out. Paul, that's what my father does! He raises money for Israel. Lots of it!" She pulled herself into his arms.

"Can we do anything?" asked Mose. Paul shook his head, and Mose and Marti left.

"Has any shooting started?" asked Paul.

"Not that my father was aware of."

"Why would they think Israel was getting ready to attack them?"

"Because Israel didn't have a large military presence at the independence day parade. Syria said Israel's Air Force was preparing to strike first."

Paul was trying to order all this information. "Slow down. Syria is accusing Israel of preparing for war, because they had a smaller than usual display for independence day celebrations. It's been Syria and al-Fatah that have been raiding the northern kibbutzim. There has to be more to this."

"I told my father to call me over here if he got any more news, but he'll be busy on the phones getting donations. We're mostly in the dark!" Her body remained tense.

"It still doesn't mean war. It's not the first time there's been war scares along the borders. This will probably pass too." Paul hoped his voice was convincing.

They remained locked arm-in-arm, each trying to make sense of the news. At times like this, Paul also tried to make sense of Sarah. He worried about her condition, but her thoughts were focused on Israel and her cousin Hannah. Hannah, Sarah's alter ego living in the heart of the conflict. In time they pulled far enough apart to look into each other's eyes. Paul asked, "Did you tell Mrs. Meyer or any of your sisters?"

"No, I got the call just as the event was breaking up. People were still talking and congratulating the winners. I changed clothes and rushed over here. You understand this better than anyone there. I needed you!"

"Will Mrs. Meyer worry because you left?"

"Maybe. Should I call?"

"Yeah. No. Let me call. Your voice might worry her." He went to the phone with Sarah still keeping an arm around his shoulder. He dialed the SDT house. After a short conversation, he hung up the phone. Sarah's eyes were locked onto him tighter than her arms. She pressed her lips together but said nothing. "It'll be all right," Paul said deliberately.

"You don't think there will be war then?"

"I didn't say that." It was time for the truth now, he decided. "I just believe that it will be all right. Israel will be all right when the crisis is over."

Sally poked her head around the doorway. "Anything I can do?" she asked.

Sarah finally took her eyes from Paul, dabbed her right one with her little finger, and smiled. "Yeah. You can pop some popcorn and bring your studying in here. Otherwise, I'll be all over Paul, and he won't get his essay done. Is James with you?" Sally nodded. "I hope I didn't interrupt anything," continued Sarah.

"Nothing that can't be restarted. I'll be right back." She turned and yelled out, "Party in Paul's room!"

"If I work on my essay, what'll you do?"

"Give me some paper, and I'll work on French verbs." She hugged him very tightly.

Wednesday, May 17

KOA radio reported similar information about the crisis on its seven-a.m. news broadcast. Its account doubted whether Israel had moved troops near to the Syrian border. It claimed the United Arab Republic had given or was going to give notice to the United Nations that peace keeping forces in the Sinai should be removed. Sarah spoke with her father briefly after the report. He had little to add to his statements of the previous night, but he did provide some news about a possible Israeli response.

"Eshkol is standing firm about shipping lines being kept open in the Red Sea, and I believe the United States will support our position."

"The radio this morning said all of the Arab nations were ready to support a war against Israel," said Sarah, repeating the Syrian diplomat's claims KOA had reported earlier.

"That's Arab propaganda. You will hear lots of it. Ignore it." Dr. Phillips' words were always spoken in soft tones, without a trace of alarm. "We believe several Arab states will refrain from giving blank checks of support to those wild leaders. Jordan has been pretty antagonistic toward Egypt of late."

"Call here first if you hear anything new. Somebody will be around to take your call. Have you heard anything from Uncle Abraham about Hannah?" asked Sarah.

"She's back at Shamir. Got back on Monday. All leaves and passes were cancelled, I guess, in preparation for what may occur. Martin was sent back to the Negev. They're both fine, Sarah." Eugene Phillips needed to get back to fundraising. "Don't let this news interfere with your studies. It will probably amount to nothing more than a brief scare, but your final exams are important."

"I'll study, Father. Tell Mother hi for me. Is she worried?"

"Susan is being Susan. She's not interested in hearing about these details. 'Tell me if war breaks out. Otherwise, it's nothing.' That's what she says."

The *Camera* had more details. Syria and Egypt were meeting to combine forces, and war plans were being drawn up. Arab diplomats were charging that the United States was behind the Zionist military buildup, especially the CIA.

"Yeah," said Paul sarcastically, "that's just what LBJ wants, another war. I suspect what he's really telling Israel is to back off."

"I met Abba Eban a few years ago at a dinner with my parents in New York. He walked into the restaurant and came right over to our table to speak with my father. Such an eloquent man. I'll bet he can be pretty persuasive if he has to."

"After being Kennedy's vice-president, I'll bet LBJ has had enough grace and charm to last a lifetime. Wonder how Kennedy would be handling this?"

"So do you think Johnson will dictate his demands to Israel then?" asked Sarah.

"America's primary concern is still Vietnam. We'll stand by Israel, but LBJ will want to keep the lid on this." Sarah looked worried again. "That's a good thing, Sars. It'll keep Israel from over-reacting."

"I need a nap. I didn't sleep well last night, and I've got a little trig homework to do before tomorrow."

"I'll go to Norlin for a few hours. Do you want some dinner first?"

When Paul returned from the library, he found Sarah asleep in his bed. His first thought was to join her, but she looked so relaxed and comfortable after a few days of being tired and worn down by the events in Israel. He did not switch on the light; the light from his living room shining through the doorway was enough. He wondered about her thoughts just now. He wondered about everything—it was his nature—but especially how this special woman had come into his life and stayed there. Was he so special as to deserve her love or just a lucky guy at the right time?

He retrieved his poly sci text and returned to the bedroom. He turned on the reading light next to a wicker chair opposite the bed and began to review. He would let her sleep for another hour.

Sally entered the apartment about nine and went to the bedroom.

"Hey, Sal, what's up?" Paul whispered.

"Oh, you're home. The candle in the back window was still burning, so I thought Sarah was here alone. She asked me to wake her about eight-thirty, but I just remembered."

"I forgot to blow it out. Let's go into the other room, so we don't wake her." He switched off the reading lamp and tiptoed out. "Do you want anything to drink?"

"Maybe some orange juice, but I'll get it." She poured two small glasses. "Is she all right?"

"Honestly, I don't know. She's so caught up in this Israel thing." He paused. "Thanks." They both sat down at the small kitchen table. "It's real to her, Sally, like it's her roots."

"She has family over there; it makes a difference. Her cousin is like her twin. It binds."

"Yeah, that does make it more personal, but it's the Jewish thing. Remember the night you guys made dinner, and she drank too much Mateus? We were all talking about our families. God, that was hilarious. We couldn't stop laughing, and Dan talked about going back to Leadville and running the greenhouse because he understood his town; it was where he belonged."

"Mose said he needed to go back to Oxnard in order to understand the place of his birth."

"They're good people, Sal."

"We're all good people, silly. You included. I think we voted on it, and it passed four to one."

"Who voted against it?" asked Paul.

"Mose, of course. Now that I think about it, it was five to one. Sarah voted twice." Sally finished her juice. "Part of her isn't like you and me and Dan. Just like Mose is different from us. We're from here. Small town. We belong."

"We don't have several hundred years of baggage to haul like she does. We kid about it, but she's serious. She's no longer trying to avoid being Jewish. She wants to understand." There was a long silence.

"We're all pretty young. Do you think any of us have the right to understand?" Sally's focus shifted. "I've got a kid who's living with another family. I'll never see him. I know what searching is about, and that's what Sarah's doing. She's a whole lot smarter than me, but it'll still take time." Sally was looking into Paul's eyes. She reached over and took his hands. "Have you got the patience to see her through this?"

"Holding hands with my beau, Sally? I knew you two had a thing." Sarah was standing in the doorway wearing Paul's Colorado Basketball tee-shirt and her underwear. Paul got up and walked over to her. "No kiss, my dear. You didn't give me one when you came home."

"How do you know that?"

"Because if you did, you would have crawled in bed with me. I know you can't resist this sexy bod."

"That's true," said Sally. "I hear you all the time."

Sarah relented and gave him a kiss and a loving hug. Then she went over to Sally and hugged her. "I pray for you and your little boy." She returned to Paul and wrapped her arms around his waist. "Yeah, my dear, do you have the patience for me?"

Thursday, May 18

Sarah was explaining what it meant to have the reservists called up in Israel when Paul arrived at the SDT house. He stood in the hallway where she could not see him directly, while she spoke to the twenty-odd sisters about the most recent developments in the Mideast. She seemed composed, but he knew on the inside, she was a tempest. Mrs. Meyer came up to Paul from behind.

"She's not the same these days, is she?" Paul was unsure as to whether it was a question or a statement, but he decided to put a positive spin on Sarah's recent behavior.

"Oh, I think she is. She's just so worried about her cousin and family. They're up near the Syrian border, so all those Arab raids scare her."

"You've really been good for her this semester, Paul. As we've discussed, I was worried about the two of you early on, how rapidly you came together. I could sense an unsettledness in her last fall, but we kept her busy with house doings hoping to keep her settled. She gets an idea, and it's hard to hold her. I'm sure you've experienced that, haven't you?"

Paul laughed slightly. "Yes, ma'am, I have, but it's a part of what makes her so special."

Sarah was putting her positive spin on the events a half-a-world away. "The Arab world is not united. Jordan and Saudi Arabia have deep suspicions of Nasser and of Syria. The congressman with whom I spoke this morning says the Israeli people are calm. They're making some preparations for a possible conflict, but they do so periodically. What we can do here is donate money." She smiled her convincing smile, and Paul thought he recognized her dad in her. "Yes, I know, I ask for money every day."

"She is impressive, isn't she?" said Mrs. Meyer.

"Yes, ma'am, she is." He turned toward Mrs. Meyer. "Thank you for the other night. I know it was completely against house rules and all."

"That's enough. Sometimes an old woman has to go with her instincts and trust her girls and her girls' boyfriends. My time with my husband was cut short, and we missed some things because we put them off. I wish I hadn't. I trust you, Paul, with Sarah's heart."

"Hello, Sars."

"Can you always keep your arms around me?"

"I'm doing the best I can."

"Don't you ever get tired?"

"Are you kidding? You energize me."

"I can't believe the semester's over. This has been the best time of my life," said Sarah.

"Yeah, for me too." The night phone conversation seemed always to have at least one serious moment.

"Are you sure? Because you've always had a good life, haven't you?"

"I've been lucky, Sars, but this has been the best. Trust me."

"I do, my dear, I do. Are you going to stay up and study some more?"

"A little history, the causes of World War I. I think Orr will ask about that," said Paul.

"How'd I do with my presentation to my sisters?"

"I'd give you an A-plus, but the proof is in the amount of money you raise."

"I'm sorry it takes up so much of my energy."

"We have time. We're on the verge of something big, Sars, you and me. All of us. We live in the time of the possible. Of that, I have no doubt."

Sarah nodded her head. "You say that because you and I have glimpsed the power of, for lack of a more specific word, love. We're needed by each other, and that, my dear, gives us power."

"It makes us one on our journey, that's for sure."

Friday, May 19

The phone rang at Paul's apartment at five a.m. He knew it was bad news before he lifted the receiver because early morning calls were always bad news. He also had a feeling it was Sarah. He took a chance.

"Hello, Sars, what's up?"

"Oh, Paul, the UN forces are being moved off the Sinai border! The southern border is exposed to an invasion now!" Her father called to give her the news just before she called Paul. "If Egypt crosses the border, it's war!"

"Slow down." Paul was trying to remember what the guest speaker to the Cold War class had said about UN peacekeeping forces a few weeks earlier. "Could the UN transfer those troops onto Israeli territory, so they could still act as a buffer? Has U Thant ordered them out?"

"I'm sorry, I shouldn't have called. You have a test this morning."

"No, Sars, I want you to call me and tell me these things. Besides, I can shower and then study a little more." He had stayed up until three studying, getting just over two hours of sleep, and had planned to sleep in until eight, but he was not going to tell her. "Why don't you get dressed and come over here. We'll get the *News* and see if the radio has any more information, and we can get some breakfast."

"Are you dressed?" she asked.

"No, I'm standing here in my shorts."

"God! It's five-fifteen, and I'm worrying my boyfriend in Boulder, Colorado, about an event that may not happen. Do they have pills for this sort of weird behavior?"

"That's one way to look at it." He let the silence sit in the phone for a moment. Then, gently, "Will you come over and have breakfast with me? Cheerios?"

She began to relax. "Yeah, but I need to shower and put myself together. It'll be an hour or so."

"You know I've seen you at five in the morning a few times, and you've always looked good to me."

"One could question your taste, you know. You're dating this high-strung Jewish girl."

"Just come over."

"Okay."

As Paul hung up the phone, there was a quiet knock on the door, and Sally poked her head in. "Everything alright?"

Paul smiled. "Sarah. She just talked with her dad about Israel and was a little shaken."

"I meant with you?"

"Oh, yeah, I'm fine. Thanks. Go back to bed." He leaned over and gave her a kiss on the cheek.

"You too."

"We'll see. Thanks."

Paul put a small pot of coffee on to brew and took his shower. He walked over to the corner across from The Sink to buy a paper. *The Rocky Mountain News* showed a map of the area from where UN troops were being evacuated. It appeared as though the way was now open for Egyptian troops to move through the Sinai Peninsula and into Israel. Another story grabbed his attention, however. "Dr. King Challenges Draft Laws." For a moment he was angry at himself for not attending the speech at DU. He had planned on going for several weeks, was anxious about it, but with his Cold War final and Sarah's needs, he had decided at the last minute not to go, and he did not tell anyone about it. He read the quote by the Reverend, "I oppose the war in Vietnam because I love America. I want to see our nation stand as a moral example to the world." *I should have gone,* he thought. A picture inside the paper showed a small group of white men protesting King's talk while holding a sign that read, "Rights for Whites." Paul wondered what rights were being denied to them, certainly not the right to be bigots. And, of course, the war in Vietnam continued. Paul returned to his paper, but then wondered if he could complete his new major in two more years. Maybe with summer school he could. Sarah arrived a few minutes later looking terrific in her darker than usual eye shadow.

"Sorry about this morning. I'm okay now." She gave him an intimate hug.

"Did you talk to your dad about when you have to go home this summer?" he asked.

"They finally relented. I can stay until commencement in order to see some of my sisters graduate, so my ticket is scheduled for Saturday afterward. Then I'll be back around the twentieth."

"What about your trip to see Hannah?"

"We're going to wait to see what happens, but if I don't go to summer school, I'll go in July. Otherwise, late August . . . if there's no war."

"It'll be good for you, you know."

"You could go with me?" She was still holding out hope.

FAC was a blow-out for the CU students, despite another soggy day in Boulder. Most of the final exams would be completed by Wednesday of the following week, and the students would pack and hurry home, so this Friday was the last one of the semester. A local band was playing, and the crowd cheered when the fuzzy-haired lead guitarist played "Going, Going, Gone."

Paul and Sarah begged off when the group went for a pizza after FAC ended. The others knew what that meant, as if Sarah's body language on the dance floor at Tulagi's had not given her desires away. The gang went to Bennett's, while Paul and Sarah went back to the apartment.

At the apartment Paul stacked four albums on the stereo, which, as it turned out, was not enough. After the week of stress about events in other parts of the world, they were relieved to know only about the desires and needs of each other. The first time they made love that evening was with energy and a sense of emergency. Then they talked and planned and relaxed. Later, their lovemaking was gentler and more prolonged. "I think I'm beginning to get this," said Sarah softly after she had rolled off his chest.

"Hello, Sars."

"I love you even more than I thought I did before."

"Before when?"

"Before the first time, before your accident, before I came back after spring break, before yesterday. Just before."

Paul ran his hand through his hair and laughed silently at her statement. *What a simply wonderful girl I have*, he thought.

"Know what?" asked Sarah.

"What?"

"I'm wet again."

Alone in his office at the Pentagon, with just a single desk lamp to light the large room, Robert McNamara recognized what he had set in motion these past months, but he could not imagine where it was going to wind up. Earlier in the day, he had submitted his memorandum to the President recommending a compromise with North Vietnam, the same one he had discussed with LBJ on May 8. McNamara's doubts about the progress of the war, at least about its current path, had finally convinced him to oppose the military's requests for additional troops.

Saturday, May 20

"Sarah, the news will be broadcast later in the day, so I wanted to call you," said Eugene Phillips cautiously.

"What is it, Father?"

"Israel is mobilizing its troops. U Thant has ordered the UN troops off the border." There was silence. Dr. Phillips wished he could reach through the phone and touch his daughter. He wondered how and when her journey of awareness and concern about the Jews of Israel had started, then realized it did not matter. "Uncle's family is prepared. They've been through this before." Again, he paused, waiting for his daughter's response. One can be born Jewish, which could be a burden, but the journey of becoming a Jew could be daunting. "Will you be calling Paul?"

"Just as soon as we end this conversation."

"Will he be awake?"

"He'll say he was, just waiting for me to call."

Dr. Phillips sensed a smile on the Boulder end. "He's a fine young man, Sarah."

"Yes, Father, he is."

She went to the bathroom and then called Paul. She tested him. "Were you awake?" It was six-ten."

"Oh, yeah. Working in the garage."

"Israel mobilized."

"Do you want coffee?"

"I'll be there by seven."

He bought the *News* again, but it did not yet have the news about Israel's mobilization, only that the crisis in the Mideast was escalating to a boiling point. And the war in Vietnam continued. Sarah arrived dressed for synagogue in a conservative brown outfit. She was met at the top of the stairs by Paul, who hugged her tightly.

"How bad is it?" he asked.

"Really . . . bad," she answered slowly to emphasize her response.

"Well, come in and tell me what your dad said."

They talked for the better part of an hour about a variety of topics, but never too long from the crisis in Israel. They drank coffee, held hands, read the paper, and talked some more.

"I've got to go to synagogue. Will you come with me today?"

He was resting his head against his left hand while he sat at the table. He looked away for an instant and then came back to her eyes. "No, I'm hardly dressed for it, but it's still a place you need to go by yourself. You get the chance to talk to others who understand this whole thing more than me."

"No, they don't, and they don't understand me like you do either."

She was right. "Some parts of you they do, because they're from the same place." He smiled. "I'll be here when you get back, and then we can go to the library."

"I'll just go back to the house and change, and then I'll call you. You can pick me up there."

At their usual table in Norlin Library, Sarah spread out her books, then nestled her head in the crook of her arm and fell asleep.

Sunday, May 21

The studying began in earnest around one. Marti was informed of the rules, as was James, who needed no prodding. The group had grown too large for Paul's apartment only, since Jeff was also taking part in the regimentation. Mose and Marti worked across the hall, but both apartment doors stayed open. Paul's radio had on "Fabulous KIMN." "Groovin" by the Young Rascals was the number one record for the week, but it was the comments of the disc jockey Jay Mack and his two imaginary buddies, Niles and Farley, who kept the troupe from getting too serious.

Sarah had her biology final on Monday, but Paul had both history finals, the completion of the US History and part one of his Cold War exam. Dr. Orr was going to challenge him right to the end. They had staked out the pillows on the floor for the afternoon, but they generally used each other to rest their heads or prop themselves up. "I've been over this stuff so much, I don't know what else to cover," he said.

"Then let's go for a walk. It would be a shame to waste the afternoon sun," she whispered. She stood first and stretched before helping him up. "We're going for a walk. Anybody need anything?"

"Punch out," teased James.

They walked west along Pennsylvania toward the cemetery,

arm-in-arm. "You're having a hard time studying again," said Paul.

"What's so hard is the waiting, and I'm so isolated from it all. I'm trying to imagine what it must be like for Hannah and her family. Waiting on Egypt and Syria, waiting on the Israeli government, waiting on LBJ. Waiting for war."

"It still might not happen."

"Might! That's just it. Maybe it will, maybe it won't. So, we wait. But for what? What is Eshkol waiting for?"

"For time. For LBJ. For any avenue leading away from war. Eshkol must be under enormous pressure," said Paul.

"My father wonders if he's up to being a wartime leader."

"Let's hope we don't find out," answered Paul.

They walked along in silence for another half a block before she spoke again. "When we met with Rosenthal, you predicted war. Now, you hedge. Are you trying to protect me?"

Paul was slow to answer. Then, "Yeah," he said.

She stopped and turned to him. "Do I need to be protected on this?"

"No. Not anymore. Wrong word," he said gently. His next sentence was spoken deliberately. "I don't know the right one, but I'm trying to help you ease into this. You're making a big jump just returning to Judaism, and immediately your new nation is being threatened."

Sarah leaned into Paul, placing her head into his neck and wrapping both arms around his waist. She spoke softly. "I ask myself what I'm doing, and you already know. I'm returning to Judaism, huh?"

"Yeah," he said pulling his arms up to her shoulders and squeezing. "Seeking that which you already are."

She tilted her head back to see his face and smiled. "That's pretty profound, and I accept that."

There was a short wait at the Gondolier, and they had to sit in two crowded booths. Dan had returned and joined them, making eight. Sarah, Paul, Dan, and Jeff sat at one booth. Mose, Marti, Sally, and James at another. They were back studying by seven-thirty, with Dan tutoring Sarah with her trig and Paul organizing three-by-five note cards on the floor about America's twentieth-century wars. No one seemed as stressed about finals as they had been about mid-terms. The evening session broke up about ten, when Paul turned on the news to see if Carl Akers was going to give any information about Vietnam and hoping there was nothing about the Middle East. It was minimal, news Sarah already knew.

"Well, this Jew needs to get home for some sleep," announced Sarah.

Paul parked the pickup across the street from the SDT house a half-hour ahead of their normal drop-off time. He let the radio run off the generator but found a station playing continuous classical music with no talk. "How about if I just hold you for a while?"

In time Sarah finally spoke. "Quiet, huh." She shifted her head so that she could see him. "I love you in so many ways. I hope you never believe that it's just a college passion, a time of my life I went through, and you happened to be the one." She gave him a chance to respond, but he waited. "It may have started that way, but you didn't fit that role. Mrs. Meyer said she was going to talk to me about choices after we'd been dating for a month or so, but your actions, your treatment of me, made her keep postponing it. She told me last week you were her favorite boyfriend, and she thought you treated me better than any of the boyfriends of my sisters. She's really worried about me, but feels you'll protect me. She said you'd guide me through this crisis. I know she and my father have talked on the phone about my moodiness."

"She and I have had a few talks, too. I know she trusts me, or else she'd never have allowed you to spend the time with me that you do. It's not something she's comfortable with, but her instincts tell her an exception needs to be made in your case. We're of the same belief you're something special . . . and deserve special treatment." For the second time that day, Paul was removing his protective cloak from her—and holding his breath.

Her mind raced, but she understood what was happening in their relationship. She gave the most subtle smile, then leaned in and kissed him, while she held his cheeks in her right hand. The porch light blinked twice. "I'm going to go straight to bed. Promise me you'll do the same."

Monday, May 22

"Morning, Paul. It's supposed to be in the 80s today." Dr. Orr's morning greeting generally spoke of the weather.

"Crazy weather. Rains every day and then suddenly, it's summer. I've never seen anything like it."

"You're young. You will. Shall I call off our final exams so we can all enjoy such a day?"

"No, sir," answered Paul. "I'd hate to have all my studying go to waste." They smiled, and the young man poured himself a cup of coffee. "No sugar. I'm trying something new."

They were quiet for a moment, each sensing the end of a relationship. They both started to speak at the same time.

"I'm sorry, go ahead," said Dr. Orr.

"I was going to ask your opinion of FDR, especially during the Depression . . . whether or not he was effective."

"I'll let you answer that shortly." Orr swiveled in his chair toward his books, then stood and walked around the desk to pour himself another cup of coffee. "You've been quite a student, Mr. Garrity, beyond what I anticipated. I received a call last year from the Dean of Students asking for a favor. Seems as though you had some people in your corner." He stood behind Paul holding his coffee in his left hand. As he turned back to his desk, he placed his right hand on Paul's shoulder. "You more than justified their faith in you." After a moment he returned to his chair.

"I couldn't have done it without you."

"No, Paul, you could have."

Mose pushed his pace up the hill on 10th Street as he ran south looking at the Flatirons. His body hummed in the warm afternoon sun, and he wondered if it was made for track more than basketball. *All those seasons of hating suicides and conditioning*, he mused. At Baseline Road he turned back for the last mile that would return him to 1203. It was downhill, and he lengthened his stride. Now his thoughts were focused on his running, where before, for the first nine miles, they had wrestled with his business final, how to break up with Marti, and next year's starting five. The addition of the seven-foot kid from Pueblo could bring immediate help. And he thought about his mom.

The graceful, powerful stride of the six-foot-five swingman eased a block from the apartment as he began to shut his body down. He reached The Colonial just as Paul was returning from the SDT house along Pennsylvania.

"Lookin' good, Robinson."

"Walk with me for a few minutes while I cool down." Mose's body glistened as they walked west along Pennsylvania. "This is a great town to run in. Hills. Scenery." His breathing returned to normal almost immediately.

"How long have you been out?" asked Paul.

"I don't know. A little over an hour or so. Best I ever felt, but the weather helped." They turned around at 11th and headed back. "How's Sarah?"

"Stressed, but she's holding up. I need a direct line to the Israeli leader to see if he'd postpone the war for a while, at least until finals are over, so she could get her studying done and get some sleep."

"Hasn't seemed to have affected her desires for you any," teased Mose.

Paul gave him a gentle shove off the sidewalk as he smiled. "No, that's still as intense as ever. I've never known anyone like her, obviously, but she just never lets up. I'm not complaining though, but it's a good thing I'm young."

"You're lucky. You're in the type of relationship all college guys dream about, and it seems like it's destined to last."

"Yeah, but with Sarah you never know. She could decide to be the tambourine babe for a rock band and head out on tour the next week," said Paul.

"Except she loves your ass too much. That's why she's renting Dan's room for the summer, you know, so she can stay with you. She told me she wasn't gonna take any classes."

"Maybe I'll hire her to help us finish the apartment upstairs."

"She'd probably like that, hanging out with the two of us," said Mose.

"She already does. She's pretty fond of you too, you know."

"How could she not?" Mose flashed his grin that made all mothers love him.

The news out of the Middle East was ominous on May 22. Egypt was moving troops across the Sinai, while Syria was reinforcing its army in the Golan Heights, both moving closer to the Israeli borders. The remaining Arab states were lining up in support for a war against Zionism. Sarah spent the afternoon talking on the phone with her father and Congressman Rosenthal and then relaying the information to her sorority sisters. By the time she arrived at 1203 at seven, her emotions were taut.

"You probably don't care that Henry Aaron hit two homeruns yesterday, do you?" said Paul as he hugged her at the door.

"Selfish of me, huh."

"They had a piece of news about the call-up of reserves, which leaves the kibbutzim short of manpower. I guess girls from the cities are going to help with the farm chores."

"They're getting on a war footing, just waiting for Egypt to close the Gulf of Aqaba," said Sarah.

"What did Rosenthal say? Did he offer any hope for diplomacy at all?" asked Paul.

"Sure. You know he's going to put the most optimistic viewpoint out to me. He still tries to protect me as best he can. He holds out hope for the UN or the Soviet Union to restrain Syria."

Paul probed again. "U Thant . . ."

"Fuck, U Thant!"

Paul had never heard Sarah use that expletive, and she had said it with such anger, but he understood. They both believed the Secretary General had removed the peacekeeping forces in haste, thus emboldening Nasser. Paul put his forehead on Sarah's. "How about if I massage your shoulders for a few minutes?"

"How about a kiss first, then the massage?" She offered her first smile.

Mose and Dan wandered in a half-hour later, each with a book and some notes. The massage had ended and the radio was on. Paul was in his usual spot, propped against the couch, and Sarah was at the table, reviewing her trig.

"Need any help?" asked Dan.

"Of course. You've been my savior," she said.

"I didn't think Jews had a savior." Dan sat next to Sarah and began to perform his miracles.

Mose took the chips from the counter and opened a can of soda from Paul's fridge. His assigned seat was the green chair on the inside wall, where he re-read class notes for statistics.

Sally and James arrived a few minutes later and settled in on the sofa. James had heard the stories about the mid-term study sessions, but he found them hard to believe. "This is impressive," he whispered to Sally.

After about an hour, Sarah closed her trig book and went to the bathroom. When she returned, she snuggled up to Paul for a kiss and whispered something the others could not hear.

"How am I supposed to concentrate with you two carrying on like that?" complained Mose.

"She just said it might be time to take a break," said Paul.

"All of us, or just of the two of you?" smiled Sally.

"All of us," said Sarah. "Let's go walk around The Hill and get some fresh air. It's a nice night. A half-hour would do us all good, and then we can come back for a couple more hours. Hell, I'm the only one with a curfew. You guys can stay and study all night long."

"Hello, Sars."

"Hello, my dear. Are you still studying?"

"Dan and Mose are still here. We'll probably stay at it for another hour or so. Are you going to stay up?"

"No. I should after falling asleep at your place the last hour. Sorry about that."

"Never apologize for sleeping on my lap. My leg did fall asleep, however, which led to a funny tingling sensation elsewhere."

"You're too funny. Thanks for driving me home. I wish I was with you now."

"This weekend, you know."

"Anne is so jealous."

"I didn't know she had a thing for me."

"You know what I meant."

"Yeah. Are you doing okay, Sars?"

"You know me better than I know myself. What do you think?"
"I know you will be, but I worry about right now. Not knowing about your cousin and her family makes it more frightening, doesn't it?"

"Yeah. If I could just call her each night, or if the TV reports weren't so limited, then I think I could handle this. But I hate not knowing, and especially hearing the Arab reports, but so little from Israel."

"I forgot to tell you, but Orr said he thought the whole thing was in the hands of the major powers, and they might be able to prevent war from breaking out. So, maybe . . ."

"If Egypt closes the Gulf of Aqaba, Israel won't accept it, and there will be war. Even Rosenthal admits that," said Sarah.

"Nasser will close it. It'll just depend on whether it'll be permanent."
"Oh, Paul."

"I'm coming over for a while. Tell Mrs. Meyer. Okay?"
"Hurry, Paul."

Tuesday, May 23
Paul was confident his political science score would be good enough to keep his B, but he was just as sure he had not scored well

enough to raise his B in Art History. It did not matter; it was over. He grabbed a *Daily* at the UMC and waited for Sarah. The headline told him what he already knew. "Mideast Crisis Worsens." Nasser had closed the Gulf of Aqaba.

Sarah handed her trig test to the proctor and asked if he was going to be grading it. There were only four other students still taking the exam at twelve oh-five. She wanted to know how she had done. Eighty percent kept her B; 79 probably meant a C. She charmed him into grading it just then. It took just over ten minutes.

Sally completed her Spanish final and headed for Norlin Library, where she hoped to find a quiet place to review for her sociology exam at two. She was confident her GPA for the semester would surpass Mose's, but she would have to ace her sociology exam to have a chance at beating Dan. Sarah and Paul were out of reach this semester. She smiled to think that after winning the grade point contest last semester, she might do better and yet finish fourth this spring. Paul's relationship with Sarah had served to inspire him to excel in the classroom, whereas hers with James had only distracted her from studying. *Of course, it had been worth it*, she thought.

Sarah arrived at the UMC fountain unnoticed by Paul, who was still reading the *Daily*. "Remember those days when you used to watch for me?" He spun around to see his girlfriend in shorts, knee-high socks, and a brown blouse. And a big smile. "Eighty-three percent! Wait until I tell Dan."

"I'm proud of you. So, it's all going to come down to your bio grade and my lit final." He stood and gave her a hug.

"No, my dear. It's all coming down to your lit final. I stopped by to see if the bio scores were posted. I got my A, so we'll see if you're competitive enough to hang with me. How'd you do on your art test?" Paul frowned. "Too bad," she said with a mock pout. "It's probably over already. Dinner at the Greenbriar is going to be so delicious."

Everyone returned to Paul's apartment in the evening for another round of preparation. For Paul and Sarah, Wednesday would be their last finals. The others all had one more on Thursday morning. Sally and James left about nine, sensing that Paul and Sarah wanted some time alone. They dragged Mose and Dan with them.

"Do they ever talk to you about me and my obsession with Israel?" she asked as they moved to the couch.

"They worry about you. Sally, the most. She's so good at sensing other's moods, like just now. She knew we needed to talk. But all three of them have asked if you're okay."

"What do you tell them?"

"They're my closest friends."

"The truth? That I'm a basket case?"

"That you're really stressed over it, and it probably won't change as long as the situation remains tense over there."

"Do they understand why I'm taking it so hard?"

"Yeah."

Sarah's mind was racing again, and Paul waited for it to find a station. He was holding her hands, their fingers kneaded together. "I didn't read the paper tonight, and I haven't watched TV either, but Nasser closed the Gulf, didn't he."

"Yeah."

"Will the war start soon?"

"Not just yet. I think both sides will dance for a short time, while the US and Russia ponder their next moves. If they could just get Nasser to shut up for a few days, but he just inflames the other Arab states." Again, they fell silent.

Sarah threw her legs across Paul's lap and buried her head in his chest, and he held her tightly. "You comfortable?" she asked.

"Yeah, very." Paul knew she would either fall asleep now or ask him to make love to her.

"Hello, you're calling early."

"My father left a message for me. He talked with a diplomat from the Soviet Union today who assured him there would be no war. He said reason would carry the day. My father seemed to think war might be prevented."

"That's great news! If the Soviets and LBJ can just keep a lid on it for a few weeks, maybe war won't break out."

"You were wonderful tonight, you know."

"You were loud," said Paul.

"Think anyone heard us?"

"Nooo. At least not anyone at The Sink or Colonial. At the apartment, yes."

"I should be embarrassed."

"No big deal. They'll just tease me until they leave for the summer."

"I love you so much!"

"You can make as much noise as you want."

Wednesday, May 24

Paul slept in on Wednesday morning. After Sarah's call Tuesday night, he stayed up rereading poetry for his lit class, and then tried to write some of his own, but without much success. Sarah would have to wait for her second poem. At ten-thirty he arose and showered. KOA radio was reporting Egypt had effectively blocked Israeli shipping in the Gulf of Aqaba, but the major powers were meeting in the Security Council to try and avert the war that seemed unavoidable. Israel's foreign minister was in Washington to meet with LBJ. *I'd love to sit in on that one,* thought Paul.

"See here, Abba, I'm a little busy with the skirmish in Indochina.

Don't do anything foolish like attacking Egypt. Ya'll sit back and wait for them to start it."

"Okay, Lyndon. We'll let the Arabs hit us on all sides because we know you will be there to save our ass. Shalom."

Paul walked over to the UMC to meet Sarah and concede the GPA contest to her.

Martin Ofer stood on the tank, looking through his field glasses into the Sinai Desert, wondering when the Egyptian army would attack. Tomorrow? The Sabbath? He climbed down and looked north. Would they be ready for the Syrian attack on the Golan Heights at Shamir? "Give 'em hell, Hannah" he yelled to the sands.

Dr. Orr posted his scores for both his US History course and his Cold War class on the wall next to his office. The student identified only by number 654714 was at the top of each list.

US History93.4%

Cold War95.1%

He wondered if he could get 654714 into Yale for his graduate studies.

Paul sat on the cement blocks on the west side of the fountain enjoying the sun and watching other students move through the area. He talked to a few, but noted how many were complete strangers to him, and how large a university CU was. *My place in the universe, and even here I'm an unknown.*

"Garrity! Haven't seen you around recently. Where the hell have you been?"

"Cohen. Just hanging at the library studying for finals. Did you go to any classes this spring?"

"Not enough. I'm failing nine hours. I think my professors are punishing me for protesting the war. Part of the plot." Cohen winked. He knew better. "Waiting for Sarah?"

"Yeah, she's taking her last final this morning. I wanted to read the *Daily* before she got out. Not good news for your people in the Mideast."

"No, it's not. Since I'm flunking out, maybe I'll go join the Israeli army."

"What? And give up your legacy as a peacenik?"

"I've never been anti-war . . . just anti-THIS war. Sort of like you, Garrity. Fucking Vietnam!"

"What do you mean, flunking out? You're kidding, right?"

"Nope. The SPU will be all yours next year. Imagine. A clean-cut, suburban, non-Jew leading the war protests. At least you won't alienate every student who wants to join the movement."

"That's true." Paul and Cohen laughed. "You have a gift. What're you going to do now?"

"They'll try to draft me, so I'll get to decide whether to go to Canada or jail."

"I'll write to you either way."

"By the way I found out it was Morgan and Buckingham who bombed the booth. Can't prove it, but I know it."

"Who was the third guy?"

"Don't know. Probably just some lackey. I got a mole."

"Are you going to give me his name?"

"Nope. I asked him if I could pass him on, and he said no. Will you take this on?"

"No, but you know who would do a good job at it? That Schultz woman. Smart and reckless. She's not afraid to piss anyone off, and she sure hates the war, plus she's older."

"At least help her out. You're a damn good lieutenant, Garrity. You get things done. Hey, I've gotta run, but I'll send you my address when things settle in."

"Cohen."

"Yeah?"

"Stay out of jail. Seriously."

"Say hi to Sarah for me. See ya."

They shook hands, and Cohen headed into the UMC.

The campus was thinning out as exams entered their final days. Paul read the *Daily* and soaked up the sun's rays while he waited for Sarah. It was the last issue of the CU paper for the spring, a sure sign that the semester was over. The summer editions would not start until mid-June, and with a new editor. Paul had decided he was not going to cram any longer for his lit final. He had attended nearly every class, read every book and poem, written all the essays and earned a B. One or two more hours were not going to change it.

He saw Sarah walking down the steps at the southwest corner of the court dressed in one of her many miniskirts. She headed directly towards him.

"Well?" he asked as he stood to greet her.

"Easiest test of them all, and now I'm done for three months." She threw her arms around his neck and kissed him. "You now have my undivided attention."

"Well, yeah, except for that little crisis in Israel." He pulled his head back while maintaining the hug.

"Anything new this morning?" she asked.

"Not really. They'll dance at the UN for a few days, I think, now. Maybe give you and me a chance to enjoy the end of finals and the warm weather. Hungry?"

Paul's American Literature exam seemed strange. It was all multiple-choice questions, probably to facilitate rapid grading. The poetry section focused on the figurative language of Robert Frost's poem, *Birches*. The novel section concentrated on realism, and Paul found he was able to eliminate most of the choices for each question and come up with the correct answers. When he left the room at two-fifty, he was satisfied with his performance. Unlike his girlfriend, however, he would have only a three week break before the summer session began on June 19.

"Where's Sarah tonight?" asked Dan.

"She's helping her sisters pack, plus I guess the sorority house gets pretty wired these last few days. Seniors graduating and all. Little celebrations and lots of tears," said Paul.

"Celebrations for girls! Guys graduate and get invited to that wild party in Vietnam. Helluva reward!" grunted Mose.

"Can I get you guys anything?" offered Paul as he put on his baseball cap. 'I'm going over to the drug store to pick up a few things."

"Chips maybe."

"And some sodas."

"Have you got one final or two tomorrow, Dan?" Paul asked.

"Just the one. Then I'm heading home."

"You still takin' Sally?" asked Mose.

"Yeah, she's done before me and already packed. My grandma's gonna put her to work before dinner."

"Chips and pop. I'll be back shortly. Study hard." Those last words were said in a gloating manner, and Paul received two one-finger waves as he left his room.

Dan got up from the table, walked to the back window, and watched Paul back out of the driveway. "He's gone. I'll get Sally."

Paul returned about 90 minutes later with the sodas and chips.

"Where you been? How do you expect us to keep our grades up if we can't concentrate? You've been gone too long to have just gone to the drug store. You stopped by to see Sarah, didn't ya?" Dan finished his mock tirade while Mose opened the bag of chips and poured two glasses of pop.

"What's that?" Paul asked, pointing to the large box on his table tied with a bow.

Sally re-entered. "Where have you been?"

"Geez! What difference does it make? I stopped off at Orr's house to give him the bookshelf. We talked."

"Did he like it?" she asked.

"Yeah, a lot. What's the package?"

"Just a little something for putting up with us all year, for taking care of us here. Open it," she commanded.

Paul furrowed his brow and shook his head as if to say it was unnecessary, but he pulled one end of the ribbon and opened the box. It was a basketball rim.

"We sorta thought you could make a wood backboard and then fix it to the garage," said Dan.

"One more court for me to beat your ass," said Mose.

"Thanks, guys. Whose idea was this?" asked Paul.

"It's really for all three of you guys," said Sally. Tears welled up in her eyes. "I'm going to miss you all this summer so much, and you've taken such good care of me this year." She stared at them for a moment before Mose stood up and crossed over to her and gave her a hug.

"Shit, Sally," said Mose, "it's not like this fun is ending, you know. You can come up and see us all summer."

"And we're gonna do the whole thing over next year," said Paul.

Thursday, May 25

Paul used a one-inch-thick piece of plywood to fashion the fan-shaped backboard. He reinforced the area where the square bracket attached to the base of the backboard and put two-by-fours behind the main board for strength. He spray painted the board white and set it aside to dry. Then he erected two braces on the garage wall above the garage door.

Everyone at 1203 had morning finals except Paul, but they all agreed to meet at noon and have a last lunch together at the Colonial, which was serving meals clear through to Commencement. Sarah walked down to 1203 around eleven. The rain had stopped, but she still carried an umbrella.

"Must be a New York thing," said Paul when she found him in the garage.

"After this spring it's a necessity. I thought Colorado was supposed to be dry." She kissed him and asked him what he was doing. He explained the present and about Sally and showed her his progress.

"It needs a second coat and an orange square. I'll do that tomorrow. Come on, I'll get cleaned up."

"It's weird with nothing to do, isn't it," she said. "I'm not sure I know how to relax."

They walked upstairs where Paul washed up. Sarah browsed through the morning newspaper. Vietnam had been pushed from the front pages by the crisis in the Mideast. The story that caught her attention was an account of Israeli citizens, not soldiers, making preparations for war. Bank withdrawals, runs on grocery stores, making home air raid shelters, and digging trenches in Tel Aviv to slow the invading Arab armies.

Paul finished buttoning his shirt as he returned to the living room, then leaned over and kissed her on the neck. He noticed what had captured her attention. "That story struck me too. All the young men have gone to war, just like in the song."

"Don't say that, my dear," she replied softly, "because you know where they go from there."

"Sorry. I wasn't thinking."

She turned and thrust her face into his stomach and hugged him around the waist. "What am I doing here?"

He held her tightly and measured her breathing and his words. "Maybe your father could get you a ticket over there in the next week or two instead of waiting until later in the summer." He paused. Her shoulders tensed. "You've been thinking about it anyway."

Somehow before the tears came, she replied, "But I don't want to leave you. I've been looking forward so much to living here with you, to go to bed with you every night." She got no further. The turmoil of the previous month released itself in one sudden burst.

At some point they moved to the couch where Sarah's crying subsided. They remained outwardly silent for over ten minutes, but inwardly their minds were racing.

"I need to straighten myself up before everyone gets back," she finally said. She stared into his eyes for a moment and then kissed him.

"I love you, Paul." She got up and went to the bathroom.

Mose stuck his head into Paul's apartment right at noon. "Garrity! I'm done! Passed 'em all! Not even any D's."

"What a difference a year makes, huh? Where are Dan and Sally?"

"They'll be here shortly. Where's Sarah?"

Paul nodded toward the bathroom. "We'll be ready in a minute. Dan wants to have lunch before he heads out, doesn't he?"

"Yeah. I'm gonna put these books away and change into shorts. See you in a sec."

Paul took a last glance at the picture of the Jews of Israel digging up their own streets, then closed the newspaper and put it on a stack in the corner. Sarah was still in the bathroom when Dan and Sally came up the stairs.

After lunch Sarah gave both Dan and Sally hugs before they left for Leadville. James hugged only Sally.

Geez, Sarah," said Mose, "you'll see 'em on Saturday morning."

They pulled away around two-fifteen. Mose said a few words to James and then shook his hand. He would not return to Boulder until September. "It's gonna get lonely around here pretty soon," said Mose.

"I don't think I'll mind," said Paul, who had his arm around Sarah's shoulders.

She smiled. "What about Marti?"

Mose held out his hand to Paul, who reached into his pocket and flipped him the keys to his truck. "She's just finishing her last final. I'm gonna go take her to the bus stop so she can get to Salida tonight. Short goodbye."

"Isn't she coming to Tracey's graduation?" asked Sarah.

"Nah, I don't think so."

Sarah looked puzzled. Mose waved and went around back to Paul's truck.

"You've seen Mose. He's not into lasting relationships." Paul smiled. "Unlike me."

"Come on," she paused, "let's go to the Audiophile."

Her mood had perked up, and she was nearly racing to the music store on The Hill. Each time Paul asked for an explanation, she just replied, "Surprise."

Tim Rosen, one of Sarah's former two-date boyfriends, was working the desk. Sarah led Paul to one of the listening booths and then went back to speak with Tim. He handed her an album and then pointed his finger at her. "I promise," she replied.

For the next hour, they sat in the booth listening to "Sgt. Pepper's Lonely Hearts Club Band" one day before its official release. Sarah also paid for two albums to be picked up in the morning.

Mose went out with several of his basketball buddies in the afternoon to begin celebrating the end of the year and to say goodbye to the seniors. He was pretty mellow by the time he settled into the current events session with Paul at 1203.

"The whole Arab world is lined up against Israel. Its chief ally is fighting another war in another part of the world. So, explain to me why Israel is taking the hard line on this blockade." The beer was beginning to affect Mose's traditional stoic nature.

"I think it's about a lot of things, not just the closure of the Red Sea. That's sort of like the last straw. Syria's been shelling the settlements in the northern part of Israel for seven or eight years, and the Jews have no access to parts of Jerusalem, and just a bunch of shit. All that, and now Nasser can't shut up, saying Israel's destruction is at hand," said Paul.

"It's really shaken up Sarah, and I'm about to go over and kick some Arab ass," said Mose to Paul's laughter. "Where's Sarah now?"

"At her sorority house. Lots of the sisters are leaving, so there's some partying going on. She might not come over tonight."

"It's been quite a while since just you and me sat around drinkin' beer."

"We'll have plenty of time for that this summer, I think." Paul took a drink from his beer can. "Did you talk to your mom tonight?"

"Yeah, she's doin' good. Good spirits. Real optimistic."

"When are you going to see her?"

"She's sending me some money for a plane ticket. Coach said he could get me a deal to go home, so I'll leave next week sometime. Probably around the first."

They drank beer and listened to KIMN.

"You and Marti done?" asked Paul.

"For the summer anyway. We'll see what happens next fall. She was fun though. She liked you guys."

"Hello."

"Hi. I've missed you. What did you do tonight?"

"Mose and I've just been sitting and talking. He's asleep on the couch. Too much beer after not enough sleep for a week."

"What are you doing?"

"Thinking mostly. Groovin' to some tunes on the radio."

"I talked to my parents tonight about going back next week and then going to Israel."

"I'll bet they were happy about that, now that war seems more likely."

Sarah missed Paul's sarcasm. "Not really. They're worried about me being over there if war broke out. They don't understand it's sort of why, you know, I'd go. To be a part of it all. Does that make sense?"

"Yeah."

"Would you be worried?" she asked.

"Yeah."

"So, I shouldn't go?"

"I didn't say that. I just know either way, you'd regret not going."

"What do you mean 'either way'?"

"If there's no war, then there would have been no danger, so why not be there, and if war did come, and you were here, you'd regret you weren't there to help."

"What could I do though? Can you really see me digging trenches or picking apples with my city hands? The most manual labor I've ever done is sharpen a pencil."

"There are a lot of little kids needing daycare. You'd fit right in in that socialist paradise. And didn't Hannah say she'd teach you to shoot?" As soon as Paul said that, he retracted it.

"You could help me," she purred. "Come with me."

On his own Paul always considered this. His heart and his head were at odds. "I've got an apartment to finish. Besides, they'd shove that rifle into my hands."

"Could you get along without me for a couple of weeks?"

"As long as it's only for a couple of weeks." Paul wondered how her absence would affect him.

"I promised my parents if I went, I'd come back and go to summer school, so I'd have to be back before the nineteenth."

"Have you decided?" asked Paul.

"Not yet. Can we talk about this tomorrow while I move? I'll sleep with you if you come with me."

"You are such a tease, you know. We'll keep talking." Paul thought of all the hours he and Sarah had talked about their future together, and still it was not decided.

"Will you tell me what you're thinking?" she asked.

"Of course. When do you want me to come over?"

"Now!"

"No, tomorrow morning."

"I'll come and get you instead, but it'll be early."

"I'll be ready," promised Paul.

"You always are."

"Now you're getting dirty."

"Sometimes, I just ache for you," said Sarah.

Friday, May 26

By the time Mose got out of bed and wandered across the hall for a cup of coffee, Paul had already given the backboard a second coat of paint and taped the outline for the shooting square. Sarah arrived with the new Beatles albums and two boxes of books she might need over the summer. They both scoured the paper for subtle clues about the crisis in Israel. Sarah wondered if Israel could live with the situation as it stood.

"Their Mediterranean ports are still open, and they've gotten used to the Syrian shelling in the Galilee." But she knew it was an untenable condition. Paul's look confirmed her fears.

"Only the Big Guys can prevent this now," he responded, "and they might be able to keep a lid on it. The longer that war is delayed, the less chance there is it'll be fought. Call your father and see what he knows."

Dr. Phillips had little to add. His sources were all unsure of what would happen next, but they were not optimistic about a peaceful resolution. Arab rhetoric was making it nearly impossible to edge back from the brink. He tried to calm his daughter's worries about the vulnerability of her cousins at Shamir. "Years of preparation for this sort of thing, Sarah."

"Then it would be safe for me to go there then?" Sarah teased. "Paul and I are talking about it."

"Could I speak with him, please?" asked Sarah's father.

She handed the phone to her boyfriend and put her arms around his waist. "Good morning, sir."

"Hello, Paul. My daughter says it's raining out there again. You must be about to float away."

"It's been a wet spring, that's for sure. I'm working on a boat out back." He waited for the serious part to begin.

"Paul, I know this is going to sound strange coming from me, but is there any chance you could convince my daughter to attend summer school and stay in Boulder for the entire summer? Her mother and I are worried about allowing her to travel to Israel at this time."

Paul stared straight into Sarah's eyes as if he was speaking to her rather than her father. "We talk, and she knows very well I want to keep her safe." He paused momentarily. "But she'll decide. She'll choose if and when, and I'll support her." He continued. "She's supported me in my activist protests, and I'll be by her side through this. Your determination to help Israel has rubbed off on her, I'm afraid."

Dr. Phillips' laugh seemed ironic. "More like her uncle's attitude, I think." He shifted directions. "Sarah said she edged you out for the highest grades this semester, but it sounds like you did very well."

"She did. She's had a positive effect on my studying."

"Would you mind if I called you for reassurance occasionally, Paul?" It was obvious now to Paul the crisis in Israel was taking a toll on Jews everywhere.

"No, sir, that would be fine." There was silence, and he handed the phone to Sarah.

"I'm back. I haven't made up my mind yet, Father. Don't worry."

Paul and Sarah walked slowly over to Bennett's and shared a beer. CU's undergraduates had gone home for the summer, and The Hill was quiet. The singer at Bennett's played for no more than twelve customers for over an hour, but it was soft and gentle, and the two lovers enjoyed it immensely.

"Come on, roomie, let's go home," said Paul.

They strolled the one block back to 1203, and each wondered what the night would bring. Vietnam and Israel were far away.

It was quiet. There were only three people at 1203. One slept soundly, while the two others talked softly, giggling occasionally about the past semester, the coming days, religion and faith, world events in a philosophical way, and their friends. Naked, they touched and kissed at every opportunity. Two candles provided a soft light for the bedroom. Sarah's touch.

"If it doesn't get any worse over there, I'm going to stay here like I planned. I'll visit later in the summer, maybe August when summer school is over. I'll still try to convince you to come with me."

"I hope Vietnam moves to the front pages again."

They made love one more time before Sarah fell asleep in his arms, with her right leg wrapped around his left leg. The second candle burned out just after three.

Saturday, May 27

"They ought to build a tunnel through this mountain," suggested Sarah as Paul eased the Blue Bomb past the Seven Sisters on Loveland

Pass. "It would be faster, and you wouldn't have to battle the snow at the end of May." They passed through more snow at Climax but arrived at the greenhouse in Leadville in plenty of time for Tracey's graduation.

Mose, Sally, and Dan's grandparents rode up to the high school with Dan, while Robyn rode in the Corvair with Paul and Sarah. There, they joined Tracey's parents for the ceremony. Seated alphabetically on the auditorium stage, the graduates listened to short speeches by the superintendent, principal, valedictorian, and class president. The featured speaker was a US Army colonel from Leadville who had just completed a tour in Vietnam. He spoke about patriotism, duty, and containment of communism. He related personal experiences from his tour in Vietnam, focusing on improving the future for the children there, and he closed by challenging the graduates to "Stand Up for America." He received an enthusiastic ovation from both the graduates and the audience. Paul stood and clapped politely, ignoring the nudge from Mose or the look he received from Sarah. He knew this was not the arena to protest the war, and these people were not the enemy.

On the way back to Boulder, Mose was now accompanied by Sally in the back seat of Sarah's car. At Frisco, realizing how uncomfortable it was for him in such a confined space, Sally moved to the front seat with Paul and Sarah for the remainder of the trip. The sky cleared, the roads were mostly dry, and the group relaxed and commented on the day.

"I had a great time helping at the greenhouse for a couple of days. Dan's grandma called a flower shop in Pueblo to help me get a job. I think I can work two jobs this summer," said Sally.

The conversation continued unabated as they headed down the pass, past Silver Plume, Georgetown, and Idaho Springs, and into Golden. Sally was leaving on Sunday. Summer was upon them, but they all knew they would see one another periodically over the next three months.

When they arrived at 1203, Sarah called her parents to tell them of her decision to stay. "But you have to tell me if things get worse," she warned her father.

They assembled in Sally's room to watch her pack. Paul was allowing her to store her extra stuff in Dan's/Sarah's room for the summer. Hers was already rented out to a grad student who would arrive on June 15. After talking with Sally's mother on the phone, Mose decided to stay in Pueblo over the Memorial Day holiday.

"You know," teased Sally, "James wonders about us."

Sarah broke in. "Hell, we all wonder about you two." They all laughed. "We're out of here. Sure you don't need anything else?"

"Nope." The two girls hugged. "I'll see you guys in the morning before I leave. Mose already told me we weren't leaving early."

"You know what I'm going to miss this summer?" Sarah was facing away from Paul as they lay naked in bed. His arms held her tightly.

"What?"

"Our late-night telephone calls."

"I thought about that too."

"Goodnight, my dear." She turned her head to kiss him tenderly. He did not release his hug, nor did he fall asleep quickly.

Sunday, May 28

Sarah was the first to get up on Sunday morning. The two nights with Paul were everything she had hoped they would be. She slipped on her panties, a sweatshirt and jeans, and went downstairs to greet the morning and retrieve the newspaper. The neighborhood was as quiet as could be. She went back upstairs and put on a pot of coffee, opened the *Camera*, and sat down at the kitchen table. The headlines were no better than the previous week, but no worse either. U Thant was pessimistic about the situation. "Well, no shit!" she said under her breath. "Your reckless removal of the peacekeeping forces only encouraged the Egyptians." Nasser was continuing to incite the Arab world with his speeches proclaiming the imminent end of the Zionist state. On page 3, the grim statistics for American casualties in Vietnam for the week, the month, and the year were given. Total US deaths to date: 10,253. "Is there no end in sight to this mess?"

A quiet knock returned Sarah to Boulder. Sally stuck her head into the apartment. "I thought I heard someone go downstairs. Is Paul still sleeping?"

"Yeah, I wore him out again last night," she joked, but it was mostly true. They had made love on the couch to lengthen the distance between them and Sally's apartment, hoping to keep the noise down. "You tell me not to worry, but I do. I still think I want to have sex with Paul too much."

"Is that coffee I smell? Is it ready yet?" asked Sally.

"Yeah, I think so. Want some breakfast?"

"No, coffee's enough. Want me to pour you a cup too?" She poured two cups and sat down opposite Sarah where their whispered conversation continued. "I'm really going to miss you and Paul."

"We'll come down and visit."

"I know, but it won't be the same until next fall. I'm already looking forward to next year. This is the best place and the best time I've ever had." Sally blew on her coffee and took a sip. "I've had so many laughs here. You know, I worried Paul would change when he started up with you, that the special relationship existing here might be disrupted. You only enhanced it. You fit in in a unique way, and Paul has been so much happier."

Sarah tilted her head slightly. "Wasn't he happy before?"

"Maybe happy is the wrong word. He was tentative. He gained so much confidence because of you. I think he thought of himself as the least capable person up here. That's a part of him you couldn't know. You made him their equal, in some ways even superior."

"He said that?"

"No, it was never spoken. Just my observation, our observation. You gave him what these three guys gave me last fall."

"You've got it all backwards, Sally. Paul's the one who gave me confidence."

"It's his gift. He takes care of people. You're both very lucky to have each other."

The time came. "I'll be back on Tuesday, probably in the afternoon. Have the hoop up out back." It was a directive from Mose, who was sitting in Sally's car waiting for her to finish saying goodbye to Sarah. "They've become pretty good pals."

Sally turned to Paul and gave him a hug. "I'm going to miss you. Thanks for taking care of me this year. You didn't have to rent the apartment to me . . ."

Paul cut her off. "Would you get in the car? It's just summer break, not graduation. Sarah and I'll be down to see you a couple of times anyway." He guided her into the seat using his hand on the small of her back. "Geez." He looked over at Mose who was stifling a grin and shaking his head.

"Okay, Mr. And Mrs. Garrity, we're off." As Mose put the car in motion, the phone upstairs started to ring.

Paul handed the phone to Sarah. "What's wrong?" she asked with a sense of urgency.

"Nothing, Sarah." It was her father. "I was checking to see if you could be reached at this number tonight. Hannah wants to talk with you. They're nine hours ahead of you, and she can get an overseas line tomorrow morning, about nine for you tonight. Will you be there?"

"I'll be here. Is there anything I need to prepare for?"

"No, Dear. Some people in Israel are calling their families to reassure them is all." Sarah spoke to her parents for several minutes, and Paul went to the garage to keep himself busy. Sarah talked with her mother about her grades, about Tracey's graduation, about the rain. Then she joined Paul in the garage.

"Everything okay?"

"I guess so, but I need to be here tonight at nine to take a call from my cousin."

"Why do they have to live so close to the Syrian border? Do they enjoy being shot at by the Syrians?" asked Paul.

"My uncle made a choice years ago. He was going to live in Israel and create a Jewish nation. He chose to make a stand, even if it meant putting his family at risk." She sat down on a nail keg, while Paul inspected his backboard. "If you believe strongly enough, sometimes you have to forego comfort and safety. I've seen pictures of Shamir. It's all boulders and fences on the side of a hill overlooking the Jordan River. My cousins sleep in dorms. My uncle takes precautions; the whole compound is secure, and he doesn't believe harm will come to Hannah or the others." Sarah laughed. "Those Zionists are hard-headed. You can't reason with them."

"You admire him, don't you?"

Her eyes focused on a previous time. "I didn't used to. I thought he was foolish. But now, yeah, I do."

"What about your father and mother?"

"My father has raised thousands of dollars for Israel. I remember something he once told me. 'We all have a part to play.'"

"So, you do remember something your dad told you after all." Paul smiled.

"I've been pretty hard on my parents over the last couple of years. They're an older couple, at least ten years older than your parents. I'm sorry for that."

"It's part of the separation that's natural for a strong-willed daughter, you know. I doubt if Eugene holds any grudges. He's a pretty wise old doctor."

"You're right, but my mother has been hurt."

"Tell her you're sorry, give her a hug, and move on."

"I'm not as tough as you give me credit for, you know."

Paul smiled inwardly as he pulled the tape from the backboard that outlined the orange shooting square. "What do you say we go to the mountains?"

Sarah packed a picnic lunch with a jug of water—she had squeezed the skin around her hips and promised to cut back on beer for the summer—and they headed up to Estes Park and Rocky Mountain National Park. In the park they drove to the Bear Lake trailhead, where about a dozen cars and trucks were already parked. Morning rains had given way to midday sun and warmer temperatures. They did not get far before they found an open spot just off the trail near a creek.

"I'm safe here," Sarah mused as she sat on a rock by the fast-running creek. "Not *here* here. I mean in America. I risk nothing; I'm hardly even Jewish. If it wasn't for my sorority, I wouldn't have any connection with Jewry at all. In all other ways, I could be a Tri-Delt." They both laughed at her remark.

"We screw too much for you to be a Tri-Delt," Paul responded, "and they don't accept Jews." That particular smile of affection came over both of them. They both loved their lovemaking. "You're changing, I'm changing, but is it youth or culture or Israel's dilemma?" It was a serious question. Paul tossed a willow twig into the stream. "All things fall into the stream and head for the sea." He stared into the creek and bit his cheeks.

She narrowed her eyes as if to say, "That's so dumb!" before actually saying it. She splashed him with water from the creek; then they searched for a secluded spot away from the trail to add proof she could not be a Tri-Delt.

That evening Paul watched Sarah toss and turn while she dozed on the couch. She had fallen asleep as soon as they returned home, around six. Boulder's wettest May in over a decade kept the temperatures bearable in the second-floor apartment, and as the rain began to fall again, Paul covered his girlfriend with a blanket. The current crisis was taking a toll on her, but he realized he was tired too. He touched her on the shoulder, and then went to the refrigerator in search of dinner.

Around eight, she stirred and sat up. "What time is it?"

"A little after eight. I was going to wake you in about a half an hour."

"What are you reading?"

"A novel Cohen gave me about Vietnam."

"You're amazing. You read everything."

"Got a lot a catching up to do from all those years when I didn't read, from when I was a math guy." He smiled, remembering all those times he had done book reports on sports books.

"Do we have anything to eat?" asked Sarah as she wrapped her arms around him from behind.

The phone in Paul's room rang precisely at nine. The two students gave a glance to one another and grimaced, probably for different reasons.

"Yes, I can hear you. Will Shamir come under attack?" asked Sarah.

"We're well fortified. If there is war, the battles will be a little north and south of us. We get shelled, but it's been going on for years. Anyway, the Syrians cannot hit the ocean from the beach," said Hannah.

"Will you guys go to the bunker when the fighting starts?"

"Sarah, there might not be a war, but if there is, we will not be going into hiding. Judith will go to a cellar, but the rest of us have a rifle and a post. Most of us cannot wait. It is time to end this constant harassment by the Syrians."

"Where's Martin?"

Hannah spoke with confidence. "He's in the Negev. He is fine. We are all eager. If war comes, we will be ready."

"Will there be war, Hannah?"

"It is out of our hands now. If the UN and America cannot get the straits open, then we will fight!"

"What can I do?"

"Keep sending money." Hannah laughed. "I have to go now. Do not worry for us, Sarah. We will be fine."

"Shalom, Hannah." Sarah hung up the phone gently and kept her hand on the receiver. Paul watched her carefully and waited. Without moving, except for turning her head to look at him, she finally spoke. "There will be war, and it will be soon."

"Is that what Hannah said?"

"No, not in so many words, but it's why she's calling. She said it was out of Israel's hands."

"Who will decide then?"

"Everyone but Israel. The Arabs, the UN, the Soviet Union, America. They have to prevent it, but who can silence Nasser?" It was a rhetorical question. "No one now; he's gone too far with his posturing."

The phone rang again.

"Did you get to speak with Hannah?"

"Yes, Mother, I did. We just finished."

"See, everything is going to be fine."

"No, Mother, it's not, but I appreciate what you're trying to do for me." There was gentleness to Sarah's words.

"Sarah, dear," Sarah cut her off politely.

"Mother, I know what's happening. You can't protect me from it. I'll worry, but Jews all over the world are worrying. I'm no different. I'm a Jew too. Israel will fight, and we will worry."

"What else can we do, my dear? What else can we do?"

"What else, indeed."

Curled up on the couch, they watched the ten o'clock news. In New York Jews had rallied near Broadway and 72nd in support of Israel, but a counterdemonstration by Arabs had resulted in a near riot. Jeering, spitting, eggs, tomatoes, and bags of water were the weapons. After the police broke up the battle, over 20,000 Jews marched up Riverside Drive. Along the way a few Arabs chanted, "Aqaba is Arab" and "Bring the Jews to America and peace to the Mideast."

"I'm not even there," whispered Sarah.

Monday, May 29

In the morning, they drove down to a used furniture store on west Pearl and picked out a three-drawer dresser for Sarah. They loaded it onto the bed of his truck, tied it down, and headed back to 1203. In his garage Paul sanded the top, glued together the backs of two drawers, and added one-quarter of an inch to one leg so it would not wobble. They carried it upstairs and into the bedroom where Sarah set to work unpacking her things. Paul returned to the garage to attach the rim to his backboard.

For lunch Sarah treated Paul to a burger and fries, and then they mounted the backboard on the garage. She stood on the roof and held the board to the braces he had erected on Thursday, while he inserted lag bolts through the four pre-drilled holes. She tightened the nuts with a crescent wrench. When it was secure, she climbed down, with Paul providing support with his hand on her butt.

"Yep, that's firm."

"Smart ass!"

Paul put the level across the rim and was satisfied. "Now, as long as Mose doesn't hang on it, I think it'll be okay. Care to make the first basket?"

"Might take a while, my dear."

"I'll rebound."

It took her three attempts before she banked one in from the left side about five feet away. They shot around for another half-hour, even playing a little one-on-one, with Paul backing her down under the basket. She would jump on his back when he bent over close to the hoop, trying to keep him from raising his arms above his shoulders. She made a new rule, the Phillips' Rule, whenever one of them made a basket, they had to kiss.

"Mose'll love this rule," Paul said.

"Only applies to you and me. Doesn't matter whether I'm on your team or the other team . . . or even if I'm just watching. When you score, I get a kiss."

They took their first shower together in the afternoon and discovered a new way to make love.

"Let's dress up and go to the Lamp Post for dinner, and then we can take in a movie," suggested Paul as they toweled off. He touched her hair. "It's really grown out since you cut it."

"Dinner there would be pretty expensive, my dear."

"My dad slipped me an extra twenty last week when we were down for dinner. Bonus for good grades."

"My father has always put money in my account for each A. Now you know why I study so hard."

"And how you can afford your clothes," smiled Paul.

Paul studied Sarah's face as she gazed into the fireplace at the Lamp Post. They spoke very little before their food was served, content with holding hands and the ambiance. As the food began to arrive, she turned her attention back to him. He had not minded at all, confident her inattention was only because she was comfortable enough in his presence to stay quiet with her own thoughts. She leaned over and smelled his salad, actually the salad dressing, and made a funny face.

"Roquefort?"

"A king's delight!" Paul answered.

"I thought that was watermelon."

"Actually, it's something else entirely," he said.

"Promise me when we travel through Europe you'll try the local cuisine. You're so picky, and so generic, so meat and potatoes."

"You still want to go to the movie?"

"I don't think so. Let's just go back to the apartment and watch TV."

Sarah was in a good mood, relaxed and happy. They had avoided news from any source, kept busy, stayed by themselves, and been very physical all day. He had promised her a better day last night, and he had kept his promise.

That night in bed, she massaged his back and talked. "Ignorance is bliss, but I'll need a paper tomorrow. One day is enough. By the way, what did you do with it?"

"It's in the trash can in the garage," said Paul.

"Thanks. I kind of needed a day off to re-charge. I did think about things over there a few times, though. When we were playing ball this afternoon, I thought about my cousin Robert who wants to play for Israel's national team. He loves basketball. And at dinner, I have to confess that before the food was served, I was wondering about Hannah and Martin, and whether or not they have ever gone out to dinner on a date. There are no restaurants on the kibbutz, just one large dining hall."

"Not very romantic, huh?"

"I wouldn't think so," said Sarah.

"Remember how we would sit in the corner at the Grille at the UMC and get lost in our own world? Maybe Martin and Hannah can do that too," offered Paul.

"I hope so." She stopped rubbing his shoulders and rolled over onto her back. Paul turned onto his side and propped his head up on his left arm. "Over spring break, in New York, Hannah said the city was so noisy. In Israel, at least in the Galilee, it's quiet, and the sky is still a mystery at night. 'All the stars are still here' is what she said." Sarah stretched out her arms above her head and smiled. "Tell me about what you thought when you first met me. I'll close my eyes and put images to your words." Paul touched her face with the fingers on his right hand but was rebuked. "No touching. It will distract me from your words. Your touch has a way, you know."

"Okay, let's see." Paul pulled back his hand and decided to try to be funny about this game. "I remember the look on your face when Mrs. Meyer asked you to introduce us, and you didn't know my last name." The corners of Sarah's mouth flinched. "I didn't know what to think about that, whether to worry about it, but you saved us by touching my chest as I left."

She opened her eyes, turned, and gave him a kiss on the cheek. "I should have given you a kiss." She laid back and closed her eyes again. "Continue."

"I walked about a block, just to be cool, and then I ran back here. I called Kevin to tell him, and then I rounded up Mose, Dan, and Sally and told them about you. I think they thought I was nuts. I was less mature then than I am now." Sarah laughed slightly.

His recollections went on for another ten minutes before he decided she was ready to sleep. "We can continue later. We've got time."

Sarah snuggled up. "Thank you, Paul Garrity."

Tuesday, May 30

Eugene Phillips had a difficult time waiting until eight to call his daughter, but knowing it was two hours earlier in Colorado and Sarah would still be sleeping delayed his impulses. He was distressed with his recent dilemma. On one hand, he wanted to protect his daughter from the dangers of the Israeli crisis, to protect her as he always had from the outside world, to keep her as his child. On the other hand, he was proud of her growth, proud of her desire to know about Judaism and Israel, proud of her decision to demand he share what he knew about the events of the Mideast. In the end, it was the promise she had extracted from him to tell her everything. He dialed Paul Garrity's number.

Two thousand miles away, Paul Garrity was not sleeping. He slept very little during the night. Around five he got up, brewed some coffee, and started reading his Cold War notes from Dr. Orr to see if he could make some sense of Sarah's devil. The phone startled him.

"Hello."

"Hello, Paul, this is Eugene Phillips. I know it's early and I apologize, but I would like to speak with my daughter."

Paul rubbed his head. "Yeah, sure, just a minute." He put the phone on the counter and went back to the bedroom to wake her. "Sarah," he said softly as he put his hand on her shoulder. "Sarah, your dad's on the phone."

Her eyes flew open. "My father?" Naked, she grabbed Paul's sweatshirt off the hook on the back of the door, slipped it over her head, and went to the phone. "Father, what's going on?" she said with concern.

Paul wondered if she covered herself so she would not be exposed in front of her father. He could hear only her portion of the conversation.

"But Hussein hates Nasser. Nasser's tried to get him killed; he's ostracized him from the Arab world; he's constantly called him a tool of the United States. Why would he sign a pact with him?"

Paul knew what had happened. Jordan had signed an agreement with Egypt. "Blood is thicker . . ."

"Israel is surrounded now. It can only be a matter of time until war breaks out, until Israel is invaded." There was some panic in her voice. Paul watched her as she listened to her father. "Has Rosenthal spoken with anyone in Washington or is that just a prediction?" She turned toward Paul. "So LBJ is telling Eban he can't promise his support if Israel strikes first. Israel can't wait. Mobilization for them can't be a permanent condition. The economy will collapse!" Paul had shown her the article in the *News* about a prolonged standoff in the Mideast and why Israel could not afford to partake in that process. "So you're saying Hussein had to join to save his throne? To hold off the Palestinians?" Paul was trying to understand Dr. Phillips' statements. "Could I even get there now?" Sarah glanced up at Paul at this last remark and bit her lower lip. She looked away. "What could I do? What could I do! Well, I could watch over the children while their parents fight the Arabs! Armies are more than just riflemen!" Her chest heaved as she made this last point. "I'll talk to him, of course. We talk about everything!" It seemed to Paul as if she resented what her father had just asked her to do. "I'm sorry, Father. Is Mother okay?" Her head dipped slightly. Paul remained motionless. "I'll call you this evening. Thanks for calling." Sarah hung up the phone and turned immediately to Paul. "Decision time."

He saw her mussed hair, her long legs, and her dark brown eyes, but he thought only of her heart and where it was taking her.

They went back to bed to warm up rather than sleep. She continued to wear the sweatshirt. Neither spoke for several minutes about anything of importance, but they both knew she would have to begin the discussion.

"Did you get all of that," she finally asked.

"Most of it. The important parts."

"There will be war now, you know."

"Maybe. It didn't happen last week when I was sure it would break out. Adding Jordan to the mix still shouldn't change the positions of the Soviet Union and the US"

"My parents think you can talk me out of going."

Paul smiled. "They've misjudged me from the beginning, haven't they?"

"You could, you know." Her brown eyes fixed onto his. Finally, she released him, sat up, and removed the sweatshirt. "We'll never wear pajamas to bed, okay."

Because it was Memorial Day, the *Boulder Daily Camera* was delivered in the morning. The headline confirmed what Sarah's father had told her: King Hussein of Jordan had signed a defense pact with Egypt. Whatever differences the two leaders had were cast aside. The animosity existing between them was forgotten in the face of the greater enemy, the Zionists. In Israel the war preparations continued. Lines formed at hospitals to give blood, and the postal deliveries were being made by civilians, as call-ups depleted the work force. On page seven, a story chronicled America's response, or lack of one.

"Secret diplomacy," complained Sarah. "LBJ won't stand up in support of the Jews. Do you think it has anything to do with the fact most of us Jews oppose his stupid war in Vietnam?"

"Actually, I don't. By staying quiet, I think it gives him some room to maneuver, some time to use diplomacy. LBJ may be the only one who really doesn't want a war to break out. Maybe he's convinced that Israel doesn't need America's help to defeat the Arabs." He raised his eyebrows. She looked at him funny.

"Can Israel win alone?" she asked.

Paul stared intently at his girlfriend. "If I didn't think they could, I wouldn't let you go, if that's your decision."

"Am I just being a stupid American Jew who's caught up in the moment? Can I really do something?"

"That's your mother talking. Of course, you can help."

It rained again for the seventh day in a row. AJ Foyt won the Indy 500. Paul and Sarah spent the morning and a part of the afternoon cleaning the last two downstairs apartments, then they tackled the large bathroom.

"Boys are so gross."

Mose called from Pueblo to see if Paul needed him before Wednesday. Sally's mother was just treating him too well to leave early.

"Did you call your mom?" asked Paul.

"Yeah, she's still doing good. I'll be back around noon, and you can pick me up at the Broadway bus stop. Did you get my hoop up yet?"

For dinner Paul cooked spaghetti while Sarah wrote in her diary. While the sauce simmered, he sliced the French bread, buttered it, and slipped it back into its foil to be heated later on. Finally, he opened a bottle of wine, poured two glasses, and sat down on the couch next to Sarah.

"Thanks." She did a toast "to peace" and kissed him.

"Your hair has sure grown since February. Are you going to cut it again?"

"Nope. Going back to what it was like when we met in January."

"Do you know what attracted me to you last year?" Paul let his question linger for a moment. "Your looks. Quite simply, I thought you were pretty. I didn't know anything else about you. Your hair was even longer than this year. I somehow thought you were an upperclassman."

Sarah shook her head. "Explain."

"Can't really, but I saw you occasionally at the cafeteria, and I just wondered about you . . . from a distance. Still do."

"In a good way, huh."

"Yeah. Up close."

She closed her diary. "You can't read this, you know. Someday I'll let you, but not now." She took a sip of her wine and then put her head back against the couch. "I'm going to wait another day or so to see what happens. If things get worse, I'm going. If not, I'll stay here with you."

Paul turned on the couch. "Can your dad get you tickets? What's the route?" He acted calm, but his insides churned. He had lied earlier. He had no idea whether Israel could win a war against such a united force as was gathering at its borders. He only knew he was going to support her in whatever path she chose. Her leap from the train had been a long one. The butterflies in his stomach were greater than for any baseball or basketball game in which he ever played, his apprehension at a level he had never experienced. He had jumped from the train also.

"Everything seems to be open to Tel Aviv still. If war breaks out, there's no guarantee that anyone will fly in. I'll just have to see."

Wednesday, May 31

Paul was relieved the phone did not ring on Wednesday morning. *No news is good news*, he thought. He got up and went to the bathroom before eight. *Too much wine.* The apartment was darker than it should have been, but one look out of the window explained why. The clouds were thick, and rain was falling. Was it really time to start the ark? He dressed quietly and closed the door behind him. He made coffee, grabbed some change from the dish next to the counter and left to buy a newspaper.

Sarah heard his footsteps on the stairs and smelled the coffee. She stretched and then went to the bathroom to fix herself up. Paul was back before she was out of the bathroom.

"Anything in the paper?" she called out when he checked on her.

"Nothing new. Just more about Hussein and his brother Nasser. Actually, there's a front-page story about Vietnam, more bombing near Hanoi. Maybe that's a good sign."

She emerged from her bathroom cocoon as a beautiful butterfly. She hugged her boyfriend and allowed him to kiss her.

"Why the make-up?"

"For you. How about some coffee? It's so quiet and peaceful. Is it raining hard?"

"Not yet, but the forecast says this could be the day. Maybe as much as two inches. Any plans for today?" asked Paul.

"Just read and mess with you." She took a coffee cup from the cupboard and picked up the paper.

"I'm going to run over to campus to advertise the rooms for rent. Put up notices at the UMC and at Regent's. They'll go quickly. Then, nothing. Are you hungry?"

"God, no!" she replied patting her belly. "Any idea when Mose will get back?"

Paul shook his head. "About noon. Can you pick him up if I don't get back?"

"For a price." She smiled and moved closer.

As quiet and peaceful as it was in Boulder, the opposite condition existed at Shamir and Jerusalem and in Tel Aviv. Sandbagging store fronts, taping windows, refitting buses for war use—all while daily chores were being done. But the Israelis were not alone. Jews, especially from Europe, were mobilizing to help. Young men were flying to Tel Aviv to support the effort, and money was being raised in all parts of the world for the defense of Israel.

In the Knesset Israeli leaders knew time was drawing short. They could not maintain their war readiness indefinitely. If LBJ could not reopen the Red Sea, they would have to.

Paul exchanged the five-dollar bill for quarters and called from the pay phone booth next to the bowling alley at the UMC.

"Congressman Rosenthal's office. May I help you?"

"Ah, hello, is the congressman in?"

"Who may I say is calling?"

"This is Paul Garrity from Boulder, Colorado."

The line went quiet for a moment. Paul did not think he would be patched through, even if the congressman was at his office in New York. He pulled out his list of questions just in case.

"Hello, Paul. You caught me at a good moment. What can I do for you?" The friendly voice of Benjamin Rosenthal was also loud.

"Thank you for taking my call, sir. I know you have more important issues to deal with right now, but I have a few questions."

"Well, as I said, you caught me just between visitors. It has been pretty hectic around here of late. How is Sarah?"

"Pretty nervous, sir. Actually, she's very stressed out."

"She's not alone. Jews everywhere are quite anxious, as you can well imagine. What can I tell you?" The congressman's concern was felt through 2,000 miles of phone line, but his manner put Paul more at ease."

"I'd like to ask you a few questions, if I could."

"Certainly."

"Will there be war?" Paul just blurted out the toughest question.

"I can only tell you what I know, but I will try to give you the best I can. I believe there will be, Paul."

"What makes you think so?"

"Several things. My sources tell me a sort of calm has settled over the people of Israel and even in the Knesset, as if a realization has occurred that the decision has been made. Also, Moshe Dayan is back. He'll be named defense minister soon. And Prime Minister Eshkol has formed a National Unity government. Do you understand what all that means, Paul?"

"I think so, sir. It's like a war cabinet, isn't it?"

"Yes."

"What's your feeling about Israel getting our support?"

"You ask intelligent questions, Paul. You certainly impressed me when I met you this spring." Rosenthal's words were genuine. "The President. He cannot say so publicly, but I'm sure he will support Israel. Some officials have given Israel the green light. They have come around to the same conclusion the Jews have. Nasser is no longer bluffing, and he must be silenced if Israel is to survive."

"How long, sir," Paul paused, "until it starts?"

"That I cannot say for sure, but very, very soon. A few days. Maybe ten days. No longer though. The longer Israel waits, the more Egypt will prepare, and the more casualties will occur."

"Israel will actually go to war on its own?"

"Our country is, officially, opposed to a pre-emptive strike, but I am afraid Israel sees no other way. They will never accept the permanent closure of the southern waterway."

Paul scribbled notes as fast as he could. An operator reminded him additional coins were necessary to continue. He deposited two more quarters. "How long will it last?"

"Again, I cannot say. It will be decided in the United Nations by the Soviets and the Americans. Ironically, Israel will fight the war, but it will be ended by those who refuse to prevent it."

"One last question, sir. Is it safe to go?"

"To go? You can't be thinking about visiting Israel just now, can you?"

"No, sir. It's Sarah."

Sarah burst into the apartment and hugged Paul. "Where have you been?" she asked. Mose entered shortly after, holding up his hands to indicate no hug was forthcoming.

"Just over on campus." He did not want to talk about his phone call with Rosenthal just now, so he kissed her and turned to Mose. "When did you get back, Robinson?"

"An hour ago. We went out for lunch. Sally said to say hi. The hoop looks good, man!"

They went for dinner around seven. Mose was in an exceptionally good mood, probably because he had been pampered for three days by Sally's mom.

"Are we going to start on the apartment tomorrow?" Mose asked as he cut his roast beef.

"I don't think so. There'll be interruptions from people looking for a room, and I'm enjoying her company too much to get started yet. Maybe later in the week. You can shoot hoops if it's not raining." Paul leaned into Sarah's shoulder in a show of affection. "Also, I owe her a dinner from the grade race, and I want to pay off." He looked at her. "Greenbriar or the Flagstaff House?"

"Is it safe to say you guys didn't miss me the last few days?" laughed Mose.

There was bantering back and forth throughout the meal, with Mose getting in the best shots. Sarah did not try to protect Paul, enjoying his discomfort as much as Mose. It was too bad, she thought, that Sally was not spending the summer in Boulder with them.

Sarah plopped down on the couch when they returned and moaned. "I've had a stomachache all day."

"Nerves?"

"I think so. I just can't put this whole mess out of my mind."

Paul raised a beer at Sarah, who shook her head no. He opened a cola for himself, took a drink, and then joined her on the couch. She rotated so she could lie flat with her head on his leg.

"I talked with Rosenthal today." She watched him closely. He put his right hand on her hair and looked down into her eyes. Her left hand slid up his left arm. "He thinks time has run out, that war is imminent." Paul rolled his lips inward. "Israel won't wait much longer for others to solve this problem."

"What do you think?" she asked, emphasizing you.

"Same. That's why I called . . . for confirmation." He was measuring his words. "Sars, I think you need to call your father and line up those plane tickets. If fighting starts, you won't be able to get in, and you'll regret not being there. You've come too far to sit this out." More than support for Sarah's journey, more than permission, Paul was giving his approval, his full-on endorsement. Safety be damned. What had begun as an exploration was now a passage, and the Boulder leg was ending. He simultaneously took hold of her hand and let it go.

Tears welled up in her eyes and she curled her lips inward. "But how do I leave you?"

Tears formed in Paul's eyes too. He smiled slightly, reassuringly. "Because you know I'll be here when you get back. The war won't last long. You can visit your family on the kibbutz and then hurry back."

Sarah blinked her tears out, then rolled her head into his torso and hugged him tightly. After a few minutes, she pulled back. "I need to call home before it gets any later."

"He can get me home on Friday." She looked conflicted with a momentary faraway gaze. "And to Paris on Sunday night. He's working on getting me to Israel from there."

"Sounds like he's been checking the schedules ahead of time," said Paul. She walked into him as he sat on the counter. "Are you okay?" he asked, knowing she wasn't.

"I'll go in your place," offered Mose, who had been listening at Paul's door.

"No, you won't. You're too big of a target. But thanks. This is something I've got to do . . . for myself."

"What else did he say?" asked Paul.

"I'll have to go to the Israeli Consulate and sign some papers, but it's close to my home, and I have the feeling my father has gotten them all in order. Evidently, I'm not the only American Jewish person who wants to go, but most of the others are men. About a hundred or so, my father thinks."

"Is he okay with you going?" asked Paul.

"He's worried, as is my mother, but they raised a Jewish kid. What should they expect?" She seemed more at ease than she had been just fifteen minutes earlier.

"What did your mom say?"

"She's happy I'll be home for Shabbat." She paused. "Is there a band at the Tule tonight?"

Paul looked at Mose for an answer and got nothing.

Sarah stepped back and pulled Paul from the counter. "Well,

boys, let's go find out. I want to dance."

There was no band, just a DJ at Tulagi's. Sarah laughed and danced hard, as Paul tried to keep up. Mose found a local girl and danced too. The crowd was sparse, but it was perfect . . . and Sarah had no curfew.

Lying in bed, Sarah cried. "Get use to this, my dear. It could be ongoing for the next few days."

"I'm excited for you. I'll worry, but I'm proud of you for going." He was proud of her, but he was scared for her, and he was going to miss her terribly under these conditions. He knew they would be out of contact.

"How many times can we make love before I leave?"

Paul gave serious thought to the question, until he was interrupted by Sarah. "What?" he asked.

"It was a request to start on number one." she said.

They made love tenderly at first, but with greater physical intensity as the minutes passed by, and when they finished, she cried again. They fell asleep bound together as tightly as two people who had only known one another for five months could be.

JUNE

Thursday, June 1

The day started as the night had ended, two naked bodies intertwined.

"How long have you been awake?" asked Sarah.

"Not long. Just before you," he lied. He had been awake most of the night, holding tightly to his lover, listening to her breath, feeling her heartbeat.

"I have to pee!" she said with a smile.

"So do I. You go first." It was not quite seven.

When they both had flushed the beer, they dressed and made coffee.

"I think I want to go to the Flagstaff House, and I want Mose to go with us."

"A chaperone?"

"Don't you think we need one?"

"Definitely! I'll call for reservations."

She smiled. "We all have to dress up."

"Tie?"

"Of course. Mose too."

"He might refuse the invitation if you force him to wear one."

"He wouldn't dare."

"Hungry?"

"Famished."

The Columbine was a greasy spoon just around the corner from 1203 on Broadway, but it served the best breakfasts. Paul and Dan and Mose had gone there often first semester, but not at all second semester. Paul ordered bacon and eggs; Sarah ordered oatmeal.

"Why do you suppose LBJ still refuses to go public?" she asked. It was a familiar question from her. The president's silence had frustrated her from the beginning of the crisis.

"Dr. Orr would say because of oil." Sarah looked puzzled. "Even though we support Israel, we have to do this dance with the Arabs to get their oil. That's too simplistic, but it's a big part of the equation. They can say publicly whatever they choose, as Nasser has done for the past few weeks, but we can't."

"But we will support Israel, won't we?" Again, she was looking for assurances.

"Rosenthal said his sources assured him the Israelis won't need US help."

"What do you think?"

"I think he's right, and I wish the South Vietnamese didn't either.

Honestly, Sars, I don't know what the military situation is."

"We haven't talked about Vietnam for a while, have we?"

From the Columbine they crossed Broadway at University Avenue and headed onto campus across the old stone bridge, walking and talking slowly, arm-in-arm.

"What's Israel like anyway?" asked Paul. "I mean with trees and vegetation and all. Or is it just desert?"

"Oh, no! The northern half is green with fields and forests. I guess the valleys north and west of the Galilee are quite beautiful. We were taught in Hebrew School about the land of milk and honey and the Fertile Crescent. From Jerusalem south, though, it's the Negev, which is a desert. The Dead Sea is barren, too, I guess, but it's supposed to be beautiful in its own way."

"How will you meet up with your family once you get there?" Paul's concern was obvious.

He knew she was about to reassure him and did not really know how. "If there is no war, then I'll take a bus, but if war has started, then," she paused, "then I'll hitchhike or get a ride on a tank or something."

"You'll go to the kibbutz, won't you?"

"Of course. Remember, I'm going to take care of all the little kids there while everyone else fights or works. What's your concern here?"

"I don't want you in Tel Aviv. It seems to be the city the Arabs equate with Zionism. 'On to Tel Aviv' seems to be a rallying cry."

Their walk had no destination, but in time they found themselves at Brackett Hall, on the east side of campus. "Show me your old room," she said. "They'll probably let us in. Nobody should be there except the R.A."

They climbed the half-dozen steps on the south side and knocked on the R.A.'s door but got no answer. "Come on," said Paul, "it's just down the hall." Room 120. Mose had been in 121. Dan was 124.

"How'd you guys get together, you know, start hanging out?" she asked.

"Interestingly enough, Dan and I both brought basketballs from home. A bunch of us were playing over at the gym almost immediately, including Mose. Then we ate our meals together, went to football games together, and just became pals. It's funny how people form relationships." Paul smiled. "And we all shared the toilets and showers, a true bonding experience."

"Do you miss not playing basketball?" she asked as they left Brackett and headed back west toward the UMC fountain.

"No, not so much anymore. I still play all that pick-up, and that's all I need. Plus, I'm usually smart enough to be on Mose's team. Lesson in life, I guess. Who you're with in life matters. Keep that in mind." He stopped and smiled at her.

She hugged him and kissed him on the cheek. "Oh, I know, my dear. I know."

When they arrived at the UMC, it was obvious someone had emptied soap into the fountain again, as it was filled with suds.

That afternoon Sarah called Sally, Anne, and Dan and told them about her decision. Then she called Mrs. Meyer, who was visiting her family in Fort Collins. She was able to get the number and reached her there. Mrs. Meyer was concerned but told her that her life was always an adventure. "Be very careful, Sarah. Call me when you get back to Boulder. Say hello to Paul for me."

Paul rented out a downstairs apartment to a grad student. Mose was thankful for a dry afternoon and went for a run. It was cool, but there was no rain.

"Are they all worried?" asked Paul.

"Except Anne. She's a Jew and understands. She thinks everything always turns out right for me anyway."

"Does she want to go too?"

"No! Anne? God, no! She has more sense than I do, but she wants to hear all about it when I get back."

"What did Sally say?" said Paul.

"She wants you to go with me. She said Mose could run this place and you could protect me."

"Obviously, she has no concept of what's going on over there. What else did she say?" asked Paul.

"She's working with some women's clinic and starts on Monday in a florist shop. She seemed very happy."

"And Dan?"

"He's worried about you," said Sarah.

"He didn't say that!"

"No, but I could tell. He's going to call you this weekend. Wants you and Mose to come up. You better go! I don't want you sitting around reading books about the Mideast and worrying about me."

"When you leave, I'm not leaving the apartment. Just staying inside until you get back. Draw the shades."

She drew him into her arms. "Promise me you won't worry too much. Remember what you told me, that you wouldn't let me go if you felt it wasn't safe. I'm going to be very careful and come back safe and sound. Okay?"

"Okay. You better start getting ready for dinner. It takes you longer than me."

It took about twenty minutes to drive partway up the mountain to get to the Flagstaff House. Located on the side of the mountain, just north of the Flatirons, it offered a spectacular view of Boulder at night. Paul's parents had taken him, Mose, Dan, and Sally there in the fall when Dick Garrity had received a promotion. It was crowded on Thursday night with seniors and their parents anticipating Friday's commencement ceremony. The maître d' led Sarah, Paul, and Mose to a quiet table opposite the kitchen entrance with a great view and close to the fireplace. Sarah was impressed.

"What did you do to get this table?" she asked.

Mose started to answer, but Paul cut him off. "They saw you and were impressed, I guess. Happens wherever I take you." She leaned over and lightly kissed him on the cheek.

"Worth it already, huh, Garrity?" said Mose.

Paul switched topics. "I wish they made those Dick Tracy phones you could carry around with you, so I could keep in touch with you over the next few weeks."

"I'm going to call you whenever I can, and I'll write every night. I'll bet I'm back before most of my letters arrive."

"Have you heard from Hannah recently?" asked Mose.

Sarah shook her head no. "Oh, that reminds me. I'll need to stop by the house tomorrow and pick up my mail." She touched Mose's forearm. "I'll even write you a letter, Robinson."

The waiter arrived with the wine list.

"I'm too young," smiled Paul.

"Not me. I'll take a merlot." She lied, but the waiter did not ask for an ID.

"I'll take a beer," ordered Mose.

Paul held up two fingers indicating that he would take a beer too.

"Are you excited?" Mose finally asked her in a serious tone.

"Unbelievably so! It's strange. All my life people have been telling me about this place, Israel, and I didn't pay much attention. Then I hook up with Paul," she squeezed his hand under the table, "and he gets me all excited about what's going on over there." She smiled. "That's not all he's got me all excited about." She turned to Paul. "I love you," and the tears in her eyes appeared again. She bit her bottom lip. "Excuse me, I need to go to the ladies' room," and she left the table.

"Did I do that?" asked Mose.

"Don't worry about it. She's just going through every emotion possible. It won't be the last time she cries tonight."

"This has to be hard on you."

Paul deflected the serious response. "Well, the upside to it all is she's even more passionate than normal, if that's possible."

"You've been a lucky guy this semester, Garrity."

Sarah returned shortly with her eye make-up back to perfect. "Must have gotten something in my eye."

"That was nice."

"Are you referring to what just happened or to tonight's dinner?"

"Dinner. I wouldn't use nice to describe what just occurred." She smiled and took another deep breath. "I couldn't do this if you weren't supporting me, you know." Paul lay still. "I'd be like my sorority sisters. No!" she interrupted herself. "I'd be like I was a year ago. Safe and ignorant." He remained quiet. Only his hands spoke. "I'm not very brave yet, but you've given me enough courage to overcome some doubts about myself."

"I did that, huh? All I was trying to do was get in your pants."

"It didn't take you long to achieve your goal, did it?"

"Seriously, Sars, I'm proud of you."

"For what? All I'm doing is going on a trip . . ."

" . . . to a war zone."

" . . . and doing what I want to do, not what I should be doing. Sort of like falling so much in love with you, a Gentile apartment manager, basketball nut, carpenter, history major."

"Whatever. You know, you're a little melodramatic about my part in all of this. Your going is pretty remarkable at this time. You're scared, but you're going, and you're going to miss me, but you're going."

"Do you have any idea what you're trying to say?" she teased.

"Something about going. Hard to explain."

"Just be quiet and hug me while I fall asleep." She rolled into the crook of his shoulder and closed her eyes. "Paul . . ."

"Yeah?"

"Will you sleep tonight?"

"About like last night, I guess."

"So not much then, huh?"

"Shh."

"I love you."

"I love you and I'm going to miss you, but I'll be here when you get back."

"Paul."

"Yeah?"

"Maybe when I'm older, I'll do what I should, not be so intransigent."

"How much older?"

Friday, June 2

Eugene Phillips did not wait this time. He called his daughter at five Boulder time. "There was shooting yesterday with the Syrians. Two Jews died. Are you sure you want to do this?" he asked with great concern.

"Yes, Father, I've decided. Meet me at the airport. Did you get everything?"

"We'll go to the consulate to sign the papers when you arrive. Why am I letting you do this?" It was a rhetorical question asked with genuine anxiety.

"Will the consulate still be open?"

"I have some privileges afforded to me. Someone will be there. Your mother and I will meet you at the gate."

Sarah had packed her suitcases the day before. She hung up the phone and went back into the bedroom where Paul waited.

"My father just wanted to check on me, to see if I was still coming." She pulled back the covers and climbed in.

"You know I'll read about it in the paper, Sars."

"There was some shooting up by Shamir, a little south. Syrians. God! They started the whole thing. I hope they don't get away without being held accountable."

"Even if there's no war, they'll get theirs," said Paul.

"I'm sorry. No war or political talk in bed. That's another rule. How much time do we have before we need to get up?"

"We need to leave here by eight."

"I probably can't talk you into going with me, can I?"

"No, you probably can't. I never got a passport." It was an answer to deflect a deeper response.

They got out of bed an hour later and had cereal and orange juice for breakfast. Sarah showered and dressed for the plane trip to New York, a black pants suit with a brown blouse.

"Got everything?" Paul asked.

She looked around the bedroom and then took his picture off her dresser. "I think I'll take this one too. I've got a whole set of pictures to show Hannah."

"Won't the glass break?"

"I'll carry it on the plane in my purse and then roll it for the trip to Israel. I need to say goodbye to Mose. Do you think he's awake?"

"No, but go in anyway."

"I wish I knew how long I was going to be gone." To Paul, it appeared as if she was questioning her decision. "Then I'd know if I've packed enough."

Paul suspected what was coming next, so he steered her out of the room. "Go see Mose. I'll get your bags. Whatever you don't have, you can borrow from your cousin. Go!"

She crossed over to Mose's apartment while Paul took her bags down to the truck. Since it wasn't raining, and none was predicted until later in the day, they decided to take his truck. There was a lot of action at the Colonial, senior girls getting ready to graduate. *Just two more years*, he thought. He went back upstairs.

"I guess I've got everything." She wrapped her arms around his neck. "A couple of weeks won't be too long, will it?"

"No. Maybe I'll even clean the apartment while you're gone." He kissed her, then as they left, he yelled out, "See you, Mose. I'll be back before noon."

At Stapleton Airport in Denver, Sarah checked two bags and carried an oversized leather purse with her to the gate. "I'm scared. What if I'm just in the way when war breaks out?" Tears again.

"You won't be. You have a knack for helping, for getting things done. Don't doubt yourself now."

She hugged him tightly. "I really am scared, but I'll take your words with me." She took his tissue. "I knew I shouldn't have put on so much make-up. I just wanted to look good for you. It's the last time you'll see me for a while."

"Do you think I'm going to forget how you look while you're gone?"

"Sorry." She dabbed her eyes. "Okay, I'll be okay." She put her forehead on his.

"I'll call tonight and tomorrow morning and tomorrow night and before I leave for Paris on Sunday."

"Sars, you're going to love this trip. Don't worry."

"I just remember how much I missed you over spring break, and I'm going to be gone longer this time, and I love you more now."

"I know, and I you."

"Mose promised to keep you busy with basketball and the upstairs apartment and taking care of him." Sarah was rambling, trying to keep from sobbing. As it was, tears were rolling down her cheeks. "What if the war lasts longer than is expected?" Her eyes fixed on his.

"I don't think it will, but I'll just have to be lonely a little longer." He kissed her wet nose. "You're going to have lots of stories to tell me when you get back. Did you pack your camera?"

"Uh huh." She sniffled as the final call for boarding was announced. "Gad, this is hard. I won't be able to call you once I get to Shamir."

Paul turned Sarah and walked her slowly to the corridor leading to the plane. "One more kiss, and then you have to board." They ignored her makeup, and when they pulled back, Sarah wiped a bit of lipstick from Paul's lips. "Last thing," he said taking a folded envelope from his back pocket. "My second attempt at poetry. It's still not quite poetry, more of a composition." He slipped it into her purse and then hugged her more tightly than ever. "This poem is to protect you for as long as you're there."

"Thank you for helping me with this. I love you, Paul. I love you so much! I'll call tonight."

"I love you, Sars. I'll see you soon. The time will pass quickly." He had held her hand as long as he could; now she would travel on her own. She walked backwards for three steps, paused as if she might run back to his arms, then raised her hand gently before placing it over her heart. She turned and headed for the plane. Paul stayed at the window until flight 304 for New York taxied away from the concourse. He hesitated for a few more moments before returning to his truck.

Not having had more than four hours sleep in any night in more than a week, his body surrendered to the front seat. He closed his eyes as he slumped over the steering wheel. He no longer needed to stay strong, to conceal his own emotions. In addition to his fatigue, he felt a tinge of guilt for allowing her to go alone, but Sarah had to go for her own needs, and he needed a break to process their journey. She would be all right now that the decision had been made, and while he would be scared too—and very lonely—he could recharge and be ready for their next phase. Paul rubbed his forehead against the backs of his hands and pictured Sarah as she had waved goodbye. He thought of his poem. *No matter what, no matter where.* He smiled and straightened up. With Sarah securely on board for her passage, Paul started his truck and headed back to Boulder to continue with his . . . that search for understanding.

The Hill awaited.

EPILOGUE

June 5-10, 1967

The third Arab-Israeli war began on Monday, June 5, 1967, when Israeli jets attacked Egyptian bases. It was Sunday night in Boulder. Sarah was stuck in Geneva, Switzerland, until Wednesday when Swiss Air began flying into Lod Airport near Tel Aviv. By then, the war was firmly in hand for Israel.

On that Wednesday, the Israeli army captured all of Jerusalem.

The United Nations brokered a cease fire which became effective on Saturday, June 10. Israel had soundly defeated its Arab neighbors and taken control of the Sinai Peninsula, the Gaza Strip, the West Bank and Jerusalem, and the Golan Heights. Kibbutz Shamir was no longer a stone's throw from Syria.

Tuesday, June 12

"Hello."

"Paul! It's Sarah. Can you hear me okay? I don't have much time to talk on this line. Only one minute is allowed. Oh, Paul, I miss you so much!"

"Where are you, Sars? Are you safe?"

"Yes. I'm in Tel Aviv, and people have been dancing in the streets for two days. Everyone is so happy. Everyone is a Zionist today! I love you."

"The papers are calling it 'The Six Day War.' Is your family okay?"

"Yes, yes. I'm with Hannah. Oh Paul, it's so good to hear your voice!"

"I love you, Sars. I'm so happy for you."

"What did you say? It didn't come through clearly."

"I said I love you."

"Paul, I need to stay here for a while longer, maybe until the end of the month. I can't explain it in so short of a time but trust me. Okay?"

"You know I do, Sars. I understand."

"I have to get off the phone now. I love you, my dear."

"I love you, Sars. I miss you too." Paul hung up the phone slowly and looked at Mose. "Bad connection; I'm not sure if she heard the last part of the call. She's safe though." He turned toward the table and shook his head. "Just one minute."

Mose smiled. "At least she'll be back here shortly."

Martin Ofer sustained serious injuries fighting the Egyptians in the Sinai during the Six Day War which required extensive surgeries, but he eventually recovered and returned to Shamir.

Paul traveled to Israel in July, staying two weeks at Shamir. He and Sarah spent three days in Jerusalem. On his return, he stayed overnight in New York with Sarah's parents.

Later in July, Hannah Mandel suffered a concussion in a tractor mishap.

The Student Peace Union at the University of Colorado dissolved over the summer due to lack of leadership and direction. Paul Garrity flirted with the SDS movement but switched to volunteering for Boulder community social issues. He worked for the Eugene McCarthy campaign in 1968.

Disenchanted with the war in Vietnam, Secretary of Defense Robert McNamara resigned on February 29, 1968.

Ross Garrity died from a drug overdose in Los Angeles in February 1968.

During a visit to Kibbutz Shamir in July 1968, Paul proposed to Sarah.

Dan Savage enlisted in the Army in the fall of 1968. He served his time in Germany.

In March 1969, President Nixon ordered unrestricted bombing of Cambodia (indiscriminate carpet bombing) using B-52s.

In April 1969, Paul received notification from his local draft board that his 2-S draft deferment would end with his graduation, and that he was to report for induction into the ARMED FORCES OF THE UNITED STATES five days after receiving his diploma.

In June of 1969, Sally got three-fourths of an earlier wish: Paul Garrity, Sally Long, and Moses Robinson graduated from the University of Colorado. Paul was drafted and deployed to Vietnam.

In 1971 amid the growing anti-Greek atmosphere on American college campuses, the Sigma Delta Tau sorority at the University of Colorado in Boulder closed its chapter permanently.

In 1971 the Department of Defense listed Corporal Paul Garrity as missing-in-action along the Cambodian border.

June 2, 1997

My Dear Paul,

Congratulations on your accomplishments with the UNHCR refu-gees. Working in places where there are so many refugees existing in such extremely desperate conditions, I fully understand the value of your work—and the dangers. You always took care of others without regard for your own safety. Your wife seems pretty remarkable too. You must be surprised by this letter, coming after so long. I have started this letter hundreds of times over the years. I'm trying again.

While our time ended so long ago, I remained in touch with a few of my sorority sisters. Anne Rostow-Stanley stayed in the Denver area after graduation and kept me up on many of the events there. It was she who came across the newspaper story about your career and passed it on to me. It is obvious you are well respected, but I would have expected no less. I experienced the passion and witnessed the drive in a young scholar who became the champion to so many in need. I knew the boy who trans-formed into the man in the story.

Youmust have wondered what happened to me after your ordeal as a soldier in Vietnam. I know because we loved each other so deeply and your feelings were my feelings. That corner of your heart you reserved for me has its counterpart in Tel Aviv.

Well, my dear, I live the life I came for, doing my small part, living life as a Jew in the land of Israel. I wake up each morning, have my coffee while I peruse the newspaper, get to my school at six, and take care of my children. Then, my staff and I do it again the next day. You pointed me in a certain direction, and I needed to fulfill that destiny. (I recall a conversation we once had about destiny versus fate.) I could not have stayed that first summer if I didn't believe that I would be returning to Boulder in the fall—coming back to you. But two weeks became four and four became the summer—and so on. First, there was Martin's injury, then Hannah's accident, and then Shamir's childcare teacher passed. I was thrust into real-life situations at the end of war and was needed. There was purpose and immediacy, so my return kept getting delayed. We talked and decided I would stay on the kibbutz until you graduated. Then we would be married and take on the world. You know all of that though.

After nearly two years of letters and plans to leave Shamir and return after your graduation, to pick up where we left off in '67, you received your induction notice, and Vietnam swallowed you up. It was Sally who wrote telling me that you were reported missing. I sensed an element of anger from her at me for my time away from you, that somehow it was my fault. She suggested that I remain in Israel . . . until your return. The last letter I received from you came from Long Binh Post, Vietnam, in 1971. That was our last communication. Over two years passed, the war ended, and I heard nothing. I believed you died and weren't coming home from the war that you so hated, that you weren't coming back to me. So, to assuage my grief and my guilt, I moved to Tel Aviv and threw myself completely into my work and my life in Israel. To cope, I convinced myself that it's what you would have wanted for me. During the Yom Kippur War in October of '73, I returned to Shamir to help where I could. I stayed for two months. War had sent me to Israel; war brought me back to Shamir and—in a way, to you again. In truth, those years are a blur even now. I didn't receive any letters after you returned from captivity. I didn't know. For years I assumed you hadn't survived, and I was devastated. The mystery of those lost letters haunts me still. They arrived in a bundle in 1980—that's when I learned of your ordeal and prolonged recovery, but more importantly, of your survival—in your own words. It was such a shock. That was seventeen years ago. I have no understanding of why I didn't respond then. I'm so sorry.

That year you went missing, through my uncle's contacts, I was able to get a job working in a daycare/school in Tel Aviv. I finished my degree here and then opened my own center in the northeast neighborhood in 1977. It's called '1203' after your old apartment, and it continues to be my life. We serve about 80 children each day. All of them are Jewish, but a few were Palestinian in the years immediately after opening, and, yes, some of my prejudices have mellowed, but not all. I know how you cringed when I would rant about the Arabs.

My work always kept me busy, too busy to develop any personal relationship early on, but eventually I met an older gentleman, a good man, who managed another center nearby. I hired him to help manage 1203. We were together for eight years before he passed away. Yes, he knew about us. I told him. His gentleness helped me through my struggle. While we never had children, we always considered the children at the center to be our own. I have pictures on my refrigerator as proof. My parents continue to live in New York; they are aging well living in a Jewish retirement community. Father was terribly fond of you, as you know. I have visited America a few times but never traveled west of New York. I hope your parents are well.

I'm rambling.

Paul, I missed you so much when I left. So many tears. It was almost unbearable, and I constantly planned on return-ing. It was always my intention to return to your arms. I often wonder about the life we could have lived. For those six months in 1967 . . . and the immediate years afterward . . . you were the center of my universe. You're still very much a part of it. None of what I did or became would have happened without your encouragement and love. A very unselfish love. One of my regrets is I didn't insist you come with me. Would that have been fair to you? You had your own destiny, and Israel was not it. I had my destiny, and it was. I remember you teasing me one night by saying that destiny doesn't allow for sentimentality. Yet, there are moments . . . .. When we were together in Boulder, I had a feeling that you were more designed for the field than the classroom. You would have made an inspiring professor, but something told me you belonged on the front lines, your natural affinity for the kind of work you're doing now. Maybe that would have carried you to me.

I still have those letters and all the ones from before, but I won't reread them now. It would be too painful. Maybe when I retire. I don't believe I will ever return to Colorado. It holds no real meaning for me without you. I wish you would visit me here in Israel one day. I would cherish showing this part of my being to you. I still have your room key that you made into a necklace and have worn it frequently since I left you and Boulder. While I never needed it to open your door, it opened others. Somewhere I misplaced your first poem, the goofy one, but your second poem sustained me in many lonely moments; it has kept my heart beating all these years. I gave my engagement ring to Hannah when she and Martin finally married. It's her wedding ring.

I'll close here while I still have the courage to mail this one off. The letter I planned was to be much longer with so many questions for you—about Mose and Sally and Dan, mostly about you, but I realize it doesn't matter. What does matter is that I loved you with every beat of my heart for our time, and when the time came, I was able to let you go and live the life that was meant to be.

After three decades, it's what I tell myself ~
Shalom, my dear Paul,
Sarah

June 12, 1997

Dear Sarah,

As you can imagine, I'm stunned by both the unexpected arrival of your letter and its stark revelations. Every assumption I made then, about our ending, was wrong, and what I've carried within ever since is now shredded, probably like your reaction back in 1980. But because your words are so gentle and heartfelt, those memories have flooded back. Over the last two days, I have tried to piece together how every action or opportunity went wrong, especially from the time I returned to the States after my captivity. That's a difficult concept to comprehend, so on the day after I received your letter—two days ago—I drove to Northwestern University on the shores of Lake Michigan and walked. I walked for six hours to think. My wife, Abby, calls it "walking it through." And last evening, I sat down to put my thoughts into this letter to help me understand. I hope what follows helps you too.

Sarah, I really did accept our separation while I was finishing my degree and you worked in Israel after the Six Day War. Your work had real meaning and value. Our letters, phone calls, my half-dozen visits . . . and the time apart . . . were part of our growth. It was so difficult—but right. Our plans to marry after I graduated and then for us to live a year in Israel before I would start graduate school . . . but Vietnam interfered. The months I spent in solitary captivity, however, forced me to re-examine that; I often thought the jungle jail might be a punishment for the choice I made of delaying our marriage to "do my duty." Partly to protect my mom. It was the only fight you and I had. You had the courage to go . . . and I didn't have the courage not to. You were so angry and hurt that I postponed the wedding since I was to be away for another two years. Your love sustained me during that ordeal. What I couldn't get my head around when I returned was why you stayed silent after I was released, why you didn't answer my letters. I assumed you gave up on me when I chose to go to war.

And now I learn that you never received my letters . . . or those from Mose. I didn't know that you had moved off the kibbutz to Tel Aviv or that your parents had relocated too. It wasn't you who went silent; it was me to you. You believed that I died in Nam. You lived with that for nine years. My God! That had to have been torture. I'm so very sorry.

This letter will be lengthy—several pages as I will try to summarize my time since we last communicated—and may begin to answer some of your questions. First, I ask myself why didn't I call, or why didn't I call your parents when I didn't hear from you? The simple answer from the psychiatrist at the VA in Denver was that I was suffering from PTSD and was scared—scared that you had blown me off, that you had moved on. That was my excuse then, but it seems inadequate now. That first year back in America was pure denial. I concluded that I didn't deserve any of the good things life had given me prior to Vietnam. At the top of the list was you. Next, those letters. While I couldn't reveal my feelings or my struggles to the psychiatrist or my parents, I did to you in those letters, as you now know, but didn't then. And I believed that you chose not to respond. It never crossed my mind that my letters didn't get to you. That's when I left Colorado and went to California to live with Mose and Sally and get on with my life. (More on that later in this letter) Who had my letters to you? Was it intentional or just a postal error. I need to let that issue go.

We can't go back, Sarah, but what I want to do is begin to build a relationship rooted in our past but based on reality. On now. The newspaper article revealed much about my wife. I have discussed this with her, and she is completely support-ive. She knows that I lived another life before I met her, as did she. If you are willing, I would like to call, the call I should have made in '73. I want to learn about your school and your students. I want to learn about your gentleman, the man you shared so much with, who took care of you. I want to tell you about my sons. And maybe, just maybe, I can visit you in your land of Israel with my family. I'd like to hear your voice again.

Let me begin.

Sally and Mose

Dan and Tracy

Oxnard

Dr. Orr

Bidong

Cambodia

Chicago soup kitchen

UNHCR

Guatemala

Gaza

Why, Arizona

Eastern Africa

My sons, Moses and Sal

This just scratches the surface, I know. Maybe too much too soon with more questions than answers. We have a huge time gap to fill. It will take some time and patience. We both have our careers still, careers that in many ways are similar.

Thank you for writing, for reaching across the years, for taking a chance. I hope you can forgive me, Sars, for not trusting your love when I came home from Vietnam . . . for hurting you when I left for the Army. At this moment, with your letter—your heartfelt words—it seems like it was just yesterday.

Love,
Paul

June 23, 1997

Dear Paul,

Parts of your response warmed and comforted me; other parts brought a few tears. Your description of Mose as a junior high teacher was precious; he was always such a teddy bear. Our little CU clan all doing well . . . the tidbits about your sons. Other parts were so you, especially the accounts of your work and its rewards. You working in Gaza . . . so close, but unable to make contact with me because of "worldly events." Maybe like our love back when . . . the world just got in the way. In my note, I didn't tell you that the structural additions to my center have been completed which will allow me to expand my services to another twenty or so children. My center now has a basketball court. I'm quite excited about that.

It has been three weeks since I wrote the first letter to you, three weeks of near constant consideration of what might happen because I mailed it off, and of how you might react. Obviously, I had much trepidation about reconnecting, about revealing your missing letters. I'm sure that my letter has caused you some turmoil and apprehension also. Thank you, my dear, for your kind offer of a phone call, but no, this exchange will have to be enough. In my earlier note, I wrote that I would like to show you my Israel, but reading your words tells me that it is no longer necessary. That bridge has been crossed. To know after all these years that you treasure our time—when it was our time—as much as I do will have to suffice. Maybe a brief note to one another in the case of a major happening will be okay, but anything else would be stilted. We were once, of course, but now we have other lives that must be lived. The magic that was The Hill in 1967 cannot be duplicated but knowing that you are loved and needed, especially by your wife and sons, brings me peace . . . and finally . . . closure.

Paul, know that I am so very proud of you for the work

you have done, that you continue to do. It's necessary and very unselfish of you and your wife. Last night, I removed your room key from my neck and placed it in my security box along with your letters. My love for you will be forever, but our journey cannot. I am—and will continue to be—well. Be safe.

Shalom my dear,
Sars

Paul's Second Poem to Sarah

June 1967

Hills symbolize challenges—or vistas.
Boulder's Hill, our setting, our starting place.
Early on . . . simply infatuation?
Physical passion? A college affair?

Passengers at the station punched tickets,
Committed to . . . a passage . . . with each other.
That train we boarded accelerated
The excursion soared . . . became . . . Destiny?

A crush grew into love—and a promise.
Two hearts to one. That symbolic train ride
Became a fastening, unbreakable . . .
Resolute, yet tender and supportive.

You asked, "In some way, no matter what, no
Matter where, love me forever." Softly,
I whispered, "Count on it, Sars." A promise.
I promised then; I promise now. Always.

The End